LEAFY RIVERS

Jessamyn West's new novel, set in the Ohio Territory in the early 1880's, is a handsomely paced adventure, charged with increasing suspense.

Leading a superbly realized, varied cast of characters is Leafy Rivers, the young bride, caught up by emotions she does not altogether understand and cannot quite control, racing against time to save a life and a marriage that may already be lost. Among the others who live on these pages and linger in the reader's memory are Simon Yanders, a man whose loss has taught him generosity, whose grief has made him alert to joy; Cashie Wade, irresistibly wild and free; and Reno, Leafy's husband, whose love is matched only by his ineptitude. These are merely a suggestion of the vibrant people who play vital roles in a continuously fascinating saga.

In addition, this moving novel offers a magnificent journey through woods of Americana that have rarely, if ever, been explored.

To a gripping narrative Jessamyn West has imparted universal meaning of a high and rare order. *Leafy Rivers* marks a new triumph for one of America's most distinguished authors.

Leafy Rivers

Jessamyn West

HARCOURT, BRACE & WORLD, INC.
NEW YORK

1415796

For Nicky and Berni

LEAFY RIVERS

one

🖋 *Prill*

At four o'clock on the afternoon of July 16, 1818, Prill Converse
went to the back door of her home in Blue Glass, Ohio. Actually,
the Converse farm was seven miles south of Blue Glass. But the
Converses, if they wanted to give strangers some idea of where
they lived, named Blue Glass. Blue Glass itself was unknown
outside Belmont County. But it was certainly better known than
Sand Creek, on the banks of which the Converse farm was located,
or the old Fork Road, by which you reached it.

Prill Converse needed a man to carry a message for her. Out on
the farm three were available: her husband, Bass; her son, Chancellor; and Clate Henry, the hired man.

Of the three, she preferred her son. It would be a pity to take Clate, hired to hoe corn, away from his job. Bass had no more sense of time than a turkey—and this was a message that needed to be delivered before nightfall. She often tried to imagine what it would be like to live in the timeless world Bascom inhabited. Bass would start somewhere with the best intentions in the world; then he would catch sight of a breachy cow on the wrong side of a fence and nothing further would be heard of him until long after the errand he'd set out on had been taken care of by someone else.

Prill looked around, hoping she'd see Chancellor and be able to hoo-hoo to him quietly. If she rang the dinner bell she'd bring all three men up to the house; and Bass, because the message was serious and about his daughter, would feel he ought to deliver it.

There was something godlike about Bascom. A thousand years were as a minute in his sight. In the first months of their marriage she had been unable to believe that such tardiness wasn't deliberate. Time ticked in her veins; pendulums swished back and forth behind her forehead. No one needed to wake her. She could tell when night had faded with her eyes closed. Joshua had stopped the sun; but she would like to see the man who could start it up for Bass. She had struggled for twenty-five years to make Bass understand that the sun did move. But you can no more put a sense of time into a man who doesn't have it than you can put tides in a pond.

She and Bass managed to get to church, sit down to table, and go to bed at more or less the same hour. But by the time Bass arrived, she had, as often as not, moved from eagerness and anticipation into anger. Our whole life would have been different, she often thought, if Bass could have known the woman I was the hour before he was an hour late.

She was a round, short woman and she stood on tiptoe to scan cornfield, apple orchard, barnyard, meadow-pasture, woods lot. As she watched and listened, she heard the growing rustle in the

4

leaves of the big sycamore that shaded their house. The day had begun as a weather-breeder. She had stepped out of bed that morning into air as still and warm as a saucer of new milk. Now the day had stopped holding its breath, and she was glad. She was ready for a change. The day in its warmth, the season in its fullness could go no further. July was the month when summer, like bread in the oven, might change color, but it would rise no higher. It was at its height.

Though she could hear the wind she could see no movement, except the occasional twitch of a leaf like an eyelid gone out of control, there was a sign that told her Chancellor was near. She could smell tobacco. Chancellor was a grown man of twenty-two, but out of respect for his father he did his smoking away from the house. Bass was against tobacco. His mother—preacher, teacher, and mother of eight—said that Bass had been given an odd turn because *his* father had chewed tobacco while she was carrying Bass. Bass didn't want that to happen again. Nobody, to Prill Converse's knowledge, was carrying any child of Chancellor's; and, for that matter, even if you admitted that Bass had an odd turn or two, there was no proof that his father's chewing was responsible.

Head up, sniffing for the fumes she didn't find unappealing, Prill followed her nose toward the barn. Houseflies, even as she walked along, clung to her. The hogs out in their wallows were complaining. Crows flew over low and pumping hard. Every so often the crickets and katydids held up their chirping to listen to something she couldn't hear. The sky was cloudless. But change was on its way; it had a long tongue like a toad's which could reach out and make itself known from afar.

Chancellor, when she came into the barn, looked up but didn't move. He was sitting on one sack of timothy seed and was lolled back against another. Old Barney, the barn cat, was on his lap, and Chancellor was puffing his pipe and patting the cat to some silent tune inside his head. Prill was quick to notice patterns like that, and Chancellor was quick to make them. Though each was quick, neither moved slapdash, hit or miss, catch as catch can. Prill felt nearer to Chancellor than she did to her husband and her other two children. She didn't like to think she loved him more, but she did understand him better. Chancellor, in a way, was her thoughts made visible.

In looks, Chancellor was a cross between her and Bass. He had inherited his father's lean, loose-coupled plowboy build. But he had her coloring, and that made all the difference. Bass was straw-colored. He could have been run up, so far as color goes, from the material available in any hayrick. Not Chancellor. To get his colors you'd need a blacksmith shop (at the very least). Black eyes, blue-black hair, white skin, red mouth. Iron, flame, white-hot metal. He had her colors, but they had been laid onto a shape flattened, elongated, Roman-nosed, Adam's-appled, and in every other appropriate way masculinized.

Which was a very good thing. Chancellor had some dainty ways. If he'd had his mother's small bones, plus his father's bleached colors, plus his own cat-loving, tea-drinking, ruffled-shirt propensities, he might have been in for trouble. As it was, standing over six feet and weighing close to a hundred and eighty, he could cut his fingernails with his mother's embroidery scissors, instead of paring them with a jackknife, carefully match the color of the rig-outs he wore (everyone was pretty sure), and keep a cat perpetually on his knee, without anyone caring to make anything of it. By the luck of his bold looks, his mother thought, Chancellor was much freer than the fresh-faced, button-nosed little fellows with wavy hair and dimples who, to give the lie to their looks, had to chase girls and guzzle drink no matter what their inclinations.

"Where's your father, Chancellor?" she asked.

"Over at La Belle's."

"Who's looking after the work?"

"I am."

It didn't seem likely; but Chancellor had his own way of mastering time. He didn't, like his father, ignore it. He stretched

6

it. When he moved, he made the fur fly. Afterward he lounged and was called lazy, though not by his mother.

"What's he doing over there?"

"They've got a sick heifer."

That told the story. Bass had a way with animals. Maybe they recognized that he didn't have any traffic with clocks. Maybe he smelled right. Maybe his humming and whistling worked on them like a snake charmer's flute. Whatever it was, if an animal ailed, Bass got the call. Added to his skill was the fact that his services were free. Prill knew Bass enjoyed his all-night sessions in stables. And the big buckwheat-cake breakfasts that followed. But there was a price to be paid for his absences in neglected farm work.

"If you're going to be a horse doctor," she'd urge, "put out a shingle and charge. We're not so well off you can be at the beck and call of every man with a sick shoat on his hands."

"I'm not trained," Bass would say. "I don't want to make any kind of claims."

"You doctor," Prill would tell him. "That's a bigger claim than words."

"Nobody can say I promised anything," he'd tell her, putting on his coat and getting out his gunny-sack doctoring apron.

"I wish I was a wife in sheep's clothing. I'd get better treatment from you than I do looking like a woman."

Bass would laugh in appreciation of the joke. But he didn't stay home with the joker. He'd set out, making no claims at all, saying to the farmer who asked him, "You're every bit as good a hand at this as I am"; but nothing he said took care of the chores at home. Chancellor and Prill did them.

These memories, though she was glad enough at the moment to have Bass out from underfoot, made Prill speak bitterly now.

"They've got a sick heifer. We've got a sick girl."

"Leafy's not feeling sick, is she?" Chancellor asked.

"She's going to have a baby. That may not be a sickness, but it's work. And it needs a doctor. And now that she's going to have a baby, she deserves to be called by the name she was born with."

"She changed that by getting married," Chancellor reminded her. "You don't want her going by her maiden name now, do you?"

"Don't joke, Chancellor. You know what I'm talking about. She was named Mary Pratt Converse. 'Leafy' is no name."

Chancellor, without giving the matter a minute's thought, could drop a nickname on someone, person or animal, and whatever name had been used before would be lost to human memory. Chancellor never asked anyone to use the nickname he made up; but, once heard, it was irresistible. It was as if all language was kind of makeshift until Chancellor put his tongue to it.

"It's a good thing," his mother told him, "you haven't taken to renaming crops and animals. We'd all be tongue-tied or faced with learning a new language. Look at that cat."

This was easy for Chancellor to do. He was still holding it. "Barney?" he asked.

"You don't even remember it ever had another name. I raised that cat from a kitten, and its name was Amos. And, thanks to you, except for her father and me, Mary Pratt might be a name forgotten on a headstone. Leafy Rivers! What kind of a name is that?"

"I'm only responsible for 'Leafy.' She married Rivers."

"She can't help the name of the man she married. You could've helped nicknaming her."

"Mary Pratt didn't help me any—never 'yes' or 'no,' but always 'I'd just as lief.' "

"People can't change their natures. You know that. And I feel sorry for a baby with a mother called Leafy Rivers. Poor little thing. Had as well have a mother called Sandy Creek."

Chancellor laughed. "I'm not joking," his mother said. "Now you hitch up and get Doc Daubenheyer here. Mary Pratt had her first pains this morning, and it's time she had some more."

"What's Reno doing?" Chancellor asked.

"Sitting by his wife's bedside holding her hand. You think you should have that job while he goes for the doctor?"

"No, Aprilla," Chancellor said. "I think I'm the one to go for Daubenheyer."

His mother changed color at the use of that girlhood name. When Chancellor resurrected it, as he did occasionally, she heard bells ring from way across the Ohio. She heard her name called by brothers and sisters; said softly by her mother, sternly by her father. She loved that name; she thought it rippled like a branch and smelled of spring flowers. She was ashamed of the pleasure it gave her to hear Chancellor use it. It was a flip thing for a son to do—call his mother by her first name. And it was unnatural for her to take pleasure in it. She went on as if she hadn't heard it.

"You bring Daubenheyer yourself, Chancellor."

"I'll have to drive him home then."

"I know that. But that way we can keep him as long as he's needed."

"Mind if I take Offie with me?"

She minded that name, but after objecting to so many things she let it pass. "If you can find your brother, take him with you," she said.

As she went back to the house, Prill wondered why it was that Chancellor, who handed out names to other people like calling cards, had never been handed one himself. Did he mind the omission? Did he hand out pet names as a sign for others to do likewise? He had a name that called for shortening; he had the coloring and build that would have made another boy Slim or Blackie. She tried them in her imagination. Slim. Blackie. Chance, instead of Chancellor. They wouldn't do. At the porch she turned to watch him back Charlie between the shafts. Poor boy, he was stuck with that big name she had given him.

✍ Chancellor

Charlie, along with Reno, was one of the few beings whose name Chancellor hadn't tampered with—why, he didn't know. Charlie was a fine animal, a claybank with a switch tail of darker color, a speedy notionate little roadster, a natural pacer. Chancellor loved his style and spirit and obstinacy. What Charlie gave you seemed to be a special gift and to have nothing to do with duty or training. His name didn't matter. Call him Hoecake or Peaspod, he'd put his brand on them and make them stand for something special.

Chancellor hadn't nicknamed Reno because Reno seemed like a nickname already for a man whose real name was maybe Hubert or Delbert or Wilbur. The truth was he didn't really know Reno; and, deeper than that truth, he didn't really have any urge to. Why, he couldn't say. If he had to put his finger on any one trait, he'd say he didn't care for people who wouldn't take a chance, and Reno struck him, in spite of his accident, as being a careful man.

"Well, Offie," he said, as they rode through the woods that separated the cleared land around their place from the cleared land around the Lucey farm, "it's too bad you got here too late for the Indians. They sure would've liked your red hair."

Offie ran his hand over his tufty head.

"What good was scalps to them?"

"Proof they'd got you. Like nailing a chicken hawk to the barn door."

"Did they kill you first?"

"If they had time."

"Could you live without a scalp?"

"Depends on how deep they cut."

After they got out of the woods, Offie said, "Let me drive?"

Chancellor put the reins in his hands, and Offie, who was really afraid of Charlie, said, "Ain't he liable to shy?"

"He is."

"What if he shies now?"

"We're in for a fast ride, I reckon."

"He's stepping out already."

"Hold him down."

"He's took the bit in his teeth."

"Jerk it out."

Offie was a good boy, but plump and timid.

"I can't."

"You haven't tried."

Offie braced his stubby legs and pulled. Charlie slowed down. "He's trained to obey," Chancellor said, "but he's no mind reader. You have to let him know what you want."

"I let him know," Offie said proudly.

"Let him know we're going to turn left at the next fork."

"Ain't we going for the doctor?"

"I've got a little call to make first."

"Venese Lucey?"

"Know anybody else who lives down that way?"

"You going to court?"

"Maybe. If you give me a chance."

"You ain't the only one."

"Only what?"

"Courter."

"I'm not the only one in Blue Glass with eyes for a pretty girl."

When they pulled into the Lucey place Chancellor said, "I won't be gone long. You don't get out of sight of the rig."

Chancellor skirted the Lucey house. Val Lucey, who came from the South, had built himself a house very different from Bascom Converse's two-story Philadelphia brick. Both families had started with log cabins, but the Lucey house was still half log cabin, with a second half of clapboard joined to it by a dog-trot—and by honeysuckle, morning-glory, and star jasmine. When Val got around, as he said he intended, to moving the log cabin on rollers out to his barn, and replacing it with a second clapboard half, he was going to have to perform an operation on the living tendrils that held the two halves together.

The Lucey front yard was a sorry sight. It was packed dirt

without a bush or tree on it. This was exactly what Elizabeth Lucey wanted. She had seen, in her trip through the woods from Carolina to Ohio, enough trees to last her a lifetime. A vine she could tolerate, but nothing, not even a lilac bush or peony, with power of its own to lift itself up, cast a shadow, and block the way. One thing she had left in her yard—a big hickory stump, waist-high, stripped of its bark. Mrs. Lucey treated this as furniture. She scrubbed the top of it, she stretched cloths for bleaching across it, she stacked it with milk pans to sun.

The stump was bare this afternoon, and Chancellor thought it looked, in the clear slanting light, white and menacing, like the one mean tooth left in an empty mouth. Or a tombstone. Though what it actually was, he supposed, was a skeleton; or at least the stump of one. Mrs. Lucey kept it there as a message for the rest of the forest: Stay away from my door, if you don't want this to happen to you.

Venese was more like her father than her mother. The trip through the woods that had made Elizabeth Lucey want never to see another tree had made Val a woodsy. He did what farming he had to; and he kept up the pretense that his trips to the woods were to bring back game. He did come back and he did bring game. But except that he had been brought up a God-fearing man and felt a responsibility for his family, he would have followed whatever it was in the forest that called to him.

Chancellor walked upstream along the creek that flowed a hundred yards behind the Lucey house. The day, born a weather-breeder, was beginning to settle down to doing its job. Deep in the woods, trees were breathing with a hoarse, croupy sound. A grasshopper, picked up by a sudden gust, sailed past his face and landed on the water like a slim side-wheeler. It went down, all paddles churning. Bars of light, shining through the trees, fell across the creek so that the water appeared to be sliding along inside a prison cell. The sand, where the light fell on it, was golden. It was an easygoing stream; but walking beside it, Chancellor began to whistle a loud marching tune. It was no signal to Venese. And it wasn't music. Venese had told him a hundred times that a crow's song was prettier. He wasn't whistling because he was happy—or unhappy. Or whistling in the dark to keep his courage up. There wasn't much he was in the dark about.

But whenever he got near Venese, a tightness would settle in his chest, then move up to his lips, until the only way he could get relief was by whistling. He would whistle without knowing it, wake up to the fact, and keep right on. "What the hell?" he would ask himself. "There's no law against whistling. And if there is, I'll break it."

He and Venese had a meeting place, a quarter-mile upstream from the Luceys', a bower formed by fox grapes that had climbed to the tops of the slanting creek trees and had then fallen downward to the creek itself. At the base of the trees the vines sheltered a place as private as a parlor but prettier and handier: water flowing by with its soft lup-lup, and fox grapes, in season, hanging down for the taking. They were leathery to bite into, but sweet and tangy once you got past their skins. The bower was Venese's. She had found it and she had introduced Chancellor to it.

Venese didn't come outside to haloo, or to give any other sign that she had heard Chancellor coming. And Chancellor hadn't expected her to. But when he parted the vines she was there waiting, and with that extra glitter waiting always gave her. Every time he was with her, Chancellor was for the first second or two taken aback to see how much of her looks he had forgotten. The truth was, once with her and after he had touched her or looked into her eyes, that color, complexion, shape of nose, set of ears, and matters of that kind weren't noticed. Venese was a towhead with agatey eyes and an olive skin. That much he could see, in the first two seconds before his attention went, with their talk, all to her eyes; or, with their touch, all to the feel of her warmth and springiness.

She went into his arms, and he could feel her smile with his lips.

"You've come," she said.

Venese had a funny trait. Or so it seemed to Chancellor. She didn't care for promptness. With her, he planned to be late; the way with others he would plan to be on time (except, since being on time came natural to him, it wasn't necessary). What Venese got on easy terms, or on time, or exactly as anticipated, lost its relish for her. He relished her any time, any place, the earlier the better—and he often felt humiliated not to be welcomed in the same way. And he felt that by threatened absences, postponements, nonarrivals, he belittled her. You baited animals that way: taught hens, with grain held back, then doled out, to follow a crack with their beaks to the floor; started dogs slobbering, with the smell of food you hid behind your back.

He was late today without planning, so there was no ugliness in his mind. Still, he couldn't help twitting her. He held her away from him and said, "Leafy's your friend today."

"I didn't know she ever wasn't."

"Special friend today. She made me late."

Venese didn't answer. She wanted her wants known, but not talked about.

"I'd ought to be a hunter like your pa. Show up once a month."

"No."

"Hoo-hoo at the door, lay down the deer, and run."

"No," said Venese, "you know that's not so."

After a while she said, "With you I'm a papist."

"Just so I'm your pope."

"I'm not joking."

"You don't ever kiss my toe."

"All right, you don't want to hear."

He could've said, "I'm doing what you taught me." Instead, he said, "I'm listening."

"Papists don't worship on a full stomach."

"I've never seen anything wrong with your appetite."

14

"I'm not talking about food. I'm talking about you. Before seeing you, I like to go without seeing you for a while."

"Well," he said, "I can oblige you now. I'm on my way to town to get Daubenheyer for Leafy."

Though they had planned to spend the rest of the day together, going on at seven to the Camp Meeting in Blue Glass, Venese made no fuss about the change. She bade him a fond farewell, for she liked separations almost as well as meetings.

"You going to preach tonight?" she asked.

"I got that all out of my system a long time ago. You know that. You be ready when I come."

"I'm always ready."

"I'm coming on time tonight. You be ready."

"You're preaching already."

What he had intended was a command, not a sermon. He put his face against her shoulder and heard the fast clap of her heartbeat.

"Too bad we ever have to talk," he said.

"I like to talk," she said. "I like it as well or better than anything else."

He knew she did. Talk led to arguments. Arguments led to separations. Separations made meetings necessary.

"Venese," he said, "you better try to get saved tonight."

When he got back to the rig, Offie asked sociably, "Did you court?"

"What's court mean to you?"

"Spark."

Offie had spent six months out in Indiana visiting Reno and Leafy, and six months with a pair of newlyweds might, Chancellor thought, have made Offie more courtship conscious than most nine-year-olds.

"What's spark mean?"

"Kiss and hug."

"You think I ought to tell you?"

"I didn't say 'ought.'"

"But you'd like to listen?"

"I didn't say 'like.'"

"Good."

"But if you want . . ."

"Shut up, Offie," Chancellor said.

But his mind was at least as full of Venese as Offie's. He'd known plenty of girls who wanted to keep their fellows on tenterhooks. But Venese was the only one he'd ever heard of who wanted to feel the hooks herself. He was pretty sure she loved him. He knew he loved her, and it went against the grain, loving her, to hurt her, even on her say-so. More, on her say-so.

He remembered the first time he'd seen her. The Luceys weren't old settlers in Blue Glass, and they'd had more trouble getting to Ohio than most. They had been over a year making it from Carolina. All of them except Val had been down with the milk fever. The youngest, a boy of four, had died. Their two best mules had drowned. And Val himself, no woodsy when he started the trip, had sliced his leg open with an ax and had almost bled to death. The wound hadn't healed, and he had arrived in Blue Glass with a running sore. But the worst hit, it seemed, by their year-long ordeal, was Mrs. Lucey. She'd got something worse than milk fever—woods fever. She trembled if a leaf stirred. She was as nervous of shadows as other women were of bobcats and redskins. She wanted to see before, behind, and sidewise at the same time. This kept her pretty constantly turning—even when she went out to take the air on her stump. With a mother like this and a father like Val, who, by the time he reached a place he could stop, had developed a liking for going, the Lucey children had to look out for themselves. Val would disappear, excusing himself from more steadfast work by saying he had a running leg. As a matter of fact, he had two. Lizzie Lucey, with her worry about being hemmed in, couldn't stand still long enough to be of much help in getting her children rigged out for school. The Blue Glass pupils, no fashion plates themselves, were knocked si-goggling by the outlandish-ness of the Luceys when they first made their appearance.

Chancellor first met Venese on a morning before school be-gan. The schoolhouse was set on a little rise above the sheds where the pupils who rode to school tied up their horses. As he climbed the rise after tying up his own horse, he saw a ring of his friends watching something shut from his sight.

"Who's fighting?" he called to Dutch Burdorff, who was on the outside edge of the ring.

"There ain't no fight."

"What's going on?"

"A girl's laying down, being set," Dutch said.

This didn't make any sense to Chancellor. "Set?" he asked, thinking of hens.

"Like a table," Dutch said. "She's got on a tablecloth for a dress."

She had, for a fact. Even those who had never seen table-cloths knew that, and Chancellor had seen them. The one Venese was wearing was white and fringed. It had been draped on her with an eye to not spoiling it as a tablecloth if something better in the way of a dress ever turned up.

What her classmates had done to Venese couldn't have been done without her co-operation. Everything edible that any-one had brought to school was set forth in a dinnertime pat-tern along her narrow, flat, tableclothed frame: hunks of johnny-cake, hazelnuts, fried tenderloin, soda biscuits, jackknives, a tin dipper, a piece of sorghum taffy. All she had to do if she didn't like the ordeal was to breathe hard. But she was breathing easy, so as not to upset anything. She couldn't have looked more content if she'd been chosen Queen of the May and had been garlanded with ropes of leaves and crowns of flowers.

Chancellor wondered if she was maybe deaf, for what was being said about her wasn't nice. He decided she wasn't, for her agate eyes went from face to face. She was taking everything in. He decided she was more like an Indian, captured and too proud to murmur. He intended to rescue her.

He shoved through the circle, grabbed Venese by the arm, and hauled her upright, sending the spread-out victuals flying. The sorghum taffy stuck to the tablecloth, and that he removed by hand. The Fairmont pupils picked up as much of their lunches as appeared unharmed, then backed away, quietly. If Chancellor Converse didn't want Venese Lucey set like a table, they had no intention of trying to spite him. He'd just as lief kill you as kiss you, and if you were a boy he'd probably rather. Chancellor knew their opinion before he yanked Venese up. He wasn't taking much of a chance—or so he thought.

But he didn't know Venese. She hauled off and hit him in the stomach. She wasn't large, but what she'd gone through on that trip from Carolina had made her tough as jerky. Her fist wasn't any bigger than a tack hammer, but it was just as hard. While Chancellor was doubled up recovering from that blow, Venese tack-hammered him again, this time in the nose; while he was dabbing at his bloody nose with his shirttail, she spread herself, tablecloth and all, right down where he'd rescued her from, and yelled, "Set me again."

That ought, he supposed, to have been a sign to him. He should've walked off and left her.

"Come on," she yelled to the dispersed scholars. "Set me again."

But there wasn't much point setting a human table that *wanted* to be set; particularly with Chancellor Converse ready, as soon as his nose stopped dribbling, to punch them for doing so. So there she was left, her invitations unheeded, alone, unset, flat on the ground in her tablecloth dress.

Chancellor, without asking her pleasure, jerked her to her feet again. She would have stretched out once more except that without pulling Chancellor down with her she couldn't. She looked to Chancellor like something treed, and, though expecting to be shot, defiant.

"You let me go," she said.

"You stand up," Chancellor told her.

"I don't have to if I don't want to."

"You have to as long as I've got hold of you."

He hauled her, resisting, toward the schoolhouse door, where he was met by Buck Trudge, that year's schoolmaster. "Take your hands off that girl, boy," he said. Chancellor did so, daring Venese with his black-eyed stare to flatten herself out once again in front of Trudge. She had too much sense for that.

✍ Doctor Daubenheyer

When Chancellor and Offie reached Blue Glass, the town already lay in the shadows of its western trees. The hills to the east of town were the color of rose hips, and fingers of smoky light reached out of the aisles of the forest and lay across the village streets. Though Charlie was a high stepper, plumes of dust followed the buggy. The wind, fanning all day through the woods, had stirred up the evergreen resins and bruised the foliage of the big leaf-droppers. Somewhere downwind there had been lightning. Chancellor could taste sulphur at the back of his throat. Though it was near sundown, there wasn't a breath of evening coolness on the air. The three of them came into town sweating.

People who had seen Philadelphia called Blue Glass "New Philadelphia." People who hadn't did so more often. There was talk even of changing the town's name to that. What did Blue Glass mean, anyway? Was it somebody's miswriting of Blue Grass? Somebody's description of the look of Sand Creek in cloudy weather? Named for where some settler's wife broke her favorite pitcher? No one knew, and if the name had once had meaning it had lost it. Whatever there was to choose between Philadelphia and Blue Glass was in the newer town's favor, many thought. Chancellor's grandfather Levi Converse had left Philadelphia, where his people had lived for over a hundred years,

to find a place cleaner, less crowded, less noisy, less smoky—
and less evil. The winter before he left, thieves had broken
into his home, stolen his plate, and chalked obscene messages
to the maids on the bricks of the kitchen floor. That saucy piece
of nastiness had turned him Ohio-ward more than the thievery.
He was no longer a young man. He had grown sons. But with
a continent to choose from, the man who was willing to put up
with suggestions like those he read that morning on his own
kitchen floor was about on a level with them. By March he was
on his way toward something less defiled.

Blue Glass wasn't free of defilement. There was thievery, ob-
scenity, and even smoke in Blue Glass. There were few days
when smoke from a burning in somebody's deadening didn't roll
into town. And there were no days when the town didn't echo
to the sound of cow, horse, ox, and sheep bells; to axes, mauls,
froes, and blacksmiths' hammers; to looms thumping, trees crash-
ing, and spinning wheels whirring. To say nothing of the sounds
made by stuck pigs, kicked dogs, and children yelling just for the
hell of it. But the sounds in Blue Glass, perhaps because they
had, westward, a whole continent into which to spread, didn't
grate on the ears the way the boxed-up sounds in Philadelphia
did.

Blue Glass stretched (for the two squares it existed) along
an east-to-west road and was moving, like the country, west.
Chancellor, though he could have taken a short cut to Daubenheyer's, went the length of the main street for the sheer pleasure
of seeing it. There was no point in hurrying. Junius Daubenheyer wouldn't be home from his rounds until close on suppertime. After corn, hogs, and trees the town was a sight. They
passed three taverns, two general stores, two blacksmith shops,
two churches, and the town meetinghouse. The meetinghouse
had had its floors trodden by play-party dancers, its walls bowed
out by big box suppers, and its rafters shivered by singing
schools. Itinerant fiddlers, zither players, and basso profundos
gave concerts there. Travelers and reformers lectured there. And

when there were no outside performers, the Blue Glassers themselves took over with spelling matches, geography schools, chalk
talks, and shadowgraph dramas presented in pantomime behind stretched sheets.

"I almost acted in a play there once," Chancellor told Offie.
"Why didn't you?"

"I had my choice: act if I wanted to but leave home if I did."

Offie appeared to be choosing from several questions. "Can
you act?"

"I never found out."

The first Blue Glass houses had, naturally, been of logs. Some
still were, but, as suited a New Philadelphia, it was now a town
of brick and clapboard, white and rosy. Even the log houses
that still stood had been so disguised with whitewash, picket
fences, dooryard gardens, and monthly roses framing the windows, they had lost their pioneer look.

Beyond Blue Glass, between it and the trees that were still
unfelled, were the fields of corn and wheat, timothy and clover.
Orchards of sheepnose apples and May Duke cherries had come
into full bearing. Most houses had a patch of flax, and many
had a stand of tobacco. But for all of its trim buildings and de-
pendable crops, Blue Glass was still an island in a sea of trees—
and in some places the waves still broke right in town. And no
one minded this. It gave them, like all island people, two ways
of living. They could stay home in their neat clockwork town,
piece quilts, shoe horses, and attend zither concerts, or they
could shove off into the green woods sea, be lost to everything
but wing flap, leaf fall, and the rustle of passing game. Or
they could do what Val Lucey did: ply back and forth between
the two. Whichever they chose, it was a rich time for choices:
plenty to stay home for and hang onto, plenty to launch out
toward. Everyone felt that, and had the cockiness choice gives.

Chancellor slowed Charlie down to prolong the viewing. After
the haphazardness of farm and woodland, the town was as neat,
pretty, and unnatural as a checkerboard: houses lined up and

facing other houses. Dr. Daubenheyer's house was out at the west edge of town, built when neighbors, not Indians, were beginning to be what you tried to avoid. It was the finest house in town; not the biggest, but the most elegant. Junius Daubenheyer had come into possession of it by marrying, after the death of his own wife, Woodson Clampitt's widow. Clampitt had owned the lumber mill. Anything made of wood he had right at hand. Anything that couldn't be made of wood he had the means to buy.

Before Chancellor had finished hitching, Junius Daubenheyer was beside him, slapping Charlie, joshing Offie.

"Offie," he said, "what can I do for you? Course of mercury? Glass of castor oil?"

"Always looking for a patient," Chancellor said.

"I can remember one or two in the past who looked me up," Daubenheyer replied. "Mentioning no names, of course."

If Junius Daubenheyer and Chancellor Converse had been girls, they would have been accused of having chosen each other for friends because, being opposites in appearance, the good looks of one offset and enhanced the good looks of the other. If Chancellor looked as if he had been forged in a blacksmith shop, Junius had the looks of a man put together in a meadow with sunshine and daisies. He was hazel-eyed, well fleshed, and with a warmth under his skin and in his red lips that was better than medicine for the ailing. He had arrived in town jolly, and since his remarriage had seemed even jollier. Blue Glassers thought the two friends should go into business together: dark Chancellor as undertaker in charge of the patients sunny Junius couldn't save.

"What's the matter, June?" Chancellor asked as Junius took a look at Charlie's teeth. "You shifting to horse doctoring?"

"I'll leave that to your father."

"You conducting your business out in the yard?"

"I didn't know this was business."

"If it's business, I get invited in? No business, I stay out?"

"Don't get so fine-haired, Chancellor. After a day of typhoid and summer complaint I was enjoying a breath of fresh air."

"If fresh air's what you want, I'll give you a snootful. I'm here to drive you back to Leafy."

"So that's what's ahead of me."

"It's better'n milk fever and summer complaint, ain't it?"

"It's not less work."

"I was thinking of the patient, Doctor."

"That's the trouble with this business. Nobody ever thinks of the doctor."

Chancellor put a hand on his friend's arm. "Mama thought of you. She sent me so I could drive you over and back."

"Don't she have any confidence in my getting there and knowing how long I should stay?"

"She thinks you're still a bridegroom."

Junius snorted. "I can give my bed a miss now and again without suffering. Come on in, Chancellor. You, too, Offie."

Chancellor was accustomed, in his own home, to good furniture and careful housekeeping. Even so, the Clampitt house made him feel like a clodhopper, like a man caught without cover in a sheet-lightning storm. The place glittered with polished brass, shined glass, waxed furniture. Highlights went dancing off with sharp birdlike beaks. He almost threw up his arms to protect his eyes. Sunshine after an ice storm didn't provide more sparkle.

The woman responsible for all this glitter was no middle-aged housewife, but a little widow still in her twenties with a voice like a mourning dove—and a shape like one, too: slender in the limbs and plump in the body. No one in Blue Glass was hardhearted enough to wish a man the misfortune of losing a wife. But if he had to lose one, he couldn't do better, it was thought, than to lose Rosa Daubenheyer and inherit Alpha Clampitt. And added to the widower's benefit was the benefit to his motherless boy. Alpha and Woodson had been married ten years without having children. Little Otto Daubenheyer had lost his mother at birth. The child and the widow couldn't have taken to each other more heartily if they had arranged for the decease of mother and husband themselves.

Chancellor, Junius, and Offie entered the Clampitt house by way of a front hall. Pure waste, Chancellor thought, a room used for nothing but walking into and out of. They were met in the middle of it by Alpha, with Otto in her arms.

"Put that child down," Junius ordered, before Alpha had a chance to greet them. "What's the matter with you, Otto?" he asked. "Can't you stand on your own two feet yet?"

"Of course he can," Alpha answered for Otto. "It's just that I like carrying him."

She put the boy down, but before she straightened up she hugged him.

"Save that for me, Alphy," Junius said.

"And if there's any left over, remember me," said Chancellor.

"What would Venese think of talk like that?" Alpha asked.

"You've got my permission to ask her, Alphy."

Alpha Clampitt Daubenheyer was colored like an apple, a Rome Beauty or a Baldwin: hair russety red with streaks of yellow; all health and warmth. If you were buying women in a market you would put your money on her rather than Venese or Leafy. But not buying women, Chancellor thought, not trying to get your money's worth, you might choose, he would choose, the other two: women who could spread some moonlight over a landscape.

"Can you stay for supper?" Alpha asked.

"I don't suppose we ought to. Leafy's starting to have her baby."

"Well, she's not in such a big rush you can't stop for what's already cooked and waiting to be dished up. Is she?"

"The trouble, so far's I can make out, is that rush is the last thing Leafy's thinking about," Chancellor said. "Matter of fact, it appears she's still turning it over in her mind whether or not she'll have this baby."

"She's about nine months late for turning that over in her mind," Junius said.

"Late, she may be," said Chancellor. "But Leafy makes up for that recently by being determined. Once her mind's made up."

"You know so much about the patient, Chancellor, it beats me why you're calling in outside help."

"Oh, you know how it is, June," Chancellor said. "A man don't trust himself treating his own family."

Then he could have bit his tongue out. Junius had delivered his own baby.

two

✍ Leafy

It was getting along toward dark in the parlor bedroom. Reno
was in the chair, Leafy in the bed. She had been put there by
her mother, instead of in her own girlhood bedroom upstairs,
for the sake of handiness. Downstairs, she'd be nearer the kitchen
stove and hot water, the outhouse; nearer the coming and going
of whoever was needed, or came to visit.

Leafy had been in the bed for twenty-four hours and she
had developed the habit of considering girl and bedroom and
outdoors (visible through opened door and windows) as something apart from herself. She had known the three of them before, of course, but each under different circumstances. She

had decked out the parlor bedroom many a time for company: plumped up the featherbed, filled the pitcher that stood in the washbasin with water, gathered spring beauties or cinnamon pinks to freshen up the smell of the unused room. But she had never seen or expected to see the room from flat on her back in the middle of the sleigh-footed bed.

Or expected to see from that position the farmyard buildings and the trees beyond. The door to the back porch, which she faced, framed a scene as foreign as China. The house was built on the slope of a slight rise. The farmyard buildings—barn, carriage house, smokehouse—had their foundations out of sight on the far side of that rise, so that all she could see from her bolster were half-buildings with oversized roofs. Rickshas and pigtails were all that were needed to put her in a geography picture she had once pored over called "The Celestial Kingdom."

The girl in bed (from whom she tried to keep herself separate) had a baby inside her—a big fat baby, to judge by the size of the girl's stomach—and this swollen girl was even more foreign to Leafy than China, someone she had never seen pictured, an object more transformed than the parlor bedroom. Leafy tried to look at and think about all three, girl, room, and outdoors, like a traveler, a visitor surprised and speculating but not concerned, a passer-by.

When she took her eyes from the picture framed by the open door, she saw the rag carpet, lifted by the wind, rise and fall in slow waves. As she watched, the waves spread up and into her body and the wind that moved the carpet governed her breathing and the flow of her blood. She felt seasick, the way she did in a swing when, after hard pumping, she let the old cat die.

"Reno," she said.

"Yes, Leafy."

"Set a chair on the carpet, will you?"

She always hesitated before asking Reno to do anything for her. A man with a knob of wood for one foot didn't move as easily as a man with two feet of flesh and blood. Try as she would, she couldn't help seeing how that block of shaped and polished ash pressed, for all its padding, against the red scarred stump of Reno's footless ankle. When he took a step she felt a pain, not in her ankle, but inside her at the V-shaped top of her diaphragm. Even the sound of that wooden block, felted as it was, touching the floor hurt her. Reno said it didn't hurt him. He said his scarred stump was as free of feeling as wood itself. He was even-legged. The ash block made his footless leg exactly the length of his good leg, so there was no hitch to his stride. Except that in looking down you had the shock of seeing one trouser leg footless, you would have thought the slight stiffness of his gait no more than a touch of lameness caused by a passing twinge of rheumatism.

Leafy tried for Reno's sake to treat him like a two-footed man. He didn't want to be spared—and since the block caused him no pain and hadn't made him gimpy, there was no need to spare him. The person she was really trying to spare was herself. Reno said, "I'd have walked halt the rest of my life if I *hadn't* lost that foot." And she could see the pride he felt in remembering how the loss came about. But she felt no pride remembering. She wanted to keep her mind as much as possible away from how it came about; and that was the reason, likely, the soft wooden knock of Reno's artificial foot, more like the thump made by a woman weaving at a loom than that of a natural man walking, pained her.

When she had asked Reno to move the chair, he had the puzzled-schoolmaster look she loved; he was a man who didn't act without reason.

"There *are* chairs on the carpet, Leafy. I'm sitting on one."

"Over there, I mean," Leafy said. "Where the carpet's billowing."

"It's tacked," Reno said. "It can't blow loose."

"But it's moving. I don't like to look at it," Leafy said. "It makes me sick to my stomach."

28

The minute he understood what was troubling her, Reno got up and, softly stumping, put his chair over by the door. The blue-and-white-striped rag rug settled down at once.

"That better?"

Leafy nodded.

"Chancellor ought to be back with the doctor any time now."

"There's no hurry."

"Don't you want your baby?"

"How do I know, Reno? I never had a baby before."

She smiled at him and, because he looked puzzled, picked up his hand. He was still the handsomest man she had ever seen. It was still a wonder to her that a man with Reno's looks would look at her. When she first saw him he had been eighteen, and he hadn't changed much. Except for the foot. He was dark, of course. Tow hair and fair skin were for women. What Reno looked like was a hero. His face could be carved in marble. It wouldn't look out of place on the body of a statue.

"Oh I like to look at you, Reno."

Reno's looks, good or bad, didn't interest Reno. What he was thinking about was the baby. "You didn't answer my question."

"What question?" she asked.

"About the baby."

"I did."

"That was no answer."

"Reno," she said, "you're liable to make a liar out of me someday, working to make me say whatever it is you want to hear. I'll give up someday and say it. Whether it's the truth or not. And you may be sorry."

There was more to having a baby than making one inside your body, spinning enough hair, bone, and gristle to deck a body out. That job she had done without giving it a moment's thought. But outside, ready to receive it, should be another nest, all feathered and lined with longing and eagerness. She hadn't made that, was still deciding if she would.

"A baby takes nine months," she told Reno. "Maybe a mother takes longer."

Reno looked at her as if he had an idiot on his hands. And between us two, she thought, the baby lies. She turned toward Reno with a question in her mind: When was it all decided? What turn did we take that put us here? Was it all decided at some one minute? The parlor bedroom, with the curtains pinned back, and a thunderstorm working itself up? And Reno, not another, by my side?

"Reno, do you love me?"

This question would burst from her at the most unexpected times, like a sneeze or a hiccup. It took hold of her like a seizure. She would be thinking of something else, be framing another question, when "Reno, do you love me" jerked open her mouth and made her tongue move like a St. Vitus's dancer. Not the question, but the way it came, always frightened her. If she could say that, without intending to, she could say anything. Each time it happened, she supposed that Reno would notice her surprise; and, worrying about that, she would peer at him anxiously. Reno never noticed a thing, unless perhaps he was as good an actor as she was, or better. He seemed to think that was the most natural question in the world; at least, he answered it that way, leaving her no room for doubt. He always had, he always would; there was no one else, and especially now.

After the surprise of asking that question, Leafy changed the subject.

"Reno," she asked, "do you remember the first time you ever saw me?"

"Of course. You were fifteen, starting the eighth grade for the second time."

"But I had graduated."

"I know that, Leafy."

"What did you think?"

"I thought it was a shame your father wouldn't let you go to the Academy."

There was no use talking about that.

"What did you think of me?"

"I thought I'd have to stay on my toes to keep ahead of you."

"You didn't, did you?" she asked, surprised at the natural-ness of her own craft.

"Didn't what, Leafy?"

"Keep ahead of me. Otherwise," she explained, "I wouldn't be here now."

He smiled a little sheepishly. "My mind was on teaching you that day."

And she had wanted to learn.

"If I'd gone to the Academy I probably wouldn't have mar-ried you."

"Probably not."

When her father had said "Try another year at Fairmont, Mary Pratt," was he also saying "Be in the parlor bedroom at early dark on July 16 with a baby inside you wanting to be born"?

Though it was Chancellor, who by his caper with Fab Braxton made the Academy impossible for either one of them. Bass didn't intend sending a boy with play-acting ambitions to school. And if he didn't send the son it wouldn't look right to give the daughter what the son had been denied.

She remembered the afternoon. She had cooked dried apples for supper. Her mother had gone upstairs with one of her sick headaches, wearing a mustard plaster over her left eye and carry-ing a heated flatiron to make the plaster even hotter. When she came down, the print of the iron would be on her forehead, and in the center of the print there would be a few small yellow blisters.

Before giving in and taking to her bed, her mother had finished washing the dinner dishes, had set the table for supper and then covered it with the between-meals cloth. She had watered the coleus on the window sill, brushed out the kitchen, and pulled the unbleached-muslin curtains together to shut out the warm afternoon sun.

The door to the upstairs opened into the kitchen. Her mother stood on the lowest step looking around.

"I hate giving in like this, but I'm so sick I can't see straight." She swayed as she spoke, pressing the iron against the mustard plaster.

"What can I do to help, Mama?"

"Just be quiet," her mother said. "Tiptoe. That's the best present I can have from you for the next couple of hours." Then she closed the door carefully, so as not to give her head a jar.

Leafy, when the door closed, turned round and round in the kitchen like Aladdin in his cave. Two peach trees, blooming by the south window, made the milky light, strained through muslin, rosy. There was a faint tick as the still-live coals in the cookstove shifted place. It was warm for May, and she was barefoot. There was a touch of dampness in the kitchen floor boards, left over from the morning's scrubbing. On the window sill there was a small dribble of water, dropped there by her mother's headachy hand. She got the dishcloth and mopped it up.

Being alone made her so happy she wondered if she could have wished her mother's sickness upon her—or even her death. The thought worried her until she opened the door to the hallway to listen; she shut it reassured. Her mother's groans were loud and regular. Pacing the floor, vomiting, groaning: these meant nothing but a regular sick headache. It took silence to send her flying upstairs to see if her mother still breathed. This afternoon she had nothing to worry about; she was free for the best of all games—playing house in a real house.

She never had a chance at it when her mother was well. Oh, she could run errands, do chores: hunt eggs, clean case knives with powdered brick dust, dip candles, bring milk from the springhouse, crack black walnuts, put clabber on the back of the stove for cheese, grind coffee.

But she was never given her head, she was never allowed to plan.

"Mary Pratt, I never get up in the morning without a plan for the day in my head, and I don't want you upsetting it," her mother would say when Leafy made a suggestion. Her mother's plans weren't selfish—they were mostly for others—but it hurt her to have them upset by slowness or carelessness or lack of skill. Such things made her wince (Leafy had seen her), the same way she would have if someone had thrown butternuts in the coffee mill or used the nutmeg grater to get corn off the cob.

Her mother's foresight didn't leave Leafy a chance to provide any surprises. Even now, with her mother out of the way, she didn't know what surprise she could provide. The table was set, gravy timber brought up from the cellar, a sweet cake ready-baked and cooling. The sweet cake told her what to do. Her father liked fruit sauce with his cake. Since it was too early for fresh fruit, she could build up the fire and cook some dried apples.

While they were cooking, she went into the sitting room, planning to dust. The first thing she dusted was a book—and the last thing, too. The same book. She was leaning on the edge of the secretary, dustcloth in one hand, reading, when Chancellor came in. He didn't say a word. He looked at her silently until she felt the force of his eyes. He was thirteen and taller than her father. He had a deep voice and the beginning sprouts of black whiskers. When she felt him beside her, she began to dust the opened pages. Chancellor closed the book and put it back in the secretary.

"You doing the cooking?" he asked.

Chancellor's voice worried her. She had lost track of time. It could be sundown, for all she knew.

"Did the apples burn?"

"No, they didn't burn."

"Is Mama up?"

"No."

Even so, she knew something was wrong.

"Come look," said Chancellor.

In the kitchen he took the lid off the dried-apple pot.

"Where'd all the grease come from?" she asked.

"Worms," said Chancellor.

"Worms?"

"This time of year you've got to worm dried apples before you cook them."

"What'll I do?" Leafy asked.

"Dump them in the hog slop."

"I don't want Mama to know."

"Dump them and wash the kettle. She'll never know."

When she had done that, and after hearing her mother's groans from upstairs as steady as ever, Leafy went out to the barn, where Chancellor was currying Farmer. "You going someplace, Chancellor?"

"To town."

"Aren't you supposed to be hoeing corn?"

"I done my stint for the day."

"Papa says hoe till it's dark enough to see your hoe strike sparks."

"I seen some sparks," said Chancellor.

Leafy looked at the bright sun.

"I got good eyes," said Chancellor.

When he had finished saddling Farmer, Chancellor said, "Want to go with me?"

She did and she didn't. She was enjoying the strange sneaky and triumphant feeling she had of being alone downstairs.

"Do you or don't you?"

"I'd just as lief stay."

Chancellor vaulted onto Farmer, and headed down the driveway.

"Chancellor, wait for me."

She ran after him, and, when she caught up, Chancellor stiffened his leg and held out his foot so that she could use it as a stirrup for mounting.

"You're going to miss doing something you want to someday."

"I didn't know if I wanted to go or not."

"Not everybody's going to wait for you to make up your mind."

Leafy, behind Chancellor, had the advantage of Farmer's most cushioned spot; but it was also the widest, so that her legs stuck straight out; and it was the spot that was bobbing around the most, so that she had to hang onto Chancellor, rising and falling with him like a cocklebur stuck to his coattails. Her face was against Chancellor's back, but she had one eye free to see with.

Spring was past its first froth and into its dazzlement. Spring beauties, jack-in-the-pulpits, Johnny-jump-ups bedecked the floor of the forest. Dogwood was finishing, redbud beginning. Ferns were thick and musky. Bluebirds and orioles and thrushes sang in their slow afternoon way. Day, and spring itself, was no longer a wonder to them. Squirrels leaped from tree to tree.

"I could've had a mess of them for supper," Chancellor said.

It was the first thing he had said since they'd started, and his words gave Leafy permission to speak.

"Where we heading, Chancellor?" 1415796

"We are heading west, Sister," Chancellor said in his preacher's voice. "We are going to hunt buffalo and redskins. We will see all the Northwest Territory and the English lakes. I'll sell you to an Indian chief for a wife. Say farewell to O-hio."

The lakes and rivers Chancellor named unfolded, blue and wind-driven, before Leafy's eyes. The Indian chief was tall and handsome, dressed in white buckskin and decorated with eagle feathers.

"You'd just as lief, wouldn't you, Sister?"

"Yes," said Leafy, without thinking.

"Yahh," Chancellor yelled, and kicked Farmer. "No Indian would have you."

They went south, instead of west, to Blue Glass itself. Chancellor had been recruited by a traveling actor to take a part in his play. Once a year Fab Braxton came to Blue Glass, and he could have charged its citizens for the privilege of being in his plays, as well as admission, if he'd been of a grasping nature.

Fab didn't look like an actor to Leafy—though she had never seen another one. He didn't even look like a Camp Meeting preacher. He was of less than medium height and of more than medium weight. He had tobacco-colored hair and a lot of it. His red face took on so many expressions he hardly needed a mouth or words to talk with. You could read his face. Leafy liked him.

"Well, son," Fab said to Chancellor while looking at Leafy, "you brought me another recruit?"

"This is my sister," Chancellor said, as if that answered the question.

Fab wasn't accustomed, as Leafy was, to letting Chancellor lay down the law.

"You got a name, sister?"

"Leafy," said Chancellor.

"Bub," asked Fab, "is *your* name 'sister'?" Then he turned again to Leafy. "Leafy what, pretty? Bush or tree? Vine or weed? Book? Now if I was to turn you over my knee and spank you, I'd be turning over a new leaf, wouldn't I?"

"My name," said Leafy, "is Mary Pratt Converse. Leafy is a nickname my brother gave me."

Leafy spoke as her mother had taught her, in a low, clear, carrying voice.

Fab Braxton lifted his plump hands chest high, brought them together in a soundless clap, and said, "By God, I believe you. You may be Leafy to your brother, but to me you are Mary Pratt Converse. Do you want to be an actress, Mary Pratt? You have got the voice for it."

Leafy didn't answer.

"Time will fade the freckles and supply the teeth."

"I can recite," Leafy said.

"Well, now, that's a start. When do I start rehearsing you?"

"I couldn't be an actress," Leafy said.

"Why not?"

"They are exposed to temptations."

"What temptations?"

"Drink and men."

Fab Braxton again lifted his hands chest high and clapped them together softly. "By God," he said, "where did you pick up this information, Mary Pratt?"

"Pa," said Chancellor, who was, after all, the actor in the family, not Leafy.

"Does your father consort with actors and actresses?"

Chancellor, though trying to impress Leafy, couldn't keep from snickering.

Fab turned on him sternly. "Honor thy father, boy. The old man may be a sight smarter than you dream."

Leafy couldn't bear to leave her father to the defense of a stranger. "Papa never gives even the appearance of evil."

"Oh, he's right," said Fab. "I'm against that, too. Never give the appearance of evil. That's been my life's motto. Wouldn't be here today without it. Well, boy," he asked, "do you know your part?"

"I do," said Chancellor.

"I'll try you out first," Fab said. "You'll do better if you can see who you are."

Fab lived in a three-sided lean-to the days he spent in Blue Glass. From this he brought out tailcoat, collar, cravat, black crayon, and mustache. Before her eyes Leafy saw Chancellor turned from thirteen to thirty.

Fab backed off to eye his handiwork. "Mean," he said. "Black-hearted as they come. You must have it in you, boy. I couldn't have pasted it all on."

Chancellor was right. He knew his part, but he disappointed Leafy, who had expected him to be as fiery and fist-shaking as he was on a stump in the forest preaching. But he had an excuse. Here he had to use the words Fab had given him, and he couldn't be expected to court a girl named Amelia the way he courted sinners and God. Besides, all he wanted of Amelia was her money. From sinners he wanted love and repentance, and for them he expected the life everlasting. But he satisfied Fab.

When Chancellor finished, Fab lifted his hands in his gesture of pleasure.

"Well, boy," he said, "now you've traveled. Now you've been someplace besides yourself. It's kind of a letdown to come home and be nobody but yourself again, ain't it?"

Fab, who had been playing Amelia to help Chancellor practice, hadn't completely stopped using her voice.

"Now you're limited," he went on, giving Chancellor no chance to reply, "squeezed down to your own size, one backwoods boy only."

Chancellor seemed to be clearing his throat.

"You don't claim to be more, do you?" Fab demanded.

"One's enough," Chancellor said, sassier than he would have been, Leafy thought, because of Fab's Amelia voice.

"One's enough, eh? That's your opinion, is it? And I reckon you think the one you are is what makes it so?"

Chancellor, a lot too smart to get pulled into conversations over his head, stayed out of this one.

Fab went on as if Chancellor *had* been pulled in and *had* given the wrong answers.

"You're wrong, boy. The greatest of all contained multitudes."

Leafy thought he must be speaking of Jesus, but what Fab said next made her wonder. "In him, maidens, kings, villains, and lovers. In him, little children and old men, fools, spring songs, and winter winds—and always—death."

"Are you talking about Jesus?" Leafy asked.

"No, child. I am speaking of the Bard."

Fab's voice had put aside Amelia and was now wholly his

own. While he spoke, he divested Chancellor of his play-part trappings; and Chancellor never budged even when Fab ripped from Chancellor's upper lip, along with the mustache that belonged to Fab, some of the down that belonged to Chancellor.

Leafy understood only enough of what Fab was saying to add mystery to the music. She had to guess at more than half of the meaning. She guessed she had heard her duty preached, then her wishes understood, and, finally, what neither duty nor wishes suggested: she guessed she had heard news of goodness, love, and sorrow. But Fab himself was none of these. Fab was pure joy. Without appearing to know what he was doing, he put his arms into Chancellor's coat and stuck the black mustache above his own wide mouth.

The words Fab spoke held Leafy, and they freed her. How they could do both, or even either, she didn't know. She told Fab this, using her face and eyes to speak with, as he had done. She looked at Chancellor, got no recognition and expected none. But the sight of him listening to Fab was something she had wanted, got, and never lost.

She knew where they were. She took that in and stored it away, too: they were on the edge of Blue Glass, which was also the edge of the clearing and in front of a lean-to that housed costumes and a man who could recite. There in May, at the edge of evening, Fab Braxton, lately Amelia Overturff, proud beauty brought low by love, declaimed words that were as real as crows or turkey buzzards, words that could and maybe did shoot upward to the tops of dark trees, or outward toward the smoky colors of the sundown, and so westward finally to the great Ohio itself. She didn't know of a thing that could stop those words once they'd started rolling.

She heard dogs called home to supper, yapping over cold bones and leftover mush; and she had to stop in order to remember what such sounds were and who could be making them.

When Fab had been Amelia, he had lingered to palaver with them. Now, when he had finished, he turned his back on them and, with coattails swinging, marched into his lean-to and let down the blanket that formed the fourth wall.

It was finished. Except in her mind. She rode home still clasping Chancellor; but I'm a different cocklebur, she thought. And Chancellor, too, was changed. His thin waist, beneath her hands, tingled like a pump handle when the water begins to climb. With her one eye she saw the May dusk powdery with blueness. It was settling down like something you could reach out and grab up by the handful. And dusk's blue was mixed with the scents of flowers and of the woods and with Farmer's sweat—all of which Leafy ordinarily breathed in without smelling. But tonight Fab's words had stirred up all of her senses, and she knew what she smelled, both by their right names and by all the names suggested by Fab's reciting: spring and sweetness, change and sorrow.

When they were halfway home she said, "Chancellor, I could listen to Fab recite all night; I could listen all day and not get hungry once. Do you think he's got some magic like snakes have for birds? That was just what somebody wrote, but when Fab recited it, it sounded like real people talking."

"Shut up," said Chancellor.

"Well, I just wanted to ask you . . ." Leafy began.

"Do you want to walk home?" Chancellor asked.

"No."

"Keep still then."

When they got home, the house was already lighted. The table, which their mother in spite of her headache had set after midday dinner, had not been used. From the kitchen they could hear the creak of a rocker in the sitting room. That was their father. Their mother was never easygoing enough to rock. When they opened the door, they saw her in a straight-backed chair where the light from the center table fell on her darning. The mantel clock was ticking a softer sound than the rocking chair. The door to the front porch was open. Through it they heard a bobwhite call.

"Chancellor," said their father, in his voice that was quizzical even when he wasn't asking a question, "I suppose what we've heard is true?"

"How do I know what you've heard?"

Their mother took a deep breath, but their father went on quietly, the way he'd started.

"You been down at Blue Glass, practicing to be in a play?"

"I went with him," said Leafy. "I was there every minute."

"Your brother took you?"

"I wanted to go."

"You couldn't get on the horse without his help."

"I could."

"Mary Pratt," said her mother, "don't give your father any back talk."

This made Leafy mad. Nothing her mother could say about her father pleased her: jump on him or take his part, one was as bad as the other.

"Chancellor, it's you I'm talking to. You knew you were doing what you'd been told not to."

"I finished my work."

"And when you finished your work I said you could go to Blue Glass and practice to be in a play?"

"No," said Chancellor.

"What did I say?"

"I forget," said Chancellor.

Leafy looked at her father. She wished at times like this that he would become another person: that he would get red in the face, yell, shake his fist, stamp his foot. She would like to believe that this was not the same father who picked splinters from her feet, played the French harp, and told long, funny stories. But he was the same. There were the same wrinkles at the bridge of his nose which he had when he laughed, in spite of himself, at one of his own stories. His blue eyes were calm and quiet, as usual, and sad. His sandy mustache hung down over his mouth, which was a little lopsided from laughing at stories he told on himself. He rocked in the same slow, meditative way. The only difference to be seen between her father this evening and any other evening was the razor strop on the floor by his chair. Leafy tried not to look at it.

"Chancellor," their father said, "I don't see how you can forget what I've told you."

Leafy didn't see how he could, either.

"All right," Chancellor said. "I lied. I remember."

"What did I say, son?"

Chancellor changed. He was as different as night from day. He flamed up far stronger in his words and stance than he had reciting for Fab. He was on his stump now.

"You said crawl," he said. "You said be nothing, and stay out of sight, and don't make a sound. You said don't be fine-haired, don't be biggity, remember pride goes before a fall and there's probably a million better people in the world than you."

Their father waited until Chancellor had finished; and had finished all his hard breathing and trembling, too. Then he said, "What I told you, Chancellor, was that you'd be better off, in the long run, if you didn't make any claim to set yourself up and be listened to. That's what I said. There's no point saying, 'My intentions are so and so.' Do it, and intentions don't need mentioning. People won't be given a chance to call you windy then. To say, 'There goes Chancellor Converse; he's all wind and no weather.' I want to save you that. There are playbills already out. Your name's on them. On the night of June 2, Chancellor Converse sets himself up to be letter-perfect in a part. He figures to get up on a platform and make a show of himself. He figures he's good enough to charge money for people to see him. How do you know you won't flounder? Make a fool of yourself? Be a laughingstock? You want people saying you craved the limelight? What gave you the idea you could act, anyway?"

"Fab Braxton."

"Chancellor, didn't you ever hear the story of Madam Crow?

Ugly as sin, but she had a piece of cheese in her mouth. Mr. Fox came along. 'Madam,' he said, 'you are beautiful as an angel, and I hear tell you can sing like a nightingale.' Truth to tell, Mr. Fox would've waxed up his ears rather than listen to her cawing, if he didn't have something to gain. But he did. I guess you know who got the cheese."

"What cheese have I got that anybody wants?"

"Your services, boy. No play actors, no profits for the play-master. I'm not against his putting on plays. All I'm against is your making big claims. You sit low, you keep your head down. Ten years from now people won't be saying, 'That's the fellow who tried his hand at acting and made a fizzle of it.' "

He paused and looked appealingly at Chancellor.

"You know I'm telling you the truth, don't you?"

"No," said Chancellor.

Their mother said, "Chancellor, don't call your father a story-teller."

"I'm not. I'm saying I can't know if what he says is true 'til I try. And he can't know I'll make a fool of myself 'til I've done it."

"I can know there's no use taking chances. No use making promises and giving out prophecies you more than likely can't keep."

"*You're* prophesying. You're saying what you can't know 'til I try."

"I've made a mistake talking about this *one* time. What you'd do with this one claim, I don't know. Succeed, maybe, and stick your head up higher than ever to be shot at next time."

Their father stopped and appeared to be really looking at Chancellor for the first time since he'd started talking.

"You *want* to be an actor?"

"Hell, no," said Chancellor.

That "hell" made Leafy's head jerk back.

"You're talking like one already. You come on out to the woodshed with me."

Ordinarily, after a trip to the woodshed (and Chancellor was the only one who ever made that trip with their father) they all, if it was mealtime, sat down to eat together. Not quite as if nothing had ever happened, but at least as if the world hadn't come to an end. But this evening Chancellor went directly from the woodshed to his room, and no one tried to stop him. Leafy pulled out her chair and sat down; but Fab's reciting and Chancellor's whipping had closed her throat. She couldn't swallow a bite and she, too, left the table. She expected to be called back, but, as she went up the stairs, there wasn't a sound from the kitchen, not even the rattle of knife or fork.

She tried Chancellor's door, but he had put a chair back under the doorknob and when she called to him he didn't answer. She had a room of her own but she still slept on a trundle bed in her parents' room. When they had lived in the log house, unless she had slept in the loft with Chancellor, there had been no other place to sleep. Here, where there were four bedrooms, three upstairs, and the parlor bedroom downstairs, her father thought she ought to be sleeping in her own room. She often heard him argue with her mother about it.

"One of the chief reasons for building this house was to give Mary Pratt a room of her own."

"Mary Pratt's got a room of her own," her mother would answer. "All her things are in there. The bureau's filled with her stuff, and her dresses are in the clothespress. She's got her own washstand, pitcher, and bowl in there. She just sleeps here. She's got the Pratt throat. She's subject to croupy attacks in the night. And she's timid. I wouldn't have the heart to shut her off away from everybody. I'd feel I ought to go with her."

"Better leave her where she is then," her father would agree. "For the time being, anyway."

Sometimes Leafy was roused by the murmur of her parents' bedtime talk, but usually it had a drowsy comfortable sound like rain on the roof or wind in the trees. Tonight, perhaps because she had gone to bed so early and had finished her first sleep, their talk, instead of lulling her back to sleep, brought her wide awake. Or perhaps Fab's reciting had made her ears more sensitive than usual to all sounds. Her parents' voices were low, but she didn't miss a thing. They weren't quarreling. She knew that when she heard it; then her mother's voice would be quick and breathless, impatient with her father, who was slow and balky, making joke of what wasn't funny to her mother. Each spoke quietly tonight, each questioning. Each might have been a teacher disappointed not to get the right answer. Or people lost together, neither blaming the other for that, but hunting the good place they'd set out toward and missed.

What she heard she'd heard before. Times when she sat on a footstool between their knees on buggy trips; or times while they, in the kitchen, talked, and she in the sitting room put down her book to listen. It was an old story. She knew it as well as they did.

"Bass, you'd think I'd be the one afraid to stand up and claim anything."

"It's not that I'm afraid."

Her mother dropped that word. "It's a wonder I'm not the one, whatever's the reason. I'm the one ought to feel meechin'. Ma was barefoot, smoking a pipe, when your mother was going to Meeting in silk."

"What's that got to do with it?"

"This. It makes it harder for me to understand you. You'd think I'd be the one who wanted to take a back seat. You had real schooling. I scraped together enough to satisfy a district board I could teach. Your kin's looked up to and has been since the beginning. I'm not going to talk down my own folks—and I don't have to, to you. You knew them. Well, then, why are you always bending over backward? Always talking under your breath? Always breaking your neck, and mine, so's not to be noticed?"

Her father's reply was easygoing.

"You still holding it against me, Prill, that I opposed your being head of the Sabbath school?"

Her mother made a loud, angry, sputtering sound. "If I want something to find fault with, I don't have to hark back that far. There was plenty before and there's been plenty since. Bass, what's in you that makes you want to scrunch down so little? I made the last bid at the auction. You heard me, but you wouldn't let me stand up and say so. When Leafy said the cat had seven kittens, you shushed her."

"She was bragging."

"It's the truth."

"It may be the truth. I've got a thousand dollars in the bank. It'd be bragging to go around saying so."

"If you have, why don't you send Chancellor off to school?"

"Work'll do Chancellor more good than schooling."

"They'll say you're closefisted."

"I'm not going to start cutting my coat to suit my neighbors' talk."

"You take a back seat, Bass, because you *like* it? Just because you *like* it back there in the drafts, and where you can't hear? You'd set there even if nobody seen you do it?"

"I can't say as I mind people's seeing I'm not pushy."

Leafy heard the ruefulness in her father's confession, the laugh at himself. She wanted to get out of bed, run to him, hug him, and say, "It's all right to take a back seat, Papa." Her mother *was* pushy—for her children anyway: "Speak up, make yourself heard, memorize it, get up early, aspire." She said to Leafy, "Wouldn't you like to be a preacher like Grandmother Converse?" What she meant was, "Wouldn't you like to be praised?" If she'd said, "Be a saint, be good, pray in secret, fast," Leafy would've listened.

Now Leafy saw her mother, who had been brushing her hair, as she did every night, with swift, head-punishing blows, throw down her brush and begin to walk about. Back and forth, her

46

shoes still on, but almost soundless on the bare boards, the energy of her feelings barely letting her feet touch the floor.

"No, *you* don't object. You don't object if people say you never claimed much as your due. Always willing to take second best, even when it came to a wife."

"They don't say that."

"If they knew my folks they would. And you knew them. You didn't set your cap, as all your brothers did, for somebody you had to stand on tiptoe to reach."

"You were a very pretty girl, Prill."

"Girl? I was an old maid; a self-taught schoolteacher who'd lifted herself by her bootstraps . . . and before she had any boots."

"Why did you choose me, for that matter? I was homely, back-ward, poor. . . ."

"I chose you because I thought you were better than the others. That's why. You're not a pretty man, and never will be one. I don't care about looks. I chose you because you had some learn-ing. You owned some books. You had a clean mind. And some folks you could be proud of. That was more than I could say of the other beaus I'd had. I chose you because I was looking up. Because I was proud to claim something. And you chose me because you were looking down and afraid to make claims."

"That's not true, Prill. I courted you because I loved you. And I thought you married me for the same reason."

"What if I'd been rich? And my family was better than yours? Would you have looked at me then? Would you? Could you love anyone rich and educated and high-placed?"

"Maybe it ain't too late to try."

"Bass, you'll joke with me once too often."

"What's brought all this on, Prill?"

"Don't play dumb with me, Bass. I don't hold with Chancellor's cutting didoes with some traveling mountebank any more than you do. But telling him always to take a back seat! And whipping him if he don't."

"Prill, you run down your own folks. More than I do. And you talk up mine. And I oughtn't to have to tell you what the difference is. Chancellor was acting like a Pratt tonight. Big talk. Big plans. Big mouth. 'Look at me. Jack-of-all-trades. I'll try my hand at anything.' That's what you got shut of yourself. I can't make you out. What do you want for your children?"

"The same as you, Bass."

That wasn't the end of the talk, but Leafy had heard it before. They did want the same thing. Their ways of getting it differed: one favored backing up, the other going forward. It made a tug of war, and Leafy felt that the rope they pulled on was wrapped around her and with every word tightened.

After they had gone to bed, and she could tell by their breathing that they were asleep, she got up and tiptoed down to Chancellor's room. Knocking was something she would no more have thought of than bowing to him. When she tried the knob this time, the door swung open. Chancellor was wide awake, reading by candlelight. She looked at him for a while without speaking. She had expected his face to show what he felt: she thought she'd find Fab's recitation there and Bass's whipping; even an echo of their parents' bedtime talk, which he hadn't heard. She was boiling with all these things herself, angry with her mother, and worried about Chancellor. But the sight of Chancellor, so calm, made her mad at him, too.

"You going to not be in the play, Chancellor?" she demanded.

Chancellor didn't close his book, but he was polite enough to look up.

"Yeh," he said. "I'm going not to be in it."

That didn't suit her either. Nothing had suited her tonight; and she had hoped that Chancellor, who usually knew his own mind, and hers, too, would straighten things out. She thought it was wrong of her mother to rant and rave at her father for trying to keep Chancellor from growing up biggity. She thought it was wrong of Chancellor to give in to her father. How could

48

she think both of these at once? She wanted Chancellor to tell her.

"Don't you want to be in the play?"

"I was practicing, wasn't I?"

"Why don't you run away from home?"

"How could I be in it and run away?"

"You could run away to Blue Glass."

"That's what you'd do?"

"Yes."

"You're afraid to sleep alone in your own room."

"Mama doesn't want me to."

"Papa doesn't want me to be in the play."

"Yes, but that's not the reason. You don't care what he thinks."

"It's a silly play."

Leafy stared at her brother. "I thought it was beautiful." She began to walk back and forth like her mother.

"Don't flounce around like a wet hen, Leafy."

"I could *feel* you riding home," Leafy said. "You shook. You didn't think it was silly."

"Afterward wasn't silly."

Being agreed with took the wind out of Leafy's sails. It gave her confidence to confide. "They were arguing again. About you."

Chancellor didn't appear to be interested.

"Papa don't like your setting yourself up, and claiming attention. That's all."

Chancellor threw his quilt back with so big and sudden a motion the candlelight wavered and almost winked out. He was sleeping in his shirttail, without his drawers, since this was summer, and Leafy could see the red welts left on his legs by the razor strop. They weren't bad, for her father didn't believe in overdoing things, but there were plenty of them, and her stomach tied together at the sight. For a minute she thought Chancellor planned to bang her on the head with his book, but he lectured her instead.

"Papa's preached that sermon once tonight, and he practiced it once, too, out in the woodshed. If you want to preach it, get out of here. I know it by heart already."

"I don't want to," said Leafy.

"I delight to hear it," said Chancellor. "And if you think I shouldn't open my mouth, you set me an example. If you think I should turn dumb, and set like a bump on a log so's no one will take notice of me, don't come in here like I wasn't dumb and could talk."

Chancellor was about as dumb as a guinea hen. Since the Bible was the book he was reading, Leafy quoted him a little, hoping anything said there, even if it did take their father's side, wouldn't upset him to the point of slapping or shoving her out of his room.

"The meek," she said, "shall inherit the earth."

"Inheriting the earth's nothing I want. I got too much earth as it is, out in the cornfield."

"It means," Leafy explained, "the earth and the richness thereof."

"If that's what the meek's going to inherit, why don't Pa have more? He's the meekest one of his family and he's got the least."

"Maybe," Leafy said, "he didn't start soon enough. Maybe he's trying to keep you from making the mistake he made."

Chancellor went to the window, head up and tail over the dashboard. "I don't aim to be meek," he said. "Not me, not ever."

Beyond the window was the apple orchard. Blooming time was past, but stray blossoms still clung here and there to the trees. They looked like white moths against the dark foliage.

"You gave in about the play," Leafy reminded him.

"I don't aim to be meek, but I do aim to be cagey," Chancellor said. "I'm not going to be whipped to death for a silly play."

three

✍ *Leafy*

Toward the end of her first day in childbed Leafy thought, This has been the longest day of my life.

It was still light, still warm, still gusty. The clock in the sitting room struck six, and the sound was blown to her in a spray like rain. It was past suppertime, but her mother was holding off supper until Chancellor got back with the doctor. Leafy had had a tray with food to tempt an invalid: stewed chicken and cream gravy, rice molded in a teacup topped with a sprinkling of nutmeg and accompanied by dip. To spare her mother's feelings Leafy got Reno to clean the tray. Then, just as he'd finished, in came his father-in-law to urge him to come out to supper.

"Reno," he said, "Clate's out there champing on the bit for his supper. And Prill'd be pleased to get some of her cooking down somebody while it's still hot. Mary Pratt'll likely pull through if left alone for the time it'll take us to swallow our victuals."

Reno, thus urged, left the room carrying the tray. And Bass, having talked his son-in-law out of the room so's not to delay supper any longer, paid no heed to his own arguments for dispatch. He sat down comfortably in the chair Reno had vacated.

Bass didn't mention the baby or ask Leafy how she felt. Too bashful, maybe, Leafy thought. He had washed up before the supper he thought he was going to eat. His hair still had wet comb tracks, and his bright freckled skin was high-colored from scrubbing.

"Play your French harp, Papa," Leafy said.

Bass always had three things in his pockets: a three-bladed knife with a staghorn handle, a snap-mouth purse, and his French harp. Bass didn't require asking to play, but asking pleased him, and Leafy knew it. His foot began to tap. A tune was taking shape in his head. He knocked whatever spit might have been left over from the last playing out of the harp. He was an expert at tonguing. He could get single notes clear as a fiddle cry. Then, chording, he could swell the harp up to organ size, if the ear was to judge.

Most of the time Leafy could tell why one tune followed another. After a soldiers' marching song, then a Camp Meeting song, sinners marching to Zion. He would play their tunes, but he didn't hold with Camp Meeting.

Bass was a Quaker. They all were, but Bass was a Philadelphia Quaker, which was the purest kind. Philadelphia Quakers considered the Blue Glass variety pretty outlandish.

Prill had been born a United Brethren down in Kentucky and had been baptized with water in a branch, not just the Holy Spirit like the Quakers. But because Bascom Converse would have been dropped from the Meeting rolls if he had married out of Meeting, Aprilla Pratt bethought herself if she could not be a follower of Jesus without the water baptism, foot-washing, and the singing of hymns she'd been brought up to believe in. She decided she could, and became a Quaker by convincement; though Bass always said that what she was a Quaker by practice and a United Brethren by convincement.

She was safe now, Leafy thought, whichever way it turned out. God wanted to be worshiped. Before her mother had let her Quaker in-laws change her from fancy Aprilla to quiet Prill, and put on her gray bonnet and First Day shawl, she'd been baptized, had washed the feet of strangers, and raised her voice in many a song.

There was no Quaker rule against Camp Meetings, and many Quakers, her father and mother among them, attended. Bass seated them in the back, of course, and, except for covering his eyes with his hand during prayers, didn't make any outward sign of joining the goings-on. Some Quakers did. They testified to a deepening of grace or of the conviction of a second birth. These birth pains were so strong some Quakers toppled over and lay on the ground with only the whites of their eyes showing and their bodies as rigid as those of any Baptist or United Brethren.

Her mother, because of her early training, felt it her duty to bear witness at these meetings. She did so in a brief, calm, heartfelt way. Leafy herself had been saved at six, but so quietly and matter-of-factly that no one, including herself, had been upset.

Though her father held his peace when Quakers toppled over in the aisles, said nothing when his daughter got converted and his wife bore witness, Leafy knew he suffered. She had seen him flush up when her mother rose and had watched his knuckles whiten as he listened. But he never tried to stop her.

Chancellor was another kettle of fish. He didn't, like his mother, have any Christian experiences to bear witness to. Or any great sins, so far as anyone knew, to repent of. Chancellor didn't let either of these facts stand in his way. He repented and he bore witness. He got converted the summer after his father made him give up acting, with the biggest whoop and holler that had been heard in Blue Glass since the last raid of the Miamis.

All that summer, after his whipping, Chancellor had been on the lookout for something. He didn't tell Leafy what it was, and she didn't think he knew himself, didn't know whether it was something he would find or see, do or invent. But one thing was certain: he was going to discover the secret of the world. He could talk to her about it, because she wanted the same thing. The difference between them was that Chancellor was pretty sure he had to do something. She thought it all might burst upon her suddenly and with no effort on her part. She would be walking along slowly—it didn't have to be spring; it could be fall, dead leaves in the pond and the persimmons, after the first frost, glimmering as if a candle had been lighted inside them—and, inside her, the answer would come brimming.

Chancellor had to do something, though. Maybe it was learn; so he studied hard, and except for a 94 in orthography, he had 98 in everything else. Maybe it was do something dangerous, so he accepted every banter and imposed dares upon himself: drank a pail of water with tadpoles alive and swimming in it, and then, for a while, anyway, Leafy supposed, alive and swimming in *him;* chased a blackwhip snake which could have turned at any moment and lashed him; memorized twenty-four Psalms in twenty-four hours. (Nobody had thought to say, "Long ones.")

He scared her and he excited her with his bravery.

"Why?" she asked him.

"Got to see how far I can go," he said.

"Maybe you'll get so far you can't come back."

"Maybe that's where I want to go."

Chancellor talked to her more than he ever had before, that summer. Sometimes she thought he was talking to himself, but he liked her around so that if anyone saw him they wouldn't think he was crazy. Once, when she was in the privy, he was waiting outside when she unlatched the door.

"What took you so long?" He was grumpy because he had a book in his hands to read.

"I can take as long as I want to."

The privy was for women and girls only. A man didn't use a privy unless he was too old or too sickly to squat—and Chancellor, who could go jumping from tree to tree like a squirrel, could certainly manage squatting. There was nothing wrong with him but laziness and a liking for nice things. Their privy was kept scrubbed as clean as their kitchen; it never smelled of anything but lime, sunshine, the honeysuckle that grew over it, and the pine boards of which it was made. There was only one other way to have as much privacy: kneel in prayer. But there wasn't any way, even kneeling with your elbows propped up on a chair, to pray *and* read. Chancellor had come prepared for a little reading. The book he had with him was the Bible.

Chancellor's Bible reading puzzled Leafy. Bible reading was a duty, and Chancellor read it like it was a forbidden pleasure. He showed the Bible to her now, as if he were sneaking some storybook out to read. A story, she thought, would be more suitable for where Chancellor was going. It also wasn't suitable for her and Chancellor to be having a conversation where they were. When women went to the privy, men looked the other way—they certainly didn't join them at the door for a chat.

"You oughtn't to read the Bible in there."

"You talk like a Pharisee. Jesus didn't care where you did things if what you did was good."

"There's a time and a place for everything."

"Not according to Old Turtle."

Leafy was outraged when Chancellor used this name for their father. She knew what it meant, she understood that it was appropriate, but it hurt her. She walked out of the door, giving Chancellor, Bible and all, a wide berth. When she didn't hear the door close, she turned and looked back. Chancellor had been banking on her curiosity. He was standing inside, like a man in a covered pulpit, Bible in one hand, the other pointing upward to heaven. Except for the Bible, she would have thrown a rock at him.

When Chancellor left their father out of it, Leafy listened to him. Sometimes she thought it wasn't holiness that was bothering Chancellor so much as an urge to outdo everybody. He was going to climb the gospel tree higher than anybody else had ever climbed it, rassle two angels instead of one, and suffer more boils than Job. Sometimes she thought Chancellor was bitten by religion because God was a mystery, and Chancellor was set on understanding everything. Sometimes she thought he was testing their father, saying, "I dare you tell me in church to stop making a holy show of myself."

Then there were times when Chancellor made her ashamed of such thoughts. Times when he would talk to her with not a bit of the show-off (preaching from a stump or being funny from the privy door) in him. He heard the church bells ring and said, "I want to know what they are saying." He said, "If Jesus came to Belmont County, who'd follow Him, if He didn't head west?" Chancellor talked half the time like a man traveling mostly for the danger of it. But what of that? The thing that mattered was the way he was heading!

The summer of Chancellor's acting ambitions was notable for something else. Chancellor spoke out at Camp Meeting.

Bass hadn't found time to take his family to Camp Meeting that summer until the next-to-the-last service. But by putting off the uproar for as long as he could, he succeeded in getting his family there at the most feverish minute of all. It was coming down to now or never for revivalists and sinners alike. Those not saved tonight might be lost for eternity. The revivalists were determined to find the one right word or song or prayer to open hard hearts, if it took them all night—and sinners who knew their chances were ebbing were willing to wait. They wanted the log jams of their sins and refusals blown sky-high so that the gospel mercy could come flooding in.

The Converses rode over to Camp Meeting in the spring wagon, starting after an early supper. The August evening was hot, the road dusty. Besides being religious, the occasion was social, and Leafy and her mother wore their best, protected by dusters. Leafy sat beside Chancellor on the backless seat behind their mother and father. She turned sidewise, using Chancellor as a back rest, and felt in his body the same quivering tautness she had noticed riding home behind him from Fab's.

Long before they arrived they could see through the trees the smoky glare of torches and could smell the scent of burning resin. Leafy sniffed something else: the smell of the crowd, or maybe of Chancellor, sweating with excitement. By the time they were across from Fab's lean-to, they could hear the sound of the Camp Meeting, a quarter of a mile away.

"Sounds like a swarm of mad wasps," said Bass.

Leafy corrected that in her mind. They were Christians, not wasps; or if not Christians, sinners wanting to be Christians. It was their longing that gave them a sound so different from people at a logrolling or a barn-raising. Though the sounds *were* Christian and sorrowful, not wasplike and mad, they did make her own scalp prickle. The sounds rose and fell like the light of the torches, so that the words were unintelligible. The shadows of the people, as Leafy first caught sight of them, jumped and pranced like black men in a jungle. She was glad that all her decisions were behind her and there would be no struggle for her soul. She would stand, of course, as a sign that she had accepted Christ as her personal saviour. Even her father did that.

Her father chose, as he always did, inconspicuous seats. Once seated he buried his face in his hands. In that way he was perhaps able to think that he was back in a Philadelphia Meeting. The first revivalist helped him to think this. He was a quiet man with a carrying voice, something like Fab Braxton's, though sweeter. He didn't rage or stomp, rassle with the pulpit or fall to his knees pleading with God for mercy on sinners. No tears, like smoky little pearls in the torchlight, rolled down his cheeks. He just stood up there, medium-sized and reasonable, and quietly called them home to love.

He called, Chancellor told Leafy afterward, particularly to him. That was what Chancellor thought, anyway—though others seemed to think the same thing. They came down front in droves. They spoke in tongues; they trembled under the power. The invitation offered was as irresistible as waters of a living spring to dry throats. Sinners could no more turn their backs on it than a man in a sleetstorm could turn his back on an opened door and a warming fire.

And that preacher wasn't Jesus. That's what Chancellor said, over and over to Leafy. He was only a man talking about Him. He spoke quietly, and Chancellor rose quietly and walked down front quietly. Half the tent was moving in that direction, and Bass, behind his hand, saw nothing. Chancellor was dumb as a stone at first. He didn't have any choice, he said, about anything he did. Actually, he said, he didn't walk down front; he was walked. He didn't, at the altar, fall on his face; he was felled. He didn't decide to rise; he was lifted. He didn't open his mouth to preach; the words that came from his mouth were the overflowings of joy. If he hadn't opened his mouth he would have died, drowned in a gush of feeling.

Chancellor opened his mouth and preached in each of the two ways revivalists had: with the power of threats and with the beguilement of promises. He could hold his own with any son of thunder when it came to threats of doom. While this was his manner, Bass didn't recognize him.

When, in his more usual voice, he spoke of the life everlasting, Bass, hearing a familiar voice, lifted his face from his hands. There was Chancellor, the Reverend Lige Tabb by his side, watching Chancellor happily as he preached. Bass opened his eyes wider, like a man who thinks he must still be dreaming. Then he, too, rose and walked, like any other sinner, down front. But there, in the opinion of most who saw him, he acted like one who needs but hasn't yet heard the call. He took Chancellor by the arm, spoke a few words in his ear, then he propelled him back the way they had come, past the last log bench, the last torch, and into the darkness beyond. Leafy was as shocked as anyone. To silence someone praying or speaking of God was a slap in the face of God Himself. The whole congregation turned to look at the big boy interrupted in his bearing witness. The Reverend Tabb made a motion to follow Bass, and for a minute Leafy thought Chancellor might be snatched away from her father and set back to preaching again. But there were others besides Chancellor to be thought about; many at the altar hadn't won through to salvation yet, and the Reverend Tabb elected to stay with them.

Afterward, Leafy asked her brother, "Why did you let Papa take you out?"

"What did you want me to do? Start a fight in Meeting with my own father?"

"You could've planted your feet."

"It don't make any difference," Chancellor told her. "Stay in or walk out wouldn't have changed anything."

Stay in or walk out might not have, but the preaching Chancellor had done did cause some changes. Bass decided that it would be more "settling" for Chancellor to stay on the farm that fall instead of going, as he had planned, to the Academy. And having decided to keep his son at home he wasn't in any very good position to send a daughter away to school—even in case he had wanted to.

So Chancellor, in addition to saving his soul that night, had preached her right back into repeating the eighth grade at Fairmont. And, since Reno was the teacher there, had preached her into marriage and this childbed.

She had asked Chancellor a hundred times about that night,

what he had felt and what had happened. And Chancellor, though he said what had happened was beyond human telling, had freely answered any question she would ask.

But she had always had too much delicacy to ask her father why he had done what he had that night. Hundreds of people got converted every summer, lots of them more than once. But never before that she had heard of had a father yanked a newly converted son out of church, interrupting him in the act of bearing witness. Someplace in the world it might have happened, but never before, she was pretty sure, in Blue Glass. Did her father ever feel shamefaced about it? Un-Christian? Did he ever think that for a man whose policy it was to take a back seat he'd got pretty far up front that night?

Leafy had thought of these things as she listened to Bass play his French harp. She had tried to bring the two men, both of whom were her father, together: the man softly foot-tapping, one mustache end quirked upward by a smile, and the other, the man with a razor strop, the man who had marched Chancellor away from his preaching.

It was bad enough to be caught in a tug of war between her father and mother and want to please both. It was even worse not to know which father to please. Chancellor thought she said "I'd just as lief" because she didn't know her own mind. She knew her own mind here. "Please Father." But he was two men, and what pleased one riled the other. And whatever she said she was likely to feel the tug-of-war rope, pulled by Father against Mother and Father against himself, tighten around her throat.

For the first time since that summer nine years ago, she dared let her father see what had been in her mind about what he had done.

"Do you ever wish you hadn't stopped Chancellor the time he started preaching?" The question made her heart thump, but her father answered easily.

"No," he said. "I think what I did was right."

It was the highest calling there was for a man. Teachers, farmers, legislators couldn't hold a candle to preachers. Everyone knew that. Her mother, when she had seen that Chancellor had the gift, as well as the call, to preach, was planning at once for him to be another Lorenzo Dow or George Fox. A man called of God, but not underestimated by men. But even she soft-pedaled what Bass had done and tried to explain it away to Chancellor. "Your father was worried for you, Chancellor. He thought you might make claims you'd be sorry for afterward. It don't need to make any difference to you in the long run."

What his father had done to his first sermon seemed to grate less on Chancellor than his mother's plans for future sermons.

"Five minutes was enough," he said. "I got all the preaching I had in me out of my system that night."

When her father didn't go back to his French harp, Leafy said, "If you hadn't stopped him, do you think Chancellor would be a preacher today?"

"Nobody can say for sure, but I doubt it. Nobody can stop a grown man from preaching the gospel if he has a real call. And Chancellor don't carry himself much like a man with a call nowadays."

Leafy didn't know how much her father knew about the way Chancellor carried himself nowadays. She didn't know how much she knew herself. But if you were cut off from preaching and cut off from learning, and were Chancellor, what was left to you?

"I suppose he could've run off, the way I did."

She didn't know what she had said until her father repeated, "Run off? What're you talking about, Mary Pratt?"

Before either of them had a chance to say another word, her mother, with Dr. Daubenheyer, came to the door.

"Howdy, Bass," Dr. Daubenheyer said. "Leafy, you don't look very sick."

"Bass," Prill said, "your supper's cold. You think you'd feel free to eat now?" Prill's tone was even but accusing.

Bass didn't appear to notice. He slid his French harp into his pocket and followed Prill out of the room.

When they had left, Leafy said, "Mama oughtn't to talk to Papa like that."

"Look at the way Papa acts," said Daubenheyer.

"Acts? He was talking to me and playing his French harp."

"He was doing exactly what he wanted to do. And the hell with everyone else. But all you note is what your mother says, not what your father does."

"I'm sick. He was cheering me up."

"You don't need cheering up. You need exercise. Now get up out of that bed."

"I've got my bedgown on."

"I didn't think you were naked."

"I'm going to have a baby."

"What makes you think so?"

"You said so yourself."

"I didn't set a day or an hour. Or plan on your coming down with creeping paralysis."

"I had pains this morning."

"For thirty minutes. Then they stopped."

"Aren't you even going to examine me?"

"It would be a pleasure."

Leafy angrily swung her feet to the floor, expecting a terrible twinge. There was nothing.

"What you need's to move around, wash windows, scrub floors, polish andirons."

"You know that's all done here."

"Walk, then. That's something you've proved you can do. Get up and walk. The longer you postpone having that baby, the harder it's going to be for you."

"I never heard of anybody putting off a baby's being born."

"There's quite a few things you've never heard of, Leafy, in spite of your travels. That baby's still a part of you. You lay there, not moving a muscle, it knows it's not welcome. Now you get up off that bed and start walking."

"Ask Reno to come."

"Reno's not going with you. You've got Reno buffaloed. If you want to set, he'll let you. No, you're going to take a walk with me, Leafy."

"You know what everyone else should do, June. Nobody would ever think you'd made any mistakes yourself."

The words came without bidding, and the minute they were out, Leafy regretted them. "I'm sorry," she told him.

Daubenheyer didn't answer for a while.

"That's the way a man learns, Leafy," he said finally. "That's the reason I can help you."

On the edge of her bed, leaning over her stomach, Leafy looked up. "Talking the way you do, I wonder you've got any patients at all."

"Most of them don't need talk like this. Now get dressed. Put a duster over your bedgown, if you want to. I don't aim to make any public trip."

four

⚞ *Dr. Daubenheyer*

It was full dark when they started, the wind still up, the sky heavy with stars. Daubenheyer led the way at a steady, moderate pace. He steered clear of the roads, as he said he would, choosing paths across pastures and through woods lots.

"What if I stumbled and fell?" Leafy called to him.

"Might be just what the doctor ordered."

"What if I stepped on a snake?"

"Heavy as you are, I reckon you'd kill him."

It was the strangest thing she had ever heard of. Darkness had not brought coolness. She was sweating where the linen duster held her bedgown in close to the folds of her body. She was sweating where her breasts touched the upward swell of her belly. She was sweating between her thighs and under her arms and where her hair kept the wind from her forehead. She was uncomfortable, but not tired or in pain. She could probably walk all night. Laved with her own sweat, without stays or shimmy she moved as if swimming through dark water.

They went quietly, but crickets and katydids stopped their chirpings as they approached; and as they passed, the sounds closed in behind them again like waters behind a boat. Corn was still too green and sappy for any of its dry autumn whisper. Even so, Leafy could tell with her eyes closed and by sound alone when they passed fields of corn. Flax had a starchy smell to her, and stands of tobacco were rank and weedy. Tree limbs in the woods lots were creaking, and away off on the other side of the Ohio, sheet lightning lit up the sky like the pulse of a big lightning bug.

Daubenheyer waited for her to catch up with him.

"It won't give up," he said.

"What won't?"

"The storm."

"It's farther away than it was this morning."

"It's jousting around. It'll close in fast when it gets ready."

"What if we get caught in it?"

"A summer storm? Who cares about that?"

"I don't like lightning."

"Lightning's got nothing against you."

When they came to a cluster of stumps where the Dolphus cabin had been before it burned, Daubenheyer said, "Cool off a little now."

She was glad for the dark that hid her. She felt that she was hanging over the stump like warm bread dough over the edge of the crock it was raising in.

"How long do you figure to keep me walking, June?"

" 'Til I get tired, I reckon."

"What if I had my baby out here?"

"Half of Blue Glass was born without a roof over its head. And without a doctor. There's no trick to it."

When Leafy didn't answer, he said, "You've taken your time as it is. Two years since you've been married."

"Not 'til September."

"You don't have to tell me. I was there."

There were some parts of that night he didn't mind remembering. It had been a treat to walk into a house as transformed for an occasion as the Converse house. It was as good as going to a play. A stage was set (though he wouldn't have guessed that a wedding was what it was set for), and it raised your expectations. Something unusual was going to happen, and in anticipation you became a little unusual yourself. Across the ceiling of the parlor, Prill Converse had strung real leaves, already turned red and yellow, and paper hearts, colored red. It was on an Indian summer evening, warm enough for open doors, and overhead there was a constant flutter of forest foliage and homemade hearts.

It was going to be a proper wedding, bride and groom kept out of sight until the ceremony. But no sooner had Daubenheyer greeted a few friends than the bride's mother came to him.

"June," she said, "could you go upstairs and see Mary Pratt?"

He said yes, though he didn't know what was being asked of him. At this late date was he being asked to explain to Leafy the duties of a wife? Or to cheer her up because her father hadn't arrived yet with her grandmother, who was going to do the marrying?

"She's in her room upstairs," Prill said. "She's expecting you. I told her I'd send you up as soon as you got here."

Leafy was in her room, in nothing that looked bridal to Daubenheyer, a gray wool with high neck and long sleeves.

"Aren't you dressed yet?" he asked.

"This is my wedding dress. Mama made it for me. I'll need something warm for winter."

For winter it might be warm. Now it looked hot and uncomfortable, though inside the gray tube the girl was bridal. She was burning as bright as a candle in a pewter candlestick. Daubenheyer, who had known her since she was eight or nine, thought he had never seen her before. She still wasn't beautiful, but she was bewitching: green-eyed, red-lipped, transparent-skinned, like something grown in the shade but touched at the minute with a blaze of light.

"Leafy," he said, "you knock the wind out of my sails."

She smiled at him. He didn't suppose she had the kind of looks that were much praised, and even now it wasn't her looks, but her excitement that was compelling. Or was it excitement? The skin over her cheekbones was tight. Her mouth, when not stretched in a smile, quivered.

Perhaps he ought to warn her about marriage. Mothers kept mum to their daughters about its disappointments for fear of having old maids on their hands, and out of the natural reluctance of the persons who've been had to admit it. The higher you fly in your imaginings, the higher, in fact, you fall, he thought he might remind her. Fifteen minutes of "I will's" and a couple of prayers aren't going to change your sweetheart. A good-looking, easygoing, ignorant schoolteacher won't become a god by saying, "I, Reno, take thee, Leafy." He's a backwoods boy, and he'll bed you on cornhusks and be asleep with his mouth open thirty minutes after he beds you on those husks. And you, my girl, will be wider awake than you ever were in your life before and saying, "Is that all?" Don't blaze up so now, Sis. Remember, after burning there's bound to be ashes.

Because he had stared for so long without saying a word, he had worried Leafy. "Do I look all right, June? I wanted white, but Mama said this would be more practical."

"You don't look practical. You don't need a ceremony. You could face Reno with that look and the two of you would be wed, without preacher or prayer book."

Leafy laughed. "Preachers and prayer books! There won't be any. It's a Quaker wedding. We marry ourselves."

"What's your grandma going to do? She's a preacher."

"Oh, she'll pray. But she won't marry us. The Quakers don't."

"I keep forgetting you're Quakers. The house don't look very Quakerish tonight. All those bright colors and the red hearts dancing."

"That's Mama's United Brethren blood coming out."

"You got any United Brethren blood, Leafy?"

"I expect so. I wanted a white dress and white bells and white lilies."

"Where'd you find those in Blue Glass?"

"Mama could make them, if she had a mind to."

"Your mama asked me to see you," Daubenheyer said, fearing the hour of the wedding would strike and whatever he was supposed to impart would be left unsaid.

As soon as he said that, Leafy's face collapsed; she cupped her chin in her hand.

"Oh, June," she said, "I'm dying of a toothache."

A toothache! Prepared for all kinds of bridal-chamber confessions and prewedding fears, he laughed aloud.

"It's no joke," Leafy told him.

"Show me which one," he said sympathetically.

Her mouth was filled with white patches—burns from the oil of cloves she'd been using—and bad teeth.

"These should've been stopped up long ago."

"I'm a crybaby about my teeth."

"No one should've listened to you."

"Papa's tenderhearted with me."

"If you call it tenderhearted—to cause you this trouble on your wedding night—I don't. Which one is it? Or are they all aching?"

She showed him which one. "Have you got something to kill the ache? Something that don't smell?"

"It ought to be drawn."

"All right, do it."

"I thought you were a crybaby."

"I've got Reno to think of, tonight."

"D'you want a mouthful of blood at your wedding?"

"No. Don't you have a stronger drug? Something to deaden it?"

He decided that it was the toothache—as much as, or more than, anything else—that was firing her up. Holding in pain and anticipating a mystery sweeter than kisses, that was enough to alter the looks of anybody's plain younger sister.

"I've got something out in the rig, Leafy," he told her. "You may not know you've got a left side to your face after I put it in your tooth, but it'll stop the pain."

He ran down the stairs and right into Rosa. His wife was a tall, lanky girl, pale, with burnt-sugar-colored hair, and her baby showed in her like a cherry in a peapod. She was laughing. "Oh, feel, June," she said. She took his hand and laid it against the big curve of her body. "He's kicking to the tune of 'Weevily Wheat.' He thinks it's a play-party and he's started dancing."

Daubenheyer shot up from the stump as if stung by a copperhead. He could still feel the movement of that baby against the palm of his hand. *That* didn't matter so much. He could still feel Rosa.

"March, girl," he said to Leafy. "If sitting's what we're after, there are better chairs at home."

He marched fast and sometimes out of sight. Leafy didn't care. Walking fast, she got some benefit from the air. She reckoned she knew where his thoughts were, talking about her wedding night. She wondered that the history of June's wife didn't make her more concerned for herself. A man who could make a mistake about his own baby could make a worse one, it would look, about somebody else's. But she wasn't worried. She walked the woods the way she had spent the day in bed: thinking of the way she had come, not where she was going.

✍ Leafy

She knew the country around about Blue Glass better than June. He was a doctor when he came to town, and had been busy doling out pills and delivering babies while she was free to ramble. She'd carried everything through these woods before this but a baby: a saltcellar in the spring so she could salt the new oak leaves before eating; a basket in the fall for beechnuts, hickory nuts, pawpaws, persimmons, and sarviceberries. In May she had fought Johnny-jump-up against Johnny-jump-up, the weakest losing his head in a pulling contest. She had lain with her face in a summer patch of grass watching ants lumber along like elephants. She had licked trees for sweet gum and maple sap and pine resin.

The path led down into a swale and through a pocket of cool air. June's footsteps ahead of her were as faint as echoes. Occasional clouds now crossed the sky, patternless as whey in a churn of buttermilk. She took off her duster and felt better. For all of June, she thought, his mind where it must be, she might've taken off her bedgown, too, and walked through the woods as naked as a jay bird.

Walking, walking, she thought. I've walked myself right into this walk. My feet have taken me to where I am. If I'd been content to sit home in a rocking chair, I could be there still, rocking and knitting—if I had ever learned to knit.

She hadn't actually walked toward Fairmont (and Reno, too, as it turned out), but run. Skipped, as a matter of fact, in her eagerness, big and old as she was, like a first grader.

If she had set her foot down, stiffened her neck, pouted, carried on, her father would have given in about the Academy. But she wanted to please him, especially since he was probably in the wrong and since her mother was berating him. The more she was doubtful about him, the more she always defended him. She wanted to spare him the embarrassment of having to admit mistakes. She argued against herself on his side.

"There's a lot of books at Fairmont I'd like to read over again," she said, when she'd swallowed her sorrow. "I never did manage all the twelves, or get all the capitals by heart. I'd be too lonesome away from home anyway, just when Offie's so sweet and I can help with him. Why, I wouldn't go to the Academy if somebody hired me."

Nobody offered to hire her, so she went back to Fairmont. She told herself not to be sorry for herself. She was better off than most Blue Glass girls. Most of them never got to finish the eighth grade, let alone repeat it. They were put to work, if not inside the house, then out. She and her mother were the only women in Blue Glass who weren't expected to put in gardens and help at planting and harvest time in the fields. Bass, by Blue Glass standards, was generous. It was only in the light of the education he had had himself and what his brothers were doing for their children, and what Prill had managed without help, that he didn't show up well. And he showed up even less well in his reasons for his act than in the act itself. If he had kept Leafy home because he was short on money, or because, though he had money, he was as tight as the bark on a tree; if he had kept her home because he thought girls with too much education made poor wives, or because he needed her help in clearing and farming his land, he would have been understood. But he advanced none of these reasons, only something indefinite, a suggestion, half question and half muffled behind his mustache, that it was "best not to expect too much."

Whatever the reason was, Leafy went back to Fairmont, better togged out by her mother than girls who were Academy bound.

"You look like a scholar, no matter where you're going," Bass rallied her on the morning school started.

This was a joke, and Leafy laughed. What she looked like, and she knew it, was a fashion plate. Prill was making it up to her for having to go back to Fairmont like a repeater who couldn't learn. If they took notice of the big girl who was in the eighth grade for the second time, no one was going to say her clothes were hand-me-downs. At fifteen Leafy was woman-sized and woman-shaped, destined to grow no more. ("Not counting out," Leafy told herself, as she felt the outward thrust of the load she carried.) But for all she was woman-sized, she had been child-minded. That walk was only four years past, but now she would rather talk to any old lady of forty than the schoolgirl she had been then.

It was a sign of her childishness that morning that she had boys on the brain. Not that she showed it, like the Magruder twins, or Rhoda Overbeck, or the Millspaughs. Either she'd been born with too much pride to wear her heart on her sleeve or she'd been taught not to show it.

Once, on the way to Meeting, she'd stood up in the carriage and waved to a boy she knew without waiting for him to wave to her. She had also shouted his name to get his attention: "Rudy, Rudy."

Her father had pulled up his team then and there, had turned around, pretending not to understand the cause of all the commotion.

"Mary Pratt," he demanded, "have you been taken with a cramp? Or caught sight of a bear, maybe?"

Chancellor sniggered. Her mother said nothing.

"Well, Mary Pratt, what's the meaning of this hullaballoo?" he asked again when she didn't answer.

"I saw a boy I knew."

"Were you afraid he wasn't going to see you?"

"I saw him first."

"And you were so bad off for someone to wave to, you had to hoo-hoo to a boy who's taking no notice of you?"

"He's in my grade, Papa."

"I guess he knows it without your screaming it to him."

"He might even want to forget it," Chancellor said.

But her father wouldn't let Chancellor make a joke of what was serious. Usually there was one subject on which her mother and father never disagreed: boys. Boys for her and girls for Chancellor. But that morning her mother spoke up.

"Bass, are you forgetting that Mary Pratt is a little girl, nine years old? Isn't this a pretty early date to start putting ideas in her head?"

"I know Mary Pratt's age. And if she was nineteen, there might be some excuse for her making a show of herself. But she's got no cause at nine to start screeching and jumping up and down for fear she'll be overlooked. Why, that poor little codger's hanging onto his scalp for fear it's going to be lifted."

Her father, though he wouldn't let Chancellor do so, ended his talk with a joke, as he often did when her mother got serious. But in some ways, he, and not her mother, had been right. Ideas about boys were already in her head at nine—to say nothing of fifteen. She'd given up screeching to them by that time, but by that time it wasn't necessary. She trembled in their presence. And they trembled, too. Their eyes took on a soft and shining look. When she asked herself, "What's so wonderful about a boy?" she didn't have any answer. Perhaps there wasn't anything so wonderful. People were always being disappointed: farmers with their crops, preachers with their converts, parents with their children. Perhaps boys were the beginning of life's disappointments. But she was bound to find out.

Though boys, when she returned once again to Fairmont in her fifteenth year, loomed up bigger on Leafy's landscape than anything else, she wasn't dead to the landscape either. Because it was so strange to be returning to something with which she was finished, she remembered that ninth September of her walks to Fairmont more than all the others. The first day was warm, with crows still cawing as fiercely as in midsummer, but because the school year was beginning again, Leafy felt the tilt of the earth toward winter and the excitement of extremes which winter brought. She relished that excitement: the thermometer the lowest it had ever gone, the deepest snow, the biggest hailstones, the farthest spread of glare ice. The most animals dead. And in the midst even of that tragedy (though if she had been in charge of the universe she would never have permitted it) she rejoiced. She was alive. She had survived.

September was half leftover summer, half promise of winter to come. The maple leaves were evenly divided between July green and Indian summer red. Blue haze, like ribbon through the eyelets of a bodice, was laced between the trees on the horizon. There was wood smoke in the air. (There always was.) Hogs, rooting for mast under the oak trees, chomped and conversed. Guinea hens, accustomed to school children passing last spring, had grown unaccustomed, and they screamed their warnings of strangers. Some corn was already in the shock. Birds, heading south, passed overhead in a flock so tightly packed they looked like one big ragged bird in flight. A warm wind tumbled the red and yellow leaves, and Leafy imagined winter's white blowing flakes. She had run ahead to meet winter, she supposed, because she was ready for something desperate, for some escape, for something to try her strength. Books were a part of the trial and the desperation. Because she was officially finished with them, she was planning to get more out of them than was humanly possible, and this intention kept her scared and excited.

And she remembered it all; especially because Reno had been waiting for her there at the schoolhouse.

She walked to school with Orinda Chambers. Orinda was seventeen and had to tramp clear from the Rising Sun neighborhood to get her education. Everyone thought she had given up, after two years' absence taking care of her motherless brothers and sisters. Instead of staying home with the young ones, Orinda was herding the young ones to school. She was a red-cheeked, bramble-haired girl, and the front of her dress, from having it always covered with an apron, was bright and unfaded. She was plump, but small-waisted, as if the apron strings had permanently dented her. Her father was well-to-do and accustomed to letting Orinda have her own way. She wore her mother's rings and brooches to school, as her mother had done when she went out in public. She was light on her feet from the exercise of running after young ones, and outspoken from having been too close to life and death to mince matters about little things. She was Leafy's friend and treated her like one of her own brood.

"Did you graduate last May, Leafy?" she asked. "I couldn't come to commencement, but seems like I heard you did."

Before Leafy could answer, Flo Millspaugh spoke up. Flo, who was eighteen, went to school for two months each fall as a letup from work. Nobody knew what grade she should be in, and Flo was the last one to know—or care. She flirted with such big boys as were available, memorized a few more good recitations to give at box suppers, learned some more songs, and at Thanksgiving went back to work in kitchen and farmyard, refreshed.

"Leafy graduated last May," Flo said, "but one peek at the new schoolmaster and she's ready to try again. I didn't think I'd be back again, either. I thought I was getting a little big for slates and lunch baskets. But after I saw Mr. Rivers I figured I was just the right size. And you, Orindy, you been gone for two years. What gave you such a sudden hankering for learning again? Same thing?"

Leafy was mad. She was being accused of being forward with the boys. In the first place, it wasn't true, and in the second place, she wouldn't admit it if it was.

"I didn't know there *was* a new teacher," she said.

"Don't deny it, Leafy. I admire your brass. If I'd had a signed paper saying I was finished, I'd likely not had the gall to show up again. What're you going to give for your reason to Mr. Rivers?"

"I never mastered my tables," Leafy said.

Flo almost suffocated laughing. "So it's tables you're interested in. He'll think it's beds."

Orinda stood up for Leafy. "Flo, we all know where your mind is. But you start out with your bragging and you're liable to come out the little end of the horn again."

Flo swung her hairy roan-colored braids. Ten months of the year she wore her hair coiled in a way suitable to her age. The two months she was a schoolgirl she went pigtailed like a twelve-year-old. "Bragging? I wasn't doing any bragging."

Orinda said, "You're bragging you know what's in Leafy's mind. And I can remember Tom Fazzo. You set your cap for him. Then when he headed west you had to go meechin' off like a cat that's missed her mouse."

You couldn't hurt Flo's feelings. She laughed some more. "Say, he was a pretty fellow, wasn't he?"

"He was a no-good rolling stone," Orinda said.

Flo agreed. "He sure wouldn't stand still long enough for me to get the bit in his mouth."

Leafy envied Flo her honesty. She wasn't a liar herself, but the whole truth was nothing she'd ever been encouraged to tell.

"Leafy," Flo said, "everybody knows your pa'd send you to the Academy if you wanted to go. Your cousins are all over there. Why don't you go?"

Leafy picked out a piece of the truth suitable for the occasion. "They have to memorize one whole chapter of the Bible every day over there, Flo. One whole long one."

"That'd never faze you, Leafy."

"How'd you like to live on mush and milk the way they do?"

"I'm used to it," Flo said.

"And have Miss Ellen Mabry looking down her nose at you twenty-four hours a day?"

"That's too long," Flo agreed.

Flo let Bass and the Academy alone after that and talked about Mr. Rivers instead.

When Leafy walked into the school building, and saw Mr. Rivers at his desk, she had to admit that Flo was a real truth-teller. He was as handsome as Tom Fazzo, and looked as if he might stand still, too. Mr. Rivers, this being his first year of teaching, was cutting no corners. He registered the young ones first, then the big boys, and last of all the big girls, "young ladies," he called them. Leafy hung back, watching the other "young ladies" lean across Mr. Rivers' desk, getting one hundred per cent registered, with a flouncing of ruffles, a tossing of braids and curls, and even, when Flo was registered, some hand-guiding to help in spelling her name.

Leafy, when her turn came, stood straight, an arm's length from Mr. Rivers' desk, treated him like a teacher, herself like a scholar, and the building like a schoolhouse—and the other young ladies like ninnies. She figured that, if nothing else, she could at least provide him with a change. With so many girls courting him, maybe he would take notice of the one who gave him the go-by. And she planned to be taken notice of.

Unless you had your heart set on some quirk in looks like red hair, or a cowlick, or a cleft chin, Reno Rivers would take the prize for looks. He was too near, even at arm's length, for Leafy's nerves. She kept her eyes down for fear her admiration would show through.

Mr. Rivers had been all business when the other girls leaned over him. If he saw any difference between her and the others, he didn't show it. He was still all business.

"Name, please?"

"Mary Pratt Converse."

Flo, who hadn't let being registered separate her from Mr. Rivers, gave one of her big happy hoots.

"Mary Pratt Converse! Martha Custis Washington! Her name's 'Leafy.' "

Mr. Rivers lifted his beautiful gray eyes from his register. "I'm talking to Miss Converse, Miss Millspaugh. Age, Miss Converse," he went on, as if Flo was of no more consequence than a fly that had buzzed.

"Fifteen."

"Grade?"

"I'm repeating the eighth."

"Repeating the eighth," Mr. Rivers said, kindly, as he wrote.

The kindness grated on Leafy.

"I graduated last May."

Mr. Rivers propped his pen in the inkwell.

"I'm not prepared to teach beyond the eighth."

"I don't see how you could learn up to just one spot in every subject, then stop there."

"I should have said licensed to teach beyond the eighth. There are some subjects I know beyond that."

There were precious few, as Leafy learned later. Mr. Rivers, for all his dignity, was two weeks past his eighteenth birthday, the son of a poor scrabbling father who liked reading better than farming. Reno took after his father but had the good sense to admit his liking. His schooling had been scarce, but he had memorized enough in six weeks at a summer institute in Cincinnati to convince the Fairmont supervisors that he could teach. He looked like a sweetheart to the young ladies; and their parents would have preferred to hire somebody settled, a married man or a spinster past the age of hope. But married men needed more money than they were offering; and spinsters of any age were in short supply, to say nothing of those who could teach. Besides, R. J. Rivers, as he signed himself, had, in spite of (or maybe assumed because of) his youth, the sweeping dignity that goes with broad white foreheads and waving manes of hair. And though the girls saw R. J. Rivers as a sweetheart, their parents thought they saw signs in him of the true pedagogue and possible statesman.

Leafy could see him both ways, and both ways saw what she liked. She had strong leanings toward both sweethearting *and* learning, and never had imagined the luck of finding the two in one man: to read a book with a man's arms around her! At fifteen she hadn't known this plan would be neither practicable for her nor popular with her husband. But when she looked at Reno Rivers this was what she saw them doing. This was marriage, she supposed, as contrasted with courtship, which was kissing.

Looking at Reno Rivers was one of her problems that year at

Fairmont. She didn't know whether she was snake or bird in those eye encounters. She would find herself staring at him, then make herself look out a window, sizing up a cow or a passing cloud as if she'd never seen either before. So much conscious use of her eyes made them ache at evening like a wood-chopper's arm or a cornhusker's hand. She actually thought of going to school with a bandage over her eyes. Seeing and hearing Reno Rivers both in the same day was more than her nerve-strings could bear.

She discovered that in the learning line she knew almost as much as he did—which wasn't surprising, since she'd had so much more time than he to spend with books. He was smarter than she was in anything that went by rule or reason: arithmetic, logic. But since most things didn't go by reason, but by flashes, Leafy discovered that she flashed faster. Reno wasn't a plodder, but he was methodical, temperate, dreamy, sentimental. It wasn't her eyes, staring at him, that told her this, of course, but the two years of courting, and two of marriage she'd had since that first day at Fairmont.

Reno was a fine teacher for the young ladies and the big boys, but the primer class, not a very reasonable lot, gave him trouble. Because he was trying (like Leafy) to appear older than he was, his dignity prevented him from babying them into wanting to learn a-b, ăb; e-b, ĕb; i-b, ĭb; o-b, ŏb; u-b, ŭb. He simply set them the task of learning. That was what they were at school for and that was what he, as schoolmaster, was hired to see they did. But they didn't learn, and when they didn't, all the encouragement Reno had for them was to put them in dunce caps, stand them in corners, or keep them after school. This kept the beginners quiet and didn't harm Reno's dignity, but it did nothing to speed up the a-b–ăbing.

Leafy began to help.

She did it in spite of her desire to make Reno fall in love with her. For this was her desire and she knew it. What she didn't know was how to go about making him fall in love with her. The primer class was easier to deal with. They, at least, knew that they were *supposed* to learn. They had had that dinned into them. Reno had to wake up to the fact that he was supposed to fall in love with her. She hinted a little. Some of the hints, as she understood later, had been worse than useless. And her teaching, which she was afraid would be a stumbling block to romance, and love, pleased him.

Very soon after school started, she began to have too little to do. She learned the twelves in no time. She knew more elocution pieces than Flo. She could bound every state, nation, and body of water in the world. She could define strait, isthmus, peninsula, continent, island, archipelago, cape, bay, volcano, geyser, lake, channel, and dew pond. She knew all the parts of speech and how they combined to make figures of speech and could give examples offhand of the latter. She could write her name with enough scrolls to make Mary Pratt look like a bird with plumage and Converse a feathery nest for the bird to brood in. She could spell cargoes, cantos, calicoes, tyros, and tornadoes. She had learned everything there was to learn in the eighth grade, second time around, and even with courting the schoolmaster, against great odds, she was frequently unemployed.

One day when she was giving her eyes a rest from looking at Reno, she saw what the primer class was really up to. They were no more a-b–ăbing than woodchucks. They were drawing pictures on their slates, chewing sweet gum, eating pawpaws, and asking to be excused to go to the outhouse more times than would be necessary for full-grown horses. They weren't noisy. They had a healthy respect for the force with which their teacher could thump them down into corners and clap dunce caps over their ears. They rolled their little round eyes about, keeping pretty good track of Reno. They had signed an agreement in their own minds: they wouldn't interfere with Reno's teaching others if he wouldn't interfere with their not learning. Reno didn't know about this agreement, and probably didn't want to. His life was easier that way. But Leafy saw what was going on. Offie, for one, was chewing sweet gum like a cow with a cud, and not doing a single other thing, not even drawing pictures or making spitballs.

She went over to his bench and sat down with him without, at first, any pedagogical purpose. Offie and the others his age were as sweet to handle as kittens, and she could not resist, in the emptiness of her school day and the ineffectiveness of her courtship, the pleasures of fondling. She was full of conscience, too, and had no wish to see Offie grow up as ignorant as a fence post. She had Offie, and then his classmates, a-b–ăbing by the end of the first afternoon. It was a game for her, and so for them. By the next day their slates were washed clean, and she had searched out from vacant spaces between teeth the last lumps of sweet gum.

She did it all reluctantly. She was turning her back on all her principles. She stood with her father in his belief that it was wrong to put herself forward and claim attention. The primer class was perhaps the smallest body before which she could make such claims, but she was making them. She was also against her mother's urgings to make the most of herself, to be spry, to be forehanded, not to hide her talents under a napkin, or let the grass grow under her feet.

She didn't, in her fifteen-year-old's strategy of courtship, believe that she would endear herself to Reno by suggesting to him that she thought he needed help. And without thinking or strategy, or being her father's girl, or her mother's opponent, she shrank from acts that showed others their weakness. She was also afraid that Reno, seeing her playing with children, would think she was one of them, but she kept right on playing and teaching, a drinker afraid of drunkenness—but not quite afraid enough to stop.

If Reno saw what she was doing—and he must have—he didn't say a word. The girls saw and said plenty. They would, one and all, scorn to worm their way into a man's heart by any such currycombing ways. Why not do his washing, mend his socks, and iron his shirts? And even so, they warned her, what a man liked was spirit. She wouldn't get any place by offering him her neck for his foot.

Though they had to admit spirit wasn't getting them anyplace, either. Reno Rivers had left a girl behind him in eastern Belmont County and he rode back there every Saturday to see her. If Leafy, by teaching, could get him a little weaned from eastern Belmont and inclined toward Blue Glass, they might all have a better chance.

One afternoon in November, Leafy and her little brother waited after school to be picked up by Bass and Prill. Offie needed shoes. He was barefoot. His feet had taken such a sudden splurge of growing that he couldn't crowd them into the pair he owned, and his father's and Chancellor's shoes were so large that he couldn't keep them on even by knobbing his toes. They would get Offie shoes in Blue Glass; and Prill had in mind to buy, while she was there, some heavy flannel for winter underwear.

Leafy sat with her back to the teacher's desk, and to the teacher, sometimes looking out the window, sometimes memorizing her poem. There was a light skim of snow on the ground and more was falling. She could see Valentine Vorst and his two big boys gathering corn in their field across the road from the schoolhouse.

Offie was putting buckeyes in the fire for the pleasure of hearing them explode. Leafy thought he should be stopped, and she could have stopped him. She had the whole primer class so well trained they all jumped if she said "pea turkey"; but this was the schoolhouse and the schoolmaster was in charge. Let him say "pea turkey" if he wanted to stop the din. She could stand it if he could. He was writing to his girl in eastern Belmont County, she supposed—and was too lost to the world to hear a buckeye explosion. In spite of the racket, she murmured the lines of her poem to herself: "The Turk lay dreaming of the hour." She listened to the November wind, whistling down off the English lakes, crying "winter, winter," around the corners of the building. She heard the whisper of occasional flurries of snow against the windowpanes. The teacher's pen squeaked back and forth across the fine paper he was using. Offie's buckeyes blew up, spattering like small volcanoes and filling the room with their smell of hot roasted potatoes.

Wind and snow, murmur of poetry, lift and fall of arms as corn was tossed into the Vorsts' wagon; buckeye smell and sound; scratch of pen, and sorrow swallowed because she knew where Reno's mind was. Then the pen ceased its scratching and a chair was pushed back. She waited for footsteps, and everything outside the schoolroom vanished.

"The Turk lay dreaming," she made herself say.

A sheet of paper was placed inside her opened book. The steps returned to the desk.

"Dear Miss Converse," she read.

My dear Mary Pratt, I do not want you to think that I have not noticed what you have been doing with the primer class. I have. Perhaps I said nothing for fear if I spoke it would be my duty to ask you to stop. I don't mean to say that I could not have handled them, and taught them. I could. That is my job and I could have done it. Otherwise I should resign.

But I have been thinking, Mary Pratt, that in return for *your* help, I should try to help you more than I have done. Perhaps with algebra or advanced orthography, or rhetoric, which I took at Institute.

I want to do this. I am not suggesting these studies as payments, but as privileges. I know you have a very alert mind, and it would be helpful to me to study with you.

I am going to copy a poem here I wrote the other evening with you as my inspiration. There are some things poetry can say better than prose. This is one of them and I hope my poor verses can convey my true sentiments better than the foregoing faltering lines of prose.

The village master taught his class;
As pedagogue, he tried to play his part;
Though he had eyes for but one lass,
The mistress of his heart.

She did not steal his heart from him.
He gave it freely, 'ere he knew
That kindly Cupid, by some whim,
Had shot him as he flew.

The wound was deep, the ache was strong,
He quivered with alarms.
For day and night he did but long
To hold her in his trusty arms.

But she so young and innocent
He dared not make avowal.
Rather than risk a base intent
He'd be a monk and wear a cowl.

He asked his pen to say for him
What he himself would never dare;
That for one maiden tall and slim,
He'd lose the world—and never care.

Your sincere friend and well-wisher,
R. J. Rivers

Leafy read the words in a gobble, one eye still on the first word, it seemed, while the other had reached the last. She knew what to call it, though she couldn't name the ingredients, like a piece of mince pie. She called it "love." Then, and afterward, when by rereading it, sleeping with it, wearing it in the top of her shimmy, she knew it word by word, forward and backward, it said, "Love." The poem itself didn't use the word. That was one of the reasons she thought it so remarkable. That was what made it so poetic, its roundaboutness. Anyone could say, "I love you." It took a real poet to *not* say it, and yet let the fact be known.

The minute she knew the fact, all sounds ceased. She and Reno were alone in a hush. The falling snow curved around the schoolhouse like a pure white eggshell. What the poem said was clear enough. It was unbelievable because it was her dream, and it was the nature of dreams to be untrue. She had no plan for action inside a real dream. She stood up, letter in hand. It was suddenly the easiest thing in the world to look Reno right in the eye. It was a great relief. It was as restful as tears after holding them back or making an open hand out of a clenched fist.

She was walking toward Reno without knowing it, but knew she had done so when she touched him.

Reno rose from his desk and spoke to Offie.

"Howard, you go outside and bring in a load of firewood."

"There's some in the wood box," Offie said.

"I want more."

Offie left reluctantly. When the door closed behind him, there was a kiss. Leafy had no idea how it happened, who gave it, where it landed, or how it felt. Kissing was like death by lightning. If it happened, you didn't know it. And vice versa. She thought there was only one. And that was a good thing. Offie was back in jig time with an armload of chips. He dumped them down and dared anyone to think of another excuse to get rid of him. No one did.

In Leafy's mind she was as good as married, though it took them another two years to reach the ceremony. There was her age, Reno's lack of money, and her parents' reluctance. Time took care of the first; they decided the second wasn't important, and Prill finally got Bass's consent. "Do you want another Chancellor on your hands?" she asked him.

Before his first year at Fairmont was up, Reno had the offer of a school that paid more, or that promised to pay more, than Fairmont. A school fifty miles west, at a settlement called Saw Dust. Reno thought he should take it. He believed in pushing on. He could clothe the unknown with qualities the known didn't have. Saw Dust, he had heard, was growing at the rate of ten families a week. Twenty-five boats at a time were tied up at its wharves. They were talking college. He would go where there was a town he could grow up with and branch out from grade-school teaching into higher education. And property ownership.

Bass and Prill thought he should take it, though they would have encouraged him to answer a call to the foreign-mission field, head west with a wagon train, or try east for further educational openings. Fifteen and eighteen were too young for matrimony. Especially since eighteen was penniless and came of shiftless stock. Prill, whose people had done considerable shifting about themselves, had less to say on this score, though she knew the dangers.

Leafy thought he should take it because he wanted to, and because, inexperienced, she accepted the way he sized up his chances at Saw Dust. She was more ambitious and tenacious than she had any idea at the time. She had been hurt, at first, that Reno was prepared to endure separation. But she knew, too, that either going to school to Reno another year or staying home and watching the other girls flounce past the house on their way for a day with him would have its drawbacks. If she had to suffer, she preferred to do it for reasons she could respect: separation and unsympathetic parents, not jealousy and spite.

She bade him go. She would stay home, spin, weave, hem, and continue to learn. She would go to school to the new master. She would send Reno problems they could work together by mail. He could send her poems he wrote. She could copy out poems for him. If he finally got to be president of that college they were talking about building in Saw Dust, he would find he had a wife who could hold up her head in learned society.

The teacher, for her third year as an eighth grader at Fairmont, was Donal Demarest, a young man dying of lung fever. He was proceeding west for his health, had played out at Blue Glass, had paused to rest and earn more money. Leafy taught the primer class again, not because Mr. Demarest didn't know how, but because he didn't have the strength to. Before the school term was over she was teaching every class but the seventh and eighth.

When Mr. Demarest died, she was offered the school for the next year and took it. It was already decided that she couldn't marry until she was eighteen. In the year she had to wait, she would earn something to add to Reno's savings.

Before she had a chance to get a letter off to Reno with the news of her appointment, she had a letter from him.

Miss Mary Pratt Converse,

My own precious girl: As I have told you, the only payment I have received thus far for my teaching this year—is promises. I have not had to spend anything, as I have been boarded round. Now I am *promised* a fine bay buggy horse in addition to my wages for next year, if I will agree to keep on here. I have seen the horse, but the silver is still as scarce as ever. "Once burned is twice cautious."

Now I'll tell you what I have in mind. Most of the talk about the great future of Saw Dust has turned out to be just that. It is proving to be no more than a stopping place for people pressing on to the beautiful Whitewater Valley in Indiana. If we had the money in hand, that is where I would take my precious girl. Teaching is but day labor after all, and to get ahead in the world requires the ownership of something that increases in value, to wit: land.

What I have in mind is this. If Mr. Demarest should prove too sickly to teach at Fairmont another year I would be willing to return there. As you know, I was asked to return for a second year before I decided on Saw Dust. Perhaps now that I have more experience they would be willing to pay me more. I will wait to send in my formal application until I hear from you.

I am sorry to hear that you got your ring broke, but like Chancellor and your mama I think you should not have let Bert hold your hand, then he would not have got the ring. I have always had a pride, pardonable I hope, in the ring I gave you, and it makes me mad to think Bert broke it. I would like to know what good he thought it would do him to take it from you. I am sure it would be no pleasure for me to take a ring from a girl that didn't want me to have it, and Bert surely has sense enough to tell whether you wanted him to take it.

Let me ask you a question, dear. Why is it you have so much trouble with boys wearing your rings? Mort used to wear the other ring I gave you. Tom Johnson and Emmett and I don't know who else. Do other girls have similar troubles? One thing I am sure of, no girl has been bothered with me taking her rings. I don't care half as much about its being broken as I do your letting him have it. I gave it to you because I loved you and thought it would be an ever-present reminder of the fact.

Leafy, it is hard for me to be away from you all this time. I get so lonesome sometimes I hardly know what to do. I know that if I could get to see you, you would dispel all the gloominess. I think of you nearly all the time, especially as I am going and coming from school.

Who in the world has a sweetheart like mine? I can't tell you how much I love you. You are what I live for. Good night, sweetness, your devoted, Reno.

P.S. Sunday eve. It's getting dark. I am alone and lonesome. I wish I could see you a little while, pet. I would like to hold you tight and kiss the sweetest lips in the world. Leafy, you mustn't go with other boys. You were a good girl to refuse to go with Mort or Lafe. I will kiss you a dozen times extra for every time you refuse some other fellow. (I'm afraid now you'll go for sure.)

Reno's letter was a mirror in which Leafy was able to see herself—for a little while at least. What was she up to, getting her ring stolen and broken, writing Reno about boys? What did she want him to do? Carry her around on a chip? Think she was a bee-gum tree and the boys were hiving? Did she want to see how far she could try him? Badger him into cutting loose from school at Saw Dust and rushing up to Blue Glass to settle Bert Huff's hash. Was that what she wanted? If so, she was bad off for treats. She couldn't rest nights for thinking of what she'd done. What had come over her? Two things, she thought. She was like a child who has just learned to make fires. She couldn't resist starting them, little ones she was pretty sure she could stamp out. But why did she have to tell Reno? Because she wanted him to remember, off there in Saw Dust with the big girls leaning across his desk, that his girl, back in Blue Glass, didn't lack attention? She was ashamed of herself and determined not to egg Reno on in that way. If she had to keep proving to herself, by letting boys fiddle with her rings, that, for all of her freckles and seventeen years, she could toll a boy to her, she didn't have to tell Reno about it.

So she stopped. And she made what amends she could. She got the Fairmont job for Reno and never mentioned to him that it had been offered to her first. She kept Reno's ring on her finger, and the kisses she collected from him weren't in payment for fidelity. While he taught, she worked at home getting the gear ready they would need in the Whitewater Valley. She plied needle and loom, braided rugs, plucked ducks, stuffed bolsters, dried pumpkin and corn, made peach leather, and hemmed sheets. When she and Reno started their trudge for the Whitewater Valley, their provisions were so plentiful as to be a burden.

Lying in childbed, she remembered it all. What had happened in that schoolroom seemed more real to her than what had been going on in the parlor bedroom.

five

🖋 Chancellor

Chancellor had a bite of supper, after delivering Dr. Daubenheyer
to Prill. Then he set out for the Luceys'. He wasn't much surprised when Mrs. Lucey told him, when he stopped to pick up
Venese, that she had stepped out a half hour back. He knew
Venese well enough to know that she, since he had announced he
would be on time, would try to add some element of chance to
their meeting by half hiding herself. Would he find her or not
find her? And she wouldn't do this to make him anxious, but to
make herself anxious. She would be in the fox-grape bower, or
in a boat on the river, or walking slowly down the tunnel-like
game track through the first-growth trees. And she'd never make

a sound to tell him where she was. She'd set up a gamble to lose him, not because she wanted to lose him, but because she didn't know how to live without a gamble. Or maybe, and he didn't like to face this, she loved gambling more than she did him. He didn't believe this, but he'd be a fool not to see that she liked the combination. He didn't have to imagine (because she often told him) how she was feeling now, wherever she was. Maybe even watching. Dressed for him. Waiting. Eager to go, the evening empty without him. Yet having to take the chance of his walking by without seeing her . . . seeing him but unable to call to him. It was backwoods fear turned wrong side out, not trembling and sickhearted for fear the panther or redman would see you, but trembling and sickhearted for fear of being *missed.* That's what she said. He put up with it for two reasons: he loved Venese; and when she won the gamble she greeted him like a blind man who'd never expected to see the stars again, or a drowning man who finally touches land; or the girl whose sweetheart comes back from the grave. He didn't know how he would feel about parting with these pleasures—uneasy as he was about accepting them. They were treats Venese earned by suffering. She took the chance of missing him, she lived the pain; and the letup of pain, for her, was real. She *was* blind and drowning and bereaved, and she'd earned her stars and air and resurrection. But how long can I travel under such false colors, he wondered.

He was not willing to stop that minute, anyway, and he wondered if he was picking up the other half of her habit, getting as hypoed on hunting as she was on hiding. Or even if his eternal honing after something out of sight, beyond reach, unknown, had made a hider out of her. Just to satisfy his needs.

He didn't believe that, though. They were both notional, and their notions happened to run on parallel tracks.

He walked his usual way along the creek to the fox-grape nest, the night closing in dark and warm. The stars spread big with heat, the coming storm still rustling about with quick, soft, furry-cat jabs. Hardly a touch of claw yet. He thought he might run into June and Leafy. The woods were full of walkers tonight. Leafy out hunting her baby, like a little girl looking under cabbage leaves. June trying to blot out a bad memory with a good one.

The walker he met was Val Lucey. He smelled him before he met him, rank and rich on the downwind as a buck in September. And it was Val's own smell. He was carrying no game. It was too dark to see Val, except in outline, but he hadn't the hump on his back of any animal, or the buckskin garland of thong-laced birds across his shoulders.

Val was first to call out.

"What you prowling around for, Chancellor?"

There wasn't much use trying to fool Val about the purpose of his prowling. He reckoned a man who kept track of turkeys and deer knew the whereabouts, and the why of the whereabouts, of his own daughter. And he reckoned Val knew he was hunting her. But he felt some delicacy in saying so—whether to shield what, when he had to face it, appeared to be a weakness in himself or to shield the strangeness in Venese.

"I just felt like making a break for tall timber," Chancellor said.

"Kind of ketchy weather back in there," Val said. "You better come on home with me."

"I aim to go on to the Camp Meeting tonight."

"You ain't aiming to go on foot, are you? You got a rig back at my place, ain't you?"

"Charlie's back there," he admitted.

"Charlie's pretty high-strung. I wouldn't plan on leaving him hitched too long, if I was you."

"I was planning this evening for my pleasure, not Charlie's."

"What's the pleasure of a Camp Meeting, Chancellor?" Val asked sociably, taking his gun off his shoulder and leaning on it as cozy as if slanted against a barn door. When Chancellor didn't answer, he said, "What's *there*? What you hunting? Or maybe you're just an onlooker?"

"No," Chancellor said, "I'm like you, Val. I'm a hunter."

"How old are you, Chancellor?"

"Twenty-two."

"Grown man."

"I hope so."

"What you figure on doing?"

"Hunting," said Chancellor, thinking another hunter couldn't fault this.

"Hunting *what?*" Val asked. "When I hunt I bring something back. I grant you I'd make better out of it as a farmer if I stuck to my furrow. But my family don't suffer. They're housed and fed. They know the taste of more delicacies than you do over at your house. What do you bring *back?*"

"You asking this because of Venese?"

"No. I'm not one to whip the devil round the stump. When I start asking you questions about Venese, you'll know it. I'm asking out of curiosity. What makes the merry-go-round, boy?"

"I spend considerable time walking furrows, too."

"That's where your feet are. Where's your head?"

"Maybe I'm a born poke-easy."

"Come on, Chancellor. Don't fob me off, calling yourself names. Give me the word with the bark on it."

"If I knew the word maybe I wouldn't be hunting. I'll be up at the house later, Val."

Chancellor walked past Val, still planted as sociably on his gun as a housewife on her broom.

"You're following a cold track," Val told him.

Chancellor said over his shoulder, "You want to tell me where it's warm, Val?"

"This way," Val said, and he headed away from the creek, Chancellor on his heels.

Chancellor didn't ask any questions. What question was there he could ask that he'd like to hear the answer to? And he had answers of his own, answers to questions Val Lucey would never ask. Unconsciously he was soft-footing it, treading like a still-hunter. "No use for that," Val told him. "You can't catch a weasel asleep."

Val himself, leading the way, was reminiscing. "This clumping along a narrow woods track, the fit as tight as the path for a bullet down a barrel, puts me in mind of our trip from the Carolinas. Venese was the oldest, and we was young ourselves. We treated her like she was Liz's and my age, only stronger, from having gone through less. We held her accountable for herself and for the passel of younguns. She took it all, and the more she took, the more we put on her. And she throve on it. In the beginning she had the terrors. We all did; but Liz and I had to hide it for the sake of the younguns. This place, smoothed out as it is now, is a still-howling wilderness compared to what had been home to us. We looked on our trip, at the start, like a park stroll. Outdoors, to be sure, but a good time of the year and under the shelter of trees. Under the shelter of trees! That tells the story. We'd as well have made the journey underground, crawled the whole distance through a culvert. Except for one thing. The trees being alive you had a different feeling for them than you had for the dirt of a cave, or the timber or stone of a culvert. They're alive, and, like anything live, they had feelings. They could be won over. Or so we hoped.

"But they're like an animal, too. They take advantage of you if you're afraid. Liz was afraid, and they knew it. Where she was, the sounds were worse and the shadows blacker. I've proved it out. I've come up to her unbeknownst and seen it with my own eyes. Venese was afraid, but she never gave in like Liz. Never ran; trembled, but never called for help. They fought her, and she fought them back. And they outnumbered her a million to one, to say nothing of size. Trees were a real trouble. Apart from what we maybe imagined. They hid the going from you. They slowed you down, heaved up roots at you, made walking, with the leaves they'd dropped a million years, like a trip through a featherbed. They made everything worse. But chop them all down, grub them up, burn them till the land's as smooth as I hear it is west of here, and you've still got the rivers and the weather and the varmints and the Indians and the sickness and the breakdowns and the accidents. And the homesickness. Chop them all down, grub every root, burn every topmost spire. Blow away every shred of wood smoke; *see* where you're going. And still you don't know where that is. The mules drown, your wife sickens, the meal molds, the baby dies, you chop your own leg half off.

"You never done any fighting, did you, Chancellor? I had a little spell of it once, nothing but a little Indian fracas. Lasted six weeks. But I took notice of one thing. The boys who started the scaredest, and rassled it down, ended the meanest fighters. They'd won one war before they started on the redskins. And it gave them a taste for fighting and danger. Them boys, the scared ones that got over it, they hunted other wars. Or headed west for fighting's sake. I wasn't one of them. I come west for land and money. I started for those reasons, anyway. Venese was the one put me in mind of those boys who fell in love with fighting. She was trained up in a battle. She was no more than a baby, and a crybaby to boot at the start, and we made her fight shoulder to shoulder with us. She didn't have any choice but toughen up or die. If she'll ever be reconciled to peace now, I don't know. She don't know nothing but walking through a forest of danger. Everything else is a comedown. She ain't the only one to be marked, of course. Liz has to stay out in the open because of it. And I ain't ever left it. If this all gets to be a clearing, I reckon I'll move on, till I find more forest land."

"Why?" Chancellor asked. If Val could ask about a man going to a Camp Meeting, he could ask about a man staying in a forest.

"Maybe it's like a man let out of prison after a long spell," Val said. "He don't feel at ease without walls and gratings. The way I feel without the big butts hemming me in and the crowns overhead for roofing. Then," he said, "if you get deep in there, deep enough, not another human anywhere near to make them mistrustful . . . they take you in. You step out of your skin. Everything that's plagued you drops away. You swell up to their size, you color to their darkness . . . you age to their years. You hear what they hear . . . rustlings and chitterings, singing and screams." Val stopped walking, and Chancellor caught up with him.

"It beats me," he said, "where I find enough sand in my craw to turn home. I don't know as I admire myself for doing so. Something's promised, if I go deep enough. I don't know whether turning back's God-fearing or plain fearing. Well," he added, "it's a straight shoot from here."

"Straight shoot which direction?" Chancellor asked.

"You know that big sycamore at the edge of the sarviceberry plantation? We'll head that way."

The feeling that he was nearing Venese made Chancellor, as it always did, begin to whistle.

"Ain't you being overly kind?" Val asked.

"It's the first time anybody ever called my whistling a kindness."

"It's a warning."

Chancellor didn't feel free to tell Venese's father that for Venese a warning wasn't a kindness. Love-making wasn't a subject for confidences with anybody, let alone the girl's father; and particularly when it had its peculiarities, as his and Venese's had.

The sycamore was well known to him. No one who had hunted sarviceberries in spring, and that was everybody under twenty in Blue Glass, but had used the hollow in that sycamore for sarviceberry feasts, for protection from rain, and, if of the right age, for a little kissing and cuddling. He knew exactly how Venese had figured. The fox-grape bower was too easy. After his cutting the ground out from under her evening, by telling her to be ready on the dot, and waiting, she had revolted. She had made the chances of his finding her scarcer. And except that he knew that she suffered more waiting for him than he did searching, he never could have forgiven her.

The sarviceberry bushes grew on a southern hillside, rising above a little branch. They blossomed before the trees leafed, and Chancellor had in the past mistaken this clump for a patch of late snow. In May the red berries against the green leaves gave the bushes a Christmas look. Now in July, berryless and blossomless, they were a scrubby part of a leafy world, no more than froth rising toward the foot of the sycamore which topped the slope. The sycamore itself, its white trunk mottled with gray, and the black mouth of its big hollow gaping, was easy to make out.

Until they pushed through the last of the sarviceberries, Chancellor and Val momentarily lost sight of the tree. Chancellor was still whistling, though he was already anticipating the released tautness of Venese's body against his. She would be in his arms before she saw that Val was on his heels. But she'd like that, too, her father's presence setting up one more barrier they must break down in order to be together.

He stopped his whistling when he stepped out of the bushes and in sight of the tree. Venese was not alone, and the clothes she had on were too few to wad a gun. She could have been fully dressed if she'd had a mind to: there'd been time, since he'd first started whistling, for her to have started from scratch and dressed for a ball.

Beside her, with enough clothes on for winter or a wedding, was Brock Staples—whether redressed or never undressed, Chancellor had no idea.

Brock had been sashaying around Venese for some time. Trying to bid up her contributions at box suppers and to set himself opposite her at play-parties. If there was any more to it than this, Chancellor didn't know it. Brock was nobody, a widower of thirty, childless, and smelling around for a wife. Venese wasn't the only one he'd smelled around, and Venese was more than likely the one who had given him the scent for tonight, tolled him up here as one more item to add to the chancyness of their meeting. Maybe not find her at all, and, if he did, find her with a man. That was something she'd never tried before. How she must be trembling, having put that wall between them. Would he clear it? And how? Clamber? Jump? Butt it down?

The idea somehow made Chancellor laugh. The four of them

standing there in the come-and-go light from clouds crossing the stars and shutting out the moon. Father with gun. Daughter half dressed. Widower overdressed. Lover, for that was the right name for himself, Chancellor supposed, bound for sermons and prayers. And debating with himself whether or not a fist fight was in order. No use thinking Venese wanted that, that she was the simple kind of girl who wanted to see two fellows punching each other's noses for her. If he was going to try to figure out what Venese wanted of him, running might be in order. But Chancellor didn't feel inclined to do one or the other. A line had to be drawn someplace. He had gone as far as he could in reading Venese's mind. His inclination was to get an eyeful of the outlandish look of the four of them standing there above the shadbushes. Just the look, not the sorrowful facts. Just the four of them needing to be bored for the simples: woodsy, widower, and us two church-bound sweethearts. They were horse and horse for silliness. He laughed now, the way he had whistled before. Because he couldn't help himself.

Brock, a man who didn't enjoy being laughed at under the best of circumstances, which these certainly weren't, hit him. It was unexpected; and Chancellor, as his face caved in to make room for Brock's fist, knew he should have expected it. Brock knocked the laugh out of him—and a tooth. He heard it clink against a pebble when he spat; and had time to think, That's a sound I hope I don't hear twice. But it was the first note in the ashes-to-ashes refrain that would end him.

Brock's blow did one other thing. It knocked the indecisiveness out of Chancellor. He hit back. Brock was a target more or less like a barn door, but the footing was bad, and Chancellor was standing downhill from him. The barn door also had a certain degree of maneuverability. Chancellor missed, went down, was poleaxed coming up, and went down again. He was dazed, but didn't feel pain. He never did when his blood was up. This made fighting easy for him and dangerous for his opponent. He didn't know when he was hurt. He was still inclined to laugh. Fighting Brock was as silly as wrestling a cow.

They worked, trading blows, uphill to a level spot above the sycamore. Venese reappeared, fully dressed. A lady might be caught love-making in her shimmy. But something more modest was required for watching a fist fight. Val was still there leaning on his gun. Probably waiting to drag the loser home and salt him down for winter use. Likely sees us as two bucks in rutting season, Chancellor thought. Hears us that way, anyway. Gruntings and snortings; sharp whistle of air in and out of windpipes; the wet-meat sound of lungs flogged by the convulsive heaving of chests.

Brock was no sharpshooter and didn't try to be. He was a big target and he aimed for a big target: the belly. Chancellor's belly wasn't big, but it was the only one he had, and Brock kept him doubling over. If Brock had been smart enough or fast enough to undercut as Chancellor straightened, the fight would have been over. Meanwhile, Chancellor was ruining Brock's face, hunting for a spot that would end the fight like a bullet, not keep it dragging on like a sickness. Venese had vanished from his mind. He was striking because he had been struck, not because he had caught Brock with his girl and his girl with half her clothes off.

This might not be the most high-minded reason in the world, but it was reason enough for Chancellor. He found the spot on Brock's chin he'd been hunting for, and Brock dropped, and lay full length, snoring lightly.

Before Chancellor could get his breath he was wrapped round by a pair of arms from behind. He thought it was Venese. Was she trying to save Brock?

"You can have him," he said coldly. "I've finished with him."

The arms turned him around. "Brock? Brock?" It was Leafy asking the question. "What're you talking about? I'm saving *you*. At least that was my intention."

She said these last words apologetically, sliding downward in spite of Chancellor's outstretched hand.

Daubenheyer, winded, began talking as he reached them. "A walk was what I planned, not a run."

"That's plain to see," Chancellor told him. "But as soon as you've caught your breath you can do a little doctoring."

Venese was kneeling by Leafy; Val had Brock's head propped on his knee. Both patients came to without help from Daubenheyer. Brock clambered up and stayed up. Leafy, steadied by Venese, stood, then, knees buckling, fell back again. Daubenheyer caught her before she touched the ground.

"Something's happening," Leafy said in a low voice.

"Good," said Daubenheyer. "I was beginning to think this trudge had been wasted. Chancellor, are you in shape to give me a hand?"

The two of them made a chair seat for Leafy with their crossed hands. The procession headed for the Lucey place. Leafy, carried, in front. Behind Leafy, Venese. Behind Venese, Brock, half grunting, half groaning. Behind them all, Val, with gun over shoulder, walking like a jailer with a convict gang.

Chancellor, looking over his shoulder, said, "Val, how's it feel getting out of the woods and back to civilization?"

His future father-in-law, if Val was still that, gave a grunt that was half-laugh, half-groan.

At the Luceys', Chancellor took time to wash and to rinse out his mouth before driving June and Leafy home.

Venese stopped him at the front door. She was as self-contained as ever, but the skin across her cheekbones was pulsing. Her heartbeat was visible that high.

"Are you still going to the Meeting, Chancellor?"

These were the first words she had said to him that evening.

"Yes," he told her.

Having said that, he closed the door between them without a good-by.

six

✑ *Leafy*

Leafy woke up—if she had been asleep—or came to—if she had been unconscious. She thought she had been unconscious.

She had fainted once before in her life, at thirteen, when she had measles and had jumped from her bed in the morning forgetting that she was sick. She had made it from bed to kitchen, and there she had, she thought, gone blind. When she regained her sight she was again in her bed, but her body did not need the bed's support. She was supported by air, weightless, blissful, experiencing the kind of happiness she had supposed was reserved for the faithful in heaven. Since then she had often longed to faint again, had willed herself in moments of misery to go blind and find that air-supported, gently rocking bliss. She had never managed it, but now, though she could not remember the blindness by which she expected fainting to announce itself, she was conscious of the same flooding of delight. But like one awakened from sleep by a dream, she heard the echo of two sounds: the clock in the sitting room, chiming a number she lost track of, and her own voice saying, "Olin, Olin."

Olin. Olin. She looked around the room to see who might have heard that. She was alone except for June Daubenheyer, who sat in a rocker by a stand-table on which a candle, its light shielded from her, was burning. June was looking at her as if he, too, might have been awakened by a sound.

"Did I say something?" she asked.

"Somebody did," June said, "but it might have been me. I dozed off."

She thought he was being kind to her. "What did you say, Olin?" she asked, heard her mistake, and went on quickly. "I think I am dreaming."

"You've been sick," June said.

"I didn't have my baby," she told him.

"No. You lost the water," he told her. "The baby will be later."

"It would've been better both together?"

"Yes. Could've slid him along like a log down a millrace."

"Now what?"

"Shove and push," Daubenheyer said. "Grunt and groan."

"I don't feel like shoving and pushing."

"You will later."

"I feel like sleeping."

"Go ahead. You can have a little rest now. I've got something that'll make you feel more workbrickle later."

"You think I'm lazy?"

"I never did 'til now."

"Are all the others on needles and pins to have their babies?"

"They're on needles and pins to get it over with."

"Is something wrong with me?"

"No. When the baby begins to kick up a fuss you'll want to have him. You'll scream and holler for him."

"I won't," said Leafy.

" 'Bout as well," said Daubenheyer. "Opening the mouth seems to open everything else."

"I won't scream," said Leafy.

"Don't figure on holding back. Don't figure at all. Nature don't care about you. You're just a pod with a seed in it. Split open and drop it. That's all nature cares about. She don't care if you're quiet or noisy."

"I care."

"Good. I thought for a spell you didn't, one way or the other. Now you rest a while. If you don't want to scream now, your time's coming later to want to."

June turned the candle, which he had been shining on her face, away from her. The light went up the wall behind the stand-table in a golden broadening triangle. June rocked a little, slowly, making the sounds which from babyhood had said, "Sleep, sleep, rest and sleep."

"Where's Reno?"

"Getting a little rest while the resting's good."

"What's that noise?"

"The wind."

Leafy yawned.

"You got any gap-seed to spare?" June asked. "I'd like to catch a few winks myself while you sleep."

But she didn't sleep. She thought back to her home in the Whitewater Valley.

Through the chance of their meeting with Simon Yanders, Reno and Leafy had found a ready-made house in the beautiful Whitewater Valley; a well-made cabin near the banks of the Whitewater itself, with a full complement of necessary outbuildings. Leafy walked in her imagination about her home there. She could stand at the fireplace there and reach every pot and skillet, paddle and spoon. She would see in her remembering the arching crown of the cabin featherbed, stuffed with feathers of her own picking. When she turned in her bed in the spare room at Blue Glass, she imagined herself turning as she had in her own home: left side toward the wall against which the bed was built; right side toward the fireplace where, all night long, winter and summer, the coals were kept alive. But most often she saw the four panes of glass that Ellen Yanders had carried from Pennsylvania to Indiana, had carried across the Susquehanna, the Allegheny, the Muskingum, the Miami.

Ellen Yanders hadn't cared about furnishings. She could sleep on leaves, live on a dirt floor, make do with one pot and one skillet. She had survived floodings and fordings, freezings and fires. But when she settled down inside a house, she wanted that house to have a door she could close and a window she could look out. That had been the difference, to her mind, between living like an animal and living like a human. A three-sided lean-to was no better than a bird's nest. A windowless cabin was about on a level with a woodchuck's burrow. Ellen's father, in Towanda, Pennsylvania, had given her four panes of glass, each pane twelve inches by twelve inches, clear, but beautifully hazed over with the green-bronze sheen of water passing over sand. Ellen Yanders had carried those pieces of glass like jewels; and Simon had had no choice but to raise up a suitable setting for them. He did so. But Ellen Yanders had only a little more than seven months to look through that window. The Yanders arrived in September; the cabin was up at the end of October; by mid-June Ellen Yanders was in her grave, dead of milk fever.

Whenever Leafy leaned her cheek against that glass and looked out, she remembered (because Simon Yanders had told her) that Ellen's last trip from her sickbed had been to that window. Leafy often wished she knew less about Ellen and the glass she had carried all the way from Towanda. When she looked out, she felt the need of seeing the world for Ellen as well as for herself. Yet except for Ellen's death they would never have had that log house and its fine window at all.

✒ Simon Yanders

Simon Yanders had made the return trip from Cincinnati to the East Fork of the Whitewater in two days; good time, but he was well mounted and knew the country. He forded the East Fork before sundown and was already thinking of his friend George Conners' tavern at Connersville. The evening was chilly. The day which had started rainy was ending windy. If he pushed on at the rate he had been traveling he could be stretching his legs in front of a good fire in three hours' time. The prospect appealed to him—if it didn't make him happy. Since his wife's death, he had come to regard happiness as a quality of youth. He was thirty now, and had given happiness, along with singing, rassling, and daydreaming, the go-by. There were satisfactions left. The hearth he was heading toward was one of them. He wasn't a man to mope or fall into inaction. The trip to Cincinnati had been on business occasioned by his election as a sheriff of the Whitewater country. The election pleased him. He had worked for it, and he expected to do a good job at it. He had given happiness the go-by along with the high spirits of being young, but he still relished new places, new experiences, power, overcoming difficulties, men, and women. He was a widower—but no one can become a widower who isn't a man. And he was still a man.

He had known before Ellen's death that he wasn't cut out for farming. The chances and dangers of travel, the gamble of finding a good place, and the hardship of getting settled had blinded him to the fact that what he liked was getting there, not settling. He wasn't a settler at all. The bottom dropped from his bucket the minute he was settled. He had no stomach for hitching his horses to any piece of equipment that didn't have wheels. What he would have done if Ellen had lived, he didn't know. It was a bitter twist to life that Ellen had died coming, against all her own inclinations, to be at his side. She had lost her life for what, as it turned out, he didn't want either. After Ellen's burying he had never gone back to the cabin. He had sold the cow; he had left the pigs he was planning to fatten for the Cincinnati market to run wild; traded the pulling team for a saddle horse. This done, he fastened the door and rode away. After a quarter-mile he had turned back for one thing: to put his face against Ellen's glass for one last look inward. He thought he might see the two of them still there by the fireside; but the day was hazed over and nothing of what had been their home could be made out in the gloom inside the cabin.

His house was on government land. He had planned to meet his payment by selling his pigs. If Ellen had lived, he supposed he would have done so. As it was, he owned a house and furnishings on property that wasn't his. The fact didn't worry him. Sometimes he visited it in his mind, wondered if it had been broken into, if pigs had climbed the steps and benastied the rag carpets, if birds had come to roost on the meat hooks and clothes pegs. But he never went back. What was buried there was buried. He had heard it said that time heals all things. Maybe. When he was sixty, he might be as reconciled to Ellen's death as to his mother's. There were women willing to comfort him, and he let himself be comforted. He didn't say, but he would have had he been asked, that he would trade every bit of comforting he'd had since his wife's death for an evening's talk with her by their own fireside.

As he came up out of the shallow gravelly ford of the East Fork he heard voices. There was no reason to be suspicious. But the habit of seeing before he was seen was too ingrained to disregard. He got out of the saddle, and proceeded noiselessly on foot. What he saw was an old story. Settlers had missed the ford. Their wagon had been overturned in midstream and had been dragged out on its side by horses fighting for their lives. A wheel was off the wagon. One horse was down. The husband, head in hands, was sitting with his back to a tree. Only the female of the party was going about her business as usual. The cow was grazing; the young wife was spreading out wet clothing and bedding onto bushes and trying to keep it, in spite of the wind which was coming up, in place.

The wife, more girl than woman, he saw, as he came closer, stopped her clothes-spreading every few minutes to run to horse or husband. She stooped, patted, encouraged, and got, insofar as Simon could see, about the same response from both. Though the horse did, when she spoke to it, make efforts to rise. The husband never lifted his arms from his knees or his head from his hands. Simon could hear what the girl said, but if he had been required to judge her tone of voice without understanding the words, he would have thought her far from any wilderness or accident: a girl cooking supper for company or getting dressed for a play-party. She was still dripping from the accident, bedraggled as a wet hen, but happy. A bad thing had happened but they had survived and were making the best of it. *She* was doing more. She was enjoying the chance it gave her to overcome a setback. The accident, Reno thought, plus all the bustle and cheerfulness was enough to make any man feel downhearted.

"Reno," the girl said, "I thought I was a gone Josie for sure. My nose was scraping gravel when I finally shot up to the air. We won't meet up with anything else as bad as this from now on. Except for the soaking, we're not in such bad shape from this."

The man spoke without lifting his eyes from his hands. His voice was muffled, but Simon could hear him. "Blaze'll have to be shot."

The girl, who had been squeezing water from a bolster, threw the bolster over the upturned wagon and went to her husband. She put one hand on his shoulder, the other on his dark hair. If he hadn't seen the girl's face, Simon would have thought from that gesture that she was mother, not wife.

"Don't say that, Reno. Blaze'll be all right. He's hurt, like you. But he'll get over it and have as much go as ever. He's better already. He don't look near as poorly as he did."

"You always think everything's going to turn out all right."

"I'm not a cowardy calf."

"All right. I'm a cowardy calf."

"You're not. You're hurt."

"I'm not hurt."

The girl straightened up. "Well, if you're not, what're you setting there for? You better get up and help me."

"This trip was a mistake."

"You wanted to make it. We saved and scraped for a year to make it. You said it was our only chance."

"Not 'only.' 'Best.'"

"How does upsetting in a river change that? We never figured on reaching the Whitewater without some mishaps."

The husband took his face out of his hands, and Simon, prepared by his words for some hangdog, weak-chinned specimen, was surprised. The fellow didn't look like anyone ready to tussle bare-toothed with a bear, but he did look like a fellow most girls would be eager to take up with and, except that at the minute he was mighty down in the mouth, a man with grit enough to be a settler.

But the grit now was out of him. "This trip was a mistake," he repeated. "It's October now. We're a month late. We're not even to Connersville yet. When we get there, we've got no place to live. And if we had a place to live, we've got nothing to live on."

The girl backed away from him. "Do you want to spend the winter right here?"

"No. But we could make it back to Blue Glass before the snow closes in. I know the way now, and how to do it."

"Reno, would you turn tail and run?"

"I'm not your father. I'm not afraid to admit I made a mistake. Are you?"

"We don't know we've made one yet." The girl dropped on her

knees by her husband and put her hands on his shoulders. "If you're not hurt, what's a month late mean? Or an upset?"

"I'm not hurt."

The girl nuzzled the man, like a mother cat with a kitten. "Come on, Reno. Let's build up a fire. It's cooling off fast. We'll dry ourselves out, and I'll cook us some supper. I'll make us a skillet of gravy and a gallon of hot tea. We're on the right side of the river, and it's a nice spot to spend the night. Blaze'll be all right by morning, and you can fix the wagon wheel then. We'll be in Connersville before the week's out. And in after years we like as not won't even be able to bring to mind the time we turned over in the East Fork."

The girl had hold of her husband's hands and was pulling him upward as she talked.

"The only way we'll be able to remember, likely, will be seeing a book with water stains," she went on. " 'Did you leave that outside?' you'll ask me. And I'll answer you back, 'Reno, that book floated in the East Fork.' And you'll say, 'Floated? East Fork? What're you talking about, Leafy Rivers?' And when I tell you, you'll say, 'You dreamed it. It's another fancy of yours.' "

She had talked him right up and even into smiling. "I reckon you can charm the rings off a raccoon's tail, Leafy," he said.

Simon chose that moment to come tromping through the under-brush. As long as they had been in the midst of an argument he hadn't wanted to mix in. Now that it was decided—or at least died down—he did what any decent man in the woods would do: encountering folks who had had a mishap, he offered his help. His intention was to give them a hand in gathering up their gear, mending their wagon, and looking after their animals. As it turned out, he spent the night beside their campfire—and in spite of the fact that he'd had Connersville and the talk and drink there in his mind all day. And it wasn't wholly because the Riverses needed more help than he could give them between sundown and dark.

The horse, in spite of the girl's optimism, had to be put out of its misery. The Riverses weren't traveling with any great burden of breakables, and what they had was, for the most part, sensibly boxed. Still, their belongings were scattered from July to eternity, and the food and clothing that they had recovered was water-logged. The wagon was stove in, all along the side that had been dragged, and the right front wheel had to have its hub rebuilt. Reno Rivers, once he had swallowed his misfortune, was a nice-enough boy, but it takes more than niceness to make a wagon-re-pairman. When Simon heard Reno had been a schoolteacher, he had his explanation. A man doesn't teach school unless he is lacking in some way.

The girl had been a teacher, too. Simon wasn't able to figure it out, but a woman who could teach appeared to be a woman with something added beyond what was usual for her sex; while the man who taught had had something subtracted from him. So though Reno was no great shakes with the wagon or horses, the girl was able to turn out a better than usual supper with her waterlogged victuals. Simon watched her cook. It was hard, after Ellen, who had been a big well-rounded woman, to see this freckle-faced sprig of a girl as a wife. I bet he was her teacher, he thought, and what she married was respect for chalk dust and admiration of long division.

"You go to school to him?" he asked Leafy.

Leafy, who was browning chunks of salt pork, stopped shaking the skillet. She was trying to figure out the meaning of the question before she answered it. She had already heard, Simon took it, some fault found with teachers who married their pupils.

"He's only three years older than me."

"Don't yell 'til you're hurt," Simon advised her. "I got nothing against a teacher marrying his pupil. Good way to find out if she's got any gray matter."

The girl had an answer to this on the tip of her tongue, swallowed it, and went back to her gravy-making. The little Jersey had yielded up her usual amount of milk in spite of her swim. Simon watched Leafy stir grease, thickening, and milk together. If the girl was made to close her eyes, shut her mouth, and stop her swaying as she vigorously stirred, she wouldn't be worth a second glance. But no one was likely to see her that way before she was laid out on her deathbed. Her frame and features when moving, talking, feeling were like the pebbles at the bottom of the branch: not worth a glance without the living water that flowed over them.

He could see that she wasn't laying herself out to please either him or her husband. She liked what she was doing for its own sake. She enjoyed putting her hands and feet through the tight pattern of fetching and carrying her mind had laid out as necessary for cooking the meal. She had gone off in the woods when he shot the horse and hadn't come back until she'd had her cry out. She said to Simon, as if in excuse, "Blaze never did a mean thing in his life, and except he was trying harder than Ginger, he wouldn't have been hurt."

"Well, that's the way," Simon told her.

After supper Reno, sitting bolt upright against the wagon bed, fell asleep. "He almost drowned," Leafy said, "trying to get Blaze out of his britchin."

"He looks tuckered out," Simon agreed.

"Reno's a real staver when he's not out of heart. But there's times a blackness settles down over him he can't see through. His brother, next older, went out in the woods and hanged himself in a spell of blackness."

"What brought the spell on?"

"Some words with his wife."

"I reckon you're afraid to cross your husband."

"Reno? He's not like his brother. He gets streaks, but he gets over them. He comes to a wall in his mind and it shuts him off from whatever it was he had in mind to do. The only thing he can see to do is turn back. Or turn left or right."

"Traveling in tacks like that, it's kind of uncertain where you end up, ain't it?"

The girl nodded.

"You know this before you wed?"

The girl shook her head. "I didn't know anything before then but my twelves. And after three years I knew them backward and forward."

"You learned how to make good gravy somewheres."

"It was root hog, or die, when it came to gravy."

"What's your plan when you run into this wall? Face around? Or head off si-goggling in another direction?"

"I don't run into the wall, so I don't have any plan."

"Sit down," Simon said.

"I better get Reno to bed." But she sat down.

"When you start on something, you've got a plan," she said. "If it's moving west, you reckon on upsets, setbacks, spillings. And still you figure to do it. If the Whitewater Valley was your best chance, it still is even after the setbacks. So I don't see the reason to turn back."

"So you talk a hole in Reno's wall."

The girl laughed. "My father offered me a fip once if I'd be quiet for fifteen minutes."

"You didn't get it."

The girl laughed even more.

"What's so all-fired funny about that?" Simon asked.

"Nothing. You held a looking glass up to me and I saw myself. It was like being home." The girl's voice was low, heavy with memories.

"You homesick?" Simon asked, recalling his Ellen.

If she was, she wouldn't admit it. "We're headed for the White-water." They listened to the East Fork for a while, and she said, "If you knew rivers, I reckon you could locate a ford by the sound."

"The sound helps."

The remaining horse whickered once again, as he had been doing since the shooting.

"It hurts me to hear him. He misses Blaze."

"He'll miss him even more tomorrow when he has to pull the full load."

He was on the verge then of telling her about Ellen. A girl who could sorrow for a widowed gelding ought to have some pity left for the real thing. The girl's response would bring Ellen to life. "Had eyes and hair of amber color. She used to say the reason I chose her was because her colors put me in mind of a good chaw." But either he wasn't ready to speak of Ellen yet or wasn't ready to speak of her to this girl.

"Are you farming in the Whitewater Valley?" Leafy asked.

"I had a farm there. I still got a cabin."

"What happened to the farm?"

"Nothing, not a thing. Oh, I cleared a few trees. But it was government land and still is. I never paid up. Never even paid down, in fact."

"Who's the cabin belong to?"

"Me."

"Do you live there?"

"No. My wife died; I closed the door and never went back. I never aim to." Before the girl had any chance to express pity, he said, "This life suits me. I'd of made a poor farmer. I'm a sheriff for the Whitewater territory now. That's the business I was in Cincinnati for."

"What's a sheriff do? Send people to jail?"

"Hang them if need be," he said. "I'm more on the order of a tax collector," he admitted. "I try to see folks like Simon Yanders don't raise cabins on land they don't pay for."

He could see the idea he had in mind move into the girl's mind, back of her transparent eyes. Before she could say anything, he asked her a question. "What's your plans? After you get through that hole in the wall of your husband's mind?"

She looked at him, surprised. She didn't know there could be more than one plan—any more than Ellen. Help her husband— that was her plan—stick with him.

After Leafy had roused her husband and the two of them

had crawled under blankets back in the shadows, Simon continued to sit by the fire. What he saw in the fire was Ellen's cabin with this girl in it: he saw the cabin bright and alive again, leaf shadows washing across the sanded floor, sassafras tea brewing, books on the mantelpiece, meat in the smokehouse, soft soap in the jar. Bringing the cabin to life was the next thing to bringing Ellen to life.

He didn't have the least notion of making a gift of the place to the Rivers fellow. A man who came up against walls ought to climb over. He'd charge *him* a fair price for the cabin. And a snug place to live in, with a good quarter-section already picked out, partially cleared, and stocked with hogs, if any were still about, was a godsend, at any price. He'd ask nothing for the work he'd put into clearing or the money he'd put into the porkers. The land wasn't his, and they would have the same chance with it he'd had: a year to pay. From the looks of their outfit they had folks back east who would give them a hand at payment time if they found themselves short. They needn't be short, though, if they'd round up his pigs, add to them, fatten them, and get them to Cincinnati in time for next winter's market. Sell the hogs, pay the land agent, and head home to their cabin again, owners of the best quarter-section on the west bank of the Whitewater.

Some muscle in Simon Yanders' chest or throat that had been tight since Ellen's death unloosened. He was planning ahead again. He was here by the fire, an October chill settling down in the woods, the two young folks stretched out, flat as cleaned hides, after their day's miseries; but what he was seeing was their future. Like some old doting pappy, he was looking forward for them. Half of his pleasure, before Ellen died, had been planning. He lived, they both had, in two lands at once: the land of what they were doing and the land of what was to come as the result of that doing. When Ellen died, he had made no resolutions: no "The future is uncertain," or "Don't count your eggs until they are hatched." Nevertheless, he had been unable in his mind to go forward into any future. He didn't will himself not to think ahead, any more than a man without legs wills himself not to walk. And until now he had forgotten what it was like to live a life that took in the future, forgotten how it spreads a man out, enlarges him. He felt like an animal shut up for a long time in a stall half his size and able at last to stretch. He had an impulse to wake the two sleepers, give them a shake, say to them, "Look what I've figured out. Look what's ahead for you."

He didn't do it because he knew they needed their rest. And they took their rest like young people, unmoving on their pallets. He watched them for a while across the embers of the fire. But in his mind's eye he saw his distant cabin, clean, warm, and well lit once again; he could see the girl Leafy's face looking out the glass Ellen had been at such pains to pack all the way from Towanda. He saw Leafy's face there at nightfall awaiting his arrival as he stopped to ask how she and Reno were making out.

The young people never stirred when a rider, his horse stepping lightly under the guidance of a knowledgeable hand, came onto the gravel at the far side of the ford. Yanders, gun in hand, went to meet him. Except for ground-hugging river mists it was a clear night lit by a late-rising but still good-sized October moon. Yanders knew the horse at once—Cashie Wade's blood bay. He felt a little ashamed of his gun.

Cashie, who had forded the river, feet held high, put them back in the stirrups. "You sheriffing night and day, Simon?"

"I'm bedded down," Simon said, pointing to the fire. "You're the one sashaying around in the middle of the night. No use asking why, I reckon."

Cashie laughed. "You old fellows think all us young fellows do is run after girls. Don't you figure we've got more high-minded since your day?"

"No," Yanders said. "That's something I don't figure."

"With figuring like that, Sheriff, you're going to arrest the wrong man some day. I'm homeward bound from Cincinnati, where I been smelling out the hog-market prices."

"How are they?"

"High. If I can keep the news from hog owners, I ought to turn a pretty penny this fall."

"When didn't you, prices high or low?"

"I have my ups and downs," Cashie said. "Like anybody else."

It was Yanders' turn to laugh. "That's your story, Cashie. Stick to it. Why don't you bed down here?"

Cashie looked across the fire to the two pallets by the wagonside. "What kind of a wagon train is this?"

"Young couple who missed the ford. Lost a horse and stove up their wagon. I stayed over to give them a hand."

"I reckon I better push on," Cashie said.

"The girl's a first-rate cook. Not bad-looking, either."

"She's married, ain't she?"

"It don't seem to have hurt her cooking a smidgen."

"No," Cashie said. "Married women are bad news to me. Besides, I'm expected at Conners'."

"And she ain't married?"

"Wasn't two days back."

Leafy, roused up by the light rhythmic clatter of Cashie's single-footer across the gravel of the riverbank, called out in a low voice to Yanders on his return. "Anything wrong?"

Yanders, out of consideration for the sleeper, answered softly. "Boy on his way home from Cincinnati."

"Boy?"

"Big boy," Yanders told her. "Nineteen or twenty."

"Traveling in the night?"

"Yes."

There was a pause, the girl still on her elbow.

"What is this, anyway?" she asked querulously. "A highroad between Ohio and the Whitewater?"

"Seems like, nowadays."

"What I figured on was wilderness."

"Things have got to be refigured every now and then."

She didn't answer this, but Yanders could see her, before she slid back under the canvas, nod her head in agreement.

A girl like that, Simon thought, convinced there were no walls that could stop her, was in about as bad shape as a man who made up walls out of whole cloth. Ready-made cabins gratis might, for all the fuss she raised, dot every ridge from the East Fork to the Mississippi. It wasn't for his own satisfaction he wished she'd blaze up a little more at her good fortune; it was for her own well-being. There were mistakes that couldn't be undone, misfortunes that robbed you of goods and health, final setbacks like death that settled down heavy as casket wood in your heart. Cabins on the Whitewater, lighted by hand-blown glass, were the exception, not the rule. True, she went quickstepping through her work, managed fair dodgers from corn meal already water-soaked and swollen, shed no tears over stained clothing and candlesticks swept away, and once even hugged Elizabeth, the cow. But she would probably have done so in any case; she had been confident at nightfall, with a horse shot and her husband down with hypo. Joy in the morning was likely her habit. Once, she did grab his hand and say, "Mr. Yanders, you won't be sorry." But the cabin, he could see, appeared to her less a provision of his than a link of the kind she could always count on in her chain of good luck.

The husband had a more practical turn. Was there some catch, he wondered? Simon didn't blame him for wondering. He felt surer, actually, that a man with Reno's doubts would pay him than a woman like Leafy who still believed heaven could rain down gifts. There was no catch. He was giving nothing away except the time he'd spent in clearing and the hogs, if any were left and they weren't too wild to be fattened and marketed. The cabin he was selling. The contents of the cabin he would reclaim at some future date. The Riverses were as much his good fortune as he was theirs. Until he'd run into them, he hadn't seen anybody he'd care to trust with what had been Ellen's.

They agreed on a price for the cabin. He rode with them to where it was in sight; then, turning toward Connersville, he headed once again toward the postponed delights of the tavern.

seven

✒ *Leafy: Whitewater*

The April snow, Christmas in springtime, lay sparkling on the ground outside the Yanders cabin. Snug in their bed, Leafy knew it was there, though she couldn't see it and hadn't heard it fall in the night. She knew it was there and knew it wouldn't stay, because of the sunlight, which shone through Ellen's precious glass window.

Reno said, "Leafy, are you awake?" "Yes" was all the answer he needed.

She might have been dreaming, for anything else that was said; in any case, Reno was sound asleep again in seconds.

Marriage, Leafy thought, was easy as falling off a log. There was nothing to it. I could be married to ten, she thought, and it would never faze me. She had listened to a few tales, though her mother had warned her not to, about the hardships of wedded life. What were they, she wondered? It was true that in getting from Blue Glass to the Whitewater there had been so many hardships that those of wedded life, if they existed, seemed no more than drops in a bucket. And whatever novelties there were in wedded life, and there were some, they couldn't hold a candle to the novelty of living in a wagon, moving through the woods (when they were able to move, in spite of mirings and break-downs), to the novelty of fighting off gnats and mosquitoes, and of wondering if they'd have to fight off those animals whose big eyes stared at them from the trees on the far side of their evening fires, fires that burned only if they'd been lucky enough to find wood not water-soaked, and if another downpour didn't quench them.

Maybe for stay-at-homes back in Blue Glass, with no other hardships to put up with, being wedded was an ordeal. But in the midst of trying to dry wet clothes, find a time and place for washing dirty ones, poulticing risings, fighting chills and fever, keeping an eye out for copperheads, a bride hadn't the get-up-and-go, once she was in bed, to find much fault with what went on there. She was too thankful to be alive and in any bed to raise a ruckus over bed rites. If they'd had time, as most newly-weds did, for a proper infare journey, she might've taken closer note of such things.

As it was, she could remember the first time they lost their cow, Elizabeth, the first time she boiled squirrels for supper (skinned and cleaned, but with their heads on, so that she and the squirrels stared eye to eye whenever she took off the pot lid), the first time the horses swam a river, but couldn't remember the first time she was married in the flesh.

Her forgetfulness saddened her. She had tried to get Reno to help her recall the time. "Reno," she said, "I've always heard tell a girl's maidenhead is her most prized possession."

Reno didn't care to talk of such things. But he didn't deny that it was true.

"Maybe I was born without one?"

Reno didn't say anything, not yea, nay, or kiss my foot, so she had to reason on without any help from him.

"If I lost my eyes, or my tongue, I'd know it. I'd remember. I know I would."

Reno stayed mum as a hog with the lockjaw.

"And they're not my most prized possession. And my . . ."

Reno cut her short as pie crust. "You lost it. I can guarantee you that."

"When?" she asked eagerly. "Where were we? How did you know?"

If he knew, Reno wasn't saying. Perhaps he didn't know, and was only trying to cheer her up. "It's gone," he told her. "Now forget it."

And he wouldn't say another word. She respected him for it. He was no dirty hired man, nor she a sluttish hired girl whose chief occupation was telling how she'd lost hers with somebody's brother, yours perhaps, if she was telling the truth.

"Do men have them?" Leafy asked, taking another tack, but not giving up entirely.

"You acquainted with any men who are maidens?"

This explained why girls had to be so much more careful than men. Men had nothing to lose. Still, though she had lost hers under circumstances in which the goings-on were too unusual for her to be expected to keep track of everything, she would dearly love to have remembered the exact occasion. It was the minute she went from maid to matron, and she would like to recall if life from then had changed for her.

It *had* changed. She wouldn't go back to being an old maid for anything. On a raw morning like this, before she was married, she would have awakened curled in a ball, trying to warm her knees with her chin. Here she was, with snow on the ground and the coals in the fireplace dying down to ashes, and she was as snug as if they were already atop the summer. Reno was as warm to sleep with as a heated soapstone.

The bed Simon Yanders had built was in a fine spot to reconnoiter room and weather before getting up. It was built in the corner of the room, fireplace to the right and Ellen's famous window straight ahead. Before you put a foot out from under the covers, sun and fire had told you their strength. The cabin wall itself formed headboard and one side of the bed. The outside corner was supported by a walnut post, smoothed down as slick as furniture and rubbed with grease 'til the grain stood out as clear as ringworm on a baby's arm. There was a webbing instead of ropes to hold up her plump featherbed, and over them were the wool-filled comforters she and her mother had made. She didn't think Andy Jackson in the White House was bedded any better; though the President was likely up betimes, drafting treaties and signing bills. Or maybe fighting a duel.

Reno turned away from her, half sighing, half snoring, and she looked at him fondly. The girls who had whispered of hardships had also sniggered about pleasures. They were as wrong about one as the other. They didn't know what they were talking about when it came to being one flesh. To hear some, you would think it was a cross between kissing, Christmas, and maple sugar. As a married woman, she smiled at their innocence. Everything her father had said appeared to have been lost on her. She'd heard him say "Most said, least done" a thousand times. The talkative girls were ignoramuses trying to hide it. Anyone acquainted with marriage would know that the one flesh of that eyeblink act was neither present pleasure nor being burned at the stake, either; it was the baby to come. A seed, tiny beyond human seeing, and naturally beyond human feeling, was planted. It was an urge given by God to man so that he would increase and multiply; and likely little pleasure even to him. Reno first sighed, then slept like someone glad to have a duty over and done with. But this was another matter Reno didn't like to talk about.

"How can you tell when you have done enough to make a baby?" she asked.

"Something tells you," he said, and would say no more.

It was the way she had figured. Hit or miss, no more sure than a water dowser who says "This is it" when he gets tired tramping. It explained why some couples had children and some didn't. She doubted they would have any; staying qualities didn't seem to be Reno's long suit. And he was by nature easily discouraged.

As for herself, she was glad to be a wife and spared the wearisomeness of a husband's responsibilities for baby-making; wide awake, morning's first duty done, and free to watch coal-glow, snow-sparkle, and the sunup's growing splendor. Marriage, as far as she was concerned, was all pleasure. At home she had been pulled in two pieces. Here she could get out of bed and do what pleased her. At home her mother would say, "Stand aside, Mary Pratt. I can work faster without you." If she went down to the barnyard, her father would say, "It'd look better, Mary Pratt, for you not to be hanging around with the hired men."

Reno never said, "Stand aside"; and since he was all the hired man they had, he was glad for all the help he could get. They were always reading the law to her at home, which might not have been so bad if her father and mother had read from the same book.

Living with Reno had taught her more than an academy. She wasn't slow at all. She could work circles around Reno, read the whole of two pages of the book they held together while he was only halfway through the first. But she had learned too much from her mother to be sharp when he lagged. Besides, Reno was proud of her. "Mama looked at a page and knew it," she explained herself to Reno.

Reno whistled. "Glad I'm not married to her."

She could plan with Reno. Reno was a great planner himself. They could talk together, building up domes of hope as high as the sky, and they lived under them without the least sense of shame. Or of regret when they tumbled down.

Reno didn't see anything unladylike about her coming down to the barn lot, and there she learned what she would never have guessed at home in Blue Glass: she liked animals. In Blue Glass a horse was a wheel, moving; a cow, a full crock in the springhouse; a chicken, an egg cracked and dropped into its new nest of corn meal and lard. Pull, drink, and lay. That's all she knew of horses, cows, and chickens in Blue Glass. A dog was watch. A cat was catch. A pig was fry. A goose was pluck. A sheep was shear.

Now that she was a married woman with no one to shush her, her world had doubled; animals had been added to people. She hadn't slacked off in her housework. She hadn't become an old farmer or drover who'd rather curry a horse than redd up a house. But for all that she had ever noticed them, God might just as well never have created an animal until she reached the Whitewater Valley.

In a way she was like Eve, except that she hadn't yet gone so far as to take a shine to a snake. But she did put her cheek to Elizabeth's cheek, and let old Emma, her pet hen, ride on her shoulder. "Next thing you know, you'll be hugging hogs," Reno said, which was a joke, because before you can hug a hog, you have to catch one. And Simon Yanders' hogs had become woods hogs, wild, dirty, and mean. She was trying to make them less fractious, to toll them to the barn lot with offerings of slop, and of acorns and beechnuts she'd gathered herself. They'd never walk the trace to Cincinnati next fall if they didn't learn to look to someone for food. She already had an old sow, Sukey, who would come up to be scratched. And though Reno was wrong about hugging hogs, there was one little runt, the castoff of a big litter, starving to death without a tit to suck on, which she had raised by hand. She had had to hold him like a baby to feed him, and she fondled him now like a pet lamb or a pussycat. She kept him out of the house, though he was more housebroken than many a hound dog she'd seen. He had his own little pig house in a corner of the barn lot next the barn and didn't run with the wild ones in the woods. It was a seven days' wonder he hadn't been eaten by an uncle or aunt, or even by his own mother, when he was a starveling. Maybe they had tried, and the memory of it kept him away from them now. When he looked up at her out of his pink eyes and through his long sparse eyewinkers, his baby snout breaking into a sharky smile, she did, if Reno wasn't around to see, hug him.

She called him Esau because he'd sold his birthright of razorbacking it, wild and hungry under the beech and oak trees, for a mess of cabin pottage. That wasn't, when you got down to the bedrock facts, the truth. He didn't have any such birthright to sell. When she found him, death was staring him in the face, and the only right on his calendar was that of providing pork for his own family. She called him Esau anyway, and gave him pottage as a free-will offering. He acted like he knew it. He dogged her footsteps—hogged them, Reno said. If he got out of sight, which wasn't often, she called him by his name, Esau, not Soo-ey, Soo-ey, as she did the other, nameless, ones.

"Esau, Esau," she would call, and he would come running, clean as a pin, pink and white with grayish spots, and shrewd little pig eyes, expectant or merry; or sad, she'd swear, when he was expecting a handout and she had nothing in her bucket for him. His tail was curled so tight you could pull out a cork with it. He was her dog, her cat, her pet lamb, her baby brother, and maybe even her baby. "If we ever have a baby," Reno said, "I bet it will cry 'onk, onk.'" Meanwhile, they didn't have one and they did have Esau. Sometimes she would wake up in the morning smiling, and wondering why. Then she would remember Esau, bedded on straw and ready for fondling, and she would laugh to herself at the remembrance of his bright little eyes, blinking up at her through his stiff eyelashes like cinnamon pinks from behind a picket fence.

Reno slept on, so she slid out of bed, quiet as could be, built up the fire and set a basin of water before it. She took off her bedgown and scrubbed herself well. The water was cold, but the big red fire warmed her up as fast as the water cooled her down. She had always liked being awake in a house while others slept. It made her feel like Adam in the Garden of Eden, required to share the glory with nobody but God. If God had made a woman before he made a man, that might've been the end of creation. A woman, used to having the run of the Garden, and all of its say-so to herself, might've raised Jesse with God if she'd been roused up one morning to find a rib missing, and a man there to spoil the quiet and mess up the neatness and to pounce on her in the one-flesh act. A woman, with uninvited company like that, would likely have fought like an Arab, not been a softie like Adam, saying, "Thank you, God. If you want to make another, feel free to take another rib." Women had more spunk than men. If a woman had been first in the Garden, with everything she needed at hand, she would more than likely have given a man, who for all she could know might be a bear with his hair singed off, the welcome of a good-sized rock. And if that hadn't settled his hash, would have greeted him, when he had pounced, tooth and toenail.

She lived through that scene as she washed, enjoying the comeuppance she was giving Adam—and God. As she dressed, it came to her that God had no doubt made man first for this very reason. He had no intention of letting women see what Eden would be like without men.

The basin of water she had bathed in was already lukewarm— from use and the fire. She left it in case Reno might like a little warm water to douse off in. She mixed corn pones and set them to baking, gathered up some slop and leavings for Esau, and stepped out into the snowy spring morning.

The snow would not last long; it was no more than a skiff, but it had fallen wet enough to lodge, and the night had been cold enough to hold it where it had fallen. From house to barn— and everywhere else the eye could see—was a fairyland. The pink and yellow of leafing willow and maple were be-gemmed where the sun caught drops of melting snow. Shadbush blossoms, actually white, were creamy against the snow. Birds, with the morning's snow adding to their spring excitement, were all in an outcry together. A bluebird, when the others were catching their breaths, got in his uninterrupted song, clear and sweet as snow.

As she went toward the barn, Leafy looked over her shoulder at the tracks she was leaving behind her. They gave her pleasure. It isn't often you can see where you have been and the way you have come. Though she couldn't see them, she had left footprints like these all the way between the Whitewater and Blue Glass, and between the clapboard house there and the cabin where she had been born. In eighteen years she had come all that distance; and ahead of her was the trackless white. She stopped, and had the feeling that time stopped with her and that she was adding to her life by not going on. She put down her pail of slop and held out her arms as if she were the world's living center and could pull the snow around her like a comforter, and the hills like soapstones and the blue sky like a coverlid. She let her arms fall. When I do that, I'll be tucked in a burying ground asleep forever, she thought.

She had a sudden heart tug to run back to the cabin and rouse Reno. The tug went along the muscles of her thighs and up into her shoulders. She half turned. Then it died out; she didn't know why. She felt a turncoat to Reno, going on, while he slept, into all the be-creamed and be-silvered world. The sun, warming as it climbed, would soon put a noonday plainness over everything. It was now or never for Reno. Still she didn't go back for him. It was magic for her because no one had called her out into it. If she went back for Reno, said, "Wake up, Reno. It's such a pretty morning. Come and look at it," Reno might say, "I've seen snow before," and go back to sleep. And he would have gained nothing and she have lost everything. Or Reno might be willing, but the corn pones smell so good that they would both put off going outside until they had eaten. And by that time, the snow would be gone, and when Reno said, "What was it you wanted me to see?" she wouldn't be able to tell him. And even if he came at once, it would be a secondhand thing for both of them: handed to him by her out of good will, and damaged in the handling.

So she didn't turn back. She picked up her bucket of leavings and walked on into what was trackless.

"Esau, Esau," she called, dragging out his name in a singsong.

Usually, Esau came running—or was waiting and didn't have to run. She looked for him this way and that, and saw on the slope above the barn someone she had expected since October: Simon Yanders, mounted on his claybank, both still as statuary. She had been ready all winter to run forward and welcome him. Show him Ellen's window shined to a fare-ye-well. The table top scoured with sand, bed legs oiled, crane blackened, lilac tree spaded. She and Reno had both expected some neighboring. A sheriff roamed up and down the country. She'd started up many a time at footfall, thinking, It's Simon Yanders.

Without thinking at all now, she went on with her calling as if she hadn't seen him. It came to her that Simon Yanders might have made more than one such unannounced call on them; had seen them and the care they were taking of his property without their seeing hide or hair of him; had sat just where he was, calculating the payments they'd be able to make him after they'd sold their hogs.

"Esau, Esau," she called, her eyes on pig house and barn lot. When Simon Yanders had befriended them, she and Reno thought they had someone in the wilderness to look to. They thought the sale of his house and the gift of his hogs meant he'd taken them under his wing. He hadn't. They were two settlers out of hundreds; reliable-looking and in such need of a house they never questioned his price or terms. From where he had planted himself, he could tally the number of trees Reno had deadened or felled, catch sight of his hogs, gauge by the smoke from the chimney whether the fire had been well banked the night before, and maybe even take note of the state of his precious glass.

I would scorn to do that, Leafy thought. I would scorn to spy. She turned her back on Simon Yanders, and Esau helped her take her mind off him. He was not in his pig house, but his tracks led away from it, out under the fence in the far corner. She started to blame Reno, who was no hand for making fences hog-tight or horse-high. But the barn-lot fence was never supposed to be hog-tight. Hogs roamed free as the forest animals, and Esau was likely the only pig in the Northwest Territory with a roof over his head and a yard laid out like that of a Blue Glass residence.

His tracks in the new snow were easy to follow. She put down her bucket and followed them; she had an uneasy feeling that Esau might look more like a side of bacon than a brother to his family. And there were wandering varmints who would like to get their jaws around a juicy little pig—though they wouldn't tackle the old boars and sows unless hunger had got the best of their judgment.

She followed him up the slope opposite the one on which Yanders sat. Well, now the spy would see that the Riverses were up betimes, tracking down their livestock. And he could figure from this that they'd have a herd to sell in the fall and he would get his payment on time.

A third of the way up the slope, under beech trees with butts she and Reno together couldn't reach around, she caught sight of hogs, working away on the snow-covered mast. There was no sign of Esau, but seeing the herd, companionably rooting and snuffling, made her feel easier. They didn't have the look of cannibals. She recognized the old sow, who had littered Esau, giving her family of suckers lessons in rooting. Winter-thin shoats kept to the outside of the circle. Old tuskers plowed where they pleased. There was no sign of a pink-and-white fatty. Hogs ate animals, including their own kind. A notionate sow would turn on her own litter. Or a wandering child. She had seen a man with one side of his face puckered into what looked like a belly button—a giant's belly button, the size of a saucer—the scar left behind by a sow who had felt hungry for man's jowls.

Reno had told her, "You're not doing that pig of yours any big favor, making a pet of him. About the time you spoil him for hogs, you'll weary of him yourself."

She wasn't weary of him, but she might have spoiled him for hogs, given him the wrong smell, and a look to whet their appetites. Hogs didn't scare her. She'd taught them that she wasn't food, but the feeder. She pushed in among them, and though one or two growled at her like dogs with a bone, she had no intention of letting a mean-tempered hog keep her from finding Esau, if he was still alive; and he was, there on the far side of his mother, in a clot of his littermates, rooting and snuffling like a pig who'd never had a mouthful he hadn't dug up himself.

Leafy snatched him up. Not to save him from anything, but in relief—the same way she would have grabbed Offie, lost, then found—grabbed him and squeezed him and, with Esau squealing, started back down the slope with him. There was a sound behind her. The sow, who had never mothered Esau, was having an attack of jealousy. It never entered Leafy's mind to drop her pet, though she felt the sow's anger like teeth at the backs of her legs. It never entered her mind, either, that she couldn't outrun a stump-legged, tit-heavy sow. And for the first two-thirds of the race she did, though Esau was an unhandy, squirmy bundle to carry, and jumping fallen logs and breaking through shadberry and spicebush with a pig in her arms wasn't the picnic she'd expected.

She caught her toe under the bowed-up root of a dead butt and fell with Esau beneath her squealing like he was having his throat cut, not loved and rescued. She didn't have the wind to do any squealing herself, but she held onto Esau like grim death to a dead man. She didn't confidence a hog's thinking.

The old sow who had been chasing her might, if she let Esau go, take out after him instead. She scrunched down over the pig, flattening him like side-meat, and her last thought was, A dimple there'll never show.

She stopped thinking at the touch of the sow's snout, and didn't begin again until Simon Yanders hauled her to her feet. She put her hand behind her. She hadn't been bitten, not deep enough to bleed, anyway.

"Where's Esau?" she demanded.

"Who's Esau?" Yanders asked.

"My pig."

"Which pig?"

Which pig? She thought Yanders should be bored for the simples. She looked for Esau herself and saw him, skiting back up the hill again toward the mast, as saucy as if he'd never been lost or fallen upon. She was after him in a twinkle, picking up a stick as she ran. If ever a pig deserved a gad, this one did.

Yanders caught up with her as she got hold of a hind leg.

"Set that pig loose," he said.

"No. He's mine."

"I didn't say he wasn't. But I ain't got the wind to save you a second time."

"I didn't ask you the first time. Besides, there's no need now."

Then she saw the sow she had supposed dead, down the slope aways, sitting up on her hind legs and peering around her like a deep sleeper waking.

"Didn't you shoot her?" Leafy asked.

"Shoot her? She'll fetch money in Cincinnati this fall."

"Didn't you care if I lived or died?"

"You didn't die, did you?"

"I fainted," Leafy said, as if this excused her.

"What do you want with this pig, anyway?" Yanders asked.

"He's a pet," Leafy said. "I raised him by hand. He's not wild."

"He'd like to be."

Yanders put a hand on the squealer, and Leafy once again hoisted Esau into her arms. "Mr. Yanders," she said, "you've got the wrong sow by the ear this time."

She tromped toward the barn, and Yanders tromped beside her. "If you think I'm going to help you tote a hog around, Mrs. Rivers, you've missed your guess."

"I don't want any help," Leafy said. "You came here uninvited and you can leave the same way."

"I didn't know I had to have an invite to come back to my own place."

"Or to spy," Leafy said.

"What do you mean, spy?"

"Coming at sunup, sitting on your horse unbeknownst to us, seeing what work we've done and when we get up and if Reno's . . ."

"Where is Reno?" Yanders asked. "He poorly?"

"Poorly? What makes you think he's poorly?"

"Where is he? You the one that does the morning chores around here?"

"If I take it into my mind to. My husband don't have a turn for ordering women around."

"Like some," Yanders said.

Leafy didn't answer that; she didn't figure she had to.

"Well, with a fire-eater like you on his hands, I don't reckon he'd dare."

"He dares whatever he's a mind to."

When she had stowed Esau away in his house, and shut him there with log and rock, she took a good look at Yanders. What she saw was what she had remembered. She hadn't missed a lick on that evening by the East Fork. It was Yanders' looks, as much as anything, that was making her stand up for Reno. It sounded as if she thought Reno was ill-favored in some way. It was belittling to Reno for her to be singing his praises, like a mother with a backward child, to this big-faced fellow.

She put a quick end to it, pigs, husband, herself. This man was a landlord and a sheriff and what he was interested in was money. She came from a family where money was respected and she knew how to talk about it in a sensible way.

"If you'd like to see the shape things are in up at your house, Mr. Yanders, I'd be pleased to show you."

"That's not what I came for."

"What did you come for?"

She couldn't tell whether he was pondering on what the reason was or on whether or not to tell her.

"I got heartstrings here," he said.

The admission melted her. She would sooner tread on a hope than on a sorrow.

"We expected you all winter. We wanted you to see how we were keeping things and what we'd done. We were hungry for a little praise."

"All right," Yanders said. "I'll come have a look. And some breakfast. If I remember, you're a pretty fair hand with a skillet."

"There's pone baking," Leafy said.

But she kept him outside for a few minutes on the excuse of wanting to hang up her bedgown and empty her bath water. "Because of the snow I didn't wait to tidy up."

Her real reason was to get Reno out of the bed—if he was still in it. She wasn't going to have Yanders, after she'd been bragging Reno to the skies, see him snoozing long past sunup.

She burst inside all of atremble to get Reno up and in his pants before Yanders caught sight of him. "Get up, Reno," she whispered. He was up, had emptied the water, turned the pone, and heated a kettle of water.

"What're you whispering about?" he asked.

"Simon Yanders is here," she said.

✍ Blue Glass

Screaming awakened her. She listened, wondering whose? The sounds that filled her ears might be echoes lapping from the walls. But the tightness in her throat fitted the echo from the walls. "Am I the screamer?" she asked herself. She opened her eyes and looked around for evidence. It was night; it was the spare bedroom; a candle was burning. Its light flickered, bending in time with the wind. Leafy watched it, waiting for it to miss a beat. It never did. Blow wind, bow candle. The candlelight was as nimble as a cakewalker: spang goes the banjo, crook goes the knee. The candle was a rope-jumper; when the rope came down, up went the heels.

What had made her scream had made her observant. Pain had whetted all her senses and they cut sharper and quicker than when dulled with ease. The familiar room was like a creek bank washed clean by the spring flood. Everything she saw looked new.

Dr. Daubenheyer, in the rocker, leaned forward looking at her. She was the new thing on the creek bank for him. The jolly doctor's round face was pale. He was listening to the echoes she no longer heard. He was listening to echoes he had heard before—someplace else. The knowledge excited her. It seemed like second sight.

"What do you hear?" she asked.

Dr. Daubenheyer, who had been looking at her, now also saw her.

"Screaming," he said.

"Was it me?"

He nodded.

"I did it in my sleep."

"Don't hold back," he said. "Don't hold back anything. Let loose," he said. "Let loose and yell. Yelling helps."

"I heard Indian women could have babies on horseback and never make a sound."

"In the first place, you're not an Indian, and in the second place, Prill'd never put up with a horse in here."

"Why does it hurt so?"

"What's inside's bigger than the gate it's got to go through."

"A farmer wouldn't plan that way for his stock."

"A farmer didn't make this plan."

"Who did?"

"They say, God."

"*They* say. If it wasn't God, who?"

"Nobody planned."

"It's all hapchance?"

"I don't want to blame anybody."

"Not even Adam?"

"That poor fellow," Daubenheyer said. "Babies was the fartherest thing from his mind."

"Hers, too," said Leafy.

She smiled, saying it. She heard herself speaking, the same way she had heard herself screaming. Someone else, to whom she could listen and for whom she wasn't responsible, spoke. She could indulge herself like a drunkard. She wasn't accountable. She swung dreamily in a slack in time. It was king's X for her.

"June," she asked, "who does your baby look like?"

"My wife," June answered.

Leafy considered this. June's wife was Alphy. If Otto looks like Alphy, Leafy thought, my eyesight's gone. What June had surely meant to say was, "He looks like his mother." Leafy didn't reply. It wasn't required of her in her state to correct any mistakes—except, if that were possible, her own.

"June," she whispered, "June."

"Yes, Leafy."

"It's started up again."

"High time."

"It makes me sick to my stomach, June."

"It's your female organs, Leafy. They're sensitive."

"I'm going to throw up."

"Bear down," Daubenheyer said, "bear down."

"Where's Reno?"

"Asleep, now, I hope. He was in here awhile back."

"When I was yelling?"

Daubenheyer nodded.

"Do you think Reno loves me?"

"He acted that way."

"Do women go out of their heads having a baby?"

"Some do."

"So they don't know what they're saying?"

"They don't . . . and nobody else does either, it's such a jumble."

She thought it might be true. Her own memories were a jumble. In her right mind, and trying to tell the story to herself, as straight as she could, it was a jumble. Everything, once it was past, changed. Sweet smiles became sweeter; cruel words, crueler. And circumstances, which might make you forgive yourself, faded from mind.

"June, June," she cried, "when we think back, do we remember things the way they really were?"

"My God," Daubenheyer said, "I hope not."

His loud voice pushed the hammock swinging inside her so that it touched what never should be touched. She started to tell him about it, but when she opened her mouth all the words ran together. She sat up, wildly, with the idea that if she got out of bed, she might run away from the pain.

Daubenheyer came to her, took her hands, then leaned away from her.

"Pull," he said, "pull. Let's get this over with."

eight

⟿ *Leafy: Whitewater*

July, their first summer on the Whitewater, had risen up like a castle before their eyes; it had boomed in their ears like a cannon. Clouds were white palaces, or else they were purple forts and opened to show the threat of chain lightning, before closing again with thunderclaps. She and Reno were Easterners, from the other side of the Ohio, where storms were tamer.

The hot sun bred new settlers like maggots. River and riverbanks were crawling with them. You could hear axes ringing and trees falling all the way to the Wabash. In the still of the night you could hear the corn grow. Its leaves pushed through the soft dirt with the silky mew of newborn snakes. Everything was prospering, swelling, multiplying. Hardly anyone was dying. Those winter had weakened petered out early in the spring. Babies, taken with summer complaint, didn't last through June. The heat made chronic sufferers easier, cut down on the coughing of the consumptives, lessened the shaking of those with the ague. Lung fever and the bloody flux never got in their worst licks before September. July was life's burgeoning time.

Leafy, in that month, felt herself as uplifted as a cloud, as pushing as corn. She had never lived in such a climate. She kept the house neat as a trivet, was born for the trade of housewifery, it seemed; but if Reno came in at an odd hour, and by a tweak here and a prod there, showed where his mind was, she was never too housewifely to drop needle or butter paddle, to shove the Dutch oven away from the coals. She was as cheerful as if uninterrupted; and actually, Reno, being a little shamefaced at such goings-on in broad daylight, was brisk as a cricket, and such interruptions as she suffered were short indeed.

But it was the summer's climate that gilded all its happenings. Sometimes Leafy thought the sheen came down direct from the sky; sometimes she believed that it sprayed out from her daydreaming, and that no matter what the season, her dreaming would have made every happening summery. The center of her daydreaming was Simon Yanders. She saw him all the time, solid and plain as a bedpost. She lived her life in his presence. She wasn't in love with him. He had never said an out-of-the-way word to her. She had seen him often since he saved her life in April, and slowly, without her knowing what was taking place, he had come to be there in the house in which he had once lived. She knew he approved of her. He praised her cooking. He laughed at what she said. Once he said, "There are more things here on this farm to keep track of than the hogs." At first, she had been afraid that he was talking about Reno, finding fault with him. Reno wasn't the most workbrickel man in the world. He wasn't in any swivet to get Yanders paid off. A man who made a deal as unbusinesslike as Yanders wouldn't, in Reno's opinion, expect any great promptness in payment. If money had been what Yanders was after, he would have had mortgages drawn up and interest rates set. They could take their time paying Yanders.

"If somebody has to miss a payment, it had better be the government than him," Leafy argued.

"The government," Reno reminded her, "will take our farm away from us if we don't pay up. Yanders is too softhearted to put us out. You've got to judge a man by his actions. Nobody but a softhearted man would have made the kind of deal with us he did—handing over his house without bond, and giving us his pigs out of hand."

"That's all the more reason," Leafy said, "we've got to see he's paid."

"Don't forget we're looking after his stuff," Reno reminded her.

"That's a big hardship."

"Well, it's not everybody he'd trust with the job."

"Whatever trust he's had, we're playing hob with it, the direction we're heading."

Reno contradicted her. "The direction we're heading, Leafy, we'll be able to pay the government *and* Yanders, this fall. Do you have any idea how much Senator Hull's hogs fetched last year in Cincinnati? Three thousand dollars! He walked them down there from this very valley, pocketed his money, and went on to Washington, loaded with gold."

"Three thousand dollars!"

"I grant you, we're not going to have any three thousand dollars. Even if you hand-feed every shoat on the place. But there'll be plenty, and Yanders will get his fair share."

"Sometimes I think he comes round here to see if we're taking care of things right."

Reno laughed at that. "Don't you know why Yanders hangs round here?"

Leafy shook her head. "Not unless it's to see if we're working."

Reno laughed some more. "No, he's an easygoing fellow. I told you that. Besides, I'm not his hired man. I'll tell you the reason he comes. He's a lonesome bachelor nowadays, and he's not used to that. He's used to home cooking, a lit candle, and the buckwheat batter raising in the crock by the fire. That's what he's lonesome for, and that's what we give him. Beside us, Conners' Tavern, where he used to hang out, can't hold a candle. Don't you belittle your cooking, Leafy. If the hogs get cholera or prices drop, I can always hire you out to George Conners as a cook. Oh, we've got more than one string to our bow, I tell you."

While Reno was giving her his explanation of Simon Yanders' visits, and while she was answering him mildly, "Maybe you're right, Reno," a whole new understanding of what Yanders had said came to her. He did have more to keep track of than hogs; and buckwheat batter and candlelight weren't the answer, either. The answer was that he was a dreamer, too. The weather that was brighter for her when he was around was also brighter for him when she was around. It was a pleasurable matter for both of them—like a bequest: something gained and nothing given up. It had nothing to do with love or marriage, kissing or clasping. She was a married woman and Simon Yanders a mourning widower and government official. By some peculiar grace each could make the world a better place for the other. Her daydreaming had, in fact, made her a better wife already, more soft-spoken and gentler. Reno himself mentioned it.

"You like me better than you used to, Leafy. Don't you?"

"I don't know as I do," Leafy said. And she didn't. She had always liked Reno.

"You act like it, anyway."

"I didn't know I'd changed."

"You have. Time was, I thought I might end up as henpecked as your father."

"Papa isn't henpecked."

"Leave Papa out of it then."

"I gave you some advice about farming."

"Advice about farming!" Reno pulled her over onto his lap. "Advice about my sittings down and my risings up. Leafy, there was a spell when not a thing I did pleased you. I read too slow and I ate too fast and I got out to work too late in the morning. And I buttered my bread before I put gravy on it. And that wasn't the way your papa done. I don't know what's changed you, but it must be love. I've got my sweetheart back again."

Reno held her close. "You glad you married me, Leafy?"

"Yes," Leafy said.

"Tell me why," Reno said. "Go on. I'm your teacher. Write a composition on 'Why I'm glad I married Reno Rivers.'"

Why was she glad? There were some reasons he wouldn't care to hear: to get away from home, for instance. There were some reasons he wouldn't understand: Marriage is a good place for daydreams. She spoke without thinking. "We were made for each other, Reno."

She couldn't have pleased him more, or have come, perhaps, nearer the truth. He folded her up like a tatting bobbin. He was holding her like that when the Kemp boys stalked in. The door was open and there was no reason for them not to, though they might have called out before they stepped over the threshold. Leafy, scrunched up against Reno's chest, had been in no position to see or hear, and Reno in no mood.

Brockton Jr., the oldest, called Ton because that was his weight, approximately, said, "Excuse us. But at this time of day we didn't expect to run into anything more private than dishwashing."

Murdie, the middle one, who was seventeen, said, "Well, we're just poor bachelors and don't know the ways of married life, Ton."

The youngest, Ozias, fifteen, didn't waste any time talking. He just looked.

Leafy sprang to her feet at once. Reno sat where he was and

glowered. "You might at least sing out before you step inside," he said.

Murdie, who had a quick tongue and enjoyed using it, admitted the truth of that. "Even the redskins give a whoop before they attack, I reckon."

"We ain't attacking," Ozias corrected him. "We're inviting."

But Murdie, proud of his wit as a dog with two tails, hadn't had his fill of banter. And there is something about a schoolmaster out of the classroom that makes a young fellow want to dare what he's always been afraid to do with the desk between them.

"Must be nice to have all the weeds out of your corn so early in the season, Reno."

This was barefaced sarcasm, not wit. Reno had only started to hoe his corn. But Leafy, before Reno could say a word in his own defense, blazed out at Murdie. "When your mother was poorly, Murdie, did you like folks poking fun at her housekeeping?"

Murdie, who had loved his mother, got off his high horse in a hurry. "I didn't know Reno'd been poorly."

Leafy, white-hot with rage when she heard Reno belittled, had a hard time to keep from laughing, seeing Reno's bewildered eyes. He must've looked anything but poorly to the Kemp boys, grunting and groaning and giving her bear hugs. But before Reno could disclaim being poorly, Leafy explained the nature of his sickness.

"Reno's got a rising," she said with dignity.

A rising, as was well known, could make all movement painful to a man—particularly if located in unmentionable spots.

Murdie stared at Reno, Reno stared at Leafy, and she stared right back at the two of them. "I'm poulticing it," she said in a matter-of-fact voice, amazed at her unexpected talent for lying, "with boiled flaxseed."

"Nothing like flaxseed," Ton agreed. "A flaxseed poultice'll draw the bung out of a barrel."

Reno, looking more and more uneasy, made a move toward getting to his feet. "You sit still now," Leafy cautioned him. "You start threshing around and you'll drive it inward."

"I know a man did that," Ton agreed. "Nothing to start with but a simple rising on his ass. . . ."

As that word escaped him, Ton shut his eyes.

Murdie, as quick to cover up trouble as cause it, made them forget the bad word with one worse, death. "Dead of blood poisoning in two days and swelled up like a poisoned pup."

Ozias, whose interest in risings, no matter where located or leading to what, wasn't great, issued the invitation they had come to deliver.

"We're getting up a party for Pap," he said.

"What kind of a party?" Leafy asked.

"A pantry-party is what we're calling it," Murdie told her.

Leafy had been to many a frolic, here in Whitewater and back home in Blue Glass: barn-raisings and logrollings, husking bees and quilting bees, play-parties and carpet sewings. But a pantry-party was a new wrinkle on her horn, though she didn't have any trouble guessing its purpose: it was a scheme of the Kemp boys to fill up their shelves with some of the food their mother, if she had lived, would have provided. It put a better face on the enterprise to call it a party for Pap. But Brockton Kemp, Leafy thought, would have to play a pretty knife and fork to keep ahead of his big boys when the plates were passed.

Brockton Kemp, like many a settler on the Whitewater, had had to sacrifice a wife to a farm—and it had been a real sacrifice, touching the whole man from heart to pocketbook. There was more land than women available in Indiana. If you had your choice, you'd be better off to lose your farm and keep your wife. A wife could help you get a toehold on some new land; but while a farm was no drawback in attracting a woman, a farm didn't have the power to make one up out of whole cloth where none existed.

Brock's garden was more sizable than that of most widowers.

Not only had his Augusta left him with three big boys, two of them as eager to find a wife as he, but she had left him with three little girls, an added handicap to any man's wooing. A woman willing to be a wife might balk at being the mother to quite so many of her predecessor's offspring: Pearl, Cuma, and Lacey, aged five, three, and one. Leafy sometimes wondered what had happened during the ten-year layoff between the boys and the girls. Whatever it was, three more babies in five years finished Augusta Kemp. She was never properly up and about again after the birth of Lacey. But in the time she had, she had brought up a nice family. Her boys were no more breachy than was common for that age. Ozias, between hay and grass, was still content to look; and while nobody doubted he'd tramp farther to see a woman body-naked than to get a bead on a five-point buck or watch a sunup, nobody really wanted a fifteen-year-old any other way. Brock himself was a mannerly wooer, all "Whatever suits your fancy" and "I'd delight to hear, ma'am." He appeared so ready to carry any female of a suitable age and state around on a chip that everyone wished him well in his search.

The two older boys were another kettle of fish, neither content to look, like Ozias, nor mannerly like their pap. They wanted what suited *their* fancy, and when they found it, looking wasn't all they had in mind. But Ton and Murdie were forgiven, too. They couldn't resist cutting the fool, even while they were woman-hunting; and their didoes were so comical, it was sometimes forgotten that a girl could be ruined just as completely during a fit of laughing as during a fit of crying.

Another thing in favor of the two big boys was that they liked each other and showed it. It gave people with scars on their own hearts from the meanness they'd done or received from their relatives a letup from aching just to watch them. It was a kind of peephole into what might have been. Murdie was reckoned smarter than Ton, and nobody held him not to be prettier. When Murdie was dressed up, and there were people who said Murdie wouldn't go to the backhouse without putting on a tie and hat, he looked finer than frog's hair. He was inclined to have a breaking out at the mouth; but he was a sugar-lip, too, and though he talked a lot, he never rubbed people the wrong way with what he said.

Ton, on the other hand, was no sight for sore eyes. He had a fat face, a long chin, and no neck, so that when he ate he had to chew gentle to keep from bruising his chest. He looked like a big poke-easy, but he was a hard worker like his mama and had her good heart. Nobody knew where he had heired the faculty of tickling your funny bone. Murdie worked at saying funny things. You could hear the cogs clanking around in his skull as he ground out his smart sayings. Ton was as surprised as anyone else at the rib-ticklers that dropped from his mouth. He'd blink like a bear just come on a bee-gum tree as he heard the laughing; the pleasure that came into his round eyes would come from that sound, not what he'd said.

And half the pleasure to Ton and his listeners alike would come from seeing Murdie wiping the tears off his handsome jaws as he laughed at Ton's innocent sayings. Both boys flirted with anything under sixty and in petticoats, and if they had their way, the petticoat would be heisted. But with all the joking and taking time off to admire each other, it was more like a game than life; and a woman who took exception to it felt as much of a fool as a player at blindman's buff refusing to be handled, or the recipient of a letter in the game of post office taking the kiss as a personal declaration of love.

Reno, with the rising Leafy had fixed on him, was in no good position to appreciate the boys; but Leafy, once over her anger with Murdie's observation about Reno's hoeing (which she'd made herself ten thousand times, but wasn't going to take from an outsider), settled down to enjoying the party the boys always carried with them—without waiting for the one they were talking up to start.

𝄞

But Reno said they'd go to the pantry-party. And he persuaded Simon Yanders, who'd stopped by that day for a look at a buckwheat batter—or the candlelight, or both—to go with them. Leafy would just as lief he hadn't. Dreaming about Simon Yanders, having long conversations with him, performing acts of grace and courage which he never saw were all she asked for. The dream would have died, she supposed, if she didn't see him once in a while. But seeing him too often would likely kill it, too. Grace and courage, and words that bared the heart, were natural as breathing, in a dream; but with Simon Yanders in the same wagon with them, she dried up, act and word. She didn't want to hazard anything. By keeping silent she remained in the weather of the dream. Exhilarated in the same way, under clear skies with the sun going down the color of cinnamon roses.

If Simon and Reno noticed her silence, they gave no sign. Simon, traveling as he did, was as good as a newspaper—better; he knew happenings newspapers never reported, and was a month early with what they did report, since it usually took that long for a newspaper to reach the Whitewater. Reno pumped Simon about his job, and Leafy cringed, not to hear the questions, but the answers. Traveling around enforcing laws that broke people's hearts seemed to her a job a good man had better give a miss. It was a job that had to be done—she saw that—but those she admired would surely never be driven to it, except by desperation. Desperation might be Simon Yanders' exact excuse, for all of his acts since his wife's death spoke of desperation: giving his hogs away, abandoning his house and furnishings. What man in his right mind would do such things?

"Did you ever have to turn any of your friends out of their home?" Reno asked.

"I did, a couple of times, yes."

"What if we get forgetful about what we owe you on your house?"

"That's my hard luck."

"You won't throw us out?"

"I don't have any papers on you. And I'm not going to fee a lawyer to claim I do."

"But if we don't meet the payment on the land?"

"That's a different kettle of fish."

"You'd send us marching?"

"I wouldn't have any choice. It's the Land Office ruling."

"I don't know's I could ever bring myself to do a thing like that."

"You wouldn't last long as a sheriff if you couldn't."

"Last? I'd be a fool to start."

"You're more than likely right."

Leafy fired up at that. "Reno could do it if he set his mind to it."

"That's what I'm talking about."

Reno got them back on the subject he'd started with. "There won't be any question of throwing us out. I reckon you had a look at our hogs?"

Simon nodded.

"Noted how fat they were?"

Simon nodded again. "Noted last spring a means of fattening I put a stop to."

Reno laughed. "They'd never eat Leafy. *She* feeds them. She's the goose that lays the golden egg."

"Humans killed that goose. Hogs ain't that much smarter than we are."

Reno laughed again. Sometimes Leafy felt that men and women were a race apart. Men didn't mean what they said the way women did. They didn't live in their words. A mean-speaking woman was mean. A mean-speaking man could be playing with words, the way boys did with stones or snowballs. After their noses stopped bleeding, they were friendly as ever. But she was too wrapped up in her dream to pay much heed to their word-tussle.

She possessed, for the afternoon, the grace of fitting the world, as if she and the world had been made with each other in mind. It went beyond grace and into power. It wasn't God, but her glance, that sent the gold-leaf sprinkle of light through the moving leaves down onto the dusty lane they traveled. She couldn't be sure that the sky's buttermilk tarnish didn't reflect upward from her looking. Oh, she knew she was fooling herself; the light was tawny because summer was dwindling, not because she was happy. But it wasn't an easy matter this afternoon to tell where what she felt ended and where what the world looked and smelled like began. She didn't try to sort them out. They ran into each other and overlapped in the way (it seemed while it lasted) creation had intended—and that only some kind of sickness prevented. She lived the way she had before she was born—and would again after she died: trusting the earth. She dreamed at night sometimes that she could rise to the ceiling or the treetops, and could hover there, not bound by human laws. She arrived at the Kemp party living in that nighttime dream.

She arrived free. Neither tied down, as the other married women were to housework and childbearing, nor searching, as girls her age were for a man who would provide them these millstones. The tough bubble of the daydream, inside which she moved, protected her. Inside *it,* what she did in the outside world couldn't hurt her. She could cut didoes she'd never think of without it. And because her mind was taken up with Simon Yanders, making some kind of a hero out of him (he *had* saved her life, hadn't he?), she was free as never before to banter with others. Nothing but what she said to him counted; and she didn't intend to say a word to him, any more than she did to the sun or the moon.

The Kemp place was buzzing like a big beehive when the top's been lifted. Only this beehive was being stocked, not robbed. It *was* a beehive, and the honey was corn, apples, berries, every fruit or vegetable capable of being dried that the Kemp boys had been able to recruit for miles around. Corn was being cut from the cob and spread on boards; apples peeled, cored, sliced thin; berries hulled; fox grapes pulled from their clusters. The ladies were the queen bees, though not every man was a drone. Herman Schultze had his homemade apple peeler with him, and he was busy every minute, either peeling apples or repairing a breakdown. When the thing was working he could turn out apples faster than any six ladies could peel. Ton Kemp was shucking corn. Ozias got the filled trays up on the scaffolding the Kemps had built to hold them. Murdie circulated, trying to prevent any notion getting started that what was going on was work. He didn't have any trouble. Murdie was a treat at any time; and a get-together, with or without Murdie, was so infrequent, any meeting of passing wagons was a pleasure. The Kemp boys had been too smart to ask folks to dinner. A big noontime meal would have cleared their shelves of as much as the afternoon's work would put back on them. There would be a supper after the husking, shucking, peeling, coring, quartering, and hulling were over, but no one would expect anything but a pickup meal for supper. The Kemps, at the rate trays were being filled, wouldn't have to look forward to a hungry winter. All they'd need was some pickled pork, smoked ham, and game, and they could eat high on the hog until spring. And no one begrudged the work. Augusta Kemp, alive, would've done the same for any one of them.

Leafy didn't know what had gotten into her. She was always quick but not always so deft. Tongue and knife were both limber this afternoon. Speech and apple parings spouted from her at about the same clip. Her tongue was eloquent and her knife sure. She took the peeling off a summer sweetings in one wax-green, unbroken spiral, then tossed it over her left shoulder, the way unmarried girls did, to discover the initials of their intended.

"You hunting for a new man, Leafy?" Murdie called.

"Just looking to see if I've got the right one," Leafy answered, thinking: I've covered some distance since Papa shamed me for waving first to a boy.

Murdie came over to help her look, and changed the shape of the paring with a poke of his toe from what was nearly an R to what was surely a K.

"Well, I see I'll be your second," Murdie said. "Better late than never, that's my motto."

Leafy, with a knife like greased lightning, produced another spiral and tossed it into what was a K without any help from Murdie.

"You want to nail it down, do you, Leafy? There ain't no need. You got me persuaded."

"You're a baby," Leafy said. "Third time's the charm," she told him, tossing another circle of peeling. The spiral shattered into undecipherable breakage.

"It's me or nothing," Murdie told her.

"That's an easy choice."

She could carry on with Murdie because he was younger than she was and didn't count, because her high spirits could lift her over any obstacle, and because over by the well, Simon Yanders was watching. She wasn't showing off for him, but he was the only one it would have been wrong to carry on with, because he was inside her dream. Nothing inside the dream could be real, and anything outside could be.

Murdie laughed his head off at her. He pushed her sunbonnet back on her head, put his hands on her shoulders, and said, "Won't be so easy, I promise you, if that time ever comes."

Reno, appearing from nowhere, snapped Murdie's hands off Leafy's shoulders.

"What time're you talking about, Murdie?"

Murdie was cool as a cucumber. "Time you wouldn't know anything about, Mr. Rivers."

"I know about now," Reno said. "You keep your hands off my wife."

Leafy blushed for shame—or Reno; that he could be so blind, and make such a show of himself.

"He was joking, Reno."

"Murdie's a great joker," Reno agreed. "We all know that.

I'm not faulting him for his joking—but when he wants to josh you, he better keep his hands in his pockets."

Reno strode off like a man who doesn't intend to speak twice. Murdie, with a great show of shackling himself for the good of all, slid his hands into his pockets as if they were handcuffs, then went through a pantomime of trying unsuccessfully to get them out.

"Guess it's safe for me to speak now," he said, and everybody laughed.

Leafy didn't know whether to laugh or cry. Murdie! Why, Reno had as well tell Offie to keep his distance. She could live out her days in daydream about Simon Yanders and Reno would never notice—while one jape from Murdie Kemp, who would pinch his own grandma's bottom, set Reno off like a spark in punk. She put down her knife and untied her apron.

"Don't let it faze you, Leafy," Murdie told her. "It's my fault. I got the wrong sow by the ear."

Leafy didn't say anything. What had happened was bad enough. She didn't intend to add to it by saying a word to an outsider about her husband.

"Come on, Leafy," Murdie urged. "We'll be one dried-apple pie short this winter if you stop cutting."

But she walked away from the workers and picked up Cuma, who was sitting on the ground gumming a corncob. Leafy threw away the corncob. That was a sure start for a baby on the summer complaint. Cuma was as warm, limp, and dirty as a puppy, but heavier. Leafy leaned her face against the soft moldy-smelling hair. "Poor little tyke," she said, "poor little motherless tyke."

With her face in Cuma's mess of curls she couldn't see a thing. That way, she ended up, as she wouldn't otherwise have been able to do, standing beside Simon Yanders at the wellhead.

"Poor little tyke, poor little tyke," Leafy repeated.

"What's the matter with her?" Simon asked. "What's so poor about her?"

Leafy lifted her eyes. Simon was looking down at her with the same expression she felt on her own face.

"Nothing," she answered, "except I took the corncob she was sucking away from her. And her mother's dead."

"She's about in the same fix as the rest of us."

"My mother's alive," Leafy told him.

"You're a lucky girl."

"I didn't think I was. She was one of the reasons I was glad to leave home."

"What'd she do to harm you?"

"She wanted me to better myself."

Yanders laughed a little. "And what did you want? To worsen yourself?"

"I didn't want to better myself, because it would make a better show and win me high praise. I didn't have that in mind."

"Well," Yanders said, "how're you making out? You avoiding high praise?"

Leafy couldn't help smiling. "Reno praises me sometimes."

"Not today, he ain't."

Leafy put her face back in Cuma's hair.

"You better set that buster down," Yanders advised. "She's too chunky to tote around, even if she is motherless."

"I'm strong. I started carrying a big fat brother around when I was ten."

"I thought your brother was older than you."

"Chancellor is. I'm talking about Offie."

"Offie? Somebody in your family's got a real hand for passing out names."

"It's Chancellor. He handed me mine. Offie's real name's Howard. Chancellor calls him Offie because he's an off-bloom. Born out of season."

"Out of what season?"

"After the main crop's over, he meant."

"You and your brother Chancellor being the main crop?"

"I didn't name him Offie. Chancellor did."

"Must make Offie feel like a cull."

"It's just a name to him."

Yanders reached over and took Cuma from her arms. "If this youngun's got to be dandled, it's my turn."

He took a long sniff. "I've smelled winter bears that was sweeter. Ain't anybody ever introduced you to soap and water, Sis?"

Leafy backed away from Yanders. He was in a hair's breadth of becoming real. . . . Not the widower, or sheriff, or landlord, or rescuer, but a young man with heavy eyebrows, blue eyes, partly hidden under long half-open lids, and a big, broad-bridged nose. She didn't want him to become real. She didn't want to be self-conscious about him. She wanted him inside her dream, tied down like the sun in the sky, shedding warmth; but at a distance, and no threat.

As she backed away, Simon put a hand on her shoulder. "I was speaking of the baby, not you, Leafy."

"I know that." But she walked out from under his hand.

"What's the matter, Leafy?"

"Nothing."

"Your husband got you buffaloed?"

"I don't know what you're talking about."

"I notice you don't feel free to say more than a word or two to me."

"That's got nothing to do with Reno."

"Maybe I've got things sized up wrong."

He handed the baby back to her, turned, and walked away. But the damage was done. She was in love with Simon Yanders, and knew it.

Blue Glass

Pain was not something happening to her. She was the pain. She was what could not be borne and which in spite of this got worse and worse. The pain had a location, but from that location it spread until earlobes, finger tips, nipples, toes, the outposts of her body, were bursting with agony. Then it became so bad there were no outposts left. All of her body disappeared, except the center of pain. Then the spreading of pain from that center in unendurable waves, in waves no human being could live through, began again and she lived through it.

She wasn't sure whether the pain taught her what to do to relieve it, or whether that what she was doing caused the pain. She gave no more thought to having or not having a baby. She did not even think baby. She thought push, push, push. Something was hurting her, breaking her in two. She would get rid of it, what was hurting her, if it was a panther or a monkey. She didn't care about shame or the future of what was born or the past that had brought it into being.

The pain which spread entirely over her, in circles widening like those in water away from a dropped stone, grew smaller and smaller again, until there was only the pain she could spread her hands across in the triangle mounting upward from her crotch. But *she* wasn't the pain any longer. The pain was a place she could measure in the triangle of her two hands.

"Don't stop, don't stop," someone said.

She opened her eyes. They were wet with tears or sweat.

"Be quiet," she ordered. The sound of a voice might be enough of a jar to start things up again.

Daubenheyer came to the bed and put two strips of torn sheet in her hands. Her eyes followed them to where they were tied to the bedposts. They were rust-colored where she had held them; her hands were raw and bleeding.

"I've hurt myself," she said.

"Pull," Daubenheyer told her, "or you'll hurt more."

She made a motion toward pulling. Her arms, or whatever commanded them, refused the job. She let the strips drop. As the pain shrank, the world flooded back to take its place. She heard the wind and thought she heard the sound of the rain that had been threatening all day.

"Is it raining?"

Daubenheyer didn't answer her. He put the strips of cloth back in her hands. "Pull," he shouted. "Work. Bear down. You've got things started. Don't give up now."

She took the strips; but telling her to pull them was like telling somebody who has walked out of a burning building to walk back into it. It went against human nature. She let them go. She put a hand under the bedcovers.

"I think I'm bleeding," she said.

Daubenheyer had no sympathy. "You should've brought the baby long ago."

"I tried," she said.

Daubenheyer made a scornful sound in his throat. Leafy held up her hands, palms out.

"My wife's had worse from hoeing."

"Alphy?" Leafy asked. She was too tired to imagine anything, let alone Alphy hoeing.

"No, not Alphy."

The answer reassured her. She still had all her wits about her. She lay back against the pillows to rest, but as she did so Daubenheyer placed himself with a thump on the bed beside her. He threw back the sheet that covered her, and with hands that felt like a blacksmith's began to knead her where the pain was resting, but it was ready to dart out the minute it was roused. He put the reins back in her hands.

"Pull," he said. "Bear down. Try. We're going to have this baby."

Leafy said, "You have it, June."

She perched on the joke for one second, safe above danger. Then the pains started, and she grabbed the harness and pulled and grunted and sweat. Her last thought was that she would probably never joke again.

nine

↳ *Leafy: Whitewater*

Being "in love" with Simon didn't change anything, except the name she had been giving to what she felt. She no longer called these feelings her "fancy" or her "daydream." And she admitted to herself that "in love" was what she had been all along; and further back even than the morning Simon had saved her from the pigs; as far back, perhaps, as the evening he had come to their rescue on the East Fork of the Whitewater.

The change in words changed her idea of herself. The last thing in the world she would have picked herself out for was a married woman in love with another man. Who could have guessed, seeing the way she was brought up, and how bashful she was with boys (bringing-up aside), that that was the way she was headed? Or who could have guessed, able to read her heart and mind, that her feelings for Reno weren't as lasting as the rock of ages? In a way they were. She hadn't changed about Reno. Oh, there were some few things about his house and farming habits she hadn't known before marriage and for which she wasn't about to clap hands. But what she'd lost in admiration, she had maybe gained in feelings of looking-after. And these were, maybe, more of a tie than admiration. What was puzzling to her was that living with Reno, being Reno's wife, made her think about Simon Yanders. She didn't know how that could be. It made marriage like a game of statues, and Reno the one who spun her into the position she had to hold. In the game, you were told to be "bit by a snake" or "seeing a ghost" or "fighting an Indian" and you froze like the one bit or fighting or seeing. Reno, it seemed, by marrying her had spun her into a position of yearning and had told her, "Hold it." And he didn't do it once, but many a time, until she forgot it was a game she was playing and thought it was life.

She didn't forget right and wrong, though. She lived her married life and her workaday life as she always had. She knew her duties and she fulfilled them, never feeling sorry for herself. What did she have to feel sorry about? She was like, she thought, unbelievers who had discovered religion. Over the plowing and churning they keep right on with, there is spread a kind of indifference. Their hearts are elsewhere, and their rewards. Butter come, crop fail, their smile through it all doesn't falter. They are living in the promised land, where such events are trifling.

Not that she made Simon Yanders her religion or thought he could take the place of it. It was bad enough being one man's wife and in love with another, but she didn't intend to get religion mixed up with it. Though she did intend for it to stay where religion was: up in the skies. If Simon Yanders wanted to speak to her out of a burning bush, he could. But if he didn't have that power, they would jog along without benefit of any whispers or handclasps: landlord and widower, married woman and tenant.

She treated "being in love" like any other idea she recognized as truth, but didn't intend to do anything about: the earth was round and she knew it but didn't intend to sail to China to prove it. There was a thing called gravity and she knew it and felt its pull when she jumped, but the fact of gravity didn't make her any jumpier than usual. Because of gravity and because the earth was round her body acted in spite of herself in ways it wouldn't have without them. She knew that, and she knew that loving Simon Yanders made her face burn and her fingers tingle and her tongue get big and clumsy in her mouth. But she lived with this (not that it was a trial) the same way she lived with gravity and the round earth; and it didn't affect her life with Reno any more than they did.

The calendar said it in black and white, and outside, in brighter colors, the world was saying it: they had been in the Whitewater Valley a year. The green forest was coloring up. As far back as August the poplars had gone yellow, and as time went on the colors deepened. Gum trees were as red as new turkey wattles. Along the slopes hickories stretched in yellows so bright they put candlelight to shame. Creeks were calico-colored with drifts of colored leaves. Fox grapes on the banks were plump and purple, asking to be bitten. Pigeons had turned feisty as hogs in their scramble for acorns—and every day was a feast day for both. The roof echoed at night with the sprinkle of acorn rain. Leafy smelled change in the air, of farewells, or beginnings again. It was nothing, she knew, but smoke, and fallen leaves, wet by rains and the sweet-sick smell of polecats wandering after dark. Still, it stretched her heart, took her back to Blue Glass, where she'd been nothing but a sister to brothers and a daughter to quarreling parents— and sent her forward to whatever was to come. To parting with her pigs; that she knew for certain, and the thought was a pang to her. She felt like their Judas, feeding them, scratching them, and all the while weighing them out in her mind's eye for pounds and profit.

She did her best to turn Esau from a pet back to the boar he had become. He was too big for petting and too hoggish, and, size and shape apart, she didn't relish the misuse of his trust. But Esau was mulish, as well as hoggish. He had been brought up with humans and he preferred them to hogs. He was a twig so bent now he couldn't be changed without breaking. He hung around the barnyard and when Leafy came out rubbed against her legs like a cat. He lay down on one side, waiting for his belly to be scratched and when Leafy obliged him a hind leg jerked in time to the scratching. Reno laughed at the sight, but Leafy liked neither the laughing nor the twitching. It wasn't funny, she thought, to think that an animal doing what it couldn't help doing was funny. And it wasn't nice to be so much at the mercy of somebody else's touch that you lost all control of your body. She would glare at Esau and jaw at Reno.

"That's nothing to laugh at."

Reno, who knew she didn't like him to laugh when Esau got the twitches, would try to keep quiet. But the memory of that leg flying in and out as if tied to a string would make him snort again.

"Would you like anybody laughing at you if you couldn't hold your leg still?"

"Now I got to do unto pigs as I would be done by?"

"You got to do unto pigs the way you'd be done unto if you were a pig."

"I don't scratch him," Reno said.

"When I hit that spot, I stop."

"Maybe that's the best spot of all, far as the hog's concerned."

"He don't kick because he wants to. He kicks because he has to."

"Sometimes that's the best of all."

"Like what?"

"Sneezing," Reno said, after a pause. "When you've been wanting to real bad. You can't hold it back and you don't want to hold back. You sneeze because you have to, and that's what makes it feel so good."

"Sneezing's not the same."

"Why not?"

"Because nobody's making you do it. Nobody's tickling your nose. Sneezing's different. You do it all by yourself."

"It's different that way all right," Reno agreed. "And I'll make you a bargain. You stop tickling, and I'll stop laughing. And Esau'll stop kicking."

Leafy said nothing.

"Tickle or not tickle," Reno said, "you're either going to have to wean yourself from that hog—or make him pants."

Leafy said nothing.

"You may not know it, but you've made him a member of the family. Either make him pants and set him a place at the table—or chase him out with the other hogs. If you don't," Reno asked her, "how're you going to feel when I drive him off to Cincinnati?"

"I'm going to feel like Esau's Judas," Leafy said.

"Or more likely," Reno said, "feel like I am."

Esau lay at their feet, widespread, blinking up at Leafy through his long lashes, waiting for the tickle he couldn't resist. Leafy gave him a kick.

Leafy watched Reno, who sat across the table from her doing sums out of the Advanced Arithmetic he had used at Saw Dust.

"Reno," she said, the same way she would've nudged a curled-up possum with her toe. Dead to the world, or playing possum, she didn't know which. Dead to the world, she thought. Not just his eyes but his cheeks and lips went this way and that, following the figures.

"Reno," she repeated. His face and eyes in the candlelight stayed quiet for a second, but then they were busy again, book to paper and back. She couldn't help smiling. Speaking, and not being heard, by someone whose hair you could rumple up by breathing hard, was the next thing to being invisible.

Reno had an idea that his work as teacher might not be over, so he was brushing up on some of his weak spots. He could and did farm; but the more he was mixed up with livestock and crops, the more he liked books. His plan now was, after marching the swine to Cincinnati, and making the payment there on the land, to get a hired man for the farm work and take up teaching again. He could make more teaching than he'd pay the hired man, and a good hired man would more than likely make out better at farm work than he was doing. "Any hired man," he'd had the grace to say. Teaching apart, Reno liked the orderliness of figuring. He liked something that could be solved, summed up and then put aside, and would likely have spent evenings studying had schoolhouses never been built.

Leafy, sharing the candlelight and the inkpot, was writing a letter home. She was already a half-dozen letters ahead of any chance to get them to Ohio, but she was in the habit of talking to the folks at home and she tried to think of some tidbit they hadn't been told. They already knew about the weather, the Kemp party, the pack-peddler, hogs prospering, corn ripening, Reno keeping up with his studies. Sometimes, for lack of a better subject, she wrote what she called a "now" letter, one calculated to make small things important. "Now the fire crackles, now the leaf drops, now the kettle boils, now the clock strikes four, now Esau grunts at the door." She thought about a "now" letter: "Now Reno's pen scratches, now the coals in the fireplace settle, now an acorn falls."

What kind of news was that? What kind of a life was that?

She wrote, "Dear Mama, now I am lonesome," and, surprised, put down her pen. She read the words as if someone else had done the writing; as if a fortuneteller had said them to her, and their truth, up to that hearing, unknown. The shock she felt was so great that she looked at Reno, half expecting him, though he couldn't even hear her voice, to have heard what her pen said. But his own pen was speaking louder.

How could she be lonesome? She was not a lonesome girl. At home in Blue Glass she had run away to her own private sitting room or the floor of the sleigh in the carriage house to miss the hubbub at the house. Nobody in that house was silent. Her mother was lecturing her father, giving the hired girl orders, reciting a poem to Chancellor:

> "The elm trees are yellow,
> The apples are mellow
> The corn is ripe on the ear.
> The time of the clover and wild bee is over
> For this is the fall of the year."

And Chancellor, who could preach on a stump in a deadening with no audience that didn't have fur or feathers, was never quiet from the minute he ran down the stairs in the morning to the minute he climbed slowly back up in the evening. Offie filled in any gaps with questions. And her father, though not much of a conversationalist, was a storyteller, long-winded, but with such a knack of leaving questions unanswered until the windup that in spite of yourself you heard him out. Mixed in with this talk was the talk of neighbors and relatives; and of hired hands, come in from distant settlements, or from working alone, and with words piled up six deep on their tongue tips to say the minute they crossed the threshold.

Reno was naturally quiet. Esau was a real talker, but beyond "eat" and "scratch" she couldn't understand his language. Simon, in the conversations she held with him, certainly had been a free talker. And the conversations she'd had with Simon she could number on the fingers of two hands.

She got up from the table and went to the door, and from there she looked back at Reno. He didn't know that she had left. Or maybe he did. He moved the candle nearer his book.

Lonesome? She was ashamed of herself. To complain that way to her mother. She had heard her mother say she was "blue," but that was something else, and no cry for help. "Blue" was something that happened to you, like biliousness or ringworm. It wasn't any cry for sympathy, like "lonesome." She marched back to the table, picked up the beginning of her letter, and threw it onto the coals that were still alive—an extravagant act; paper was scarce.

As the paper blazed, lighting the room for a minute, Reno looked up.

"Reno," Leafy cried, without intending to, "do you love me?"

Leafy didn't send the lonesome letter to her mother, never used the word, even. But the lonesomeness showed through the words she used to hide her lonesomeness. Because of this, Prill let Offie, when Leafy asked for him, make the trip with Chancellor to visit the new settlement. And Chancellor, when the offer of a job as an assistant drover on the return trip came to him, let Leafy persuade *him* to leave Offie behind for the winter.

It didn't take much persuasion. Chancellor listened to Leafy's arguments: living with two teachers would make a scholar out of Offie; it would be a rest for her mother; and what would he do with Offie, anyway, herding pigs Ohioward for seventy miles?

Herding pigs or not herding pigs, Chancellor had had his fill on the way out of Offie as a traveling companion. He wouldn't have wished Offie off on his sister if she hadn't pleaded for him; and he had the added sop to his conscience of believing that a little wilderness living far from home and mother was just what Offie needed. Offie had been born in too clement a season. He was as soft and mushy as an overwatered fruit—like one of those pears that ripen in a rainy summer, pretty to look at, plump, thin-skinned, and high-colored. But when they drop they break wide open; and if you get them before that, they have less flavor than a cup of rainwater.

"Keep him, keep him," Chancellor said fast, before Leafy'd have any chance to think over the drawbacks, or he himself to think of what Prill would have to say when he returned without her baby boy.

Nobody asked Offie what he wanted to do, but he was content with the turn things were taking. He knew why Chancellor was so eager to be shut of him; and the feel of Leafy's hand, finger-combing his hair, told him her plan wasn't Chancellor's—to make a man of him or die in the attempt.

On the day when the hogs were due for their last home-coming before the final roundup for the trip to market, Reno had promised himself as a hand at a logrolling. He was willing to beg off, but Leafy, who enjoyed the job of rounding up the hogs, and who would have Offie for company, wouldn't hear of it.

"With Offie to help me," she bragged, "we can hunt them out and toll them down to the barn lot faster than you could."

Reno, who figured that his wife's opinion of her kin was her own affair, didn't say what he thought of his brother-in-law as a helper.

"A hog don't care who throws out feed to him," he agreed. "The only thing is, it'll take a lot of riding to search them all out. And we can't afford to miss one."

Leafy fired up at that. "I've spent more time on these pigs than you have."

Reno didn't deny it for a minute. "Who said you hadn't? And all the more reason not to miss one now. All I was trying to do was warn you. Old Man Luckett can better afford to be shorthanded logrolling than we can to miss one hog. I'm more than willing to give him the go-by. I forgot the hogs, slick as a whistle, when I promised him."

"A promise is a promise," Leafy said. "Besides, there's nothing to this bringing the pigs down. It's a lot easier than a log-rolling."

She didn't say it, she didn't exactly mean it, that Reno was a man who, between two jobs, would always choose the soft one.

But the possibility of that meaning hung in the air, and Leafy, hearing it echo, and looking at Reno, steady and calm and for-bearing, was sorry for it. She put her arms around his shoulders, hugged him, stood on tiptoe to kiss his cheek.

"I want to do it," she said. "I've been looking forward to show-ing Offie how it's done."

The three of them parted next morning a little after sunup. Leafy on Ginger and Offie mounted on an old mare borrowed from the Kemp boys. Reno would leg it over to Luckett's on foot. The air was warm as new milk and with no more current in it. Earlier in the month there had been frost in the early-morning air, the smell of leaves rotting, of pawpaws ripening, of bucks swinging through the woods with the heavy scent of their courting on them. Indian summer had wiped that all out. It looked backward, was a kind of mirror for what was gone. This, though it was so sweet a season, made it a sad one, too. It wasn't real, only a reflection of a summer now over.

Leafy felt this and judged it was why she was sad. They all had on their summer clothes: dressed like play actors, she thought, for a time past. Her sunbonnet hung by its strings down her back. Offie was barefooted. Reno, shirt open at the neck, showed his white throat, already bleached by a month of buttoning up. She reached down to take his hand.

"A fond farewell 'til nightfall," Reno told her, mocking the intensity of her clasp a little.

The threat of change made Leafy feel too husky-throated to reply.

"You two stay on your horses," Reno warned, "and don't get off. You hear that, Offie?" he asked. "You're the man of this outfit. You see your sister uses some sense."

That nonsense took the lump out of Leafy's throat. "You won't ever forget that one time," she accused Reno. "Well, Esau's no baby now. It's root hog or die with him now, like all the others."

164

"Know what she did?" he asked Offie. "Ran on foot into a mess of sucking pigs and pried that big fat Esau away from his mother. Except for a passing friend, you wouldn't have any sister today."

"I know better than to do that," Offie boasted.

"I hope so. Simon'll be over at the logrolling," he told Leafy. "You think I better warn him to keep an eye out for you if he comes by this way?"

Tenderness for the changing season and the parting hour curdled in Leafy. Remembering her one mistake in a year of tending hogs and seeing how blind Reno was to all of her that didn't show in outward acts, she hit Ginger a lick with the end of the rein.

"You tell Simon Yanders to mind his business and I'll mind mine," she called back to Reno as her horse sprang forward.

"Who's Simon Yanders?" Offie asked, jogging bareback at her side.

"The sheriff of this county. And the man who owns our house."

The hogs were up on the ridges, rooting and slobbering over beech mast and acorns. But at the drop of a few ears of corn from Leafy's and Offie's saddlebags they gave up hunting for themselves and took what was offered. This was an old story to them, and hogs were smart enough to remember how the story ended. Follow the giver to where a feast was spread. That it was spread in a barnyard and the gates, once they were inside, were closed didn't matter a lick to a hog. He didn't care where he ate as long as the supply was good. And any hog who cared to think past food could remember that the gates were opened the next day.

When they'd picked up a herd of fifty or so, Offie asked, "These all belong to you?"

"The ones with two nicks in the left ear do."

"Can you keep the others?"

"You know better than that. It would be stealing. Reno will chase the others away when we get home tonight."

"We're wasting our corn on somebody else's pigs."

"There's no way to help it I know of. Do you?"

Offie shook his head.

"They've got to be taught to stick together and to follow. If they don't learn that, Reno'll never get them to Cincinnati."

"Chancellor had a whip."

"Well, you can't whip a hog every step of the way to market. You can hustle them along, but a hog's got a mind of its own—more than a cow or a horse. A horse is like a dog in some ways. It'll do what you want it to do, just to please you. Not a hog. It's more like a cat. It wants to please itself. It'll march, but to get food, not to pleasure its owner. Hogs are smart. Esau's smart but I've spoiled him some, so he's more like a pet dog than a pig now. Esau knows what I want and sometimes he wants to please me."

"Is Esau going to Cincinnati?"

"We're counting on him to be the leader."

"He'll help you out and then you'll let him be killed?" When Leafy didn't answer, Offie said, "I wouldn't do that. I'd let him march home again."

"You wouldn't even make a trip like that. You wouldn't be there to be any help to anybody, hog or human."

"I'd like to go with Reno."

Leafy snorted. "You know what you thought of the trip out here with Chancellor. It'll be ten times as hard, droving. Not only yourself to look out for, but keeping track of a hundred hogs. Getting them over streams and fed and keeping them together and away from varmints. How'd that make the trip easier?"

"I didn't say anything about easier. What I was thinking about was Esau."

"What were you thinking about Esau?"

"I was thinking I would save him."

"Be more like him saving you."

"I wouldn't ever go off and leave somebody that had helped me. I'd die with him first."

Leafy rode up close to Offie, reached over, and took his hand. "That's a good way to feel, Offie. I talk big about parting with poor old Esau, but I don't reckon it'll come easy. When it comes right down to it, I might just throw my arms round his neck and say, 'I'd never be parted from you, Esau.'"

"Would you?"

"I hope not. It wouldn't be reasonable. I don't plan to. But I might."

As the day neared its short end and they headed home, nearly a hundred pigs followed them. They were getting close to the bottom of their bags of corn, but the hogs would likely make it the rest of the way without prompting. They could remember the barn lot and what always awaited them there. Leafy was tired after a day in the saddle, twisting and turning over rough ground, ducking limbs, hunting out hogs taking their ease in some half-hidden bog and more interested in staying cool than in stepping along in the heat for occasional handouts of corn.

The day that had started like a memory of summer was ending like the real thing, hot and close. She had none of nostalgia's excitement of farewell; or the promise, however great the sorrow of loss might be, that changes were ahead. What was left of the afternoon promised nothing but more heat and more of the dust the hogs were churning up amidst the layers of fallen leaves. She had leaf dust in her hair, hog smell in her nose, and midges and gnats in her eyes. Her body was itchy with sweat. Offie had cried a half-dozen times, had fallen off his horse and lost his lunch of corn pone and elderberry jam to the hogs, and was now hungry again, though he had had more than half of what she had brought for herself. She was too tenderhearted to ask, "Still want to be a drover, Offie?"

She heard muffled hoofbeats up ahead and knew, before she lifted her eyes to look, that she would see Simon Yanders. She did look, but recognized him with more than her eyes. She thought that, with eyes closed, she could have held up a naked hand and it would have trembled like a dowser's rod to signify his nearness.

Though she had expected him all day, and knew without looking when he had arrived, she swung her horse half around at the sight of him—trying to break through the herd she was leading and escape. Then she came to her senses and faced him. Escape? What did she have to fear? Half of her insistence on Reno's keeping his word to Old Man Luckett was because of the chance of this meeting. And half of her eagerness for it was because Offie would be with her. And topping it all, the surety of the key that locked the treasure of her feelings inside her. It would be wrong to let them out, and, besides that, she wasn't sure that letting them out would be to lose them. She rode on slowly to meet Yanders down the trace, so leafed over it was a tunnel. He loomed up bigger and bigger; and in the confusion of her heavy heartbeat and her daylong expectations it seemed momentarily that he was becoming so sizable that he would block the whole passageway, that there would be no way past him without touch. Then her heart steadied; she rubbed the heat and the gnats out of her eyes, and Simon Yanders, on his claybank gelding, was a long-waisted man on a long-legged horse, but there was plenty of room for passing.

It was a wonder to her that she should feel as she did. It was none of her asking. If, standing in front of some tree, or viewing foam castles on a blossoming branch, she was filled with such a delicious bitter-honey ache, no one would say she shouldn't enjoy that feeling if she fancied it. If she got carried away by it, neglected house and family for it, then she would be blameworthy. She knew that. But to stand before the tree, with the honeycomb in her chest getting heavier and sweeter with looking, nobody could fault that. How could they? They wouldn't know. She had a husband and she also knew how to feel. But one was a doing and the other was a feeling, and there wasn't any fight between the two; so she quickened her pace forward.

Simon, smiling, spoke first. "Reno told me you were out in this neck of the woods and might need some help."

"If he thought that, he should've come himself."

"He was on foot."

"I would steal a horse for someone I thought was in trouble."

"Reno's likely more law-abiding than you."

"There are some laws I would never break."

"Leafy," said Simon, "I didn't ride out all this way to argue with you about Reno or the law. Anyway, Reno was joking. He said you were bringing your hogs down to your place, so I come out this way on the off-chance of running into you. And it looks like I have."

Leafy didn't know what ailed her. Look forward to something all day, then the minute you catch up with it, begin to tear it to pieces.

"You're pretty touchy about Reno, ain't you?" When Leafy didn't answer, Simon said, "This the brother you were telling me about?"

"This is Howard," Leafy said. Offie hardly knew who was being talked about when he heard that name. "Offie, this is Mr. Yanders."

Offie, slumped down, hungry, hot, and tired, roused up at that name.

Simon laughed. "I see you been telling Howard about me."

"I told him you were the elected sheriff of this territory."

Simon shook his head and pursed his long clean-shaven upper lip. "Boy must have something on his conscience. Some tract of land he's never paid up on, maybe."

This foolishness didn't disturb Offie's stare. "Did you ever hang anybody?" he asked.

"Nope. Worst I ever did was separate a man from his land. I've seen some fellows kick worse at that than at a hanging."

"Did you ever see anybody hanged?"

"I seen a couple."

"Could you hang a man?"

"If it was a part of my job, I reckon I could. But the government don't hang people who don't pay up. So I won't likely ever be called on to string a man up."

"I'd like to see a man hung."

"Would you like to *be* hung?" Leafy asked.

"I don't *want* anybody to be hung. But if he has to be, I'd like to watch."

"If I hear of such a thing, I'll let you know. Why don't you lead out now, and give your sister a little letup? We'll ride behind and round up stragglers for you."

A little praise went a long way with Offie. For most of the day Leafy had been herding him as much as pigs. He was glad to be trusted; he took charge easily.

"Give me the rest of your corn, Leafy."

Leafy put what ears she had left into Offie's bag, then she and Simon pulled into the trees to let the herd pass by.

"Might be a few more yet to come," said Simon, halting Leafy, though the sounds of pig shuffle and squeal were now well up ahead of them.

Leafy had to look up at Simon. She hadn't intended smiling. That was like letting the cork out of the bottle of her feelings, but she couldn't help it. When she first caught sight of him, she had wanted to turn tail and run. When the talk turned first to Reno, then to hanging, she had stiffened with dislike for somebody, maybe herself. Now the pig smell and sounds were gone. The light through the chinks in the leaves was a clear sweet yellow, like Jersey cream. A bird, a rarity so deep in the woods, sailed clear and true over their heads. Simon smiled down at her with that curled lift at the corners of his big mouth. The treasure she had kept under lock and key like some Aladdin jewel melted and ran past all the locks. Her whole body was lit up like the cave when the genie came. It was a wonder to her that Simon couldn't see what had happened. The trouble was conversation. If she opened her mouth, she might run into talk of Reno—or hanging again. She couldn't think of any suitable words. She could do a little make-believe acting, but make-believe talking she had never mastered. The real lie, one with the tongue, she had stayed away from thus far.

Simon stretched out a hand to her. Hers rose to it, like filings to magnet. For one year, her hand, without her knowing it, had been getting ready for that touch. She could tell that the minute Simon's hand went around hers. She was so alive in her hand that, when Simon Yanders touched it, he touched all of her. Holding her hand, he brought his horse nearer, leaned, and kissed her with the whole of his mouth. She was ready to be lifted onto his horse, to ride pillion, holding him with her arms, to ride a runaway horse with him for whatever destination he chose. It was what she fully expected. It was the next act. Her body leaned toward it. She gave herself to his judgment.

Simon took his mouth from hers, leaned back, and, still clasping her hand, looked at her closely.

"Leafy," he said, "how do you feel about your husband?"

She heard the words, but their meaning couldn't break through the waves of feeling to her mind.

"I didn't hear what you said," she answered in a half-whisper.

He repeated them. "I asked how you felt about Reno."

She both heard and understood now. He had taken his mouth from hers to ask that question, when her mouth on his had been giving him the answer. The kiss interrupted, or ended, more like, was painful. But stopping it for that question was no excuse for stopping. A man who was enjoying a sunup didn't take his eyes from it to ask questions. She took her hand from his. She had given him the answer to the question with her kiss, not an easy answer to give; but not one she could hold back either. With that hard answer out, it wasn't in her to take another swipe at Reno with words.

"Reno's my husband," she said slowly.

"I didn't ask you that. I know that. What I asked you was how you felt about him."

"I told you that."

"You told me he was your husband."

She had told him a lot more. "I don't want to talk about Reno."

"I don't either. But there're some things I got to know."

"The first time you ever stopped by here—that we knew about, anyway—Reno said you were trying to find out things about us."

"That's something Reno was right about."

"You've run him down every chance you got. I'm not going to."

"I'm not asking you to run him down."

She didn't know what else. She had run him down with her kiss. How thick did he want her to lay it on? What worse thing could you say about a husband?

"Reno never did anybody a bad turn."

"Except himself. And you. And anybody else he gets tangled up with. He hurt himself a little, and Old Man Luckett bad, today."

"Why didn't you tell me?"

"Reno's got nothing worse than a muscle pulled in his ankle. Old Man Luckett's got some ribs caved in. When it comes to handling himself and tools, your husband can't tell his head from a hole in the ground. He takes any short cut to save himself work and don't have the gumption to see he's biting off his own nose. It's not his fault he didn't kill Luckett."

"He didn't intend to. I know that."

"I grant you that. All he intended was to save his back and give a log a downhill run. Who it flattened on the way, he didn't give any thought to."

"Reno's a teacher—not a logroller."

"He better get back to the younguns, then. He ain't safe out with grownups. He damages them."

Leafy felt hard as blacksmith nails. What she had already done against Reno required her to fight on his side now. "You're a fine one to be judging other people."

"I don't live in Reno's kind of glass house. I ain't under any oath not to throw at him, where he lives."

Leafy said no more. Words had ruined them. They had

brought down the two of them linked by hand and mouth, like bullets. Not one word intended, or any destruction in mind. It was the penalty, maybe, for opening her treasure to the air. She lifted her hand, half to see if what had died in it had died for good. She could hold it up, and did, but it had turned to flesh and bones, meat, like a bear's paw. It was a tool like a hoe. She used it to pull her sunbonnet, though there was no sun to be saved from, up onto her head.

Yanders took it for a farewell gesture.

"Well, you've answered my question all right."

"No," she said, "I told you I wouldn't."

"When you told me you wouldn't, you did."

She flared out at him again. "I told you everything. And you didn't want to know."

She turned her horse around, and riding first slowly, then in a lope, caught up with the snuffling, rooting herd.

When Leafy returned after that kiss in the woods from Simon Yanders, she found Reno already home from the logrolling. He was sitting with one foot in a bucket of water, one foot out, and his nose buried in a book. The sight, after where she'd been, and what she'd feared for him, made her weak. She had been prepared for blood and broken bones, and here was Reno as she'd seen him many a time soaking a chilblain. She dropped onto her knees and began to examine his swollen ankle.

Reno closed his book on one finger and looked at her. "What's got into you, Leafy?" he asked.

Contrition had got into her—that was what—and disgust and wonder and relief. But the truth, also, was that she was so accustomed to seeing Reno doctor himself that she'd gotten out of the habit of making much of a fuss over him. Reno made so much fuss over himself, all he really needed was a listener. She never belittled his pains, or reminded him afterward that his forebodings hadn't been very well founded. Reno would declare at nightfall that he was coming down with quinsy, or lung fever, or a gathering in the ear. Then he'd wake up in the morning spry as ever. Before she'd learned better, she'd ask after his health. But her asking riled him. He was like any prophet whose prophecy hadn't panned out. The less you said about it, the better. So Reno had come not to expect much of a to-do from her over his twinges.

Leafy said, "I was afraid you might've broken a leg, Reno. Or cut open a blood vessel." She rubbed his swollen ankle with careful fingers. "This won't keep you down long. Not that it isn't painful."

"Could be worse than it looks," Reno said.

"Oh, it could," Leafy agreed. "I know that full well. Sprains are tricky."

"How'd you know I was hurt?"

"Simon Yanders."

"He ride out to tell you?"

She had kissed Simon Yanders and had been ready to do more if asked—all wrong and against the honor of Reno—still, an easier thing, it would appear, than lying. She couldn't bring out the lie.

"I don't know as he did. He rode out and he let the news fall."

Reno said, not complaining, "You didn't hurry home very fast."

"I didn't know you were here yet. Besides, you can't hurry a hog."

"No," Reno agreed. "Time don't mean anything to a hog."

It was an old joke between them, never very funny, and not funny now, but sweet because it said, "Nothing's changed." Said it in spite of the fact that everything had. She had ridden out that morning nobody but a dreamer, and had come back a woman who had met a man in the woods and with a little encouragement would have kept going. She was a stranger to herself. And Simon Yanders was another stranger. She tried to recall the means by which they had passed from kissing to parting and couldn't. What had happened there was a part of her year of dreaming, though nothing she had dreamed had prepared her for it. She bore Simon Yanders a grudge, and she had never dreamed that could be. She blamed him for her misery.

"Did Simon help you bring the hogs in?"

"No, he kept on going."

"Which way's he heading?"

"He didn't tell me," Leafy said.

"He ought to've had his doubts put to rest about our having the money this fall—seeing what he did."

"I wouldn't trust him," Leafy said, "even so."

"Why not? I don't see any harm he can do us."

"He can put us out of his house and off his land."

"He can't if we make our land payments. And the government will foreclose on us if we don't."

"Somebody else might give us time if we needed it."

"What makes you think Yanders wouldn't?"

"I told you. I don't think he's trustworthy."

"I thought you liked him. I thought he was a favorite of yours."

"Favorite?"

"What's soured you on him?"

"Nothing."

"What happened today to turn you against him?"

She couldn't say "Nothing" again. She said, "I'm not sure." She put more hot water in Reno's bucket and began her supper preparations. She mixed johnnycake, sliced meat, put dried corn on to stew, and mixed a batch of dried-apple turnovers to fry.

"Why the feast?" Reno asked, watching.

"We've got something to rejoice in," Leafy said. "You might've had a broken leg."

"A sprain sometimes is longer healing than a break," Reno reminded her again.

"I know it," Leafy again reassured him. "But we're lucky, anyway. Pigs all in, and Offie and me safe back."

"I didn't know there was ever any question of your not being."

"Reno," Leafy said, "do you want me to stop cooking? I can

serve you and Offie up a cup of teakettle tea and call it supper if that's more to your taste. But if it won't turn your stomach to eat it, I feel like cooking us up a little feast. I feel like we've got a lot to be thankful for."

Reno lifted his foot out of the bucket to have a look at his ankle. It was twice the size of the other, puffy and yellow like the flesh of a fat old hen.

"I don't know what I've got to be thankful for," he said. "But it won't turn my stomach to eat if you want to cook."

Reno's ankle was just as slow healing as he'd feared it would be. It stayed tender and puffy, and, with it, he developed a low fever. He spent a lot of time soaking his ankle, and Leafy was faithful in rubbing it with turpentine and lard.

"Maybe what I've got's a bad bone bruise," Reno speculated. "Or maybe I've ruptured a blood vessel and the blood's poisoning me."

"If it was that," Leafy said, "your ankle would've turned black and blue. And it never did."

"It could be too deep to show up. In next the bone."

Leafy nodded. "It could be the marrow," Leafy said. "Jarred or ruptured."

Reno, who was playing draughts with Offie, his bucket of hot water between them, stopped in a jump to the king row to give Leafy a careful look. Leafy, making a pot of corn-meal mush for supper, kept on with her stirring. She had switched places with him, suggesting marrow and ruptures, and that made Reno suspicious. It wasn't any intention of hers to make things worse for Reno. She was always at his side if he wanted to hobble, cooked up every tidbit she had the makings for to tempt his appetite, took care of, with Offie's lounging help, all chores and outdoor work. Cutting corn was a backbreaking, finger-cutting, dusty job. It had to be done, and she did it. She and Offie loaded pumpkins onto the sled and dragged them up to the barn. Late apples were picked and cut for drying. The work pleased her. There was a vacancy inside her where her dream had been, and without the days of long work she would have felt empty. She was at Reno's service all her waking hours. No longer a farmer himself, it was difficult for Reno to remember that Leafy had become one. "No need to jump just yet," he would tell her as, in the darkness of the October morning, she would think of cow to milk, and horse to feed as well as breakfast to get and house to redd up before she got outside for the real work of the day. "What did I marry, anyway? A girl or some old farmer?"

She postponed getting up, though doing so ran her day into darkness at the other end. She knew what were Reno's rights as well as he did, and her plan now was to fulfill all obligations. Side-stepping them hadn't been much of a success. And meeting them, every one of them, made her feel powerful, like some ship's master steering his boat to port through storm and stress. She remembered the little girl who had wanted responsibility at home. Seeing what she could do with responsibility now, she understood her childhood craving better. It occurred to her that she was as good (or better—she was on her feet and working anyway) a man as Reno. She was prompter, faster, saw ahead farther, and at the minute at least was stronger. She didn't ask anything of Reno. She gave him her body for his morning's comfort, the way a mother nursed her baby.

One morning, up a little later than usual, the sun already shining red as firelight through Ellen's window, the coals stirred up on the hearth and the dry twigs she had laid across them beginning to crackle, Leafy stood looking down at Reno. Offie had gone out to do the morning chores for her, so she wasn't as pressed for time as usual.

"Reno," she said, "staying off your foot don't seem to help it much."

Reno agreed. "The swelling's not gone down a bit in the last week, as far as I can see."

"I been thinking," Leafy said, "it might be a good thing to try walking on it some. Maybe that's what it needs, the circulation stirred up in it. Maybe it's never going to get well just laying around, the way you do."

"Just laying around the way I do," Reno repeated after her. "So that's what you've been thinking?"

Before Leafy could utter another word, Reno threw back the coverlet, stood, and, in a gait that didn't favor his swollen ankle, made for the table. Before he got there his bad leg crumpled under him, and he pitched forward, face down, onto the puncheon floor. He lay there without moving until Leafy went to him. When she had helped him roll over and sit up, she saw that there were tears on his cheeks. She didn't want to shame him by speaking of them. She didn't want to be silent either.

"You could've broken your leg, Reno, doing that."

"I wish I had. Maybe you wouldn't throw 'laying around' in my face, then."

"I wasn't throwing it in your face. I was trying to think what else might help you."

"What you were thinking was that I was having a rest while you were doing the work."

Leafy helped Reno back to the bed without saying another word. The ankle was already noticeably more swollen. She got out her lard and turpentine and, after she had rubbed them in, wrapped his ankle in a steaming-hot cloth.

Offie

Offie watched Leafy stir up a corn-meal and molasses pudding. The sweet smell of the sorghum made his nose twitch. Since Reno's accident, Leafy had cooked up treats for Reno and had fed herself and Offie on chips and whetstones. Offie enjoyed food, puddings and sweet cakes in particular, but he could have gotten along without them, he thought, if anyone had had a kind word for him. If Leafy had said, "Soon as Reno's better I'll see you get your share, Offie," or if Reno had said, "I'm getting the lion's share of this, Offie; here, this half's for you," Offie thought he wouldn't have felt so left out. As it was, no one said anything to him. Leafy had words only for Reno. And Reno and Offie had had a falling out that made any kind of conversation between them awkward. So he was underfed, unnoticed, and, he felt pretty sure, unwanted. "Why did I ever leave home?" he asked himself.

While Leafy was tying up the pudding in the pudding bag, Offie took the crock the pudding had been mixed in and began to scrape up the sassafras-colored batter with the big wooden mixing spoon. Leafy, hearing him, and before he could get a lick of batter to his mouth, snatched crock and spoon from him. "Who said you could have that?"

Offie's feelings were too hurt for him to manage an answer. A place where you had to ask permission to scrape a pudding crock was next door to a prison. He wished Mama could see the pass to which he'd come. She'd make that Leafy mend her ways. Leafy, as if reading his thoughts, apologized. "I was figuring on giving Reno the scrapings, Offie. He always said he liked them better than what was cooked."

Reno was sick all right, but he wasn't so far gone in Offie's opinion as to require pudding scrapings. Offie turned his back on Leafy so she couldn't see the tears he might not be able to hold back. He didn't want "crybaby" added to the other names he'd been called: "fraidy cat" and "greedy gut" and "Peeping Tom."

Leafy came around in front of him carrying a big buttered hunk of corn dodger.

"This will hold you until suppertime, maybe," she said. But not a word of "I'm sorry" or a single pat, hug, or squeeze.

"Thank you, Leafy," Offie said as courteously as if he'd been handed cake with icing, and went outside. But if she thought he was going to eat a hunk of cold corn dodger while Reno was feasting on pudding batter, she was badly mistaken. He didn't know what he was going to do with that crumbly handful until he saw Esau. Esau was neglected these days, too. Leafy, before

Reno was hurt, had never been too busy to scratch and fondle her pet. Nowadays she had no time for Esau, and, as Offie came down the steps, there was Esau on his haunches, one ear flopped forward like a shepherd dog's and both eyes on the door.

"Come on, Esau," Offie said, tolling him onward, which wasn't necessary, with a nubbin of dodger, "I've got something for you."

The afternoon had been warm and sunny, and the western sky between the tree trunks was still rosy. Offie led Esau up the slope toward the barn and there sat down with him. Esau's position, on his tail, chin up, and eyes attentive, was as dignified as Offie's. Esau, hand fed from the beginning, was a neat and tidy eater; gentler by far than Offie's pet hen back home in Blue Glass, who didn't have any scruples about pecking up a little skin off of the palm of his hand along with the corn.

After Esau had finished the dodger, Offie talked to him a little. He didn't know whether Esau thought pigs were humans or whether he thought humans were pigs. In any case, he sat there and listened, and, when Offie told him that the two of them had better stick together, seemed to agree. Scratching the pear-shaped top of Esau's head, rubbing his plump sides, Offie discovered that if no one would pet you, petting someone else, even a pig, was the next best thing.

When Offie had first come to Reno's and Leafy's one pig looked like another to him. His father kept pigs back in Blue Glass, but he kept them in pens, and Offie had never spent any time feeding them, let alone talking to them and gazing into their eyes. He could tell big from little, sow from boar, and spotted from solid-colored. That was the extent of his knowledge of pigs. But after a few days with Esau he knew what Esau was feeling: not just when he was hungry or wanted to be scratched, but when fits of playfulness or thoughtfulness came over him. And Esau knew, too, he was sure, when Offie felt downcast or ready for a little running and high-jack. Esau, unlike the folks in the house, paid him some heed, responded to his moods, and listened to all he had to say.

Leafy, when Offie didn't come in to dinner one noon when called, walked out to where he was giving Esau the treat of some hand-gathered beech mast mixed with a few stolen bacon rinds. Leafy said nothing about the bacon rinds, though she saved them for flavoring. She just stood watching him for a minute, until Offie, who didn't have much tolerance for silence, said, "Esau's my best friend."

"A pig can't be anybody's best friend, Offie. You know that."

"He can if you don't have anyone else."

"A pig can't be a friend at all."

"Esau can."

"He's a pet."

"He's your pet. He's my friend."

"He can't talk," Leafy said. "You can't have a friend who don't talk."

"He talks to me," Offie said.

"Tell him to say something."

"You wouldn't understand him. That's why he don't talk to you."

"Offie," Leafy said, "I've been glad for you to have Esau to play with while I've been so busy. But there's no use your pretending he talks or that you can understand him when he grunts and squeals."

"He don't talk to me with grunts and squeals."

"He don't talk at all. He's a pig. Because he was a runt, he got raised like a dog or cat. But he's a pig, he's being raised for pork, and he'll go to Cincinnati with the rest of the herd to help raise money to pay for our land."

"Could you eat Esau?"

"I'm not going to eat Esau. But somebody will. We can't spend the rest of our lives with a two-hundred-pound hog lolling on the front porch. We'd just as well move out to the pigsty ourselves."

Offie made no answer to this.

"Come on, Offie. Dinner's getting cold."

Offie didn't move.

Leafy started back down the slope from the barn but toward the house. "Come on, Esau," she said. "Soo-ey, pig, soo-ey."

Esau looked at Leafy, but Offie held out the last of his beech-nut-bacon-rind mixture, and Esau settled down with Offie as if Leafy had been a passing stranger, not his foster mother who had risked her life for him.

"I tell you one thing, Esau," Offie said. "Nobody's ever going to eat you."

Esau spoke in the language Offie understood: shone his pink eyes up at Offie and nuzzled his snout into Offie's cupped hand. The door slammed behind Leafy. Offie heard it but didn't care. He didn't feel shut out of a thing. Let Leafy cuddle Reno. He had Esau.

ten

Leafy: Blue Glass

Leafy looked up at them. They stood about the bed, their faces hanging down toward her heavily. She had sometimes been one of a circle doing the same thing with a snake. Shamefaced, but watching to see if there would be one more twitch. Well, she couldn't twitch any more. Build a fire under her, the way they did with a balky horse, and she wouldn't move. She said, "Please get back, get away; don't stand so close; you shut off the air; I can't breathe."

Her mother said, "She's out of her head."

She repeated what she had said. Not loudly—she didn't have the strength for loudness—but very clearly and slowly.

"I need more air. I'm burning up. Please don't bend over me."

Her mother said, "Don't talk, petty. It just uses up your strength."

The doctor said, "She don't know what she's saying. Don't try to stop her. It just plagues her."

Reno dropped to his knees; he put a hand toward her. She drew back. What still lived, inside her, drew back. She couldn't move a muscle on the outside. She couldn't bear to be touched either. She was too hurt, too raw and throbbing.

"I don't want you to touch me, Reno."

"It's so pitiful," her mother said. "She's trying so hard to tell us something and can't."

Reno's dark eyes looked right into hers. They stayed there as his hand hovered; then his hand moved away. He got up and took a step back from the bed.

It had been daylight a long time, and now it was dark but the dark was like the people bending over her; the dark made it hotter. It pushed the heat toward her, and the burning lamp smelled like heat. She tried to throw back the sheet that covered her.

"Oh, I don't like to see that," her mother said. "It's a bad sign."

"She doesn't know what she's doing," the doctor said.

Her father was on his knees in the corner, bowed over a chair, his face in his hands. He helped hold down the carpet which the hot wind was still lifting. His trousers hung down sad, sad like the skin on an old lady's face. She was sorry for him. Poor Papa. He was praying that if it be God's will, she be spared. Spare, spare. A word that meant, she believed, "Take the others but pass over my daughter." She didn't want what the others couldn't have. Why did he think that a God who had let her suffer this much would be willing for a little letup in pain now? She was blank of prayer herself. She hoped God had nothing to do with it. If He had something to do with it, if He was responsible for the pain, she wasn't going to scream "Mercy, mercy" to Him any more than she would to any other torturer. If that was what He enjoyed, she wouldn't begrudge Him the pleasure. She thought of the baby who didn't know about God. The poor little tyke, hotter than she was, probably.

"Pray for him, Papa."

Her mother said, "Shall I send for Chancellor?"

The doctor said, "There's nothing he can do."

"You know what I mean."

"Send for him," said Daubenheyer.

Her mother took her father by the shoulder. She was no more respectful of his occupation than if he'd been playing the accordion.

"Bass, Bass," she said. "You'll have to go after Chancellor."

Her father looked up. He stood up slowly.

"Is she that bad?"

"Don't say that. He didn't say that. She's sick; we ought to all be together."

"He's at church."

"I know where he is."

Her father looked toward her. He took a step toward her, then a step toward the door. God was his witness. Would He punish a man who took his son from worship, and for a second time, by letting his daughter die?

Prill said, "Do you know better than the doctor?"

Leafy said, "It don't matter. I don't care, Papa. Don't go if you don't want to. Chancellor's maybe preaching. He's working hard as me to get something outside him. I've heard him, Papa. He don't even know what it is. He's in worse case than me. I know what's inside me."

Prill beat on Bass with her hands. "Go, go. The girl is begging for her brother."

Leafy felt the heat of her father's body as he came close to the bed. Even now, far back in his eyes there was some kind of a joke he would make if there was more time or fewer people. She didn't know what it could be and was too tired to think.

⚝ Chancellor

Chancellor was on his knees and had been there since the beginning of time; the faces in the Grove Meeting House went around him like stars in a dark sky. He was as alone as if under stars, though he heard all words, prayers, hymns, groans, cries. He heard each single word and cry, knew whose voice uttered it and even the special tune of each uttering. But the voices together were God's and he listened . . . he strained to hear, to catch the one word that would release him into knowledge . . . or love, into wherever it was he was bound to get. . . .

He was wet with sweat. He was like the struck rock pouring water. He lived inside the downpour. In the circle of faces wheeling around him was Venese. He reckoned he was leaving her behind. She wouldn't care.

He knew his weakness: it was to press on, to find something more. His strength would have to overcome this weakness; out of his strength he must find the power to give up his own will. Not *his* strength, or *his* power, but God's. He forgave himself all of his sins, except pride. Pride shut him away from God, tied him to earth. Scotch his pride, trample it under, and he could move into the Kingdom.

Was he giving up little to get much? Human pride for a heavenly kingdom? It was true, it was true. He tried to stop thinking; and this, too, was a part of his pride. "My Father, *Thy* will be done." He could not say it. Jesus had said it. But look who *His* Father was. With a father like that? We are sons of the same Father. What He did, I can do. Pride, pride.

"Jesus, help me. Jesus, help me."

He had come to the end of the world he now lived in. Everything he did from now on would add but not multiply. More land. More money. More words. More women. What could he handle he had not handled? He could travel the earth. Move westward. See some spread of water he, or, with luck, no man, had ever seen before. Some mountain. Some wild beast. He could touch a thousand women. He could read ten thousand books and learn, he reckoned, one thousand by heart. He could figure out beyond the knowing of any present man what the past had been. He could give new names to old things. He could put together contraptions never pieced together before. His pride told him all this. He knew it for a fact. Another fact he knew, and which threw his pride down, was that his heart would still be sore and dry. Add contraption to contraption, mountain to mountain, book to book: what've you got then? A stumbling block, a corruptible treasure, a feeding place for moths, a mountain of dust.

"My God, my God."

He didn't fear hell or thirst for heaven. He longed for a life on earth that would burn through the perishable into the eternal. The eternal was not in Blue Glass. Jesus had spoken of it and lived for it. Without it his life was no more than a cricket chirp or a lightning bug's spark. Less, a lot less. Chirp and spark were what they could do and all they could do. There was no God for them to fly home to.

"Oh Jesus, save me."

Save him from what? From the world? The world was his home, his nest, his hole, his burrow. His beauty, his surprise, his contentment. His snare, his chafing, his blindness.

"Lead me into the light. Lead me into what is everlasting. Lead me into love. Lead me into a fair scope of life, a forefended place. Lead me into the unending. Lead me."

Others had sins with which to seal their bargains. Pleasures to part with. Confessions to sign. The Lord could see they meant business.

He had nothing to give up but himself. That would have to be sign enough for the Lord. He was likely giving up Venese with this display of a man hunting the rock of ages to cling to. When what she honed for were chance-takers. But he wasn't offering up Venese in any trade with the Lord: "Take her and give me

Salvation." He wasn't the man, and he hoped God wasn't the God, for any dicker of that nature. He might be losing Venese, but if he did, it would be by her going, not by his giving. He was full of pride, but not prideful enough to consider himself a great sinner. He wouldn't try to fob God off with some little thread-bare faults, treating Him like a pauper so poverty-stricken any rag would be welcome. A living sin would be a suitable sacrifice. Strike it dead on the altar. Let it die for the Lord.

No sins (except pride) to part with; only love to get. And give; he had to reckon on that. The gospel was living water; it was a spring branch, not a cistern.

He felt love around him. The touch of love was in the hands that pressed against his head and shoulders, in the voices, the cries, the supplications. He heard, he knew: but what he felt and heard didn't enter his heart. He told himself, "In these voices and in these hands is God. If you aren't open to them, don't lift your eyes on high. Don't say 'My heavenly Father' and close your ears to what the earth has given you.

"Open my heart. Open my heart. Burn it open with love. Enter."

The struggle to open his heart was so desperate he was felled, like a tree. He no longer reached toward heaven. He huddled, sweating.

He said, "My Father, Thy will be done."

He let go. He gave up his pride and his will. His heart opened, and he was no longer separated from the earth or anything that grew out of it or walked on it. He had got beyond limits. Love didn't have boundaries. His chains dropped from him. He rose to his feet and praised God.

Chancellor, in the midst of his praising, saw his father join the congregation—and he saw someone else, too. Inside the weathered, spare old man with freckled skin and sun-bleached, red-gray hair, he saw a thin-skinned, round-eyed boy, a scaredy cat, lying low. The boy didn't blot out the man any more than an egg yolk blots out the shell that contains it. That man had given him welts, and he still bore their print. The welts on his butt were nothing . . . it was the reasons for giving them that scarred him. . . . It was a mean thing in the midst of love to see clearly that the person who had, chiefly, kept you from it was your father. He reckoned it was a test for him at the moment of saying "God is love" to be tempted to deny it with hatred of his own father. And he called out against all that he found hateful. He declared against the worldliness that takes thought of what the world thinks; he declared against the fearfulness that doesn't trust God or the world God has made; he declared against the judgment of men when God has said, "Judgment is mine," and Jesus has said, "Neither do I condemn." He declared against thought for the morrow, and for those tomorrows a lifetime away, by the laying up of treasure. He declared against those who wouldn't try to walk on water; wouldn't turn water to wine; wouldn't scourge the money-lenders, praise the lilies, accept the towel of dark tresses; wouldn't ride an ass into Jerusalem.

In so doing he declared against his father.

But God let him see, with the second sight of love and freedom, that the man he called his father was no more than a buckskin shirt and britches, hardened and weathered to iron by passing years. Inside them that boy, his eyes sliding from side to side in shy exploration of the world, lived. The boy peeped out at him. Chancellor recognized him at once. He had made his acquaintance without knowing it in French harp tunes, toe-tappings, and long-winded jokes.

He declared against the covering that was so unyielding, but he held out his arms to the one inside.

His father marched right on toward the altar, twisting and turning to miss those who knelt in the aisles, or stood praying, or who had the gift of tongues and were too full of glory to stay put in one spot.

Chancellor declared on, because the truth was in him, but not against his father. He declared for love, for God Who so loved the world and Jesus Who never forswore it, even when the nails were driven into His hands and feet. And none of these was against his father.

When his father was two arm lengths away, he stopped, and Bass's voice, high as the top quaver of an accordion note, rang out above Chancellor's.

"I stand condemned before Almighty God."

"No," Chancellor shouted.

He ran down to his father. "No one condemns you."

He put a hand on his father's arm, would have put a hand on his mouth. There was enough between them of blame without his father adding blame for himself if he burst out here . . . and remembered it afterward. He didn't want to be the one—if his father was going to kick over the traces—who scared him into it. He didn't want his father to be pointed out: "The pa his boy saved." Saved? "The pa his boy led on to making a fool of himself." That's how his father would sum it up afterward.

His father was too thin-skinned for public utterance. He'd built up his leather suit through too many seasons to break it open to weather and opinion now.

"Hush, Papa," he said. "Everybody knows these meetings go against your grain. Let alone, me taking part. There's no call for you to make a show of yourself."

We've changed places, Chancellor thought. Time was, he urged me not to make a show of myself. The words he had just spoken came echoing back like sounds made in a whispering cave. Am I shaped in his image, after all? Same tune, nothing changed but the piper?

It was not the same tune. Make all the show of yourself you want, only not under circumstances that'll make you discredit what you got because of the way you come to it.

Chancellor took his hand from his father's arm and stepped a pace back from him. He wanted to look at him. When he had been a razor-stropped boy, dragged out of Meeting for making a show of himself, he couldn't have asked for sweeter revenge: his father hanging on his words, sweating it out at the mercy seat, and his son the one who could bid him sit or stand.

That's what he would've thought at thirteen. Past twenty it wasn't that way. He was tender for his father's feelings. If this was power, it embarrassed him. It wasn't seemly—his father being who he was—to be led to the glory seat by a son.

Yet a man had to make his choices when and where he could. Expose his own tender feelings. Embarrass his father back into a boy's bashfulness, if that was required. But Chancellor's creed, and he had suffered for it, was that a man had a right to make a fool of himself. Bass ought to have the same right. Make a try at walking on water and find he wasn't light-footed enough. Will the water into wine and find not the slightest grape stain in the tin cup when it was filled. Say "Come alive" to what was dead and find he had no power over life and death. A man had these rights; and if he'd set out to follow in the footsteps of the Nazarene, likely had these duties. And shouldn't be separated from them either by the likelihood of failing or the guarantee of catcalls when he did.

It was this he wanted to make clear to his father. But before he could do so Clate Henry pushed himself between the two of them. Clate spoke to Chancellor, not to Bass. "Your ma sent your pa two hours ago to fetch you. Your sister's not going to last the night."

It seemed a lie to Chancellor. Or a mighty poor guess. The love he had felt and preached surrounded Leafy. That poor girl wasn't bound for darkness yet.

"God will spare Leafy," he said. It was neither prophecy nor prayer. It was what he saw.

But he had shamed Bass once again.

"Be careful of the claims you make, Son."

Bass's voice had as much fear in it as rebuke. It was strong with caution. It carried over voices soggy with tears and breathy with prayer.

The night was cooling off. Chancellor felt a chill cross his skin where the outside air touched his sweaty flesh.

"Leafy will live," he declared again, his voice as loud as Bass's.

"Don't tempt Fate," Bass entreated.

Chancellor looked at his father. "Fate?" He felt like some old circuit rider who sees a long-time converted sachem take up on his deathbed, not scripture, but the medicine man's prayer bag of bark and feathers, dung and teeth.

"Don't tempt Fate"? Was punishment at the center of his father's world? And God somebody you soft-soaped?

Bass had dragged him out of that earlier Camp Meeting. This time Chancellor left his father behind. He broke, running, for his rig. He wanted to take the good news to Leafy. Her time had come, but for bearing, not dying.

✑ Bass

There was only a stir of dust, dying away down the road in the glare of the torches, when Bass got to his buggy. He didn't know how he could have forgotten an errand of the kind he'd been sent on. Unless everything was God's will, and it was God's will that Chancellor reach Leafy before he did. He was slow in his heavyheartedness, and before he had Farmer untied, the Lucey girl, Venese, was at his side. She had always looked to him like someone with gypsy blood; and she was sparkling and smiling tonight like a gypsy who'd had her palm crossed with silver.

"Can I ride home with you, Mr. Converse?" she asked.

He supposed she meant her own home. "Leafy's sick," he told her. "I oughtn't to spare the time to go by your place."

"It's your place I want to go. I missed getting to Chancellor after the Meeting was over. Now I'm trying to catch up with him."

She was in the buggy before he was, and he half expected her to take the buggy whip from the socket and give old Farmer a tap. Her impatience rayed out from her like heat from a stove. He didn't feel up to hurrying. Where he was going he would be no help; and where he had been, he had maybe done harm. The hurry, if ever he had had any, had been knocked out of him. He might be sluggish for the rest of his life.

"Chancellor was masterful, wasn't he?" Venese asked.

"He always has been."

"Not many fathers get saved by their own sons."

"I'm one of them that wasn't."

He saw that Venese didn't know the answer to that. Backsliders were nothing uncommon, but most men took more than sixty minutes for the round trip. He didn't know how to explain it to her, though he could explain it to himself. He had read in missionary journals of like cases. Out in the foreign field were men exactly like himself. Black men in Africa and yellow men in China who thought they had put away their heathenism when they put on clothes. Chopped off their pigtails, gave up their concubines, forswore bound feet and eating human flesh. Then when somebody's life, maybe their own, was ebbing, they proved themselves heathen still. Back came all the heathen signs, the gods and prayers, the black magic they really trusted.

"I never did trust in God," he told Venese.

"Well, me neither," Venese agreed.

"The difference is, I thought I did. Till tonight I thought so."

"Chancellor didn't take away your faith, did he?"

"I didn't have any for him to take. That's what he showed me. I always did prefer some leopard tooth. Or monkey claw."

"Claw?" Venese asked.

"Paw. Hand. Call it what you like. And not them either. I had a kind of rabbit foot of my own making. The Bible says God is a loving Father. Well, I never seen Him that way, Venese. I seen Him as somebody ready to harm, if you didn't trick Him. My trick was to stay out of His sight. More like a bargain than a trick. I offered up myself a living sacrifice. You don't notice me, I said to God, and I'll scrunch down to mouse size before You."

The wheels gritted as they crossed over a patch of gravel. Farmer's big belly, empty of evening feed, rumbled with the jar of every trot. An owl hooted, as if calling back to the rumble.

"You never looked mouse-sized to me," Venese consoled him.

"I did to God. That's how I got on without setbacks. He said, 'Here's a man too meechin' to bother with.' I made no claims. Married a woman other men had passed by. Kept my children on short rations so they wouldn't get prideful."

"How did you get onto such a tack?"

"How or when, I don't know. But I'm on it."

"Was on it. You got saved tonight."

"I got my eyes opened tonight, to where I was. That's all."

"That might be the beginning, having your eyes opened."

Bass didn't need any gypsy girl with pierced ears telling him what salvation was.

"What I got tonight was mesmerized. A man came through here once who was a hypnotizer. He put on shows. I seen him once. He hypnotized Asa Barrows. He said, 'Asa, you're a bird.' So Asa flapped his wings and whistled like a bobwhite. Then the showman told Asa he could fly and to fly off the platform. The platform was two feet high, and Asa flapped his arms and flied off it without any trouble. Next he told him to fly off a chair. The chair was three feet high, and Asa flapped and flew. But when the hypnotizer set up a ladder ten feet high and bade Asa climb and fly, Asa came out of his trance in short order. He'd counted those rungs the way no bobwhite could. He was a bird just so long as he wasn't asked to do anything a man couldn't do.

"I was saved the same way. I was saved till I had to act like a Christian. Then I went back to what I'd always been."

It was the place for Venese to ask him what that was. Accustomed to him at home as a storyteller, they asked him such questions. Venese was mum, but he didn't let her silence faze him. The person he was looking in a mirror to see was himself; and when he stopped talking the mirror hazed over.

"I was mesmerized like Asa till Chancellor showed me the ten-foot ladder. Leafy at death's door, and Chancellor was trumpeting his faith in the Lord to heal her. That woke me up in a hurry. I didn't want Chancellor a laughingstock or God thinking we had any special claims on His attention. Or any need to teach us better."

Venese said, "You were saying, 'God's will be done'?"

"No, I wasn't. I was against saying anything. I didn't want attention called to us. I didn't want God teaching Chancellor a lesson and Leafy suffering for it."

"That's not Christian."

Bass didn't suppose Venese knew Peter from Paul, the way they lived over at the Lucey place. But what she said summed up the situation.

"I know it's not. That's what I've been telling you."

At the Lucey turnoff he said, "If they'll worry about you at home, I'll take the time to drop you off there."

"Chancellor's the one I don't want worrying."

What Bass thought was that Chancellor, caught up as he must be now with his preaching and with being with his sick sister, wouldn't have much time left for worrying about this wild girl with rings in her ears.

"Chancellor and I are getting married."

"That's news to me. Chancellor's never mentioned it."

"He don't know it yet."

"Has he mentioned it to you?"

"He's mentioned it, off and on for six, seven years."

"He's likely going to be a preacher. If tonight's any sign."

"I took it for a sign."

Bass didn't see Venese making any preacher a very suitable wife. On the other hand, if his own mother was any one to judge by, being married to a preacher was no bed of roses either. He told Venese so.

"If your idea is to stand first with your husband, a preacher's a poor choice. He'll get home when everyone else's cared for."

"I couldn't want a man who wanted nothing but me," Venese said. "I couldn't stomach a man that little."

"He'll be out marrying and burying. Carrying on protracted meetings all over the country, to judge by tonight. You'll never be able to count on him from one day to the next."

"That suits me," Venese said. And then, as if she'd already married into the family and had a relative's privileges, she said,

195

"Could you cluck up the horse a little, Mr. Converse? We won't be out of the woods till morning at this rate."

✍ Leafy

Except for Chancellor and Bass, all were in Leafy's room. Offie sat on the floor by the door to the back porch. Reno was fanning Leafy. Prill and June were over by the washstand talking. Leafy, opening her eyes, was astounded to be able to see. Seeing was a natural and ordinary part of life; but in her pain and weakness she had thought that seeing was as much beyond her as skipping rope or putting out a wash. Seeing did take too much strength for her to keep it up any length of time. Great distances separated her from every person in the room . . . herself included. Though she *knew* about herself. Knew her hands were bloody from pulling. Knew that she was swollen and torn. Her skin was so tight across her face she had only slits to see through. For one second she was startled by a look from Offie. She wondered how he had got in her room and why he wasn't sent out. What Offie was trying to say to her was, "Forgive me before you die." She tried to speak, but her lips were too stiff to shape themselves to words. She told Offie with her eyes, "You were a little boy, Offie. I asked too much of you. You're not to blame yourself for running away, and you shouldn't be here now."

Offie got part of the message; he ran outside. She thought she might take it to mean that he had understood everything.

She closed her eyes. Perhaps they thought she had fainted. She was only resting, and every word said was clear to her.

Her mother spoke to June. "Why did I send Bass for Chancellor? In thirty years I haven't learned a thing!"

"Who else was there to send?"

"I should've sent Clate Henry in the first place."

"There's nothing Chancellor could do if he was here."

"He should be here. And his father."

June said, "There's nothing more she can do. Or me. I'm going to take the baby."

"What do you mean, '*Take* the baby'?" That was Reno.

"You know what I mean."

"You mean cut it up?" Prill was the one to call a spade a spade.

"I mean cut it up."

Prill said, "Don't give up yet. Let her try some more."

June made a peculiar sound, half-groan, half-bellow.

"When a baby's head is bigger than the mother's opening, only two things can happen. The baby will die trying to get out or the mother will die trying to get it out. Sometimes it's both. Is that what you want?"

"I want both to live," Prill said.

"Reno," June said, "this is your say-so. Leafy is your wife. This is your child. I know what I'm talking about. My wife went through this. She was a strong girl, too. And I was full of belief that she could bear her baby. She died under my eyes. I learned something that night, and I'm passing it on to you. You can sit there and watch her try. And watch her die. Then go through what I've been going through since then. Which is hell, if you'd like to know. It's up to you. You choose."

Reno said, "Is the baby still alive?"

"At the moment, yes."

"I can't give the word for the killing."

"Whose killing are you talking about?"

Reno didn't answer.

June lifted Leafy's hand. He forgot that it was raw, but a little more pain didn't seem to make much difference.

"Good-by, Leafy."

"What do you mean, 'good-by'?" Prill asked.

"I mean I'm leaving."

"She's your patient. A doctor can't leave his patient."

"She's not my patient any more. She's yours. I take the responsibility for my wife's death. That's enough for me. You take the responsibility for your daughter's."

Leafy forced her eyes open. June left the room on the run.

He jumped over the threshold as if flames were licking at his heels.

"How'll he get home?" Prill asked.

"There's horses. If he's willing to ride," Reno said.

"Do you think we did right?" Prill asked.

"I don't know about you. But I didn't have the right to say, 'Kill that baby.' "

"If anybody did, you did. You're the father."

"I'm not the father," Reno said.

Prill said, "I can't believe it. I don't want to believe it."

"It's nothing I wanted to believe."

"How long've you known?"

"Forever, it seems like."

"Does Leafy know you know?"

"Not to my knowledge."

"Do you know the man?"

"I do. I blame myself. I should've looked after Leafy better."

"There's no way of looking after a girl who won't look after herself."

"I blame myself anyway."

"I wish you hadn't told me."

"I had to tell you. I had to tell you my reason for deciding what I did."

"If it'd been your baby, you would've said, 'Take it'?"

"I'd've had the right if it was mine. Leafy and I can have more. But this is none of mine. How'd Leafy and me live together if when she came to she found out I said, 'Kill her baby'?"

"Maybe she won't come to."

"You said she would. You said you knew. You said many a girl had pulled through an ordeal like this. You said she wouldn't give up."

"When I was saying it, I didn't know she was carrying a wood's colt."

"What's that got to do with it? That don't make the baby's head any littler or Leafy any bigger."

"No, it don't. But if I was in Leafy's shoes I wouldn't want to have it."

"Why not? It's nothing but a baby. Leafy loved its father. She knows I blame myself."

"How can she? When she don't even know you know?"

"She can tell by the way I've been acting this past year. And I can tell by the way she's been acting, she loves me."

"She can tell you love her, I reckon. If that's what you mean. And that may be all the more reason she'd rather never set eyes on this baby's face."

"Leafy never wanted an animal killed. Let alone a baby."

"You'd come to hate it yourself. And her."

"I wouldn't. The man was a poor widower. He hung around our place, and I was blind. He's not a bad man. He saved my life. I'm not going to have Leafy come to and say, 'You killed Yanders' baby.' "

Leafy, grabbing the pulling ropes of twisted sheet which still lay ready for her use, hoisted herself into sitting position.

"It's not Yanders' baby," she yelled. Or yelling at least was her intention. "And I can have it."

The minute Leafy said that, Prill ran to the door. "Howard," she cried, "Howard. You ride to Pleasanton and get Doc Westrum. We're going to have a baby here."

Offie came inside the room. Leafy, still supported by the pulling-ropes, looked him right in the eye.

"It's an awful long way to Pleasanton," Offie said.

"Don't go if you don't want to, Offie," Leafy told him.

"I'm giving the orders here," Prill said. "Howard, you ride to Pleasanton. And don't you come back without Dr. Westrum. You understand me?"

"Yes, ma'am," said Offie, and left the room quickly.

eleven

🖋 *Leafy: Whitewater*

Yanders had kept his distance from the Riverses' cabin since his encounter with Leafy on the day of the logrolling; and Leafy was glad of it. She wouldn't know where to look if he showed up. Or what to say. Or who to feel mad at. Mad at herself, she knew that. Except for Simon Yanders, she wouldn't have reason to be mad at herself. She blamed Yanders for what he had—and hadn't —done. And above all for bringing Reno, who was blameless, into the mix-up. What did she think of Reno? What she thought was that he was a good man, twice as handsome and ten times as high-minded as Simon Yanders. Yanders, careening around the countryside, making a business of leading on unfaithful wives and turning poor widows out of house and home. True, Simon Yanders had a practical turn Reno'd never come by in a month of Sundays. He could shoot horses and build cabins and repair wagon wheels. He was handy with tools. But so were burglars, she supposed: those men back in Philadelphia who had looted Grandfather Converse's home had carried the tools to break and enter.

A perfect washing day came along toward the last of October, a sunny warm morning with leaves glistening like newly polished knife blades. Since washing took building up a big fire outside to heat water for boiling her clothes, Leafy postponed washdays as long as the supply of clean bedclothes held out. Then she made a day of it, started her fire at sunup, and before nine o'clock had her sheets and pillow shams, her split drawers and shimmies bubbling away in a bleaching mixture of rain water and soft soap. She liked the washday smell as much as that of cooking apple butter. Maybe better. It smelled even more like accomplishment and a well-run home.

She was dressed for the hard wet work, with a dirty shirt of Reno's, which she would boil later, tied by the arms around her waist for an apron; her hair was wrapped up like a mammy's in a huck towel. She enjoyed washdays and relished the exercise of shoving the wet mass of grimy clothes back and forth with the big wooden paddle. She was red-faced from the heat of the fire and sweaty with steam when Simon Yanders, mounted on his soft-footed horse, rode into the yard. She was no treat for sore eyes, knew it, and didn't care. She reckoned the time for play acting with this man was long past.

"Good morning, Mr. Yanders," she said coolly, straightening up, but not ceasing to work the clothes paddle. "If you want to inspect the hogs, they're over on Round Hill. The beech mast is thickest there. Offie is with them. If it's the house you want to see, Reno's inside. As you can see, I'm busy."

Yanders looked at her for a minute without speaking, something so understanding, half-humorous, half-pitying in his eyes that Leafy almost melted. But she did not intend melting twice, and kept her look hard and impersonal.

Yanders said, "My business is with Reno."

His words frightened her somewhat. Was he going to tell Reno about that kiss? Or tell him he'd changed his mind about the cabin? Or the pigs?

"Who I'd like to see is Reno," Yanders repeated as if he thought she hadn't heard him.

"There's nothing to stop you, Mr. Yanders," she said, and was ashamed of herself before the sentence was finished. She sounded to her own ears like somebody in one of Fab Braxton's plays—and play acting was what she had decided against.

"Reno'd be pleased to have company."

"He still laid up?"

"I think he's got a bone bruise. Or a ruptured blood vessel. It don't heal."

"I might have a look at it," Yanders said, "while I'm here."

Leafy didn't reply to that. She didn't like the idea of Yanders inspecting Reno along with the hogs and the house. She didn't like him standing on his own legs and handling Reno's ankle like something second-rate. She didn't want him thinking that he was the better man—and that she had made a poor choice.

"Ask Reno," she said, and bent over her kettle. She pulled a shimmy to the surface with her paddle and saw that the dirt around neck and armholes had already boiled away. She stirred the mixture of clothes and soap and rainwater into a stiff froth and didn't turn to look at Yanders as he thumped on the door.

He was inside a long time. She finished boiling, rinsing, and hanging the first kettleful and put on another. Still he didn't come out. And she scorned to let her curiosity get the better of her, to step inside and say, "What's going on?" Or to act as if whatever was being discussed couldn't be handled by Reno without help from her. If either man had wanted her, she was within halooing distance without either having to rise from his seat. No one halooed. The house was as quiet as if empty.

She went to the privy finally, from necessity. And then, not wanting to be caught stepping out of there just as Yanders opened the door of the house, decided to outstay him. She had considered herself her father's girl at home, but who she'd made her model was Prill. Prill's outhouse was always as dainty as a parlor bedroom. So was hers. It wouldn't be a chore to live there. The seats were covered, the trench well limed. A last year's calendar was tacked on the wall in case you wanted to linger and ruminate on the past. Prill would likely have knocked down the mud daubers' nests built in the angle of roof and wall; but she had kept them. They were as pretty and intricate as crochet work, and she didn't belittle them because they were worked in mud instead of thread. She *was* like her father, who was a beekeeper, in that she didn't fear them . . . not anything that flew and stung: wasps, mud daubers, hornets, bumblebees, yellow jackets. She had sat there in the early summer and let mud daubers crawl on her arm and face, have a sip of her sweat and fly on. She enjoyed the mud daubers' nest-building and egg-hatching as much as some people enjoyed orioles and swallows. The nests were brittle and empty now, and she felt the same well-wishing homesickness for them some people feel to see dry birds' nests swinging in fall on leafless trees, and their builders all flown south. She thought how much smarter she was than a mud dauber; could read a calendar and braid the rag rug she had on the privy floor. And yet if it was be shot or build a dauber's nest, she'd be shot.

The little outhouse was sun-warmed, but through the cracks she could hear the sigh of the wind and the leathery rattle of the sparse leaves that still clung to the big tulip tree in whose shelter the outhouse was built. She was lost in thoughts of summer finished and daubers flown when she heard Yanders' horse go softly single-footing away.

She ran to the cabin without bothering to give her stewing clothes a passing stir. All of the protectiveness she felt for Reno when she was with Yanders was gone. She felt Reno her equal and able to take care of himself; and she was ready to attack him for any weakness he had shown Yanders.

"What did he want?" she said before the door was completely opened.

Reno was standing at Ellen's window looking out. This was a bad sign. His foot throbbed when he stood. Something very bad must have happened to cause him to ignore the pain.

"I don't trust Yanders," Leafy went on. "I hope you didn't give in to him on anything. I think he's an Indian giver. I think he's sorry he gave us the pigs, now we've got such a good herd built up. I think he may be figuring some way to get them back. I hope you read the law to him."

"He read the law to me," Reno said.

Reno turned from the window. He stared at her like he was beat out. Reno's forehead was his most beautiful scholarly part; not high-domed like some old professor's, but a broad band, white where the rest of his face was brown. It looked as if it was aching. Her fingers, water-parched from the soapy water, were rough as nutmeg graters. She put aside the idea of going to Reno to rub his forehead.

Reno's words stirred up forebodings in her heart. She didn't mention them until she got him seated.

"What kind of law can Yanders read to us? There's nothing signed for the cabin, and the pigs were an outright gift."

Reno sat as if he didn't care a lick about any possession in the world.

Leafy said, "I don't reckon you stole anything. Or got some girl in trouble."

Reno looked at her with those big eyes of his so quick to see future promise and present defeat. He was past all joking.

"We're done for," he said.

"How're we done for?" When Reno didn't answer, she said, trying to rouse him out of the apathies, "Speak for yourself, Reno Rivers. I'm not done for."

"You are, but just don't know it 's all. I owe Yanders for those horses."

"Yanders? You can't owe Yanders. You bought both horses of Hen Giddings back in Blue Glass."

"Yanders is collecting for Giddings. He's the sheriff and he can do it."

"You told me Giddings said you could take your time paying. 'One year, five years. It's all one to me.' That's what you told me he said."

"It's what he said. I didn't lie to you. But I signed a paper. He said it was no more than a form to keep things legal. But I signed it."

"What did the paper say?"

"It said I would pay one year from date on demand."

"You took his word against what he put in writing?"

Reno didn't answer.

"I never wanted those horses. I argued against them."

"I know you did."

"We had the offer of old Polly from Papa. She wouldn't have cost us a penny."

"I didn't want to be beholden to your father."

"What you wanted was to go skiting off to Whitewater like a rich man." She knew she oughtn't to speak to a sick man that way, but it wasn't her fault that what had rankled so long was just now aired.

Reno wouldn't fight with her, maybe didn't have the strength. But he was stubborn about the facts.

"I didn't want to be looked down on—my only means of taking you west a horse belonging to your father. And Giddings did say I could have all the time in the world to pay."

"What did you think you'd pay *with*?"

Reno was silent.

"That's why you were so down in the mouth when Blaze had to be shot?"

"That was one of the reasons."

"Well," Leafy said, "what can Yanders do? He can't get blood from a turnip."

"We got blood," Reno said.

"What blood? Where?"

"The pigs."

"They're for the land payment—you know that."

"Giddings don't know it. If we've got anything that'll raise money, he wants it. He's got a legal right to it."

"What would Hen Giddings do with a bunch of razorbacks? Though fat," Leafy had to admit.

Reno was patient. "It's the money they'll bring he wants."

"Who's he think'll drive them all the way to Cincinnati, to provide him money? When he lied to you."

"He thinks Yanders will."

Leafy hooted at this. "He don't know Simon Yanders. He's a sheriff. He's not going to drove pigs through the woods to settle somebody else's debt."

"He'll hire them droved. And he'll be there at the sale. And take what's owed to Giddings before he gives us anything."

"He can't do that." Leafy meant "I'll never let him do it." Though how she could prevent him she had no idea.

Reno answered what she had said, not what she thought.

"He can do it. It's his business."

"It's not a nice business."

"I never said it was. What I said was it's the law and Yanders' job is to enforce the law."

"I'd never trust him to sell our pigs for what they're worth. Or give us our fair share. Or who he'd hire."

"He don't care who's hired. We can find our own man. All Yanders cares about is getting what's owed Giddings into Giddings' pocket before we start dipping into it."

Leafy, who had started out so strong and feisty began, when she saw that their backs were really to the wall, to cry; not sobs, but tears running down her cheeks.

"How'll we meet the land payment, Reno? The hogs won't bring enough to pay Giddings and meet the land payment, too?"

"We won't," Reno said.

"If we don't, somebody else will get our place. Then all our year's work'll be gone. And Yanders' cabin, to boot."

Reno didn't say a word. His face was gray, whether from the poison in his foot or sickheartedness, Leafy didn't know.

"What'll we do? We'll be turned out."

"We're better off than we were a year ago," Reno reminded her. "We'll have one horse clear and some cash in hand."

Leafy saw the faraway look Reno had when ideas for a better life came to him.

"What's your plan now?" Leafy asked him coldly.

"I was thinking—before this ever came up—the thing to do was for me to go back to Blue Glass and try my hand at teaching again."

"Not with me," Leafy said. "I won't go running back there with my tail between my legs."

"Well, then," Reno said, not a whit abashed, "we'll move farther south. I hear there's all kinds of openings around Madison. Heading that way suits me better, too."

Leafy paid no attention to this turnabout in the direction Reno was heading.

"Is Mr. Yanders seeing to the hiring of a drover?"

"He'll stop back here in three days to see if we've found a drover. He don't care how the herd gets there. But it's his sworn duty to see that it gets there and that Giddings gets his money."

"Friendship don't mean much to him, does it?"

"He gets his livelihood from the law, not his friends."

"Do you trust him?"

"I've got no cause to not. He's been more than kind to us."

"He has for a fact," Leafy said.

Leafy could see the knots in Reno's forehead smooth out with her words. He had enough to fight, with his lame foot and his

I.O.U.'s coming home to roost, without his wife being against him, too.

"Yanders has a drover in mind," he said, as if the whole plan was a kindness to them. "Cashie Wade. He's a young fellow, but droving's his job. He's going to speak to him for us."

"Can't we speak for ourselves?"

"Yanders knows the ropes."

"Knows the nooses, too," Leafy said, and Reno stared at her.

Simon Yanders

Conners' Tavern at Connersville was, when the season for droving was on, a drovers' headquarters. Its ten rooms sometimes housed twenty or thirty men; and outside in the drove stands two or three thousand pigs might grumble and snore. George Conners made money on man *and* beast. He bought up corn from the surrounding countryside and sold it at a good profit to the passing drovers. He even charged drovers for the privilege of letting their porkers eat the leavings left by his cows in his cattle pen. But no one thought of George Conners as being grasping. He was one of those lucky men who like the means by which they make money so much that customers forget that they are paying for what they receive. Stopping at Conners' Tavern was like going home, with none of the obligations of a home-coming. No self-blame for the trouble you were causing, no need to volunteer to lay the fire or clear the table, or to pretend an interest in what George Conners had been doing since last you had stretched your legs in front of his seven-foot hearth.

A tavern, Simon Yanders thought, was to a home what a whore was to a wife. And a good tavern, like a good whore, could provide some comforts unknown to home and wife. Even when Ellen was alive, Yanders, though not one to stray from her bed, did stray from the cabin hearth on occasion to spend an evening drinking and jawing with Conners and the travelers he was putting up for the night. Yanders was headed toward the tavern now for business, not sociable reasons. But for him, as for George Conners himself, there was no enmity between business and sociability.

He'd waited a while outside the Riverses' cabin after his talk with Reno for Leafy to show up. He wasn't eager to see her, though he thought he owed her an explanation of what he was doing. She wouldn't be reasonable; since Reno had been so overly reasonable he felt he ought to balance things out by hearing what was to be said on the other side. Legally there was nothing to be said; and nothing Leafy could say could persuade him to change his plans. He knew that what he was doing caused her pain, and he was willing to lock horns with her in an argument if that exercise would give her any ease. But she wasn't in sight, which could only mean she was hiding in the barn or outhouse. And the call to suffer for her sake wasn't strong enough to cause him to sit there switching off fall flies already half-dead, and smelling the raw-soap smell of her boiling clothes. So he rode on toward Connersville.

Given the choice, he didn't know whether or not he'd choose to have come on the Riverses and their broken-down wagon. He didn't have set opinions about either Reno or Leafy, and this made him, each time he met them, have to start figuring them out as much as if they were strangers. He'd started out by thinking Reno Rivers a slack-twisted fellow and he was ending up (if this was the end) thinking he wasn't so much twisted slack as out of the ordinary. His feelings and changes of feelings about Leafy had been too many for him to keep track of; and he was never sure which would pleasure him most: to give her a kiss or smack her hard. Not sure which would pleasure her the most either. But one thing was pretty certain now: after turning her out of house and home he wouldn't be doing the first; and the second might be something he'd get, not give.

His horse splashed carefully through a gravelly stream. In a pool formed by an eddy, colored leaves floated round and round like the specks that swirl before the eyes after sun-gazing. He passed a snake making businesslike progress toward holing up for the winter. The season was changing from fall to winter, and bad weather was to be expected whenever that tussle took place. Like that unrest in girls passing from girlhood to woman-hood, and from womanhood to old age. All through the night before, he had listened to the nuts and acorns raining down. Once Leafy had said to him, "Alone, I am the best and sweetest girl in the world." He thought it might be true. Blue jays, many fewer now, still snarled at squirrels. A ringtail coon, fat as a mast-fed porker, moved heavily through a grove of white wal-nuts. He crossed a little run and noted the fox grapes dried and gone to raisins. He skirted marshland where at night he had seen jack-o'-lanterns and will-o'-the-wisps.

A person in the wrong circumstance (though alive and so near you can see the rise and fall of the beading at the top of her shimmy showing through the gap between the buttons of her bodice) is as lost to you as if dead. Some folk are always thirsting for water from other people's wells. They have no real thirst, only an itch for change—and maybe stealing. He didn't figure to be one of these.

Just before he reached Conners' place there was a stretch of parklike land. Forest fires had cleaned off the underbrush and fallen leaves and twigs, and the big trees stood up as unen-cumbered as if planted and pruned by human hands. The sky overhead was blue as water. But a shower had passed by at some recent hour, and raindrops, thick as maple-syrup goobles, shook with a passing breeze off the wet leaves, and down onto his hands and face.

He could hear the tavern sounds before he could see the tavern. Voices, wood splitting, cows and horses, and over all the soft continuous whomping of the talkative hogs.

His business at Conners' was to see Cashie Wade. And though missing Cashie would put him to the trouble of locating an-other drover for the Riverses, still there'd be the pleasure of talk and drink and woman-cooked food to pay him for his trip.

He kept his eye out for Cashie's wagon. Cashie was eighteen or nineteen years old; seventeen maybe. There was no telling his real age any more than his real father. Cashie's mother, Ruby Wade, ran what was probably a tavern now, way west, past Vernon. But seventeen or eighteen or nineteen years ago in the same place, then called "Truitt's," Ruby Wade had spent as much time in the bedrooms as in the kitchen and dining room. And most time of all, it was thought, in Ben Truitt's bed. In any case, when she had a son, she named him—Truitt himself being dead of lockjaw three months before—Olin Truitt. Whether or not the boy was a Truitt most people didn't know—or care; and the name he came to be called wasn't so much by way of calling him a wood's colt as by way of recognizing a need to somehow define the boy on his own terms. The fact that both names persisted showed that his second name wasn't felt to completely size up the boy either. In one dining room he'd be called in one evening by both names—and called both by the same person. Simon Yanders himself used both names; though because he knew Ruby Wade, and Olin Truitt was the name she'd given her boy, he was a shade partial to it.

Nevertheless, when he saw Olin's wagon in the yard, what he asked the Conners boy, coming in with the milk pails, was, "Cashie Wade inside?"

The boy, Tim, knew who he was talking about. "Inside what?" he asked.

If that long-nosed Tim, with his thin little mouth turned up at the corners like a turkey's, had any dirty double meanings, Simon ignored them. He enjoyed a little dirty talk as much as the next man, but he was picky about who he shared the dirt with.

Tim Conners got this and he said, as if being misjudged didn't go down well with him, "Look inside, yourself. I seen him by his wagon on my way to milk."

Simon had meant inside the tavern, not the wagon, but Tim was too shifty a customer to bandy words with, so he let it pass.

Cashie, for all he was so young, probably herded more hogs between Indiana and the market at Cincinnati than any other drover in the business. At his age you'd've expected him to be hired out to some hog buyer at so much a trip, good with the whip and strong-voiced with his "soo-ey soo-eys"; and no more than a couple of dollars ahead at the end of his trudge. Not Cashie! Cashie worked for himself, bought hogs on the hoof, hired others to do the trudging, rode in his own wagon, paid off his men in Cincinnati, and pocketed the profits, if any, himself. And there usually were profits. That's why he came to be called Cashie—not because he paid cash on the barrelhead for the porkers he bought (he did), but because when his trip east was over, cash was what he carried home in the tin box in his specially built wagon.

Brought up in his mother's tavern, his father being who he probably was, Cashie, by the time he was twelve or thirteen, had learned ropes some backwoods boys stayed ignorant of their entire lives. One of these ropes was money-making. That's a rope tavern keepers either know or go out of business in the first month. Money-making came natural to Cashie. The way a natural farmer sees where he can make two blades of grass grow where one grew before, Cashie saw where pennies could blossom into dollars. It was nothing he had to fret and fume about. He had a dowser in him that pointed in the direction of gold. All he had to do was follow.

Cashie wasn't a one-rope man. Hunting, he had a sense of where the deer were. Game flashed a message to his nerve ends. Girls did, too. It was hard to say how he found time for them, with his hunting and money-making. But Cashie, though he bought and sold, wasn't any storekeeper sitting up nights with a lard-oil lamp to figure out where the leak was.

Simon Yanders knew too much about hog droving to put down Cashie's success to luck. Cashie took a gamble every time he bought a hog. He bought hogs on the hoof, paying maybe a dollar a hundred pounds to the owner. To make the gamble pay off in Cincinnati, he'd have to sell to the butchers there for two or two-fifty. He had his drovers, and the feed his hogs would eat at the overnight drove stands, to pay for. And there were certain setbacks along the way. First of all, traveling porkers lost ten or twelve pounds on the trip. Then there were always some razorbacks, either honing after the lost free-ranging life of the forest or sensing (as a hog can) what lay ahead for them in the scalding pots of the Cincinnati fleshers, who lit out on their own. You could always count on a certain number of drownings, too. There wasn't a bridge between Indianapolis and Cincinnati. In some places there were ferries, but these weren't built to hold back a hog who wanted to take a high dive. Hogs were fair swimmers, but the waters they dove into weren't always suited to that exercise. Mostly the droves were swum across shallow fords; but after downpours, the fords were often neither shallow nor safe, and some hogs, looking more than ever like the perch, to whom they were said to be the land-going cousins, swam away to become, if not fish, at least fish food.

There were other animals besides man who fancied the sweet oily taste of a mast-fed porker; as between hog and honey, a bear would choose hog, and hogs would show up with evidence of this in a pound or two of living flesh missing from a ham. Most hogs fared better than this. They hadn't grown up as wild animals, except for a little training with corn to herd and follow, for nothing. They had more sense when it came to an attack than a horse or a cow. To say nothing of a sheep. A would-be butcher, wild cat, wolf, fox, was never given a chance to do a comfortable methodical job on some single animal. What lay ahead of the pork-hungry butcher before he could eat was a fight with an organized army: old tusker boars and saber-toothed sows facing outward from a tight circle and capable, if the fight went their way, which it usually did, of making a would-be diner a dish. Stragglers could be cut down. But even a straggler had better be looked over. A two-hundred-pound boar could whip his weight in wild cats, and what he couldn't whip he could outrun.

There were accidents, of course, that made the drover's gamble more chancy than these nibbling losses one by one. Cashie Wade, the lucky one, had once lost forty hogs at a crack, when a herd of his, sheltering from a thunderstorm under a tulip tree, was hit by lightning. Forty fell down as one, roasted in their tracks. Add a few mince pies baking and a pot of pumpkin butter bubbling, and the whole forest would have taken on a Thanksgiving Day smell.

And apart from the gamble of the march through the forest, there was, though every animal made the trip intact and even put on weight, the gamble of the market. The market wasn't steady. A man had to guess at it, buy low and sell high; with the chance that if he didn't offer owners enough, they wouldn't sell, and if he offered too much, he'd sell at a loss to himself.

Still Cashie made out. Took the gambles and won. Competed with men three times his age and, except for a couple Simon could think of, put more pork over the trails to porkopolis than any other man in the state. Killed more game on the way, came home with more money in his pocket, and slept more girls in that wagon of his coming *and* going.

Yanders, after he'd put up his horse, and though he was hungry for what the tavern had to offer and eager to settle the matter of the Riverses' hogs with Cashie, stopped to have a look at the wonderful contraption Cashie had made of what had started out as no more than a small-sized Conestoga wagon. Yanders had seen the wagon before, but Cashie, being the boy he was, always adding some new wrinkle to his horn, had maybe installed a patented coffee grinder or an inside firebox.

Cashie wasn't the boy to rig up a fancy wagon just so he could ride soft. He was always a fellow to make one stone kill at least two birds; and underneath his rolling home was slung a wooden-floored, wire-sided hog house where Cashie could carry his hog invalids. The hogs were going to have to stay flat while they were in the hog hospital, but that was the point of a hospital anyway; and twenty-four hours' bed rest in Cashie's rolling hog hospital saved him many a hundredweight of pork which otherwise would have been lost to him.

Cashie's wagon, last time Yanders had had a look inside, was redd up neater than an old maid's parlor. Handier, too, with accommodations an old maid would never have thought about: a bed box mounded to the brim with a featherbed; a provision box tin-lined to keep out water; a mirror-glass, big as a skillet, hanging from the canvas top. Cashie was a kind of dandy. Still Yanders didn't believe Cashie had hung that mirror just so he could part his own hair straight.

Yanders ran an appreciative hand around the curve of a tight wheel rim. He snapped a thumb and forefinger against the taut canvas of the cover. He'd seen many a man heading the whole way west to the rich prairies (Yanders himself didn't hold with the idea that land so poor it wouldn't grow trees was going to grow corn and grain) with outfits far more ramshackle. But these fellows, if they'd been roosters like Cashie, crowing at sunup and eager for work, would never have pulled up stakes in the first place.

He opened the canvas flaps at the back of the wagon anticipating new embellishments to Cashie's already tidy rig-out. They were there. He should have dropped the flaps at once, and would have done so, curiosity or no curiosity, if given any encouragement. He didn't get any. No screaming, flusteration, cover-grabbing. Not even a blush; and there was a plenteous expanse for one to spread over. Malvina Conners, twenty years old, gazed up at him, as smiling and clear-eyed as if she hadn't been lying, her body's curve following the curve of the goose-down featherbed, naked as a jay bird. Nakeder. There were no feathers on Malvina.

Cashie Wade, fully clothed, except he had his hat and boots off, was raised on one elbow above Malvina. He had a hand on Malvina's thigh, and Yanders couldn't help noting that Cashie, compared with Malvina's milk-white, was a redskin. Cashie was smiling down at Malvina like a man proud of his handiwork. He moved his eyes to meet Yanders' and didn't favor him with so much as a frown. "You could think," Yanders told himself, "from the looks of these two that they had been born before shame was discovered in the world." They hadn't gotten the word about fig leaves. They'd surely eaten the apple, but there'd been some delay in the arrival of the angel of the Lord with His notice of the foreclosure on their parcel of land. So there they lingered, munching and savoring, ignorant of evil and as happy as if they'd been caught fully clothed on their knees repeating the Ten Commandments.

Yanders wasn't a man ignorant of his own reactions. Prophesying his own behavior, he would have thought his eyes would have been locked to that outspread body, a snowy landscape embellished with not a thing but a tufty-brown brush and two pinky-brown berries. But he gave that body the go-by. In a world where faces were as common as May apples, and bodies of any kind, let alone a body like Malvina's, were as scarce as hen's teeth in a chickenless land, he looked at her face. He looked at her face and smiled back.

Well, he'd seen that look a time or two in his lifetime. And not always from a woman in bed; usually at such times he wasn't very reflective about expressions. Once, a boy blowing a bark boat with a poplar-leaf sail across a pond reddened with fallen persimmon leaves had had a look like that. A woman nursing a baby. A little girl fondling a tabby. He didn't try to bring them all back. He stood glued in his tracks, knowing he had been there before, at a moment when the dark glass was shined and he'd seen through clearly into where somebody had become a spirit. What name to give that spirit, he didn't know. Like as not it had different names at different times with different people. Something it couldn't be called, though, was dead. Another thing was unhappy. And, finally, he thought, ₊wicked.

He closed the wagon flaps and turned away like a man from a banquet table. Anything more would be surfeit. A man lived in such moments, perhaps more in these moments when they belonged to others than in any of his own. He headed again toward the tavern, but slowly now. Between the tree trunks the evening sky stood up in planks of rose and mustard. The day was coloring up as it finished. Taking its time like those two in the wagon. Sundown as rich as sunup. He stopped in his tracks, lonesome for Ellen. When the world was pretty, he had a gift he ached to give someone; and besides Ellen, who was there? The beauty in the sky bore down on him with a weight he longed to ease with sharing. Harvesttime of the year, and he, his thirties started, with more than half his life behind him. Time for giving getting shorter with every sunset.

Cashie Wade

Cashie Wade, the still-hunter, came up behind him unheard. Cashie wasn't hurrying to find Yanders, ask his business, dress him down for opening up without knocking, or swear him to secrecy. Yanders was no blabbermouth and he knew as well as Cashie that Malvina was marrying at Christmastime; and that, betrothed or unbetrothed, she was the apple of her father's eye.

Cashie got out of the wagon because Malvina needed space to hurry in for her dressing. She was past due for supper work in her father's kitchen.

"Don't leave me, Olin," she had whispered, to show him how little she valued the rest of the world. But he left her to give her elbowroom.

Most girls and women called him Olin. Most men, Cashie. Cashie himself walked free as a bird somewhere between the two. Being called one name by some people canceled out the other. Between the two he had the liberty to be a man no one had yet stuck a label to.

"Olin," Malvina had whispered, lapping her arm around his neck like a tippet, "you cast a spell over me."

He had a mind to tell her what the spell was. He knew well enough. Brought up in that tavern, with his mother first as helper, then as owner, he'd heard women talk. Women who had some experience to talk about, too. He could have given Malvina the word with the bark on it, if he'd thought she'd truly wanted to have what had happened spelled out for her. And though he'd learned from the tavern ladies that they weren't averse to gilding the lily, to living it all over again in words, he didn't have much stomach himself for that kind of repetitiousness.

Whatever the spell was he'd cast over her, he broke it with a light slap. "Get up," he said, "before your father comes out here and takes a horsewhip to both of us."

He already had his own boots and hat on.

Malvina wanted to prove something. "Tell him I threw myself at you."

"You stay like that and there'll be no need."

"Olin, you don't care what happens to me," Malvina said happily and with pride.

"I care. Get up and get out of here now. I don't want you locked up so you can't come back tonight."

It was his first admission. Malvina bounced upright on the spring feathers. "Oh, Olin."

He gave her an eye-kiss as he backed out of the wagon. He didn't understand men who came to women like customers to a butcher's counter, hungry and wanting no more than to satisfy appetite. A man who hunted wanted more pleasures than that. Pleasures likely couldn't be measured, but if he had to choose between the shuddering fall of what he hunted and his own appetite satisfied, he'd choose the pleasure of measuring his own power on another. He admitted to himself that his was the choice of a man who'd never had to go hungry. In which case he'd no doubt be at the butcher's counter as eager as the next fellow.

He had to touch Simon Yanders' shoulder twice to get his attention; and when Simon did turn, he said, "Cashie," but didn't appear to recognize him. For a minute Cashie felt a little taken aback. Was what Yanders had seen so commonplace it didn't stick in his mind five minutes?

Yanders said, gesturing toward the fading strips of light, "There's a chill in the air."

A widower and aging, the blood thinning out with winter and years. Thinking the best was over for him, as it likely was.

"Summer's over," Cashie agreed.

"I was looking for you, Cashie."

"Well, you found me," Cashie reminded him.

"You still buying hogs?" Yanders asked.

"I've got about my limit."

"I've got a herd I need to sell to somebody I can trust."

"I didn't know you were in the swine business."

"I'm not. This is a herd I'm attaching for an overdue debt."

"That's not a very pretty business."

"It's the law. Without that, there wouldn't be any business, pretty or otherwise."

"People you know?"

"Yes."

"How many hogs? What shape are they in?"

"Prime. They've been fattened up like household pets. You can go out and have a look at them if you want. If they get them all rounded up, there ought to be in the neighborhood of a hundred. More, maybe."

"I'd have to hire another drover."

"You can do it, can't you?"

"Likely. If I'm a mind to."

"What're you paying now?"

"One dollar a hundred."

"What do you figure to sell at?"

"Two. More if I'm lucky."

"You don't figure on going broke, do you, Cashie?"

"You can do that without figuring."

"I'm giving these folks three days to find a drover of their own."

Cashie flared up. "I'm not so hard up for hogs I need to tie up with folks who don't trust me."

"It's me they don't trust."

"What you done, Simon?"

Yanders might've said, "Kissed the wife," and Cashie'd been the first to push back a smile. What he said was, "First, I give them my hogs I'd let run wild. Now I'm taking them back. How'd they know I'm not tricking them for a year's work and fodder?"

"Don't they admit the debt?"

Yanders looked at the boy. He was brunet-colored, with butternut hair and skin the color of a dressed deerskin—only with life flooding under it. His eyeteeth, a trifle longer than the others, and curving toward the center, saved him from prettiness. He had gray eyes. The shrewdness that was in his head hadn't leaked down to cloud them. Men would sell to those eyes, and women give to them. Yanders didn't begrudge him. With a little luck, bad or good, Cashie might have been his son. He was half a head shorter than Yanders, not burly, but with thick forearms and thighs.

"They admit it. That don't mean they want to pay."

"I'd have to know soon," Cashie said. "I don't want much over a thousand head all told. And I won't hire men making their first trip."

"You'd pay me in cash?"

"If the hogs are right and you let me know soon enough, I'll pay you in cash."

✍ Leafy

Yanders, as good or as bad as his word, turned up exactly one week later. Leafy, expecting him, had settled Reno and Offie inside with jobs they couldn't, without damage to their conscience, go off and leave. Offie had to stay by the fire, where a pot of apple butter was cooking down. Leafy had thought she was through with apple butter for the year. What she had made outdoors, in the regular kettle for the job, filled twelve half-gallon crocks. But when Brockton Kemp turned up with a bushel basket of windfalls, she had no choice but to set to work again. There wasn't enough sun to dry them, and it would be a pity to eat now what they'd be so hungry for in the winter.

"You let that butter burn," Leafy warned her brother, "and I promise you, you'll eat burned butter this winter while Reno and me dine on what's good."

Reno, on one chair, with his damaged leg extended onto another, was shelling corn. This was another tag-end job, too little corn to take to the gristmill, too much to waste.

"It'll make fine hominy," Leafy told Reno. "Look at those big kernels."

"Do you know how to make hominy?" Reno asked her.

"I've watched Mama many a time. There's nothing better on a frosty morning than fried pork with hominy fried in the grease."

Reno laughed halfheartedly. "If pork's what it takes, there's no question but we'll have plenty of pork this winter. The question is, will we have a place to fry it?"

"I'm going to give Yanders one more chance," Leafy said by way of answering this question. "That's why I brought the pigs in yesterday. I want him to take one more look at them, and if he turns us out then, why then there's no more hope for us. Or for him either," she added from the doorway.

She'd been out earlier to tend to the chores. It had been a warm mizzling morning, but without sunshine. Now the sun was breaking through the mist, spangling the spider webs and tipping the colored leaves with bright beads of light. She thought she had never smelled things so sharp and fresh: wet earth, rotting leaves, the smoke from Offie's slow hickory fire, and even the spicy sweetness of the apple butter. The morning was very quiet, leaves too sodden to rustle and sounds battened down by the dampness. She wondered if when one sense had nothing to work on, the others could draw on the unused energy? That on a morning when she could hear rain falling her nose wouldn't have worked so well.

When the hogs began to talk, the smells faded. Hogs knew when weather changes were coming, and those who knew hogs better than she did could tell by their squeals and mutterings what the change would be. There were even those who claimed they could predict stormy or fair by the cock of a hog's ears or the twist of his tail. All she could tell was that a change was due; and whether the mizzle would thicken into downright rain or dry up under the sun, the hogs, though they knew, didn't tell her.

Halfway between barn and cabin she turned to look back. It was a picture of home, home smells and a squatty lift of pale smoke from the chimney. She was homesick already, before she had given herself real reason to be. Esau, who'd gotten either too doggish or too human to stay with his kin and foretell weather, was at her heels. Hog talk might be as much Greek to him as to her. She scratched his head, then stopped. Esau, with the least encouragement, lay down and offered the whole of his underside for scratching, flopping from left to right to let her know what parts were being overlooked. She didn't intend any scratching bee for Esau that morning. So no use getting his hopes up.

The air was balmy for October, soft and damp but not hot enough to account for the sweat under her arms and breasts. Her lips were stiff, because she had a speech prepared for them to say. They waited like soldiers for her order. The silence of the morning was perhaps more noticeable because she expected at any moment to hear the clop of Yanders' horse bringing him, as he'd said he would, to see if they'd found a drover. He'd said they couldn't; and he'd known what he was talking about. When he'd proved he was right, then he would feel free to wash his hands of them and let the law take its course.

She felt pulled apart; half of her looking at the cabin, the other half sending her hearing along the trace, onto the layers of leaves across which Yanders' horse would come with its feather-bed gait. She held herself together by will power, by anger, by hurt pride. And by ignorance. Ignorance was perhaps her greatest help; and knowing this, there were a lot of questions she didn't intend to ask herself. Or Yanders.

When she heard the muffled clops she had been listening for, she turned her back deliberately on the cabin. Yanders rode to the barn and waited for her there, not doing her the courtesy of dismounting. His bay was streaked with sweat or drizzle. She took note that Yanders was equipped with his usual gear: gun, saddlebags, blankets. What she had planned for him set him apart from her, so that she saw him more clearly than she ever had before. He faced the sun as she climbed the slope toward him. His eyes were as much green as blue, and there was a flicker of red at the ends of his whisker stubble. She had berated herself for her year's dreaming: not the sin of it so much as the folly. The time wasted over a hawk-nosed widower who wasn't above wife-stealing, but who wanted to palaver before riding off with the stolen goods. Didn't he know if they weren't past *that,* they weren't anywhere? But looking up now, she forgave herself some of her folly. He had the power to command, all right. There was flint up there for most any tinder. Maybe it was her greenness that had saved her.

But she was saved now. Thinking about her plan ahead of time she had been uneasy and sweating. Moving into it, she found her work now was to keep her lips, which had been stiff, from smiling too broadly. The surprise she had for Yanders wasn't of a birthday or Christmas variety; but she had holiday feelings.

Yanders leaned forward in the saddle watching her approach. "You look like you got good news for me," he said.

"Yes," she agreed.

"Don't tell me you found yourself a drover."

"I'd be lying to you if I didn't."

"Who is he? Where'd you dig him up? I hope you and your husband know there's no use sending some old man or some boy out with your herd? You've got seventy miles to cover."

"A hog can travel fifteen miles a day, easy."

"Where'd you hear that? But it ain't how far as much as what direction. One hundred miles a day in the wrong direction won't help you any."

"Our drover has that in mind, Mr. Yanders."

"In mind's nothing a hog can read. Can he head them in the right direction? And keep them together? And moving?"

"He says he can."

"You got any objection to my talking to him?"

"No. Talk your fill. He's up at the cabin. Before you go up, would you mind taking a look at the stuff he has in the stable?"

"What kind of stuff?"

"Food, it looks like. And too much, from the looks of it. From what I hear, there's enough drovers' taverns spaced between here and Cincinnati to take care of as many drovers as pigs."

"It's easy to miss one. They ain't signed like town taverns."

"It'd be better to miss one than to be slowed down with provisions. Wouldn't it?"

"Depends on whether you're owning or droving for somebody else, how you think about that."

"You're not doing either. You could judge. We're beholden enough to you as it is, but if you'd light down and have a look, we'd be thankful."

She watched him, outwardly calm, and afraid to say anything more. If she made him suspicious or resentful or just plain mulish, every bit of her planning was wasted. He sat looking down at her, and she was prepared to have him ride off. He took a foot from a stirrup, cocked it in front of him, but made no further move.

"It's none of my business," he said, "how your drover provisions himself for the trip."

She held her tongue, then. Finally, he lifted the other foot from the stirrup and slid to the ground. Not until he had thrown the reins over his horse's head did Leafy take one of the big streaked Ben Davises from her pocket.

"Do you have a knife on you?"

He gave her a surprised look. "What do you want a knife for?"

"To peel my apple."

"What's the matter with apple parings?"

"They make me dauncy lately."

He pulled his big bone-handled knife from its scabbard. "This has skinned more deer than apples."

"An apple is what I got."

He handed it to her. "Be careful you don't slice off hide with paring. It's well-honed."

"Thank you," Leafy said. "I'm being careful."

She peeled the apple as they walked toward the stable.

"You going to swing the peel over your shoulder to see what letter it falls into?" Yanders asked.

She wasn't sure he had been watching that day at the Kemps'.

"I can't do that," she said, dropping a small curve of peel. "I broke it too soon." When they came to the stable, she said, "He's got his gear stored in here."

The door was open, and Yanders paused in the doorway, then put a hand on the logs, sunk in the ground and as wide as his thigh, on which the door was hung.

"I built this before the house and I built it stronger than the house. I still had some doubts about Indians when I built this. I built it like a stockade. The redman don't live who could butt or hack his way into this."

"Couldn't he burn it?" Leafy asked.

"It'll burn," Yanders admitted, "but a real bonfire'd have to be built to start it."

"Couldn't he tunnel in?"

"In the first place, redskins didn't have suitable digging tools.

In the second place, you could shoot them down like wood-chucks as their heads popped up. No, I built this hog-tight and bull-strong. It'll be here after many a house is gone."

He stuck his head inside. The place had no window, but there was enough light from the opened door to show its shape and contents clearly. "Might be a house," he said, "you've got it so redd up. Don't you keep your animals here?"

"I cleaned it out for the drover," Leafy said.

"He's fixed like a king here. He won't ever want to pull out."

"I don't plan to ask him what his wants are."

The light from the door showed up a mound against the far wall covered by a bedquilt.

"I'd like to know what he's got under that," Leafy said. "I didn't like to poke into it." She took a bite out of the apple she had finished peeling.

"I got no qualms on that score," Yanders said. "It looks sus-picious to me. As sheriff, it might be my duty to have a look."

"You'd be the best judge of that," Leafy said.

Yanders crossed slowly, still admiring his handiwork, to the far wall. He lifted the quilt, peered under, then turned to Leafy. "I don't know where you picked up this fellow. If he's a drover, he must never had made a trip before. Or else he's a peddler and figures on selling for himself while droving for you. He could victual an army camp with what he's got here."

"What sort of wares is he carrying?" Leafy asked.

As Yanders bent for a closer look, Leafy shoved the heavy door shut and rammed the bolt that held it in place through the heavy hasps.

Yanders' voice carried clearly through the logs, and expressed nothing but impatience and command.

"Swing open the door," he said. "I can't see a thing here in the dark."

"Your eyes will get used to it, Mr. Yanders."

There was a considerable period of silence. Then Yanders said, "What do you mean by that?"

"I mean you're in there for a week, Mr. Yanders. Maybe ten days."

Yanders gave a big bellow. "Who do you think you're helping, locking me up?"

"Me," Leafy answered. "Reno and me."

"What's your drover going to think of you taking over his provisions?"

"I'm the drover," Leafy said. "Offie and me. The two of us. The provisions are for you. There's enough to keep you eating for two weeks. More, if you don't wolf it down."

"Let me out," Yanders said. He was at the door now. "I could talk this over with Giddings. He might make an exception in your case."

"I don't trust you when you get to palavering, Mr. Yanders."

"You'll never make it," Yanders said. "You'll lose your herd and end up lost yourself. That brother of yours will be nothing but a drawback. Your husband'll sicken without you to poultice and fend for him. And I'll starve to death."

If Yanders had been reasonable, not pictured the lot of them dead and dying, Leafy would have had doubts. As it was, he persuaded her that he was afraid she would make it.

"I made this trip once before. My herd knows my voice and will follow me anywhere. You seen that yourself. Offie's a good hand at rounding up pigs. And he's company. You've got food and water to last you a long spell. And I didn't do less for Reno. The next time you see me, Mr. Yanders, I'll have the deed to our land."

"The next time I see you, you'll be in jail for detaining a sheriff against his will. And for interfering with the course of law and justice."

"I'll have our deed with me," Leafy said, "when I go."

Leafy walked halfway to the house, then stopped to listen. Would Yanders bellow and scream? If he did, could he be heard? And if he could be heard, what would Reno do? Crawl out on his hands and knees, like as not, to free him. Reno was a high-minded man. She didn't know that she'd have any other kind for a husband, but high-minded men put their wives to the necessity of a lot of skulduggery.

There was not a sound from the barn. Was Yanders shouting, but the barn timbers so heavy they muffled his calls? Was he too proud to scream for help like a bad boy locked in a clothes-press? Was he ashamed to let it be known that he'd been out-witted? Whatever the cause, the silence was unbroken.

It was a buttermilk evening, a mackerel sky. No wind, warmish, the air stained with the metallic blue-gray of the fish-scale clouds above. An acorn rattled like gunfire on the cabin roof. Smoke from the chimney rose in a damson-plum plume. The summer surge of birds was gone. The hogs were talking of change. More change than they knew. She stored the scene for her night's use. She was frightened but exultant. She took this first success as an omen for the whole. If the truth be known, she was locking up more in locking up Simon Yanders than a threat to their land payment. She was locking up a past she wasn't proud of. And she was having her will of a man who'd hesitated to have his.

She planned to be on her way at moon-up. Reno'd be in his first deep sleep after the pain and restlessness of the day. She'd thought of telling him, but wasn't sure he might not persuade her of wrongdoing. Or, if not that, let Yanders free. Offie, she'd rouse with whispers, get him up with no more explanation than that she needed help with the pigs. She didn't trust Offie. He was a peculiar boy, not open, like Chancellor, who had no pleas-ure unless others partook of it. Offie, the plump picture of every-body's friend, was nobody's true friend but Offie's. Not that he was ever bodacious, or unruly. He said "Yes, ma'am" to Leafy as smooth as to Prill. But all the "yes, ma'ams" in the world didn't hide the fact that this was policy with Offie, not love. He obeyed when he thought it was good for Offie, and Leafy admired his acts of selfishness without it crossing her mind that selfishness was the name for them. But he was a natural-enough boy to take to the idea of a little moonlight adventuring without threats, Leafy thought.

She had nothing left to do in the way of assembling her own supplies. She had seen to that as thoroughly as she had seen to Yanders' provisioning. Little was needed. Drover stations were prepared to look after the needs of hogs and their "hogherds." The name had been Chancellor's for himself when he had visited them. "A hogherd with his whip," he said, "instead of a shepherd with his crook." It tickled her to think of herself as a "hogherd." "Hogherdess," she supposed, since a lady with sheep was a shepherdess.

Most drovers walked. Droves couldn't be kept together so well from horseback. Nevertheless, she and Offie would be mounted. She could walk it if she had to. So could Offie, though he would complain; and they would cover most of the trip on foot anyway. But with horses to spell them when they were footsore they'd make better time. Offie could ride Ginger; she'd mount Yanders' soft-padding single-footer, the tall gelding he called Fox.

Taking Fox was, she reckoned, the nearest to a crime she'd come. She could call it a borrowing, but for all practical purposes the horse would be stolen, and men had been strung up for less.

It came over her as she watched the chimney smoke and the metallic chain-mail sky how much she'd changed in a year's time. Chancellor had remarked on it during his visit. "I'll have to name you all over again," he said. "Leafy don't suit any more." He was right. She was finished with her "I'd just as lief." Some things she'd liefer do than others. She'd liefer march seventy miles to Cincinnati with a drove of hogs than sit home and have a sly horse trader do them out of their land. She'd liefer borrow a horse and be called a thief than run the chance of going so slow that Yanders could dig his way out and catch up with them. She'd liefer lock up a man who started kissing, then stopped to ask questions, than not. She had a mind of her own now, and even a bad mind, she reckoned, was better than none at all. It came over her as a surprise that she owed the gains she was congratulating herself on to Reno. If she'd stayed home, she'd still be troubled with "Shall I?," "Shan't I?," and answering, "I'd just as lief." She was whistling before she was out of the woods, before she was in them, actually, but she knew her own mind about that night's choices anyway.

It was a wonder to her that Reno didn't see in her face or hear in her voice that she was up to something. His sickness held him close to himself, she thought, too busy with his own swellings and throbbings to be scanning other faces for changes of expression or hearkening to voices to catch the excitement trembling there.

She knew that to succeed in fooling Reno she ought to keep the evening like any other. It wasn't, and it affected her. Reno was sick, and she was a horse thief, going off into the woods with a herd of animals she might not be able to manage. To say nothing of what she'd done to the horse's owner. She couldn't help seeing the evening as a possible last. Never-no-more, never-no-more rang in her head as she went about her supper work. She loved her pots, firkins, and stools. She loved her Dutch oven, her three-legged spider, and the well-drawing fireplace. She loved her handsome, unlucky, high-minded husband. Could she bear to leave him? She was of half a mind to go let Yanders out—so soon after praising herself for being whole-minded, say, "Sheriff, what are land and possessions to me compared with my dear one?" Instead, she decided to have both.

She cooked and cared for Reno as if he were the criminal eating his last supper and destined for a necktie party at moon-rise: fried hominy in salt-pork fat and made gravy, thick with salt-pork chunks, to put over it. Fried apple turnovers in the spider. Made a boiled custard to pour over them. She about overdid it.

"What is this, my wake?" Reno asked.

She took every opportunity when near Reno to hug and fondle him. Reno said, "Save that till I'm on my feet again." And Leafy saw that for a man with one good leg and in a low fever such endearments might be read as untimely invitations.

She kept her hands off him, and Reno, well fed, freshly poulticed, and newly bandaged, fell into the heavy, half-moaning sleep of the feverish. Offie was curled up on the hearthrug, whether asleep or not, Leafy couldn't say. Another evening and she would have hustled him out of his clothes and up the ladder into the loft. Tonight she let him lay.

After the supper washing and clearing up was over she sat down at the table to write Reno his note. She told Reno what she was doing and why she was doing it. Told him why she was right, and not to worry, she'd be home in a week, the land theirs and money in her pocket to make some payment to Giddings.

She had not intended to tell Reno that Yanders was locked up out in the barn. And she couldn't be sure, however much she might entreat Reno to leave Yanders right there, however much she might remind him that this was her plan and he had no right to spoil it, that Reno wouldn't cripple right out to that locked door, fling it open, and set Yanders free.

Still, because of his hurt foot, she had to tell Reno. If his foot took a turn for the worse, he'd have someone in her absence to call on. She'd have to take her chances on Reno's freeing Yanders.

"Reno," she wrote after she finished all she had intended at first to write, "Yanders is locked in the barn. Don't go worrying about him. He's got enough food and water to last him two weeks. And a man whose business is locking up ought to have some experience in it. It was the only thing to do if I was to get the money to the land office. Don't unlock him. We don't owe Yanders a thing, and he's not the best man in the world.

He's doing his duty attaching our hogs and I'm doing mine seeing that cheating horse dealer Giddings doesn't get the best of you.

"I know this is not what you would do. But it's what I want to do, so let me do it. I'm telling you about Yanders in case your foot takes a bad turn. He'd know what to do to help, none better. If it swells more or you get dauncy or start having night sweats, let him out. I hope to be in Cincinnati in four or five days' time and back in three more.

"Don't *worry* about Yanders. He's got more food than you have, though not so good. Don't forget the ginger cake. I put it in the chest to keep Offie from getting at it before we start.

"*Don't* let Yanders out unless you have to. I chose against Yanders and for you. You do the same for me. I love you, Reno. Your wife, Leafy."

Reno roused up as she and Offie left the cabin. She'd banked the fire closely, and it shed no light. The moon was up, and there was some sheen from it through Ellen's glass. Not enough to show Reno how the two travelers were outfitted.

"I was dreaming," Reno said.

Leafy didn't want to hear about the dream, some sorrowful premonition, maybe, of being left alone. She whispered so as not to wake Reno completely.

"Does your foot hurt?"

"It always hurts." Reno touched her cloak. "You going out?"

"I heard the hogs wowsling around."

"You run every time you hear a hog wowsle, you'll end up in an early grave."

"May anyway," Leafy agreed.

"Hurry back. I don't sleep good without you."

"I'll hurry," Leafy said, and waited until Reno's sick-sleep breathing began again. Then she put her light fingers on his foot and prayed for healing. And at the door she said under her breath, "Bless this house while I am gone."

Outside, under the coppery three-quarter moon they saddled

and with the help of a few ears of corn started the well-trained herd to moving. As they passed the barn Offie said, "What's that noise?"

"The wind coming up, I reckon."

"It sounds like somebody calling."

"That's the way of the wind. Mama used to say it always sounded like a baby crying to her. Chancellor thought it sounded like a catamount."

"It sounded like a man to me."

"It can sound like anything. Mostly what we're afraid of."

"I'm not afraid," Offie said.

"There's nothing to be afraid of," Leafy told him.

She felt it to be true. A quarter of a mile from the house and all that tenderness for brooms and cranes and firkins left her. The night of sliding winds and dropping leaves wrapped her round. The hog sounds were cheerful. She was at home with animals, a fact she would never have guessed back in Blue Glass, Ohio. She reached over to pat Offie. Offie was fat but solid—and tonight he leaned his hard round shoulders away from her.

On an impulse she handed the reins to Offie.

"Lead Fox," she said. "I want to walk."

She wanted, in fact, to be near something more companionable than Offie. She called Esau in the singsong way he recognized, and he sidled against her legs, ready for a scratching. She stooped down and gave him a hug, then in the midst of her pigs walked easily along the winding downhill trace.

twelve

⚞ *Offie*

The moon they had faced when they left the cabin was now shining behind them. They caught glimpses of it over their shoulders in the odd shapes permitted by the movement of leaves. The air under the layered branches had the unsunned earthy coldness of a cellar. The forest was full of owls hooting like Indians. There had been no rain ring round the moon. But once, the brassy clouds, crossing the sky in flocks, had held together long enough to produce a cold hard pelt of rain. The raindrops were elongated, the shape of bullets pulled while warm through a knothole. They came down so slow and hard Offie had held out his hand trying to catch one before it shattered.

Except for the time of the rainstorm, the pigs had not been contrary. While it rained they huddled together under the shelter of a close-set grove of trees—hornbeams, Offie thought. But he was not an outdoor boy and paid no more attention to the names of trees than a man not a doctor does to the names of bones. Use them was enough for him. During the storm and for a while after it was over, he and Leafy sat with their backs to one of the big trees, Esau by their side and the herd spread out like a lumpy comforter at their feet.

Leafy was kind to him, too kind. She took her cloak off and put it around his shoulders and pulled him close to keep him warm. She was trying to keep him won over, and he welcomed her efforts because they strengthened his resolution to resist. He hadn't the slightest intention of traipsing nearly a hundred miles to take pigs to a market. He had known this from the very first. He had said "yes" instead of "no" because it wasn't his way to stir up a fuss when he could get what he wanted easier. His policy was to say "yes" and keep clear of wheedling, tears, and downright commands. "Yes" was a cheap word to say considering how much it bought. He didn't know why his policy had been so little noticed. People paid less attention to him than they pretended. Leafy now, snuggling up to him, talking about how well the trip was going, and wondering if her little brother was getting tired or sleepy, wasn't really worried about him. Leafy didn't give a hoot about anything except money. She was going to sell her own pet, wasn't she? If cold or tired had meant anything to her, would she have rousted him out for this trip like a hired drover?

Offie wasn't afraid, he told himself. It wasn't fear that was going to send him home, or laziness either. He was going, first of all, because Leafy didn't need him. She wasn't afraid and she'd got the hogs trained so that they marched along like soldiers in an army. But even if he'd had his heart set on making the trudge from the Whitewater to the Miami, it was his duty to save Esau from sausage. He had to herd that pig home or be a traitor. He had to turn his back on adventure and the sociability of the drover stands no matter what *he* wanted. He had to save Leafy from being a Judas to the animal she had kissed and fondled. In after days she would thank him.

His trouble, and Offie knew it, was being a stick-in-the-mud. He wanted to keep on doing whatever he got started in. He had been able to start this trip only because he had told himself he would never make it. Now, started, it was easier to keep going than to turn back. It made sense to turn back. "Do unto others as you would be done by" required it. Still, the hardships he had imagined had not happened. The hogs stuck together like a churchgoing family. There had been no signs of wild animals. Except for the one pelt-down of rain, he hadn't suffered from the weather. But his life was filled with unfulfilled promises he had made to himself and he hoped this wasn't going to be another one. He had promised himself to run away from home; to show up Chancellor; to get out from under Leafy's thumb. He had never run, or showed up Chancellor, and here he was snuggling up to Leafy as if her hard thumb were the warmest, coziest shelter in the world. He kept reminding himself of her real purpose: not sisterly love, but get those hogs to market and rake in the money.

The hogs were having a snooze. They sounded like a hive of oversized bumblebees. Their snuffy breathing made Offie drowsy, too. Leafy had promised him, when they started, that they would spend the night at a drovers' stand. But so much of the night had already passed before they reached one, she said it would be a waste of money. So Leafy was for making a night of it, and he, soon to be on his way homeward, didn't see any reason for arguing with her. Creeping out of a tavern room and rounding up Esau would be ten times the job that giving Leafy the slip here in the forest would be.

Leafy, who paid attention to such things, calculated by the look of the stars and the moon that they were three hours from sunup. They had been traveling four to five hours and had covered, by her reckoning, eight to ten miles.

"At this rate," she said, "we'll be there in time for the land sales, easy. Two more days should do it. But we can't count on keeping up this pace."

"Why not?" Offie asked, hunting for ammunition to fire up his fading resolve.

"Nobody ever made this trip without running into trouble of some kind."

"What kind of trouble?"

"Losing animals, mostly."

"How do you know?"

"This is something Reno was planning to do. He wasn't going into it blindfolded."

"How do they lose them?" Offie persisted.

"Wild animals. The hogs stray. They get sick. They drown."

"Drown?" asked Offie. He would be on a horse out of reach of wild animals. The trace stretched straight as a string through the forest; a hog not interested in following it might stray, but he wouldn't. Sickness, which had so far passed him over in his life, surely wouldn't choose this time to strike. But drowning was a different matter. His fat was too solid to float. He sank like an anvil and never came up even a first time, let alone a third. He knew this from experience. Chancellor had hoisted him twice from water over his head: pushed in once, and once stepped off by mistake from wading to swimming water. At those times no pictures of the past had flashed before his eyes. What he saw, lying there, once in mud, once in gravel, was a future, bone-dry, in a dusty graveyard.

"How're they liable to drown?"

Leafy answered him as if he was planning to drove his own herd soon.

"There's ferries some places. They cost money and they take time. And some hogs are lost loading and unloading. But there's five other good-sized streams that'll have to be swum."

"Us, too?" Offie asked.

"You're not figuring on riding piggyback, are you?" Leafy asked. Then, seriously, "We can swim the horses. And places where the hogs'll have to swim, we can wade. Unless there's been freshets."

Offie snuggled closer to Leafy.

"You're not afraid, are you, Offie?"

That wasn't the point. His mind firmly made up to turn back, he wasn't afraid to risk being loving. Nothing was going to change him now. Save Esau and avoid potholes. He would take the first good chance that came along to face the other direction.

The leaves still dripped, though the rain was over and gone. The moon had traveled to a space in the sky the trees didn't hide, and Offie could see in its shine the sleeping hogs. They grinned as much in their sleep as they did in their waking hours. Offie wondered once again whether their upturned lips bespoke good nature or simply nature's way in shaping a pig mouth. Leafy, leaning back against the hornbeam, if that was what it was, slept but didn't smile. Her mouth turned down sorrowfully. She twitched in her sleep as if she, too, was imagining freshets and missed forks.

Offie, because he would be leaving them so soon, looked at them all, sister and hogs, with dearest love. If he'd been bound to stay with them, he might have hated them as the cause of his troubles. Leaving, he pitied them: bound for butchery and hardships. His heart throbbed with love.

When Leafy, a parcel of hogs, hungry and high-spirited after snoozing, headed toward a beechnut ridge, followed them, snapping her hog persuader and calling "Sooboy, Sooboy," as he'd heard her do all fall, he had his chance. Offie led Ginger, flicked Esau ahead of him with a gad he'd shaped from a sprout he'd cut in an elder thicket. Ginger was a born barner at any time. He never set out as eagerly as he turned homeward. Esau was now his pet, not Leafy's, and Offie patted as often as he flicked. They made good time. They moved with the speed of a long-legged pig, a barn-hungry horse, and a fraidy cat. They moved silently along the leaf-silenced path.

They were almost beyond earshot when Offie heard his sister

calling his name—a faint sound, far away, deadened by leaves. They were out of sight, deep and silent in a bush-hidden dip, when she galloped past calling loudly. Esau stirred, but Offie held him silent and still. Ginger whickered, but Leafy's calling drowned out the sound. They stayed there until she came back, still crying "Offie, Offie. Esau."

When she could no longer be heard, Offie came out with his animals. Trusting Esau and Ginger, he let them choose the direction to travel. The darkness had already thinned enough in the east to tell which end of the day he was coming to. It was mid-morning when he arrived at the cabin.

Offie pulled his jacket and shirt away from his throat, lowered his head, and sniffed. Chancellor used to say, "Every polecat smells his own stink first." Chancellor was right. It was the stink of his own sweat he was smelling. He ran his hand upward under his jacket and through the opening in his underwear. He hadn't sweated water, but something slick and sticky. It wasn't anything that would dry away; it would have to be washed off like axle grease.

It was a funny thing for him to start sweating just as he got in sight of home. But the change from night under the trees to midmorning sunshine in the clearing did it, he supposed. Ginger, the old barner, now that the barn was in sight, wanted to take the last stretch at a gallop. Offie pulled him down to a walk.

He was as surprised as a man who has spent his youth in foreign parts to see how little, calm, and unchanged home was. There it had sat, unaffected while he had traveled so far and endured so much. There was no sign of his absence upon it. He had scrambled homeward as if cabin, barn, and outhouses had the power to retreat before him. There wasn't even any smoke from the chimney. Offie, glad as he was to see what he'd been riding toward, still felt some scorn for what had proved to be so stationary.

He should have unsaddled Ginger, fed and watered him. Instead, he tied him to the hitching post. He had better tell Reno what he had in mind to tell him, while he still had it in mind. He didn't like Reno. Still, given his choice of relatives and relatives-in-law, he didn't know but he'd choose in-laws.

The inside of the cabin after the sparkle of midmorning October light was dark. It seemed to him to have changed more than the outside. He had never seen it at midmorning without a fire on the hearth and a pot on the crane simmering with something for dinner. He had never seen Reno sitting on a bench, head on arms, and arms on the table; Reno, spread so loose and silent. Offie's first thought was to run outside away from a dead man.

Reno wasn't dead; he wasn't even asleep. At the first sound of Offie's shoes bearing his stout pony-weight body, he reared up, wide awake.

"Where's Leafy?" he asked. "What's happened to Leafy?"

"Nothing's happened to Leafy."

Reno lifted his bad leg from under the table, swung it with both hands across the bench so that he could face Offie.

"What're you doing here?"

Offie had counted on Reno's understanding the common sense of his decision to come home. What good could he do Leafy? He had one other good reason for his return.

"I came back to look after you."

"Did Leafy send you back?"

Offie could figure out useful lies ahead of time. He could lie in cold blood. His brain could lie. But his tongue and his eyes, face to face with someone, could not make an untruthful answer.

"I left. I was a burden to her."

He thought for a second that Reno, though not dead, might be dying. Reno's white face was blotched with red spots, and his eyes, already oversized in his thin face, got bigger; but they didn't take *him* in. Offie could tell that. Or if they took him in, they saw something else as well. Offie wanted to bring Reno back to *him;* to Offie, nine years old, a reasonable person, a millstone in water, a lover of livestock.

"Esau was being led to slaughter."

That brought Reno back. He saw Offie then. He looked around —Offie knew it—for something to throw. When he saw there was nothing within reach, he said, solemn as a judge, "What about your sister?"

"Leafy knows how to take care of herself."

"Why did she take you along?"

Offie answered honestly, "I don't know."

Reno yelled then. "I'll tell you why. Because she was a girl and scared, that's why. And she thought you'd be some comfort and help to her. Now you get me my coat and help me on Ginger."

Offie said, "Are you going off and leave me alone, Reno?"

"You've got Esau for company."

Reno, using the broom wrong-end-to as a crutch, hobbled around filling an empty pillowcase with food.

Offie said, "I'll do that."

"I don't trust you," Reno said. "You'd likely slip me in some rat poison."

"What good can you do?" Offie asked.

Reno didn't answer.

"You can't drove, with your bad foot. You'll likely get blood poisoning and die."

"I'll die where I belong then," Reno said.

Offie didn't try to reason with Reno any more after that. He was very sleepy and eager to be rid of him. He would sleep in Reno's and Leafy's featherbed while they were gone.

He had to carry a stool out to help Reno mount. Reno's bad foot was his left, and he had to mount from the wrong side. He made it into the saddle, then sat there hunched over a while. He didn't try to put his bad foot into the stirrup, but rode away with that leg sticking out like a piece of wood. Offie waited for some good-by sign before Reno was lost in the trees where the clearing ended. Reno didn't turn. He just rode away like some poor old scarecrow.

Inside, Offie took off his jacket and shoes. On the table, untouched, were two fried pies. Offie took them to bed with him. On the bed, half under the pillow, was Leafy's note to Reno. Offie read it as he munched. What he read reassured him. He wasn't alone, after all. After he had slept he would go outside and, sitting some little distance from the barn, he'd have a talk with Mr. Yanders. It would be sociable for both of them.

Leafy, and Reno, too, because Reno could've let Mr. Yanders out and sent him on to find Leafy if he'd wanted to, wanted Yanders left locked up. So did Offie. He knew well enough that if he opened that barn door, Yanders would light out after his stolen horse. Then Offie would be really alone. With Mr. Yanders in the barn, he'd have company—and someone to turn to in case of danger.

First, he'd have a nap; then he'd go out and surprise Mr. Yanders. When he woke up from his nap, it was dark, no time for visiting. He used Leafy's chamberpot—he never had liked going outside in the dark—then ate another fried pie and took off his shirt and pants. His sweat had dried, but he still had a nasty smell. He was sleepier now than when he'd first gone to bed. When he woke up again, it would be light. He would wash, then go talk to Mr. Yanders.

✍ Cashie Wade

Cashie Wade slept in his own wagon, atop his own clean featherbed. He couldn't stomach tavern beds, cornhusk mattresses laid across rope webbings and bedmates who hadn't been out of their drawers and undershirts since they went swimming on the Fourth of July.

The night before, he had slept about five miles west of the drovers' stand on Brush Creek. He was traveling behind his hired drivers, gathering up strays and doctoring the footsore. Sometime before sunup he had heard what sounded to him like a girl's halooing. But at this time of the year the woods were so full of pigs and people yelling at pigs that anyone who stopped to figure out who was screaming at what and why would come out the little end of the horn in the droving business.

Women were a rarity on the trails to Cincinnati, but he'd run across a few himself. Last year he'd herded for half a day alongside a wagon-riding grandpa whose two granddaughters were going the legwork of droving. Herding hogs wasn't anything a good stout girl couldn't do. Success in that line depended more on the hogs than the herder. If the hogs had had some training in being tolled along by the bait of an occasional ear of corn, a ten-year-old with a supply of corn could do the job. Hogs were as sociable as dogs and a lot more sensible. They didn't waste time fighting among themselves or go chasing off after every polecat and possum that crossed their paths. So though a girl's voice wasn't unknown in these parts at this time of the year and didn't mean necessarily that some maiden was being scalped wrong end to, still he had kept his ears pricked before drowsing off again.

Along about noon next day he heard a sound that made him straighten up and listen. He didn't hear it again, and it was a good morning for hearing. It was too early in the year for it, but overhead was what looked like a snow sky. Heavy gray clouds had settled down no more than an arm's length above the treetops. Sounds didn't have any room to rise in. They were clamped down like a mess of dumplings steaming under a cast-iron lid. If they got big, it had to be sidewise—and in his direction. The trees were perfectly still. There would be a wind later, but so far it was only a blade-size blower, roaming around in the withered grass at his feet and stirring up little dry-leaf whirlwinds.

The main sound in the forest he caused himself. The gilt he was treating had a mysterious hurt, a slash too big for the strike of a copperhead, but so deep and fanglike he was hard put to account for it otherwise. Copperhead poison didn't mean any more to a hog than a swig of corn liquor to a human, so it wasn't the poison that had been slowing her down. Maybe she was just a smart porker, and, noticing how some pigs rode, had decided on riding herself. If so, Cashie was making her pay for her ticket. He had slashed her punctures open and was pouring turpentine into them. The pig was screaming like a Comanche, and was of a mind now to travel on her own. But Cashie, like any other doctor, wasn't asking the patient her druthers. It was a tussle, but he got her front quarters finally into the opening of his underslung hospital. The rest was just shoving.

He was bent over, fastening the door, when he was aware he had a visitor. Rising, he saw the horse, which he recognized, before he saw the rider. The horse was Simon Yanders' big bay single-footer, Fox. But Yanders wasn't in the saddle. Instead, a girl riding astride, but with her cloak tied around her waist like a riding skirt to make her decent. She was no raving beauty, but she didn't make Cashie want to run either. She was narrow-waisted, full-breasted, had a big wad of yellow hair in a knot that was coming unraveled, and a bright red mouth. At the minute she also had a bright red nose, splotched cheeks, and scalded-looking eyes. And even her bright red mouth was swollen and turned down at the corners. What she looked like was someone homeward bound from a funeral. Since she was riding Yanders' horse, the idea that it might've been Yanders' funeral occurred to Cashie. Yanders was no woman hater, but so far he'd never got soft enough on any woman to hand over big red Fox to her. Though maybe this was the girl who could turn that unlikely trick. The girl didn't give him time to ruminate on the horse she was riding.

In a voice rough with crying and soggy with tears, she said, "Have you seen a nine-year-old boy?"

As much to cheer her up as anything, Cashie said, "In my lifetime, you mean?"

He was sorry the minute the words were out of his mouth. The tears the girl had been holding back rolled down her cheeks. "I mean now," she said. "I lost him. He didn't want to come with me and I made him. Now I've led him to his death."

"Well," said Cashie, "if you lost him, you didn't lead him."

"I led him to begin with."

"Led him from where to what?" Cashie asked, but gently.

"From home to Cincinnati."

"You're still a far piece from Cincinnati. Where's home?"

"The Yanders' place. South of Connersville."

"How'd you lose your brother?"

"I left him dozing beside a tree while I went off to round up some strays. I found the hogs the first thing. I wasn't gone more than thirty minutes. When I got back Offie, Esau, and the horse—they were all gone. They had disappeared."

"How old did you say Esau is?"

"It don't matter how old Esau is. Esau's a pig."

The girl was beginning to cry again, and Cashie, though he thought his mistake was natural, hurried to undo the damage. "Offie. I mean how old's Offie?"

"Nine."

"And he and a pig and a horse all sunk from sight together?"

"Like the earth had swallowed them," the girl agreed.

Cashie said, "Cheer up, Sis. A boy, a horse, and a pig don't get lost at one and the same time unless somebody's in charge of getting lost. I figure it was the boy."

"Offie?"

"Offie," Cashie repeated, though that name for a nine-year-old didn't set easy on his tongue.

The girl got another face when he said that. The graveward corners of her mouth turned up, the tears dried.

"You don't think he's lost?" Her nose was already whiter.

"Nope."

"Not traveling in circles? Not eaten alive?"

"Nope. Sitting at home by the fire eating johnnycake and side-meat. What gave you the notion to bring him along in the first place?"

"I was scared," the girl said.

"What did you figure a nine-year-old could do?"

"He'd be company. Somebody to talk to. And he could help with the pigs. Anyway, that's what I thought."

"You and the nine-year-old raise them?"

"No. My husband and me."

"You a widow?"

"No. My husband's laid up with a bad foot. It looks like it's mortifying. There was no one else to make the trip."

"You lose the pigs, too, while you're hunting—the boy?"

The girl, now that her mind was relieved about her brother, had plenty of spirit. "No, I didn't," she flared up. "They're just back of that rise in a little hollow. Eating and resting."

"You hung onto them pretty well in spite of all your hunting."

"I hunted," the girl said obstinately. "And I think maybe I ought to some more. 'Home by the fire eating.' That's nothing I can bank on."

"Suit yourself," Cashie said. "Like as not no one else can."

The girl drew in her horns at that. "Could I hire you to drove for a day while I ride home to see if Offie's safe?"

"I buy," Cashie said. "I don't hire out."

"If you buy," the girl asked, "what're you paying?"

"A dollar a hundredweight."

"They're paying two in Cincinnati."

Cashie agreed. "More if the market holds."

"Why should you get as much for droving pigs to Cincinnati as I get for a year raising them?"

"You asked. All I did," Cashie said mildly, "was tell you my price. You ain't required to sell."

"Not required and not volunteering."

Before she could turn Fox, Cashie asked, "Where'd you get Simon Yanders' horse?"

The girl hauled back on Fox and turned to Cashie. "How did you know this horse belonged to Yanders?"

"I know Yanders. I know his horse. What I don't know is how you got it."

"Mr. Yanders loaned him to me. For a week."

"Yanders spending a week afoot?"

"Mr. Yanders is resting for a week."

"Ain't he well?"

"He was feeling dauncy last time I saw him. And since he wasn't going to have any need of his horse . . . well, I've got the loan of him."

"Be funny to see Yanders on foot."

"He can walk like the rest of us, I reckon."

Cashie smiled to himself. The girl was fighting him without the least reason in the world; reason to the outward eye, that was. He'd seen it happen many a time before: stockade door slammed shut with a thud and he with no attack whatever mounted. They did it as if to remind him.

"Where you aiming to end up tonight?" he asked.

"I'll keep going till I reach a drovers' stand."

"There's nothing before Deever's. You'll have to travel a far piece to make that by nightfall."

"That's my present aim," the girl said. "I didn't have much rest last night and I aim to lay my head on a pillow tonight."

"It'll be a dirty one."

"Come nightfall, I won't be choosy."

"You can follow me," Cashie told her. "I'm behind my drivers and figure on hustling to catch up. I'll help you across the West Fork if you make it the same time I do."

"What's your charge?" the girl asked, pert as a jay.

Cashie grinned. "Drovin's my business. But neighborliness I don't charge for."

The girl wouldn't joke. "It would be worth a price, and I'd be willing to pay."

"I don't hire out," Cashie reminded her again. "What's your name?"

"Leafy," the girl said. "Mrs. Leafy Rivers. What's yours?"

"Olin. Mr. Olin Truitt. I'll see you again at the West Fork."

She couldn't be that agreeable. "I wouldn't wait, if I was you, Mr. Truitt."

"Oh, I won't, Mrs. Rivers," Cashie assured her.

✍ Offie

He lay in Reno's and Leafy's bed, munching fried pies, though it was past noon, for his breakfast, and thinking how well things had turned out. Getting himself and Esau home safe had been his own doing; but Mr. Yanders locked up in the barn where he could be called on in case of any trouble and Reno gone off to be with Leafy was none of his doing and simply a sign, as his mother always said, that the Lord helped those who helped themselves. He didn't think Leafy'd come to any harm alone; otherwise he'd never have left her. But with Reno along she was better off than she'd have been with a nine-year-old; and since sitting around hadn't cured Reno's foot, a bout of riding might be just what he needed. And Mr. Yanders out in the barn!

He had never before been in a house by himself, let alone been the head of a house. He relished the idea. What he said went. But who could he say it to? He took Leafy's letter to Reno out from under the pillow and read through it once again. Leafy hadn't locked Mr. Yanders up for his sake, but if she'd been planning for his comfort, she couldn't have done better. If he got lonesome he could go sit by the barn door and have a little talk with Mr. Yanders. Mr. Yanders would probably like it, too.

He hadn't remembered that the cabin was so big. Of course he'd never seen it before from the far corner of the bed, and the bed away in a far corner of the room. He counted the floor boards to the fireplace. Eighteen. He counted the boards of the loft floor overhead. Twenty. Once, there had been a chink in the flooring directly over his head. It was filled in now, but he looked up, half expecting to see an eye staring down at him.

The window *was* an eye of white light looking in at him. The red eye in the fireplace blinked at him. He had banked the fire well, and the coals, where the ashes had fallen away, were alive with dancing points of heat. He called to Esau, curled up on the hearthrug like an old tabby, but Esau, snoring away, didn't so much as twitch an ear. Leafy wouldn't care for the idea of a pig in the house, not even Esau. But Esau was pretty well trained. Besides, Offie was a good scrubber, so no lasting harm would come of Esau's mistakes.

A lonesome wind was whistling around the corners of the house, now loud, now soft. It could've been a person. Two limbs of the dooryard tulip tree rubbed together when the wind was strong. He'd heard them before, but never really noted until now how much they sounded like a door being slowly opened. The door was bolted tight. He looked again to be sure, but that was what it sounded like. If he'd been Reno, he'd have sawed those two limbs off. Then there wouldn't be any doubt in the middle of a long dark night about the door. Reno was a kind of poke-easy when it came to outdoor jobs. He'd noted that.

Maybe he would go back to his regular bed in the loft tonight. Probably shouldn't be sleeping in Reno's and Leafy's bed anyway. Up in the loft, he could open his peephole again and look down if he heard any sounds.

Meanwhile, he was cozy, full as a tick, warm as a bug in a rug; Esau on the hearthrug and the sheriff in the barn. He'd done what he'd planned to do from the minute Leafy spoke to him about going; and the way things had turned out was better even than he'd planned. So why, in the space of the room, though much larger with only one person than it had been with three, and inside the space of his chest, swelled out with pride in what he'd done, was there pain? The pain was caused by a sound. The sound was carried to him and made louder by the cold whistling wind. The sound was Leafy's voice as he had heard it calling to him as she ranged up and down the woods in the dark night, searching.

"Offie? Offie? Where are you, Offie?" she cried.

She'd kept it up for such a long time, and he knew that if he'd answered her in any way, even "Leafy, I'm caught by a bear," she would've come right to him and fought the bear.

But a bear hadn't caught him. He was caught by his plan,

doing what he'd decided on, and every time she called he'd almost choked, holding back his voice from answering. He had hated her for the pain she caused him with all her calling: "Offie? Offie?" But if he'd known that he'd keep on hearing her voice this long, maybe he *would* have answered her. Though she was better off at this minute with Reno than with him. He'd be a mighty biggity boy to think anything else. A couple of acorns, last of the crop to be harvested by the wind, hit the roof with a bullet spang. Offie knew what they were the second, or the second second anyway, after he heard them. But since he was already out of bed, he decided to pull on his britches.

He was a neat boy and, once his britches were on, he brushed the crumbs from the bed, straightened the covers, cleaned up Esau's mess, and recruited the fire. Esau, when the fire blazed up, rolled over on his back, waiting to have his belly scratched. What Offie wanted was a face to talk to, not a belly to scratch. Squatting in front of the fire, he picked up Esau's head, and nursed it like a doll baby.

"I saved you, Esau," he said. "Only reason you ain't tramping the woods on the way to being hit in the head with an ax is me."

Esau blinked his pink eyes.

"You never will be et while I'm alive, Esau."

Esau jerked a hind leg in the way he had of saying, "Scratch me."

But Offie wouldn't scratch. Scratching Esau made him a hog, and you couldn't talk to a hog. He put Esau's head back on the floor and went down to the barn.

He knew he was going to be a big surprise to Mr. Yanders, who would be expecting, if he expected anybody, to hear Reno's voice. He knocked on the barn door as polite as a caller—though he certainly didn't intend going in. Or letting Mr. Yanders out, either. He wanted Mr. Yanders kept locked up as much as Leafy, though for a different reason.

Mr. Yanders answered his knock with a mean growl. "Who's there?"

"It's me. Offie."

When he heard Offie's name, Yanders stopped growling and bellowed. "Let me out of here. If you know what's good for you, get this door open at once!"

The bellowing and the door kicking that followed it turned Offie silent.

"I'm the sheriff here. I'm an officer of the law. I can have you clapped in jail, young man, for locking up an officer of the law."

"I didn't lock you up."

"Your sister did. Tell her to get me out of here before I throw the lot of you in jail."

"I can't tell her. She's on her way to Cincinnati."

"I thought you were helping her. What're you doing here?"

"I brought Esau back."

"Whose idea was that?"

"Mine," said Offie. "Leafy'll be glad to have him saved."

"So you ran off and left your sister alone in the woods in order to save a pig? What kind of a brother are you, anyway?"

"Leafy didn't need me the way Esau did."

"You the one I heard ride in this morning?"

"I reckon."

"Who rode out?"

"Reno."

"Reno! How'd he get on a horse with that bad foot?"

"I helped him."

"Helped him to go off and do your job and likely ride to his death. Let me out of here, boy, or there won't be anything left of you to throw in jail after I lay my hands on you."

Yanders kicked and pounded the door, but Offie turned stubbornly silent again. What kind of a fool did Yanders think he was? To open a door so's he could get a thrashing and a jail term. Let Mr. Yanders pound and yell. Offie could see the hasp that held the door shut. Yelling and pounding weren't going to budge that.

The same idea seemed to have struck Mr. Yanders. His voice when next he spoke wasn't angry any more.

"What're your plans now, Offie? Offie? Ain't you got any better name than that?"

"My name's Howard. I'm called Offie because I'm an off-bloom."

"I remember now. Your sister told me once. Well, some folks never know when they're well off."

This made no sense to Offie. "You can call me Howard, if you want."

"I think I'll stick to Offie, after all. So you're in charge here now, Offie?"

"I reckon I am," Offie said.

"Well," said Mr. Yanders, "since we're both stuck here until they get back, why don't you let me out of this place and we can both live up at the house together?"

That was a likely story. "Live together." Once out, Mr. Yanders would be on his way faster than popcorn when the lid's off.

Offie said, "Leafy wants you kept locked up."

"What Leafy wants don't seem to have cut much ice with you, judging by last night."

This was pretty near the truth, and Offie didn't want to face the truth. "Ain't you comfortable in there, Mr. Yanders?"

"Sure, I'm comfortable. Good bed. Plenty to eat. What time of day do you figure it is, Offie?"

Offie looked at the sky. "Past noon," he said.

"It was you I was thinking of," Mr. Yanders said. "I could give you a hand in case of any trouble, if I was up at the house."

"What kind of trouble, Mr. Yanders?"

"Oh, no special trouble, Offie. Fire might go out, for instance."

Offie gave a scornful sniff at that. "I can keep a fire agoing without help."

"Then, this time of year," Mr. Yanders went on, "with the money from hog sales coming in, there's always a lot of housebreakers roaming around hoping to get their hands on some loose cash."

"There ain't no hog money at our house."

"Thieves wouldn't know that till they'd searched."

"They wouldn't find money or me. I'd be hidden up in the loft."

"A loft's one of the first places a gang of housebreakers turn inside out. Everybody knows that."

"I could run and get you, in case the house was broke in."

"You could run, but would you make it?"

"It's money they'd want, not me."

"They want money. But they don't want witnesses. You'd be a witness."

"I been a witness before," Offie said, trying to escape the sound of those footsteps pounding behind him as he ran for the barn. And to put Mr. Yanders in the wrong.

"I reckon we all have," Mr. Yanders said. "But not to thievery."

"I witnessed thievery," Offie said.

"So you're an old hand at catching thieves," Mr. Yanders said in a voice that made "old hand" sound as bad as thief.

"I witnessed you and Leafy out in the woods."

Mr. Yanders was quiet for a while. Then he said, "Well, I didn't know you seen it, but I saved your sister Leafy one day out in the woods from being chewed up by an old sow."

"Chewing up ain't what I seen. Kissing and hugging's what I seen."

Mr. Yanders was right up against the door now. And yelling again. "There was no kissing and hugging. There was one kiss. And I'm old enough to be Leafy's father."

Offie doubted this. Mr. Yanders didn't seem old enough to be his father, even. Let alone Leafy's.

"I never seen Pa treat Leafy that way."

"What you seen your pa do or not do don't have any bearing on this."

"I know sparking when I see it," Offie insisted.

"I reckon you're talking from experience."

"No, but I've seen it. I had myself a peephole in the loft floor, so's I could watch Reno and Leafy."

Mr. Yanders, very close to the door now, gave another bellow. The idea that Offie knew what he was talking about apparently didn't set well.

"You get on back up to the house before I make a peephole in you, Off-bloom. You get up there and stay there. Don't come down here again."

"You change your mind about coming up to the house with me, Mr. Yanders?"

"Yeh, I changed my mind. I'm better off where I am."

"What if thieves come smelling around for money?"

"I feel sorry for them, that's what."

✒ Cashie Wade

Cashie waited for Leafy at the West Fork, though not from choice. By late afternoon the snow sky had hardened up. It took on the color and looked to have the weight of a cast-iron skillet. Then the skillet went to pieces; the sky broke up, and what came down was not snow, but rain, icy winter rain. Somewhere higher up, what was reaching the earth as sleet had been hail. A hailstone, unmelted, came down occasionally, mean as a bullet, to sting a tired horse into a sudden lunge against his collar. Such leaves as still clung to sycamore and maple, hickory and tulip were pounded off. The downpour onto the leafless limbs rang wooden and hard. Gone was the summer flutter of rain on foliage.

Cashie pulled up once to see how his underwagon cargo was making out. The hogs were scrooched down as close together as bees in a hive. They gazed at him out of their sensible little eyes. He would've sworn they appreciated the storm they were lucky enough to be giving a miss. He wasn't out from under cover for more than a couple of minutes, but if his coat had been cloth instead of hide, he'd have been wet to the skin. The rain was coming in sheets, and the sheets had the icy edge and bruising strength of a block of harvested pond ice. The wind was out of the northeast, and Cashie had no choice, if his travel was to mean anything, but to head his team into it. They went into a wall, but they were better off traveling than standing, and he kept them headed toward the West Fork.

Somewhere west, the storm that had reached him had come earlier and harder. The ford at the West Fork was flooding, and there was no question of putting his team across it, let alone his underwagon cargo. Earlier in the season a man by the name of Demaree Clapp had operated a ferry across the West Fork. But as the hog traffic had slacked off he'd folded up. The lean-to shed where Clapp had sheltered still stood. Cashie pulled into it and was startled for a minute at the change in sound. Falling on canvas, the rain had produced a soft windy roar. It filled his ears like the throb of his own blood. Under the shed, the drumbeat rain moved up onto the roof where it belonged. The roof wasn't completely watertight, but it was tight enough to make the shed, compared to that waterfall he'd been under, a Sahara desert.

Cashie could make camp tidier and faster than a woman could spread a bed. There was no rush tonight, so he didn't hurry. But in jig time he had unharnessed, fed his team and his hogs. That done, he lit his lard-oil lamp. His wagon was rigged so tight, the lamp warmed as well as lighted. He had eaten cold tenderloin, fried at breakfast, and was ready to blow out his lamp and crawl into the comfort of his downy bed when he thought of that poor girl beating her way through the woods on her borrowed horse. Though he still doubted the horse was borrowed, it puzzled him how a yellow-haired girl could take a horse away from Yanders if Yanders was unwilling. But borrowed or stolen, or a gift outright, she was, if lucky, still on it; and had been now for some hours in a downfall that weathervaned between sleety rain and rainy sleet. It was unlikely that she could've made the ford, pushing the herd she was, before the freshet struck, and crossed ahead of him. She was either bedded down in some old hollow sycamore butt, her pigs, like rocks running water, huddled around her, or she was, stubborn as he figured her to be, still slipslopping along on her single-footer, urging her hogs ahead of her toward the one named and inhabited place she knew: the West Fork and him.

He wished the idea of that poor benighted girl had never entered his head; because once there, he had no choice but to pull his jacket back on, get out his ax, and build up, in the shelter of the lean-to, a beacon fire. There was plenty of dry wood stacked in the lean-to. What he needed, and it wasn't hard to find, was wood wet enough to slow down the burning; he wasn't of a mind to sit up all night tending the fire, even though the sight of it would give Mrs. Rivers heart and direction. He got the fire built to his satisfaction; it should last three or four hours and be able to warm the girl, bone wet and marrow cold as she was bound to be, when she arrived. Then he went to bed; and when she did arrive, he was asleep.

He had supposed, if she did make it, that she would, after throwing some dry wood on the fire, settle down thankfully to thaw out. Instead, she rapped on the tail gate of his wagon like a late traveler at an inn.

"Mr. Truitt," she called. "Olin."

Cashie wasn't one of these people who, when asleep, live in their dreams, and have a hard time, when they open their eyes, accounting for their surroundings. He heard Leafy's voice, opened his eyes, knew who was calling him and why. Knew, even though the voice had come to him in his sleep, not only that the girl's teeth were chattering, but that she had the all-over shakes. Her voice reached him in little punkin-seed pieces that he had to shove together to get into the shape of understandable words.

He pulled on his britches and climbed out of the wagon. The rain had let up. The dwindling moon was traveling through a clear space, and the fire, though burned down to coals, shed considerable light. He'd never seen a more woebegone sight.

White-faced, sodden, hair half to her knees, shaking as she huddled over the fire, she smiled at Cashie as though he'd been waiting for her and the news. "I got them all here," she said. "The storm made them stick to me better than usual."

It was like listening to a foreign language to make out, through the chatter of her teeth, what she was saying.

Cashie said, "You get out of your wet clothes and into my bed. It's warm. You'll have lung fever if you don't get warmed up quick. I'll give you some hot rum toddy. That'll warm you from the inside."

Leafy made a gesture of modesty, and Cashie said, "It's your choice. Keep those wet clothes on and I'll have to lay you out and bury you. I can take a good look then, if you've got anything so precious to see. I'll get you an undershirt of mine. It can serve as a bedgown."

He went into the wagon for the shirt while she stripped; but once in there he used the peephole through the canvas to see what shape of a woman she was. A naked woman was no rarity to him. He'd seen them since he was tall enough to reach their knee joints; and while they were more of a treat than a well-rounded filly, they were a treat of the same kind. His favorite shape in women wasn't this short-waisted. At forty, short-waisted women were boxes, no space between tits and belly button. But at nineteen there was nothing sweeter to handle than a short-waisted girl, with plenty of handhold above and below and the general outline as the hand traced it of a dove plumped out with flesh instead of feathers.

He tossed her, turning his eyes ostentatiously away, the shirt from the wagon. It came almost to her knees. She was already looking healthier when he joined her by the fire. He'd like someday to see her nose its rightful color. First time it had been red; now it was blue. But she could hold her words together now, keep them from spattering out in broken pieces.

"Could you spare my drove some corn?" she asked. "I'll pay you back when we get to Deever's."

He had a plentiful supply. "It'll hold them together for the night," she explained.

He didn't need advice from her about handling hogs. She was swaying on her feet. "Get into my bed," he told her again. "It's touch and go now whether you pull through this soaking without a fever."

She didn't give a hoot as to where he'd sleep. She was so sleep-starved she would've crawled into bed with six horny drovers and a dying dog.

After he'd helped the girl into the wagon he took care of Yanders' horse and gave the hogs enough to make them hopeful for more in the morning. He had never had the least intention of sleeping anywhere but in his own bed. If the girl didn't like sleeping double, all she'd have to do was hop out. She'd have a good fire for company. Though if that was what she wanted, he was capable of sleeping with her harmless as a twin brother in a trundle bed. It wasn't what most men wanted; though he wouldn't say most had any notion what it was they *did* want. He knew his own wants, though. He'd been taught; and was now himself a teacher. Women thought he was brimful of loving-kindness. He smiled into the fire. He wasn't unkind to women, but Olin Truitt was the boy he was really befriending.

There was a touch in him, and he knew it, of the small boy who provides himself with nerve shocks by the momentary stringing up of pairs of cats across back-yard clotheslines. The cats didn't live who couldn't wriggle out of that predicament, but while it lasted, their shivers and caterwaulings set up in their tormentors a reciprocal shaking that was about equal parts sickness and joy. Anyway, something you could get a taste for. Predicament might be the right word for cats. But it was wrong for women. Cats weren't asked if they wanted to be strung up. Women either, for that matter. But they were given plenty of chances to say no. It was no fun for him if what he offered wasn't wanted. He wanted what every man wanted. Only difference was, he wanted more. *He* wanted more, and it was a comic turnabout to be thanked, praised, and petted for a gift to himself. Well, it was a gift to them, too. He'd had too many thanks to doubt that. Though it wasn't what they called it: love. It was maybe loving; as his mother had ordered him, playing with a puppy, "Now be loving with the little doggy." But it wasn't love. Not love any more than the love a man is said to have for the bottle. A man who loves the bottle doesn't love any particular bottle. Between whiskey and rum, he don't have any real choice. He don't play favorites. Any good bottle'll do. Any good woman.

Cashie pushed the coals closer together and covered them with rain-soaked chunks so that white smoke went up toward the clearing sky. He had a good fire to send signals with, if he'd known the sign language and had any signals to send. To send a message, you had to have one. He couldn't make out clearly what he had to say, let alone send it off in smoke puffs for distant reading. Neither cats over clotheslines nor bottles drained explained what he'd been trying to make clear to himself. They said he had "a way with women." The women said that. The men said he had a way with money. And with game, too. Collecting or hoarding was nothing he leaned toward. Control? Get a response? Cashie was hunting for the word "power."

He was eighteen years old, already a rich man in the Whitewater Valley, a masterhand with women, a wood's colt, but no woodsy interested only in smelling out game. He had a deep longing to know the person he felt himself to be, the person who stood unnamed, halfway between Cashie Wade, the money-maker, and Olin Truitt, the boy brought up by his mother's friends.

A bear could've crawled into bed with that sleep-sodden girl. A polecat or a panther. Any beast so long as it kept its claws sheathed and its fangs unbared. She still wasn't thawed out. Out of respect for his visitor Cashie had shed his travel-sweated underwear. He got into bed mother naked and felt along the length of his fire-warmed body the coldness of hers. He figured that the bone-coldness, the marrow-ice, had melted and surfaced as far as her skin. He cuddled her close, and she folded herself as

naturally inside the curve of his bigger outside curve as a kit
to a cat. Somebody touching her body in bed was nothing out of
the way to her; and she was as distant in sleep from who as from
what. If taking had been the sole pleasure he was after, that, he
figured, could've been done without more than half rousing her.
Half rousing was less than half his goal. He wanted her awake.
And if not as kindhearted as credited by ladies, he was at least
too kindhearted to take sleep away from a girl so starved for it.

Her shape under his hand didn't contradict what his eye had
seen. Round and soft; but springy enough to step off those Cincinnati miles. He made his hand as much a part of her as another layer of her own flesh; he cupped her here and there. All
she did was cuddle closer. He ventured the spot where he would
prove his schooling. She gave a little shudder, toward, or away
from, he couldn't say. He took pity on his bedfellow. She was still
cold-skinned, soft and velvety cold like winter toadstools. Let her
sleep and warm. He was accustomed to dozing in a blind as he
waited for game. To sleep he had only to close his eyes.

He opened them, as was his habit, at daybreak. The light in
the wagon had just enough gray in it to be called that. The rain
had slacked off. The wind sent down an occasional ripple of
drops from overhanging boughs. They fell with a zither tinkle
on the shed roof. The hogs were awake and sleepily woofing.
The girl in his arms was as warm as a peach on the sunny side
of the tree. He scanned her face. He would like to see if her
nose had gone back to white, but it was too dark for colors. She
was still asleep; but a little waking now, he figured, wouldn't
harm her. She slept right on through fondling that was friendly,
and through the beginning of fondling that wasn't. He knew
when she woke up. She took on a special stillness, something
quieter than breathing, more silent than sleep. That was the
best sign in the world. She didn't want to wake up. If this
was a dream, she was telling herself, I want to keep on dreaming.
If it wasn't a dream, she didn't want to know it. What happened

when she was waking she was responsible for. Her breath was as delicate as cobwebs. She was taking in just enough to stay alive. She'd said farewell to a lot of herself to go away and live in a better place. Not her heart though. She hadn't forsaken her heart. It was as loud as her breath was quiet. There was light enough now for Cashie to see its beat under the curve of her closed eyelids. His own pulse was keeping almost exact time.

✍ Offie

The wind, which at noon had whistled, began in the night to roar. It had clouded up before sundown, a dark threatening sky overhead and a sound of foreboding from the racked leafless limbs. It was not the time of year for thunderstorms or cyclones or blizzards. But something ominous was brewing away to the north where the bad weather came from. Offie bolted the door. Then, with what Mr. Yanders had had to say about thieves in mind, he shoved the clothes chest and the food safe against the door. Finally he hung a pillow sham across the glass. If thieves were prowling around it would be just as well they didn't see that he was here alone. Through the double thickness of cloth, the yellow-green tongue of the distant storm licked into the room every now and then, snakelike.

He banked the fire down less than usual. Its flicker was company, something alive and on his side against robbers and darkness. He made his supper on the fried sidemeat Leafy had left for Reno. The fried pies were all gone. When the sidemeat was gone, he'd start on the cold pone. That was his policy: eat the best first. That way, when he got down to the cold corn pone, it would taste good, for between nothing and corn pone, corn pone would chew mighty sweet. He took pride in having figured this out and thought with scorn of haphazard eaters without plans who put in their mouths whatever lay nearest at hand.

The fire and the food made him, in spite of the booming

wind and the creaks and groans of the trees, sleepy. Just for company, he thought he'd have Esau sleep in bed with him. Esau was too heavy to lift; but the bed was low, and Esau, if he'd been of a mind, could've hopped under the covers with the greatest of ease. He'd seen hogs jump through openings in rail fences which were higher, and which required more skill; for the opening in a fence offered a much smaller target than a bed. But Esau wouldn't make the least effort, no matter how much encouraged, to enjoy the comforts of a featherbed. Wouldn't make any effort to settle down and sleep *any* place. Offie'd always known bad weather wore on the nerves of hogs. They could smell a storm afar off and give warning half a day before it arrived. Even the sudden clouding over of the sun made a hog complain. But with a roof over him, Offie thought maybe it was something besides weather that was making Esau so skittish. The hog went smelling around like a dog. Tried to get past the clothes chest and food safe to smell at the wind that blew under the door. Flopped down. Snored for a while. Woke up with a start and tried another corner. Finally, when he settled, as he had that morning, on the hearthrug, Offie joined him. He curled around him spoon fashion and covered them both with the coverlid.

Before he went to sleep he said his prayers. He never in his life had gone to sleep without saying them, and didn't suppose he could. He asked God to bless his father and mother and Chancellor, back in Blue Glass. He prayed for Leafy and Reno on their way to Cincinnati, sleeping snug in some tavern and safe from the storm. He prayed for Mr. Yanders out in the barn. He thanked God that Leafy had boxed Mr. Yanders up so tight, and he prayed God that the barn bolt would hold.

Saying his prayers put him to sleep, but not for long. He knew it hadn't been long because the coals had scarcely grayed. A sound had awakened him—it was still echoing in his ears—but what it was he didn't know. It didn't seem likely any sound could be louder than those he was hearing. The wind was screaming around the corners of the cabin, roaring through the treetops, slamming the rain against the walls with the roar of a waterfall in spring.

A tree came down: first the whistling wheeze, then the crack of live wood splintering, and finally the earth-rocking thud. The sound fitted the echo in his ears that had awakened him. There was nothing to worry about, he told himself, if the whole forest fell down. The cabin was set in a clearing broad enough to let trees pile up like jackstraws without its being touched. No wind could possibly blow it over. Only the noise itself was worrisome —and even the noise had its good side. In the midst of all the racket of wind and rain, there was no sense straining his ears to hear prowlers. He wouldn't be able to hear a dozen of them; and anyway, he doubted any man would be so greedy for hog money as to spend a night out in such a storm.

Esau, who couldn't reason about such things, sat on his haunches by the door, tilting his ears like a suspicious hound-dog. Offie uncovered the coals and built up the fire with a couple of chunks. No one was going to break in on a night like this, but if they tried, he'd rather it wouldn't be in the dark. Since Esau wouldn't budge from the door, he took his cover over to Esau, made him the warm headboard for his bed, and settled down once again to sleep.

This time he knew what had awakened him. A horse had come in at a gallop, paused as if to let a man dismount, then trotted off in the direction of the barn. Offie strained his ears to hear, above the racket of the storm, sounds of the door being forced. He hurt his eyes trying to see if the chest or safe moved. He heard nothing, saw nothing. He was threatened by a mighty crafty robber.

Sometime during his vigil he dozed off. The next time he awakened all was quiet. Rain dropping from the eaves; a little wind blowing down the chimney onto the almost dead coals. Esau still as if scalded and scraped, but snoring lightly. Offie leaned across the chest and around the corner of the safe to where he could lift an edge of the pillow sham which covered the glass. The storm was over. The clearing was littered with broken limbs and fallen trees, but the sun was out and the wet trees were rainbow-colored.

There were no signs of the horse or his rider, though he had to be near at hand. A man didn't ride in like that in the middle of the night for nothing. This would be the minute to let Mr. Yanders know of their danger. He shoved safe and chest from the door and sped for the barn, hitching up his britches as he ran.

He pounded the bolt out of the hasp with a stone, swung open the barn door, and burst in on Mr. Yanders, sleeping soundly as if at home in his own bed.

"Mr. Yanders," he yelled.

Mr. Yanders opened his eyes as if he'd been resting, not sleeping.

"I thought I told you to stay away from here, Off-bloom."

"Robbers," said Offie.

"Where?" asked Mr. Yanders, sitting up.

"Rode in in the night."

"Did they get anything?"

"They couldn't get in."

"Where are they now?"

"Waiting around till we leave."

"Well, we ain't going to do that, are we, Offie?" Mr. Yanders asked.

"No, sir," said Offie. "We're going to live together and look after things together."

Mr. Yanders had been sleeping in his pants. All he had to do to dress was to pull on his boots. When he had done that he said, "Smells like a backhouse in here," and made for the door.

Offie went out with him. There wouldn't be any *reason* for Mr. Yanders locking him up in the barn. Still he didn't completely trust him. Mr. Yanders blinked in the bright light like an owl. "Another day or two in there and I'd've lost my eyesight," he said.

He looked at the storm damage. "Nobody's going to have to do anything here for a while but chop and haul the wood in to the house," he said.

He walked around the barn, Offie at his heels, to the barnyard where Leafy kept the pigs penned up overnight and where Ginger had fed.

And there was Ginger, washed clean by the downpour, but dried rough; saddleless, still bridled, and pulling hay from the fodder house.

"There's your robber," said Mr. Yanders.

"Where's Reno?"

"God knows—laying along the trace somewheres between here and Cincinnati."

"Dead?" asked Offie.

"That's what I'm going to find out."

"How can you find him?"

"I don't know's I can. But I got no choice but to try."

"What'll come of me?" Offie asked.

"Off-bloom," Mr. Yanders said, "you should've thought of that when you gave your sister the slip."

Offie watched Mr. Yanders prepare for his journey. It took him about ten minutes. Food from his barn supply, in balancing sacks, hung across old Ginger's back. Another sack for a saddle blanket, though there was no saddle and he rode bareback. Then he pointed the horse in the direction in which Offie had ridden out with Leafy two nights before.

As he passed the house, Esau, who had been rooting around the doorstep in the fresh mud, lifted his head; then, as if he remembered not only Ginger, but the journey that had been interrupted, he followed the trotting horse in a stiff-legged gallop.

Offie, no runner, tried for a while to keep up with them. "Esau, Esau," he called. But Esau was as heartless to him as he had been to Leafy, and if Mr. Yanders heard him calling, he paid no attention.

✑ Leafy

Next day the season had passed the ridgepole of the year; it had climbed the roof of the world, faced the sun and was sliding down the shady side.

Leafy resolutely kept her mind on pigs, on the miles yet to travel, on the money that had to be collected in Cincinnati. At midday she reached a little glade too spongy to favor the big hardwoods. It lay open to the sun, and though she had been moving too fast to need warming, the sunlit clearing was a cheerful place to stop for breath and food. The herd, wonderfully docile after its day of stormy traveling, rooted around peaceably under the beech and oak trees on the ridge opposite her. She wasn't yet to the point of tending those hogs like a mother hen, but she did understand them: knew when they needed to be spelled on their march, when they required the encouragement of the whip or a few ears of corn dropped ahead of them. Fox was getting to be, or maybe he always had been, a kind of hog horse. Sometimes he saw a stray before she did and went after it, like a sheepdog after a sheep. She dismounted less and less often. She misdoubted any other animals but hers could have been held so faithfully to a path and a plan. Dogs would have been off after every scent that promised food or coupling. Sheep would long since have toppled over some cliff. Horses wouldn't have stuck together for half a mile. Two or three cows, she might have managed. But a herd wouldn't have had the hog's faithfulness to each other and to their drover.

She was managing to keep her mind on hogs all right, but what she thought about them was as admiring as if they had, every last sow, shoat, gilt, and boar, pearly tusks, silvery hoofs, and hearts of gold. The fact of the matter was, there was a sheen on the world, the entire world, and keeping her mind off last night didn't dull it any. The dazzlement just spread to other objects. Whatever her eye fell on was changed and enhanced.

The day before's downpour had left a few pools among the bleached grasses. Across one some kind of a skimmer bug darted like a skater on ice. Leafy's heart took pleasure in his success. One little bug and one little pool of water, its brown blued by the sky overhead. She felt as joyful as if the bug had been a great fish and the pond an ocean. If he had been big enough she would have stroked his back with one light finger to say, "Well done." "Bug lover," she scoffed at herself. If it wasn't pigs, it had to be something.

Spiders, when the rain had stopped, had gone to work reweaving their webs. The rusty tussocks of autumn grass were bound together like corn shocks with threads of glitter. She had been so still a field mouse stopped staring and began to chew. She could see his whiskers move. They would never meet again though they had exchanged glances longer than most. Above the slope where her herd fed, two buzzards laid themselves on an updraft and were lifted as easily as leaves.

Skating with the bugs and flying with the birds, Leafy told herself, "I've got no limits this morning. My heart's opened up to house the world"; and she struggled again to close it to all but her work. The world conspired against her.

On the tussocks of grass, drops of rain, still undried, quivered with ruby and emerald lights. Diamonds and moonstones jeweled the spider webs. The sun shining down onto wet fallen leaves brewed up the smell of a wild tangy tea. Beneath her hand the bleached grass was slippery as baby hair. "This," she told herself, "may be the world's most beautiful hour so far. And I alone here to see it."

She wasn't alone long, and the company she got wasn't interested in cobweb jewels or friendly field mice. He was pushing hogs, like everyone else between the Wabash and the Ohio, toward Cincinnati; and his herd had been pushed hard. They were content now to sit on their tails and draw a long breath. He reminded Leafy of her father, straw-colored, long and lean. A man with a sour face who made jokes. Somebody who'd taken

the world's measure, found it short, but tried, out of goodhearted-
ness, not to let folks who still enjoyed it find out the truth.
Wasn't completely successful, however. Had to tell the truth
sometimes, but coated the bitter with the sugar of jest when he
did, so that his listeners, though they got the bitter, had it sweet-
ened with laughter.

"Well, Sis," he said, looking down at Leafy, "what you got to
be so happy about?"

Leafy certainly didn't intend to let herself talk about what
she wouldn't even let herself think about.

"I'm not happy," she said, thinking she oughtn't to be.

"What're you sitting out here in the middle of nowhere for,
then, smiling like a possum in a 'simmon tree?"

"I can smile if I want to."

"I never said you couldn't, Sis. You can, that's plain to see. All
I asked was why. It's none of my business, I'd be the first to
admit. And if something good's happened to you and you've taken
a pledge to hold your tongue about it, well, more power to you.
Tongue-holding's not most women's long suit."

Leafy thought it wasn't her visitor's either, but was too polite
to say so.

"Tongue-holding's not my long suit," she said, feeling called
on to contradict everything this man said.

"I'd be pleased to hear what is. In your opinion."

"Droving hogs," Leafy said, working her way back to the subject she was struggling to keep in mind.

"Who you helping?"

"Helping myself."

"You alone out here in the howling wilderness?"

"I had a brother with me to start."

"What happened to him?"

"He got scared and went home. He was nine years old," Leafy
explained before the man could berate Offie for desertion.

"You're likely better off shut of him. Where you from?"

"Southwest of Connersville."

"How far southwest?"

"Seven–eight miles."

"Them porkers you got, or pacers? You better give Cincinnati the go-by and head for Kentucky and the races. How'd you make out in the storm last night?"

"Tramped the first part of the night. Then sheltered."

"You don't look none the worse for it. Maybe that's what put the bloom on you. Hard times are what some women crave."

Leafy said nothing. She was no expert on what women craved, or on what put the bloom on them. If this man was, let him talk. She would listen and learn.

With no opposition from her, he didn't do so, but went back to the pigs. "I got mired down last night between the West and East Forks. That's a swampy stretch, best of times, and after last night's cloudburst you could've sailed boats on it. I lost three hogs in the quicksand there and damn near lost myself. Now I've lost the fellow I'm droving for and I'm racing to catch up."

With this man, so quick to read smiles, Leafy tried not to smile again. But standing there palavering, he cut a poor figure of a racer to her mind.

"My name's Spangler," the racer said. "Roscoe. I'd be pleased to meet you."

"I'm Leafy Rivers."

"Miss or Mrs.?"

This was a thing a man could properly ask a girl. Though she couldn't ask Mr. Spangler "You married or single?"

"Mrs.," she told him.

"You a widow?"

"No, of course not."

"Of course not? Girls younger than you've been widows."

"Well, I'm not a widow. I've got a fine husband, live as can be."

"Ain't very alive, or he wouldn't be letting his wife drive hogs."

"He's laid up," Leafy said, "with a bad foot. He can't bear his weight on it."

"So you set out alone?"

"I didn't have any choice. The money's due on our place at the land sales in Cincinnati. If I don't get our hogs there and sold, we'll lose our land."

"When's the land sales?"

"Day after tomorrow."

"You'll make it with time to spare. Where you plan to spend the night? Deever's drove stand ain't too far a piece from here."

"I figure on bedding down with my herd."

"Might be more rest for you than Deever's, at that. It'll be chockful of drovers and drivers and half of them drunk. You might be better off with your hogs."

"I can look after myself."

"Sure you can. Fight your weight in wild cats, Sis, I'd bet a pretty penny. How come you got such a chip on your shoulder and such a smile on your face? Talk one way and look another?"

Leafy couldn't keep back her smile. "I don't know," she admitted.

"If you don't know, I don't reckon there's much use Roscoe Spangler trying to puzzle it out."

Spangler, who had squatted beside Leafy, rose to his feet.

"Cashie'd be the first to understand losing time in talk with a pretty girl, but he ain't going to understand my losing those three pigs last night. I better be pushing on."

Leafy stood, too, encouraging him to go. Roscoe Spangler made her uneasy. Was there really some change in her that declared itself on sight to strangers? Or was Mr. Spangler a mind reader, able to see, no matter what she said, the feelings she tried to hide with words?

Mr. Spangler, further conversation discouraged, roused up his resting animals with ringing "sooboys" and cracking persuader.

"Keep the smile and throw away the chip," he called back. "The woods are full of chips, and smiles like yours don't grow on every bush."

Leafy waved but didn't answer. With Mr. Spangler gone,

the chip fell off her shoulder naturally enough. But the smile went, too. Something contradictory had happened, and she did not know how to think about it. She had tried not thinking at all; but half of what she felt was happiness, and that had been as plain as the nose on her face to a perfect stranger. The other half, conviction of wrong, Mr. Spangler hadn't caught sight of—unless it had taken the shape, under his questioning, of the chip on her shoulder.

How could what was wrong make her happy? Could what had happened in the night be at one and the same time a happiness to her but a wrong to Reno?

She didn't like his name or Olin's to be in her mind. Particularly at the same time. Only as person against person had wrong been done to Reno. She tried to take persons out of the night's happening; she tried to put that happening back into the night as one of many: all covered by darkness, ringed round by the roar of the wind, the hogs' complaints, and ending in weariness and sleep. The night had been filled with happenings: stars falling, field mice swimming for their lives, tree limbs shattering, their crowns swept free of leaves. What had happened was on this order. It was neither for nor against anyone. Four-o'clocks opened at dusk. This was neither for nor against the sun. The rain was not against mice, nor the wind against trees. The night was crowded with happenings. People with heavy hearts cried; sleepy people gapped; the sick moaned. The tears, the gaps, the moans were not against anyone. Not even *against* sorrow, sleepiness, and sickness. They happened. They brought ease.

She would not say either name. One would never know, and the other she would never again see. She would not hold what had happened against herself, or try to peel off the world's shimmer as punishment for herself. She *could* not do that. The fair world, drying out after the storm, rocked around her like a bowl of sweetness; all its smells, stirred up by wind, freshened by rain, were now drawn out in strength by the sun. She stretched her arms toward the world's edges; she wished she could draw her arms together in a clasp of lovingness around . . . around . . . old Esau; she thought, The old pink-eyed frisker. To him she could talk, say words it would not matter if he heard.

Thinking of Esau, she was reminded of the herd that was still with her; or so she hoped, for she hadn't given hogs a thought, in spite of all her resolutions, for several minutes.

Most of the herd had now come down into the swale itself and was rooting around for those delicacies, vegetable and animal, that grew there. "Time to move on," she told them. "We've had rest and food. This isn't a pleasure trip." Having warned them, she was ready to stir them up with commands when she caught sight of movement on the opposite side of the valley. There, five or six of the herd, hardheaded old sows, if she knew hogs, had sallied off from the sensible eaters to a bench of stone, an outcropping above the slope of beech and oak trees. They were up to something—she could see that from where she was—scuffling together, perhaps digging for beetles or grubs. Their exact motions were hard to make out, but whatever they were doing she had better bring them down before they climbed higher and gave up the idea of Cincinnati altogether.

She ran, whip in hand, across the sedgy draw and up the steep slope where the herd was feeding. Her energy astounded her. Ask her a week ago if she could drove hogs two nights and a day, then spring like a hound uphill, and the idea alone would have frazzled her out. We're shut in by our ideas of ourselves, she thought. And our ideas are made up by what we've done. Chancellor might be one person able to imagine an act way beyond anything he'd done. But how many Chancellors were there? Ordinary people like herself had the doors of their world opened by what happened. They had to learn through experience.

After she'd caught her breath from her run across the swale and up the first reaches of the slope, she looked upward toward her strays, trying to figure the best way to reach them. The best way was likely the long way; the way the sows themselves had had to travel up the sloping shoulder, brown with faded grasses and brittle pea vine, and onto the ledge from the side. She chose, in the pride of her strength and knowledge of time wasted back there with Spangler, to clamber straight up the shaly rise; she went at it, to begin with, running. The footing was slippery but not dangerous. If she stumbled, the worst that could happen was a backward roll; skin her up, maybe, but not crack her skull or break any bones.

Coming, finally, directly under the ledge, she saw she had made a poor choice. Getting up and onto that would be dangerous. It stuck out over her head like a shelf in a pantry over a four-year-old climber. She had either to pull herself up hand over hand onto it or admit that she'd made a mistake, go back down through the shale she had climbed, and start again up the grassy side slope. She decided that she was equal to the pull up; then, as her feet swung clear, wondered if she'd been mistaken about that, too. It was an arm-wrenching job, face and shoulders laid flat to the ledge while she squirmed and jerked the weight of her body forward. She was onto the ledge as far as her waist, ready to hoist her body, arms bent so as to get a foothold, when she saw what the ruckus was all about. Copperheads, drawn out of their rocky nests for one last sunning, were being attacked (or maybe it was the other way around) by the sows. The fight, and feast, too, for the sows were eating as well as killing, was going on at the back of the limestone shelving where the snakes had their nests. She was at eye level with those heavy, live bodies, with the sows' long, snapping, still-smiling jaws and their little slicing hoofs. Intent on the fight, she missed for the first seconds the flat bronze eyes and flickering tongue of a copperhead no more than a yard from her face. When she saw him, she thought she could smell him, a dusty, nasty smell like calomel at the back of her throat. She was too far forward onto the ledge now to fall backward by simply letting go. She would have to squirm backward as she had squirmed forward. And she felt that if she so much as narrowed an eye the snake would strike. Her face contracted, wizened up, drew inward toward its protective bones. She became bone all over, as motionless as the heavy jarring of her heart permitted. She would more than likely die without the snake's ever striking. Just lie there while her heart wore itself out and finally stopped. Afterward, finding her bones in a snake den, they'd conclude she'd been snake bit, though actually she'd be dead of fear.

She was sinking into that kind of death. The smell increased, maybe her own smell of sweat now as strong as snake smell. The snake's flat, leaf-colored head was weaving; its eyes on her cheekbones hurt like pushed knitting needles; its tongue forked out, alive with poison; its white hound's-tooth fangs were bared ready to take hold of her by lip or eyelid.

She could hear, but dared not lift her eyes to see, the fight that was going on at the back of the ledge. The noise was all from the hogs. The snakes had no way of speaking, but the hogs were noisy enough for both sides. She'd heard that screaming before of hog against rat or attacking dog. She'd heard their groans of pleasure at the slop trough. What she heard now combined both.

She was afraid even to close her eyes, lest the movement of her eyelids cause the snake to strike. But she had closed them, for it was the sound of Old Sukey's attack that made them open wide: Old Sukey, who littered four times a year, was onto that staring copperhead like a catamount onto a calf. But Leafy felt far from rescued. The sow would like as not drive the snake across the ledge directly into her face. She would rather have taken chances on staring it down. She willed her eyes to close again, but they had got the habit of staring. The sow was maybe not as quick as the snake, but it had more to be quick with: four razor-sharp hoofs and a long, grinning jaw filled with cross-saw teeth. Snakes, to judge by Sukey's actions, were something made for the pleasure of sows; they required a little stirring up, maybe, for greatest enjoyment, but were nothing certainly to be feared. Sukey, grinning, tromped and chomped. If the snake was able to strike, Old Sukey paid no more heed to its fangs than Leafy would to a needle prick. There was no more screaming. Nothing but groans of pleasure, as before a trough of slop richer than usual with bacon rind and pot rinsings.

The copperhead that, coiled, had stared Leafy down, eyes hard as diamonds, was stretched full length now, a great soft rope of sow pleasure. It was still trying to strike, its head a battering-ram against Old Sukey's jowls, but it was either drained of poison or jaw-injured. Old Suke wasn't trying to avoid it. Finally she took that length of danger inside her lips. She worked the big machinery of her jaws like mill wheels. Froth that had been snake ran out over her lips and onto what was still snake and hung tail downward from her mouth with only an occasional surge to show that though engulfed it still lived.

With the snake safely inside the sow, Leafy, holding herself closely together, pulled herself slowly upward. She was as stiff as if she had spent a whole day on the face of that ledge. Then the stiffness was broken by shaking. The danger was over, though. She was shaking for what was past. Only one snake remained outside the den and unattended by a sow. That one she stoned to death.

She had never before in her life been in a position to lord it over snakes. She had never before been their victor. She had cowered before them and run. Now she had herself taken the measure of one of those long fellows. He lay, all his fight gone, harmless as binding twine at her feet. Before a sow could swallow him, she started the hogs down the slope toward the herd below. They were willing to leave, good-natured over the combination of adventure and food, and with more food in prospect. They outran her, but she was hard on their heels. If she had gone up the slope like a hound, she came down it like a bird. It was something to have escaped death and to have conquered a lifelong dread of snakes. But she ran celebrating more than escape. Not death left behind up there on the rocks so much as some promise of life ahead of her. She didn't know the

name of the promise or what bounties or rewards it was offering
her, but she felt sure they existed and sped toward them . . .
cracking her whip and shouting unnecessary "sooboys" for the
sheer pleasure of sound and movement. The sows had done
the fighting and won the battle. There was no reason for it,
but she felt that the victory was as much hers as theirs.

✒ Cashie Wade

He didn't have the least doubt she'd be back. What had made
him certain was her "Never, never, farewell forever."

With ladies who said, "Tonight, Olin. Tomorrow night, at
the latest," he smelled a cold track.

Whatever a woman felt in her bones, she had a need to put
the opposite into words. If they were projecting to stay, "Farewell, Olin." If they had in mind to fetch up suddenly, "Tonight,
Olin."

There was no need for fooling him. His heart wouldn't crack
if they left or run over with gladness if they stayed. Who they
wanted to fool was themselves. Say "No," then enjoy the unexpected sweetness of being swept off their own feet. Say "Yes," and
savor double-dealing. "Young man, I'm fooling you."

He was so sure of her he'd shed his underwear on a night
too frosty for sleeping bare—if you were alone. His featherbed
and down comforter were warm as a setting hen's breast; still,
he was used to something next to his skin.

Over at Deever's the drovers, from the sound of things, were
about to break their britchin. A singer with a voice like a newly
weaned mule colt sang. A fiddler who'd got his training on horse
fiddles played. Drovers, fired up with corn likker, stomped so
hard they were jarring the studding.

Staying awake, as he was, made him grin to himself. If
you're so certain of her, he thought, why don't you go to sleep
and let her wake you when she comes? If she comes she's sure

not going to spend the night sitting in a corner of the wagon for fear of spoiling your slumbers.

Still he stayed awake.

At Deever's they were bellowing play-party tunes.

> "Take a lady by her hand
> Lead her like a pigeon
> Make her dance the Weevily Wheat
> 'Til she loses her religion."

Men dancing with men for lack of better partnering. Let that Leafy arrive and the two of them would dance the Weevily Wheat in their own downy nest without benefit of horse fiddles or singers.

The girl wasn't lost, drowned, snake bit, leg broken, or hog et unless she'd accomplished those feats since Spangler saw her at noonday.

"Fine as frog's hair," Spangler reported. "And there's a girl who's got her mind on hogs, not men."

Spangler was a smart man with hogs but a blockhead with girls. Did he expect a girl sitting on a hummock out in the middle of Butternut Draw to open up to a total stranger?

"I'll step her up to your barley." They were swinging their partners over at Deever's. Casting off, casting down; and some, he didn't misdoubt, so far gone in drink as to curtsy, kneel, and promenade. He had half a notion to pull on his britches, go over to the tavern to see if any of his men, who should be getting their rest against tomorrow's march, were still up cutting didoes. Two things made him give up that idea. One, he might miss the girl, and two, he might get caught up into cutting didoes himself.

"Coffee grows on a white oak tree / The river flows sweet brandy-o." Something was flowing sweet brandy-o and that was a fact.

Eight hired drivers, twelve hundred hogs, the price paid a

dollar a hundredweight, and his profit nothing he could bank on. Twenty miles yet to travel, the Miami to ferry; and hogs, sensible as they were in the main, biddable beasts and brisk marchers, still were as capable as humans of turning notionate and ornery. Figuring hog actions and guessing at market prices did for him what sheep counting did for others.

Her weight on the bed awakened him. When he half sat up she put her hand on his bare shoulder, pushed him back onto his pillow, and pulled the covers around his shoulders.

"I spent the whole day," she said, "telling myself it was just something that happened."

"Last night, you mean?"

"Yes."

"Leafy," Cashie said, "it was."

"Not on the order of wind or rain, the way I was thinking, though. Not on the order of sunup or sundown."

"More on the order of chain lightning," Cashie suggested.

He could tell, though he couldn't see her, that she didn't smile.

"It was a human happening."

"Yes," Cashie agreed, "it was."

"And you were the human."

"I was one of them. You were the other. We were two humans together. 'Male and female, created He them.' "

"I didn't know you ever went to church."

"You don't have to go to church to know that. Adam and Eve never went to church, and they found it out."

"They sinned," Leafy said.

"God must've planned it from the beginning. He made them so they could sin. He went to some pains to fix them so they could. He had it in mind right from the start."

"Eve wasn't married," Leafy said, "the way I am."

"No," Cashie admitted, "I got to grant you that. She was a maiden lady."

"It's hard to think of her that way. It happened so long ago. She don't seem young."

"Age don't have anything to do with that."

"I'm not a maiden lady," Leafy said again.

"No."

"All day I tried to think what happened was a dream. Or that it was on the order of other things that happened to me in the night. The rain and the cold and the long march and the hogs crying and your fire built up to guide me. If it was like that, it wasn't so wrong. If it didn't have to do with a person. But you are a person, Olin."

Cashie, much as he wanted to help her, could do little—because he didn't understand where she was trying to go.

"I could fly like a bird today, Olin, and I had done wrong. How could that be?"

"Maybe it wasn't as wrong as you think. Or else you didn't fly."

"No, I flew. But I took the wrong tack, trying to think last night was on the order of sunshine. Or bitter frost. I thought that, when I wasn't going to come back. But when I knew I was coming back, I couldn't pretend I was coming to anything but a person."

"It's the truth, I reckon, Leafy."

"A storm happens to you. It may harm you, but it's not your fault. A person is someone you choose, and the wrong in the choosing is your own."

She had clasped her arms about herself and was leaning forward so that he could feel her breath on his face when she spoke.

"Get into bed," Cashie said. "I don't want to spend tonight like last night, trying to save you from frostbite and lung fever."

"Is that what you were doing?" Her voice half broke—hard to say whether with laughter or tears.

"No," Cashie answered, this seeming to be an hour for truth-telling, "that wasn't what I was doing. But it worked, didn't it?"

She still sat outside the bedcovers, clasping herself for warmth or comfort.

"We never said 'love' once."

"No, we didn't," Cashie answered, not saying it now, either.

"I'm glad. And it wasn't required."

"We didn't say 'hate' either," Cashie reminded her. "As a matter of fact, we didn't say much."

"That's the reason maybe I feel so talkative now."

"You could talk under the covers."

"I don't know as I would." She laughed unexpectedly, the dry, quiet laugh of someone suddenly appreciating that the joke's on him. "I always hooted at girls with their tall tales. And they right all the time and me wrong. They say what you don't know won't hurt you, but it hurt me."

"I don't reckon you're the most knowledgeable girl in the world yet."

"Knowledgeable enough."

Cashie didn't dispute this, and Leafy was silent. He made the motion of scrooching down under the covers and going back to sleep, thinking this might help her make up her mind what to do. There was no sign that it did; and drive her away was the last thing he intended.

"You have any trouble getting here?" he asked. "Spangler got in before nightfall."

"Spangler?"

"Driver of mine. Said he talked to you around midday. Said you were making better time than him."

"That man! He never mentioned you. After he left, my troubles started. Some of my sows got mixed up with a den of snakes."

"Snakes are fodder for sows."

"I learned that, too; and learning it was what slowed me down getting here. After it was over, though, I flew. I felt as if I had been delivered from an enemy. It was just snakes, but with them taken care of it seemed I had nothing more to fear. It was after that I knew I was coming here and stopped trying to account for you as something that happened in the nighttime, and began to call you by your right name—Olin."

"The cat's in the buttermilk,
Skip to my Lou.
Flies in the biscuit, two by two.
Chicken in the haystack,
Skip to my Lou, my darling."

"Have they been singing over there the whole time I've been here?"

"They pause for breath now and again."

"I didn't hear them up to now, I was so busy thinking of myself."

"There was the two of us in your thinking, wouldn't you say?"

She stood up, unlocked herself from the clasp of her own arms.

"Yes, Olin," she said. "There was the two of us."

The next day Cashie trailed her as well as his own men, ready to give her a hand if she ran into trouble. He wanted to make good time himself. He was feeding men and hogs and paying the men wages; and the longer the trip took, the smaller his profits would be. Leafy had more at stake than profits. If she didn't have her payment in to the land office by sundown the next day, she lost her land. He had offered to parcel out her animals among his men and free her from herding. But she wouldn't hear of it. That far she had traveled—as far as to admit Olin Truitt was a person—but he was a nighttime person, and she didn't intend to let him seep over into the daytime or to get beholden to him. And he was just as willing as she was to set the boundaries from sundown to sunup; though giving her a hand on the day and a half of travel they had left wouldn't change that for him.

Leafy stayed well ahead of him all day. She was a good drover, she was lucky, and she had a herd trained to think she was the source of all food. To Cashie's knowledge she had lost five hogs only on the trip. Three strays, one drowning, and a boar stove up in a fight. He'd hire her to drive for him any day.

There was still light in the sky when he overtook her at Drover's Tavern on the west bank of the Miami. Drover's had the largest holding pens of any of the taverns that catered to the traveling herds and their owners and drivers. They hadn't any plan to meet, but Cashie expected her to be waiting for him there. When he pulled in, she had already turned her animals into the holding pens, had paid for their night's keep, and found, someplace in her saddlebags, a clean calico blouse, blue and sprigged with pink nosegays. She had brought it along, he figured, to wear next day at the land office and had decided not to wait. The evening had turned off cold, sky white and frosty like pond ice. It was really too cold for calico and bare arms. He knew what she was doing, though. She didn't put on her jacket until he took care of his team and got his cripples out of the wagon.

He washed and combed, then came back to her. "That's a pretty shirtwaist," he told her.

"My mother made it for me."

"I don't reckon she ever figured it'd be worn by a drover."

She didn't answer that, but he knew what she was thinking. Never figured it would be worn by a horse thief and wandering wife either.

He took her mind off that. "I'd be proud if you'd eat supper with me. They set out pretty good victuals over there. Beef as well as pork. Coffee *and* tea. Mrs. Overholtzer bakes a kind of ginger cake I never seen outside of Cincinnati."

"I'm so hungry," she said, "I could eat a catamount, live."

The look in her eyes wasn't hungry. It was pride for a secret they had. She was chary when it came to words, but she didn't have such good command of her looks. It wasn't a look he hankered to see. It wasn't a responsibility he wanted the burden of.

Girls who learned their multiplication tables or how to bound the Great Lakes didn't feel any call to cipher and bound only with teacher. He could teach; and he had done so, no doubt about it, with this girl; something as important as the rule of seven and which lake runs into what river. The trouble with this kind of teaching was that girls wanted to stay with teacher, be the sole star pupil and demonstrate brightness seven days a week.

There were girls—not this girl Leafy, maybe, but girls like her—who could be taught to follow the way she'd taught her herd, so that they lost sight of the fact that any other hand could deal out the corn or any other voice cry "Sooboy." There were men who enjoyed that kind of hypnotizing; but he wasn't one of them. He would take Leafy back, if he could, to the time when he was a happening and before he'd become Olin Truitt to her. Though he had half believed that this young married woman might discover for him the unnamed stranger he'd always been searching for, the fellow who was neither Olin Truitt nor Cashie Wade, would say to him one day, "Olin, I want to make you acquainted with my friend ———," whoever *that* boy—the boy who was neither Cashie nor Olin—turned out to be. Sometimes the last couple of days he'd thought he felt that yet-unpronounced name on the tip of his own tongue.

"Better put on your jacket," he told Leafy.

"I'm not cold."

She didn't look cold. Her cheeks were as bright as the sprigs in her calico. There was something about eating in a public place with a man that perked a woman up. It was like ear notching in a hog—showed whose property she was. He wouldn't say this to Leafy, but that pink in her face wasn't all winter bloom. Wouldn't say it was the public side of the nighttime happening, but wouldn't say it wasn't either. And downright emptiness had something to do with it. The sweet smell of fried tenderloin and hickory smoke, of dried apples stewing and coffee boiling made the back of his mouth wet.

"Catamount, did you say?" he asked her. "I could eat a biled owl. With the feathers on."

Under the white film of the scalded-milk sky there was now

a tinge of glass-green. Darkness was seeping in from the woods where night had already settled. Night was held back by the tavern lights: candles inside, and, outside, flaring torches.

"They're making high-jack in there," Cashie said, listening to the waterfall sound of voices.

It was the last gathering place for drovers and their hired drivers before the Cincinnati markets. Bar mishaps on the ferries tomorrow, the worst was over. They were out of the woods and could afford to whistle.

Cashie was in fact whistling, following a note behind the fiddle's, "Here come four dukes a-riding," and walking Leafy in time to the beat, when Nance Hawkins, her long braids flopping like lasso ropes, sprang out of the shadows onto him. She couldn't have missed sight of Leafy. Or maybe she blinded herself to get in her kiss before good reason not to stared her in the face. Her arms were as long and thin as her hair ropes and she wrapped them around Cashie just as tight as ropes. Nance had only one beauty: big eyes green as toad spit; and she had her face against his so Cashie couldn't see them.

"Olin," she said, "I've been waiting for you the livelong day."

Then she let herself see Leafy.

"You've got someone else," she accused.

"To eat supper with."

"You promised me."

He hadn't promised her a thing. He answered her hard as blacksmith nails. "What I said was I'd be back. And now I am going to have supper. I'd like to make you acquainted with Leafy Rivers before we go in."

Nance tried to be hard as nails herself. "Leafy Rivers, Mossy Springs," she said scornfully. Then her hardness cracked. She was torch-lit, and her green eyes, under that smoky light, spilled green tears. They ran down the length of her long freckled face. She held her braids in front of her face to hide her misery and to mop up her tears.

She spoke to Leafy with her mouth full of braids and tears.

"I seen you come in with your sows. Why don't you go back to them?"

He was going to give a shove in the direction of the kitchen, but Leafy struck his hand from Nance's shoulder.

"You eat with Olin," she told Nance. "Maybe my hogs are better company."

Cashie took his time over supper. He couldn't keep Nance from sitting beside him, but he didn't favor her with any conversation. When he finished, Nance said, "You going back to her?"

"If I can find her."

"Well, she told you where she was going and why."

"I heard her," Cashie said.

She was where he expected her to be. In his wagon, jacket on now, sitting on the bed cross-legged, like an Indian chief prepared to powwow.

"I brought you something to eat," he told her.

She took the slabs of fried meat, the pone and fried pies, and put them down on the bed beside her.

"No use starving yourself."

"I'm not going to." But she didn't touch the food.

Cashie lit his grease oil lamp. "Makes it more homelike."

"Homelike!" Leafy said. "We're two fine homebodies."

"It's the nearest to any home I got."

She couldn't say as much. Instead, she asked a question.

"Everywhere you go, are there girls grabbing at you like that?"

"They don't all grab."

"Everywhere you go, girls?"

"You been any place where there ain't girls?"

"No." Then after a little, she added, "I suppose that's how you got the way you are."

"How am I?" Cashie asked, daring her to tell him. She'd told him the night before. He wondered if she still remembered.

She wouldn't answer that question now. Likely because she knew where a truthful answer would lead her.

"Am I supposed to be beholden to those girls?" she asked.

"Not to the whole kit and caboodle," Cashie said. "You don't have to go that far."

She smiled a little. Or at least broke the stern line of her mouth. He handed her a pone when she did that, and she picked up one of the slices of meat and took a bite as if testing her teeth and jaws. They worked all right, so she took another bite. It might be called eating.

They were surrounded on all sides by hogs. They were so plentiful their snortings and snufflings sounded like the continuous quiet rise and fall of lake water.

"They don't know what's ahead for them," Leafy said, after they had listened in silence for a while.

"Us, neither," Cashie reminded her.

A hoot owl near at hand screamed; a long throaty catlike threat.

"Is that a painter after the hogs?"

"It's an owl," Cashie told her.

"I never heard any bird make a cry like that."

"An owl ain't rightly a bird."

"It flies. It's got feathers."

"It's an animal," Cashie explained. "The Indians knew that."

"When I was a girl," Leafy said between bites, "I got into tussles with boys over my rings. They were always taking my rings off, and putting them on their own fingers. Rings that had been given to me," she explained. "Did you do that?"

Cashie knew what she meant, but he said, "Did I give girls rings?"

"No. Tussle with girls for their rings."

"I didn't care anything about their rings."

"Did they?"

"Likely not."

"Once, I was told other girls didn't have that trouble. Why did I?"

"The word likely got out you relished tussles."

In the candlelight, above the heavy skin jacket, the girl's face was narrow and bone-tired. He could see the shadows of her eyelashes on her cheeks as she slitted her eyes, thinking about what he'd said.

"I did, for a fact. I liked skirmishing with boys."

Thinking about that, she forgot to eat until he handed her one of the fried pies.

"Now that you're as good as there," he said, "maybe you'll tell me how you got ahold of Yanders' horse."

"I locked Yanders up in our barn."

Cashie whistled. "How'd you manage that?"

"I fooled him," she said, then changed that to, "I lied to him. Got him in there and slammed the door shut and bolted it."

"Ain't you afraid he'll break out?"

"He'd have to dig packed earth with his bare hands."

"You didn't need the horse for the trip."

"I took Fox because he was handy. I locked up Yanders because he was going to sell our hogs to meet a note my husband signed."

It was the first time she'd said the word "husband" to Cashie. She seemed to realize it herself. "His name is Reno," she said. "He was fooled into signing the note."

"Yanders tried to sell your hogs to me," Cashie said.

"Why didn't you buy them?"

"I already had more than I could handle."

"If you *had* bought them, where'd we be?"

"Not sitting here talking."

"Life is chancy. This is nothing we planned."

"You be a certain way and life plans things for you. Somebody else not so workbrickel as me wouldn't have had a full quota of hogs when Yanders offered to sell. Somebody not so bold as you wouldn't have locked Yanders up. We put ourselves in the way of meeting each other, being what we are!"

"We've been working toward each other all our lives?"

"Toward somebody like us."

"I'm not so bold," Leafy said. "I might not have locked up Yanders just for the pigs. Except he kissed me once, I might not."

"Half the men in Indiana would be locked up if kissing could draw a jail term."

"I was expecting him to kiss me again and he didn't."

"That's a criminal offense in any court," Cashie agreed. "Give the first and renege on the second."

Leafy wouldn't joke. "I thought I was in love with him. And I already loved Reno. And now you."

Cashie was almost able not to hear that.

"You can't go around loving everybody," she said. Or asked.

This was something Cashie felt free both to hear and to answer. "I don't know about that. I never tried. Never tried with even one, truth to tell."

"Not a one of those grabbing girls?"

"Not a one!"

"Well, Reno can," Leafy said. "He has got it in him to love one. But Reno's had a lot more chances than you."

Chances for what? Cashie felt like asking, just for the pleasure of making her bashful. But he knew what she meant. Chances for being a gentlemanly fellow who got took in on notes and let his wife ride out into the woods on a hog-droving trip. Chances you didn't get, boy, brought up in a tavern by a mother who took money for more than corn dodgers and lodging. That was the kind of chances Reno got that he'd never come close to.

But Reno wasn't the one the girl was thinking of.

"You know who you put me in mind of?"

He didn't and had no intention of guessing.

"My brother Chancellor."

"He a runty towhead? Not had many chances either?"

"You're not runty, Olin. And Chancellor's had all the chances in the world. It's what he does puts me in mind of you."

She waited for him to guess again, but guessing had never been his long suit. He either knew or kept silent.

"Chancellor's fixing to be a preacher."

"Preach! Bible thumping's the last thing I'll ever take up."

"I know that. Preaching is just hapchance with Chancellor. He was going to be an actor once."

"I ain't got no acting blood in me either."

"You've got the same kind of dissatisfied blood Chancellor's got, though."

Cashie held his breath. He thought the next word might be the one he'd been waiting for, the one that would tell him who he was. But she didn't know either. Her next words were, "Olin, I can't eat *two* fried pies."

She held the second pie to his mouth. He took her hand and ate the pie from her fingers. She fed it into his mouth as careful as a mother bird with fledglings. When the pie was gone he licked the crumbs from her fingers. She didn't take her hand away, but, when it was clean, smoothed back his hair and rounded his ears with her fingers. Then she tested the curve of his eyes under his closed lids and the turn-up corners of his mouth.

Her mind, for some reason, was filled with memories of her childhood which she wanted him to hear. Under the covers, snuggled together like babes in the woods, she told him about growing up in Blue Glass, Ohio.

"You mean Grass, don't you?"

"I mean what I say," she said shortly. "My father made me go three times to the eighth grade."

Cashie had never gone once. "That seems like a couple of times too many."

"It was. I learned all there was to know the very first time. After that I was a teacher."

Cashie, drifting off to sleep, gave her a little hug. She was as springy as new-plucked down. "Which line do you favor?"

"Which line?"

"Teaching or learning?"

"Learning, when you don't know. Teaching, after that."

They talked off and on during the night. Once, Leafy cried.

"What's to cry about?" Cashie asked.

"For things that might be different," she said.

"Different from what?"

"From what I dreamed back in Blue Glass."

"Maybe you dreamed wrong."

"In some ways I did."

"Nothing's perfect," Cashie said, and was sorry he had for fear she'd say, "You was," or even "are." She didn't, though. She said, "It's the nearness to that's sorrowful."

For all their nighttime wakefulness they were among the first to stir. Glassy stars were crackling bright in the black sky. The animals breathed plumes of smoke. Cashie brought a pitcher of coffee and a dozen corncakes out from the tavern kitchen.

"No use your going over there and tangling with that feisty Nance again."

"Tangling with anybody's the fartherest thing from my mind," Leafy told him.

"What's your plans now?" Cashie asked as they ate.

"Sell the pigs. Make the land payment and get home and let Yanders out before he tears the barn down."

"He might kiss you again," Cashie warned.

"He won't. I'm not kiss-hungry any more . . . the way I was."

They were neither one kiss-hungry now, but they kissed before they parted.

Cashie helped Leafy get her herd aboard the ferry. The drovers had boarding times and tried to make things easy for each other by keeping their animals out of the way in the holding pens until their turns came. Still there were enough hogs, drivers, and drovers running loose, shouting, and squealing to cause an uproar. The riverbank had been trodden to dust, and at sunup the air sparkled with particles thick as a mica curtain. The dark hills on the far side took on a polished pewter sheen. The tips of the river surges had, in the growing light, a gun-barrel glint.

Leafy's herd went aboard as tractable as farmers riding an excursion boat. That would be their one and only trip across the river, but it could've been a round trip, their hundredth time, with one hundred and one facing them when they hit the far shore. Fox, who wasn't traveling to a slaughterhouse, was far more fractious. Cashie had finally to blindfold him to get him to walk the bridge from bank to boat.

"I'd feel better if they didn't trust me so much," Leafy said.

"You couldn't do what you've done if they didn't," Cashie reminded her. "You trained trust up in them."

"I'd feel better if they fought me a little."

"What good would come of that? You suffering some ain't going to change their fate, is it?"

"If they didn't trust me, I'd feel better," she repeated.

"Want to set them loose?"

"No!"

"That being the case," Cashie said, "don't sell for less than two dollars. They'll try to beat you down because you're a girl. But you face up to them. You got prime stock, and you make them pay for it."

They intended to part with a handshake, but their left hands partook of the leave-taking, too.

"You reckon we'll ever see each other again, Olin?"

"You stick to droving," Cashie said, "and we're bound to."

That reply did what he intended it to do. Cut short their parting.

Cashie said, "Good-by, Leafy." But the girl, he saw, couldn't risk a word for fear, once she unclenched her teeth, her face would crumple into crying. It would have been easier on him if she had done what she wanted her herd to do: launch into a little rampaging. Give him something to blame her for. She gave him nothing but a little nod, then turned her back on him.

The ferryman's bell sounded as Cashie climbed the slope away from the water. Above the hog squeals, the cracking whips and drovers' yells he heard the first hard slap of the oars as they powered the boat to the other side of the river.

Cashie got Leafy, her hogs, and Yanders' horse, Fox, off on the first ferry that made the crossing Friday morning. He didn't wave, didn't look back, and as he went about the business of getting his own hogs and drivers across, she was in his mind, but in the back of it, along with other memories of girls and good times. It was past dinnertime before his last hog was on the ferry, and his stomach was knotting with hunger. He decided he had as well put his knees under a table and have a sample of the victuals he'd been smelling for the past hour. He was through the fried potatoes and tenderloin and was spooning into a treacle dumpling when Simon Yanders clapped him on the shoulder.

"Cashie! I been trailing you the past twenty-four hours. Thank God you decided to eat."

Cashie wasn't surprised to see Yanders. He had never supposed that barn would hold him—and he wanted to ask how he had managed to break out. But since he wasn't supposed to know he was *in*, he couldn't very well ask how he got out. What he could ask was what Yanders wanted with him.

"I don't want you," Yanders said. "It's your wagon I want."

"I was figuring on using it myself to get into Cincinnati."

"You can," Yanders said. "All I want is the use of your bed."

"Well, the bed's going to be empty. You're welcome to it. What's the matter? You feeling dauncy?"

"There's nothing wrong with me. I've got a sick man who's going to be a dead man if he don't see a doctor soon."

"Where'd you pick him up?"

"Back along the trace yesterday. His horse had throwed him, dragged him some, maybe. His foot's swelled up the size of a tub, and he's out of his head a good part of the time."

Cashie didn't get treacle dumplings often, especially not with cream dip, and he didn't suppose a foot the size of a tub could get much worse while he had the last three bites. Yanders drummed on the table.

"You've got about as much feeling as a weasel, Cashie. Taking your time while a man's dying."

"We can't cross till the ferry crosses," Cashie said, "die or not die. 'Bout as well have a dumpling yourself."

"I don't feel like eating. I got this fellow on my conscience. Remember the hogs I tried to sell you? He's the one had his property attached. If I hadn't served him those papers, he wouldn't be in this shape."

"Trying to take his hogs to Cincinnati himself?"

"No, his wife was doing that job. He was trying to catch up with her . . . lame when he started."

Cashie scraped his pudding dish for the last crumb of dumpling and dip. When he finished, he looked up. Yanders was close to him, trying to read his face. Failing that, he said, "They tell me you helped Mrs. Rivers and her herd on the ferry this morning."

"They ain't lying," Cashie said.

"You know Fox when you see him."

"I seen she was on your horse, yes."

"Why didn't you stop her?"

"She said you loaned her the horse."

"You know I wouldn't loan Fox. Let alone to some girl who don't know a single-footer from a heifer."

"I didn't think it likely," Cashie admitted. "How'd you get out of the barn?"

Yanders smacked the table till the cutlery rattled. "You two seem to have got pretty well acquainted."

"I was trying to get to the bottom of how she got hold of your horse," Cashie said reasonably.

"The bottom to that is: first she lied to me, then she tricked me. And except her brother run home from helping her drove them hogs, I'd still be in that barn."

"So Offie got home."

"Offie! Don't make me puke. That boy'll always get home. Before anyone else, too. He came home. Rivers rode out. The boy let me out."

"Why?"

"He thought I'd take care of him."

"Well, I reckon you fooled him on that score."

"For the time being. That's all I'd count on."

When Cashie heard that Yanders had already put Rivers in his bed, he said, "Looks like you took my answer pretty much for granted."

"Well, you helped the girl across the river on *my* horse. I thought you'd want me to do as much for the husband with *your* horses."

"It don't always work out that way, Simon."

"It don't, for a fact," Yanders admitted. "I been tied up helping these two since I first laid eyes on them. And they've been trouble to me from the beginning. And the only thanks I get, the girl steals my horse, the husband gets in my path with a poisoned leg so I got no choice but cart him to a doctor. And the boy'll probably grow up to take a pot shot at me from ambush."

"That bridge is some distance ahead," Cashie said.

Yanders, leaving the tavern with Cashie, didn't argue about that. He clambered into Cashie's wagon, lifted Rivers' head, and offered him a drink from the canteen. Rivers appeared to take a sip or two.

Cashie could see that in health Leafy's husband was a pretty fellow. Now, fever had taken the color of his face past fire to ashes. His black hair had no more life than pig bristles. His bad foot—there was no use trying to wrap a thing that size— wasn't colored or shaped like a human foot. The sight of it gave Cashie's stomach a jupe. While Cashie was staring at him, Rivers opened his eyes and looked at Yanders. His eyes were filmed over. Cashie wondered that he was able through that film to tell day from night. But he recognized Yanders. His voice was low and grating, the sound of a skillet pulled across a rock hearth. He made a couple of attempts to speak before he could manage words.

"Mr. Yanders," he said, "you don't have to make up anything to me."

thirteen

✍ *Dr. Daubenheyer*

His wife sat with her back against the wall of their polished hall. He sat on the polished floor of that hall with his head in his wife's lap. He was not sure how he got there. When he came home from the Converses' his intention had been to put a few necessaries in his saddlebags and to ride off. Rosa's death had spoiled him as a doctor and as a husband. His patients didn't trust him, and he was no more than a boarder in Alphy's house. The best thing he could do for both of them was to pack up, ride off, and to keep going.

His saddlebags were beside him, so he had at least got as far as packing. Beside them was another: Alphy's portmanteau. Alphy's dress, where his cheek lay, was damp. Tears? The front door was wide open, and the flower scents were so thick he might've been in the garden itself. A mockingbird who'd never heard the words "die" or "fail" was singing.

"Alphy," Junius said, "how'd we get here?"

"We sat down here to cry a little because we are leaving Blue Glass forever. Going someplace where no one will know us and start over again."

He remembered that all right. "I am going," he said.

"We are going."

"What about Otto?"

"My mother will look after Otto. He'll be in good hands. You don't care about him anyway."

"He and I killed Rosa."

"Rosa died. You didn't kill her, and Otto didn't kill her. The only person you've killed is my husband, Junius Daubenheyer. You must hate me to kill my husband."

"But you're going with me?" He touched her bag. "Why do you want to go with someone who hates you?"

"I don't know. I keep thinking you'll change. But I can't stay here if you leave."

Junius sat up. Someone had ridden in and was coming up the garden walk. Junius got to his feet. He was ready to desert wife and son, fly home and hearth forever, but not to be caught by some stranger sitting with his head in his wife's lap in the middle of the front hall on a summer night.

The stranger was Offie, round as a pork barrel and white-faced in the moonlight. The worst, Junius felt, must have happened at the Converses'. Though if Leafy had died, why would they be sending him the news?

"Offie," he cried, "what're you doing here?"

"They sent me for you. Reno said he'd give a hundred dollars to have you back. Leafy is crying for you."

"What about your mother? What did she say?"

"She said, 'Tell Dr. Daubenheyer I am praying he'll come back.' "

Junius stood irresolute. Such a turnabout for Prill seemed unlikely. To say nothing of his own turnabout if, packed and ready to leave, he returned to the Converses'.

"If you don't come back with me, I'll have to keep going," Offie said. "I can never show my face at home again."

Alphy said, "You mean shake the dust of Blue Glass from your feet forever, Offie?"

"Yes," Offie said. "Head west. Go someplace where they don't know me. I'd never be welcome at home again."

Offie appeared for the first time to take in the fact that Alphy was sitting on the floor.

"Are you sick, Mrs. Daubenheyer?"

"I was," Alphy said. "I'm feeling better. Well, Offie, you can head west with us. We're leaving Blue Glass, too. We can all go together. Seek some better place where nobody knows us."

"Start over," Offie agreed.

Junius began to laugh. It was a hysterical laugh: he had as well have been crying or screaming, and he knew it. But what he knew didn't help him to stop. The boy stared up at him as if he were witnessing a fit. And fit was as good a name for it as any. The boy was scared, but he stayed on, giving proof to what he'd just said about the change of mind over at the Converses'.

"So you'd run off from Blue Glass, would you?" Junius gasped between bouts of laughter he couldn't control.

"Yes, sir," Offie said. "If you don't come back with me. Besides, I want to go west. I want to hunt Esau."

Junius felt drunk, or the recipient of a vision, Providence having vouchsafed him the opportunity to see himself a nine-year-old in thought and action.

"Loss, loss," he sputtered. "So loss gnaws at you, too, Offie? I tell you, boy, swallow it down. What's done for's done."

"It was my fault," Offie protested. "If I hadn't left the door open Esau would never have got out."

"Who's Esau?" Junius thought to ask.

"My pet pig."

That stopped Junius' hysteria. "We are born to sorrow, Offie, and long to blame ourselves. Little girls sicken when their kittens die. Grown men throw away their lives because what was is no more. No wonder, loving punishment so much, we worship a punishing God. Get on your horse, Offie. I'll be right on your heels."

Alphy stood up as Offie went out the door.

"You're going back?" she asked.

"There's nothing more I can do. But if they still want me I've got no choice but to go."

"Shall I unpack our bags?"

"Unpack them. I think I've turned a corner. If I ain't . . . Offie'd be a better man for you. There's no marker over Esau's grave, I don't suppose. Offie's honing after something there's still some chance of finding."

Alphy, her head only to his shoulder, lifted her arms straight up to touch his face and hair.

"How long'll you be?"

"There's no telling. A couple of hours. A couple of days. Though I wouldn't think so."

It was a couple of hours. The Converse house was so lit up he saw from afar the light streaming upward into the trees.

"Oh, God," he prayed, "don't let this be death." And light didn't seem to him the way Prill Converse would meet the death of a daughter or a grandchild. He and Offie rode into a yard cross-barred by golden shafts of light. Candles and lamps in every room. The last time he'd seen the house so transfigured was at Leafy's wedding two years ago.

His prayer was selfish. He was praying for himself more than for Leafy. But God, to punish a selfish man, didn't choose to punish Leafy, too. Junius saw that, the minute he stepped into the kitchen. He saw it, but he wanted the evidence of someone else's sight.

"What have we got here?" he asked in a loud voice.

Prill, a good woman, with no "I told you so's" in her system, replied quietly, "What we have got here is a buster."

He hadn't really needed her word for it. Prill and Venese, bent over a table, were greasing a brass-lunged baby, a big pink chunk of a girl, dark-haired, and bawling like a bay steer.

"What're you doing to her?" Junius asked.

"Cleaning her up a little. She was so long on the way, she was travel-stained."

Prill carried the baby, wrapped round in Canton flannel, over to Junius. "Her head's a little pinched in, but after two days that's to be expected. Junius, except for your keeping at Leafy, walking her, making her work on that harness, she'd've given up. She was prepared to die with that baby in her."

"I expected her to do so."

"Nature had other plans."

"How is she now?"

"You'd better have a look. She's torn some."

In the bedroom Reno and Leafy were both asleep. Junius had seen sleepers in a good many positions, but never one like Reno, sound asleep, bolt upright, with an arm stretched forth unsupported so that his wife's fingers could rest on his palm.

Reno, when Junius touched his shoulder, opened his eyes. He put Leafy's hand in the doctor's, whispered, "Call me when you've finished," and went out.

✍ Leafy

"How're you feeling, Leafy?"

Leafy opened her eyes, and June Daubenheyer's face, rosy in the candlelight, told her how he thought she felt: good. To admit it seemed to her to put in question the truth of all the pain she had suffered. Anyone as sick as she had been couldn't, surely, be feeling happy, hungry, and no more played out than after any hard day's work. But that was the truth. She had not only felt like dying, she had wanted to die. And here she was now, her suffering dim as a dream, and if somebody would bring her a thick piece of her mama's light bread toasted over a smoky fire and a cup of China tea, she'd be pert as a jay bird. It was too much for her to believe. And she *was* afraid to say it for fear too much belief on her part would turn the tables. And there was one thing she still *wasn't* easy about. Ignoring the question she'd been asked, she asked one herself.

"Have you seen the baby, June?"

"I have. And little wonder we had such a siege of it. That baby's big enough to eat at the table right now. I tell you, I never did a better thing in my life than to keep you walking and pulling. I thought you were holding onto that baby out of downright stubbornness, but I see I was wrong."

Right the first time, Leafy almost told Daubenheyer. I held onto it for ten months. I was that stubborn. Till both of us had got the habit of living together.

"It took some boldness on my part, I can tell you, to get you up out of childbed and send you traipsing cross-country. But it turned the trick."

Reno was the one who had turned the trick; but this wasn't news. Daubenheyer need never know, and for more reasons than one; the first being Daubenheyer's pride in his making up with her for his failure with his first wife.

"What's she look like?" Leafy asked.

"You ain't seen her yet?"

"I don't want to. Yet. You tell me."

"She's big, that's the first thing you notice."

"Big? Reno's not big. Nor me."

"You've got a big brother, though. And babies more often look like their uncles and aunts than their pappys and mammys. She's got a thick thatch of black hair."

"Like Reno's?"

"Like Chancellor's. She's the spittin' image of Chancellor."

"That's queer."

"I just told you it happens that way more often than not. Chancellor's first baby will more'n likely be a turkey egg like you."

"Maybe I'll take a look at her."

"First, I'll have to look at you. Your mama says you're torn some. I may have to put in a stitch or two. It's bound to hurt some."

"Reno had his bad foot sawed off and never screamed once. I reckon I can stand a little needlework."

Dr. Daubenheyer called Prill in, as was right and proper while he made his examination. When it was over and after Daubenheyer had gone to the kitchen for his implements, Prill said to Leafy, "I won't crow before Doc Daubenheyer, but if he'd had his way, that baby out in the kitchen wouldn't be alive and kicking now. I knew well enough that a daughter of mine, once she put her mind to it, didn't have to have any baby of hers taken. It wasn't an easy stand to take—set my judgment up ahead of a doctor's, but I'm glad I did it."

Leafy said, "Mama, I'm glad you did, too."

"Everyone else was willing to give up. Not me."

"Mama," Leafy said, "I wish I had your spunk."

"You had it, come to the showdown."

"Who would you say," Leafy asked, "the baby looks like?"

"Babies look like babies," Prill said. "But this one's got two features that you can't mistake. Reno's hair and Bass's nose."

"Reno's hair!" Chancellor protested. He stood in the doorway, his arm around Venese. "I got the doctor's word for it the hair's mine!"

Prill went to her son, and he put his free arm around her. "Well, Aprilla," he said, "you're a grandma."

"Venese tells me I'm the mother of a preacher, Chancellor.

That's bigger news yet. Grandchildren come by nature, but preachers are chosen of God."

Prill, who had not shed a tear during the two days of Leafy's labor, began to weep because of her son's decision.

"Now, Mama," said Chancellor, but Prill lifted her apron to her face and ran into the kitchen.

"*Are* you a preacher, Chancellor?" Leafy asked.

"I preached, and if preaching makes a preacher, I reckon I am."

"He is one," Venese said. "It is going to be his lifework. He is going to seek God and labor to bring sinners to Him."

"You talk like a preacher's wife," Leafy said, "already."

"I am going to be a preacher's wife. And it was your brother Chancellor brought you safely through. He won't tell you, but I will. It was his prayers saved your baby for you. Chancellor, when his father came for him, declared to the whole Camp Meeting that love and faith would save you."

Leafy said, Yes, love and faith, but Reno's, so loud and clear in her thoughts, she was surprised that neither Venese nor Chancellor heard. Saved by June's walking; saved by Mama's knowing more than the doctor; saved by Chancellor's prayer. Everybody here tonight but Reno himself, who said the words I had to hear, ready to claim the credit for what those October nights along the trace produced. Everybody so happy to be giving, who would hand their gifts back to them? Not I.

Dr. Daubenheyer, who had saved her life, or at least her baby's life, once, by walking, came in to finish the job by sewing.

"You two step outside for a minute," he told Chancellor and Venese. "I've got to hurt Leafy a little now, and if she yells, she don't need listeners."

She didn't yell, didn't even moan. The quick sharp pain acted on her the way she supposed whiskey acted on drinkers. Woke her up to being so alive ordinary living was as drowsy as sleep.

"Tell Reno I want to see him," she said to June.

"Time you got a little rest."

"After I see Reno."

Reno pulled the chair close to her bed and took once more the hand he had held while both slept.

"Reno," Leafy said, "what made you tell Mama this was Simon Yanders' baby? That was a terrible thing to do."

"I thought it was true."

"What made you think it was true?"

"Offie. Offie told me he saw Simon Yanders make love to you out in the woods."

"Offie! Don't you know Offie by this time? Simon Yanders gave me one kiss. And never got out of the saddle. And rode off ashamed of himself. You ought not to have credited one word Offie said."

"I wouldn't have, except Yanders, going out of his way to save me, acted to me like he had something on his conscience."

"He likely has. But it don't have to be me. Why didn't you ask me?"

"We were too happy after you came back from Cincinnati. If you were trying to make up to me for something that had happened between you and Yanders, I didn't want to know about it. I was willing to let it pass."

"You may be willing, but I'm not. You go out and speak to Offie. However you feel, Offie shouldn't be let grow up to tell such lies. And when you've talked to Offie, then you talk to Mama and tell her the mistake you made."

✒ Offie

Reno found Offie on the steps to the back porch, his head resting on his knees.

"You asleep, Offie?"

"No." But he didn't raise his head.

"Offie, you look up at me. I want you to look me in the eye."

Offie lifted his head. In the lamplight from the kitchen Reno could see where Offie's eyes were, but not *into* them as he wanted.

"I'm looking," Offie said.

"Offie, why did you tell me that story about Leafy and Mr. Yanders?"

Offie didn't answer.

"Was it true?"

"He kissed her."

"You told me a lot more than that. Why? Did you want me to think something bad about your sister?"

"You didn't have to think it was bad if you didn't want to."

"Why did you tell me?"

"I wanted you to fight Mr. Yanders."

"I wouldn't have stood a chance fighting Yanders, with my bad foot. He could've licked me from July to eternity. You know that."

"I didn't stand any chance when you licked me for using my peephole either."

"So you wanted Yanders to pay me back? Offie, I ought to give you another good hiding right here and now!"

"Why don't you?" Offie asked with the assurance of someone who knows the subject will never get beyond talk.

"First and foremost because I doubt it would do any good. And second because I owe my life to you. If you hadn't let Yanders out of the barn, I wouldn't be alive today."

"I didn't do it for you."

"Oh, I know that, Offie. Likely you weren't thinking of Yanders either."

"I don't like Mr. Yanders. He wouldn't help me catch Esau. And he lied to me about staying with me."

"I don't know anyone who ought to be better prepared for a little lying than you, Offie."

Junius, coming out of the house, defended Offie.

"Now, Reno," he said, "don't you pick on Offie. He made a trip tonight wasn't easy for a little boy. Rode through the woods in the pitch dark to bring me your message."

"My message?"

"Yours and Prill's."

"To come back and take care of Leafy," Offie explained quickly.

Offie, in spite of the poor light, was able to turn some phosphorescence on in his eyes, which Reno could see. He looked up at Reno like a kitten as it goes into the sack for drowning. Reno didn't have any qualms about pushing his brother-in-law under the water, but Dr. Daubenheyer, from all he'd heard, had gone through more than enough already.

"I'm glad Offie found you, Doctor," Reno said.

"There's nothing wrong with Leafy now a couple of weeks won't set right," Daubenheyer said. "She's a strong girl. I had to take a few stitches. But by the time little Rena's a year old your wife'll likely be making you the present of a son."

"Rena?" Reno asked, feeling as if his own life was a story everyone else but him had read.

"Your little daughter."

"First time I heard that name."

"If you don't like it, you better get in there and tell Leafy so. That's what she was calling her to me. And once a name gets set it's hard to change."

Daubenheyer, after Reno went inside, lingered for a minute to talk to Offie.

"I meant that, Offie, about your riding over tonight."

"I did it to save my sister's life," Offie said modestly.

"As it turned out, her life didn't need saving. But you didn't know that. And I hope Otto will be willing to do as much for his sister some day."

"Is Otto going to have a baby sister?"

"Why, I hope so," Daubenheyer answered.

"Is that what you and your wife were doing on the floor tonight?"

Daubenheyer's gratitude dried up fast. "I was on the floor tonight because I had a sick spell. And my wife was there to help me. Now you better get on to bed. You seen more tonight than you can rightly digest."

"We all have, come to that," said Chancellor, coming down the back steps. "I feel like tonight's intake will keep me digesting the rest of my life."

Arm in arm with Venese, Chancellor went on, "June, I been breaking the news to the folks. I'll break it to you now. As soon as Leafy's back on her feet, Venese and me are getting married. I'd like you to stand up with us for the ceremony. You feel equal to that?"

"I do," said Junius. "But, Venese, I'm surprised you've let this high-stepping, side-wheeling . . ."

"Since tonight, he's a preacher," Venese said proudly.

"That right, Chancellor?"

"Right or wrong, it's a fact," Chancellor admitted.

"And you're marrying him anyway?" Junius asked Venese.

"She's marrying me because," Chancellor explained.

Chancellor and Venese walked with Junius to the hitching rack. Then, after he rode out, they continued, arms around each other, down toward the spring branch. Offie, left alone, went back into the kitchen.

His father and mother sat at the kitchen table. The candle between them was guttering, blazing up high every now and then with the sound of someone drawing a sighing breath. They sat sidewise to him, and his father was crying. Not making a sound, but tears heavy and shiny as lard oil slid down his face. Offie had never seen his father cry, or his mother either, for that matter. Crying was what children did, and the sight made him feel confused, as if his father had been sucking his thumb or playing mumblety-peg on the table with his mother.

"Don't take on so, Bass," his mother said. "Many a good Christian don't believe in faith healing."

"Healing's the least part of it. I've never had faith of any kind. And tonight, in what I took to be a rebirth of faith, I found that out. I took a public stand against Chancellor's declaring Leafy would come through safe. He was trusting in God, and I was still thinking about how much face he was going to lose if she didn't. I was thinking what a comedown it would be for him, starting his preaching, with some vaunt like that that'd more than likely prove empty. In one and the same breath I said, 'I trust in God Almighty' and 'Don't say so if there's any chance it'll cause you to lose face.'"

"Nobody else is likely to think that."

"I don't care what anybody else thinks. I seen myself for what I was tonight, and what anyone else thinks one way or the other won't change that."

"Nobody here's come through with such high-flying colors tonight," Prill said. "Not that that's anything but cold comfort to you."

Offie stepped to the table. "I went for the doctor," he reminded her.

His mother withheld her usual smile and fond pat. "You went for the wrong doctor. It's only chance Daubenheyer was willing to come back—and that Leafy didn't need any doctor."

His father surprised Offie; he reached out a hand and squeezed Offie's shoulder, as much as to say, "Your father failed, too." But his mother wasn't willing to leave matters at this comfortable point.

"Offie made up a terrible story about Leafy. He fooled Reno, and I took Reno's word for what he believed. It seems to me a good mother would've had more faith in her daughter than I did. I just swallowed down the whole story like gospel."

His father took his hand away from Offie's shoulder.

"How could a boy do a thing like that?" He asked this question of Prill, as if there was no use putting any question to such a known liar as his son.

"I don't know, Bass. Maybe we oughtn't to blame him too much. A stream can't rise higher than its source."

Offie recognized this as a kind of excusing joke. But not excusing enough to make it safe for him to open his mouth.

"Chancellor and Leafy," Bass said, "we can be proud of them."

"And Offie's young enough to turn over a new leaf. If he's a mind to. And I'm of a mind to make him if he isn't."

"You go on to bed now," his father said.

When Offie didn't move, his father said, harshly, "Go. I want to talk to your mother."

Before he started up the back stairway, Offie, their door being ajar, looked in on Reno and Leafy. Leafy and the baby were in bed. Reno sat in a chair holding Leafy's hand. They saw him, their eyes moved to him, then they looked back at each other and went on talking as if he didn't exist.

Leafy said, "I can't get over it, all of us there together at the time I was selling the pigs."

"We all knew it except you."

"I don't see how you could take it in, the shape you were in."

"They were at pains to make me understand. They thought it would help me to pull through. The two of them were right there when you bid in our land."

"The two of them?"

"Wade. The fellow whose wagon I'd been riding in. He was a friend of Yanders. Except for him and his wagon, I'd never've made it."

"What was he doing there?"

"He's a hog dealer. Like you," Reno said, smiling.

"Yanders could've took my money before I bought our land. Couldn't he?"

"He not only could've, he ought've. He went against the law, letting you use it."

"Why?"

"That's the question I asked myself. And one reason I believed the story I was told."

Storytelling reminded Leafy of Offie. She looked at him once again. "Offie, you get on up to bed. You'll wake up Rena. You've caused enough trouble around here for one night."

"I miss Esau, Leafy," Offie said.

"He's likely better off free."

"Do you think he's running around someplace in the woods tonight having a good time?"

"I think he might be."

"Then it was a good thing I forgot and let him loose?"

"It might in the long run turn out to be best. Now you get to bed before you start Rena to crying."

"You and Reno are talking."

"She's used to us."

"Rena," Reno said. "I can't get used to that name. I thought we'd decided on Mary Pratt if it was a girl."

"I changed my mind," Leafy said. "Chancellor was the one called me Leafy, and you know it was because I could never make up my mind. I can make it up now and I have made it up, and I don't like two names the same in one family. The baby is Rena for you and I am Mary Pratt for me."

"Leafy . . ." Reno began.

"Mary Pratt," Leafy corrected him. "Reno, I'm sewed up like a crazy quilt and too weak to argue. You name the boys and I'll name the girls."

Mary Pratt closed her eyes, and Reno blew out the candle.

Left in the lonesome dark, Offie postponed climbing the creaking stairs to his bedroom.

"Leafy," he began, hoping a question to ask would come to him.

"Mary Pratt," Leafy corrected him, and this gave him an idea.

"I don't want to be called Offie any more. My real name's Howard."

"All right, Howard," Leafy said, and that conversation was over before it started.

"Leafy," he began again, remembered his mistake, but when Leafy didn't correct him, went on. "Did I do wrong forgetting to keep Esau locked up?"

"I told you once, you likely did Esau a favor."

"Leafy," he said once more, but this time Reno answered. "This is no time for talk. You get on upstairs to bed."

Offie didn't move until he heard the soft clump of Reno's bad foot coming his way across the floor. Then he left the doorway and began to climb the stairs. Reno might decide that this was the time to give him the licking he said he owed him.

No one wanted to hear *him* talk but he could hear the murmur of voices all the way up the stairs: his father and mother in the kitchen; Leafy and Reno in the parlor bedroom.

His room under the roof was still hot from the midday baking. The window was pushed as high as it would go, and Offie bunched the curtains together at the sides of the window and leaned out. The outside air, though warm, was fresh, and the Milky Way across the July sky looked cool, like a streak of cream on the gray water of the stone trough in the springhouse. A piece of a moon was coming up back of the Juneberry tree. Up the lane, slowly, arm in arm, Chancellor and Venese came pacing. At the upping block they paused, and Chancellor swung Venese to its top so that she could sit. Venese leaned forward, put her arms around Chancellor's neck, and began, it looked like to Offie, to kiss him. Over and over, it looked like.

Offie left the window with the idea of tiptoeing down the stairs and going outside to watch. Before he reached his bed, the idea palled. He pulled off his britches and lay down.

"Howard," he said to himself. "Howard Converse." He had as well been saying the name of a stranger. But it was his name just as much as Leafy's name was Mary Pratt, and in time he would get used to it.